THE TROUBLE WITH LEOPARD QUEENS AND SHIFTER WARS

A CARY REDMOND NOVEL, BOOK 3

KAT SIMONS

THE TROUBLE WITH LEOPARD QUEENS AND SHIFTER WARS

Published 2020 by T&D Publishing
Cover design: © 2020 Evernight Designs
Interior book design © 2020 T&D Publishing
ISBN-13: 978-1-944600-26-6 (Trade Paperback Edition)
ISBN-13: 978-1-944600-27-3 (Large Print Edition)

This is a work of fiction. All of the characters, places, organizations, and events portrayed are either products of the author's imagination or are used fictitiously. Any resemblance to actual persons, living or dead, business establishments, events, or locales is entirely coincidental.

First printing T&D Publishing edition: May 2020
For information, contact T&D Publishing: https://tanddpublishing.com

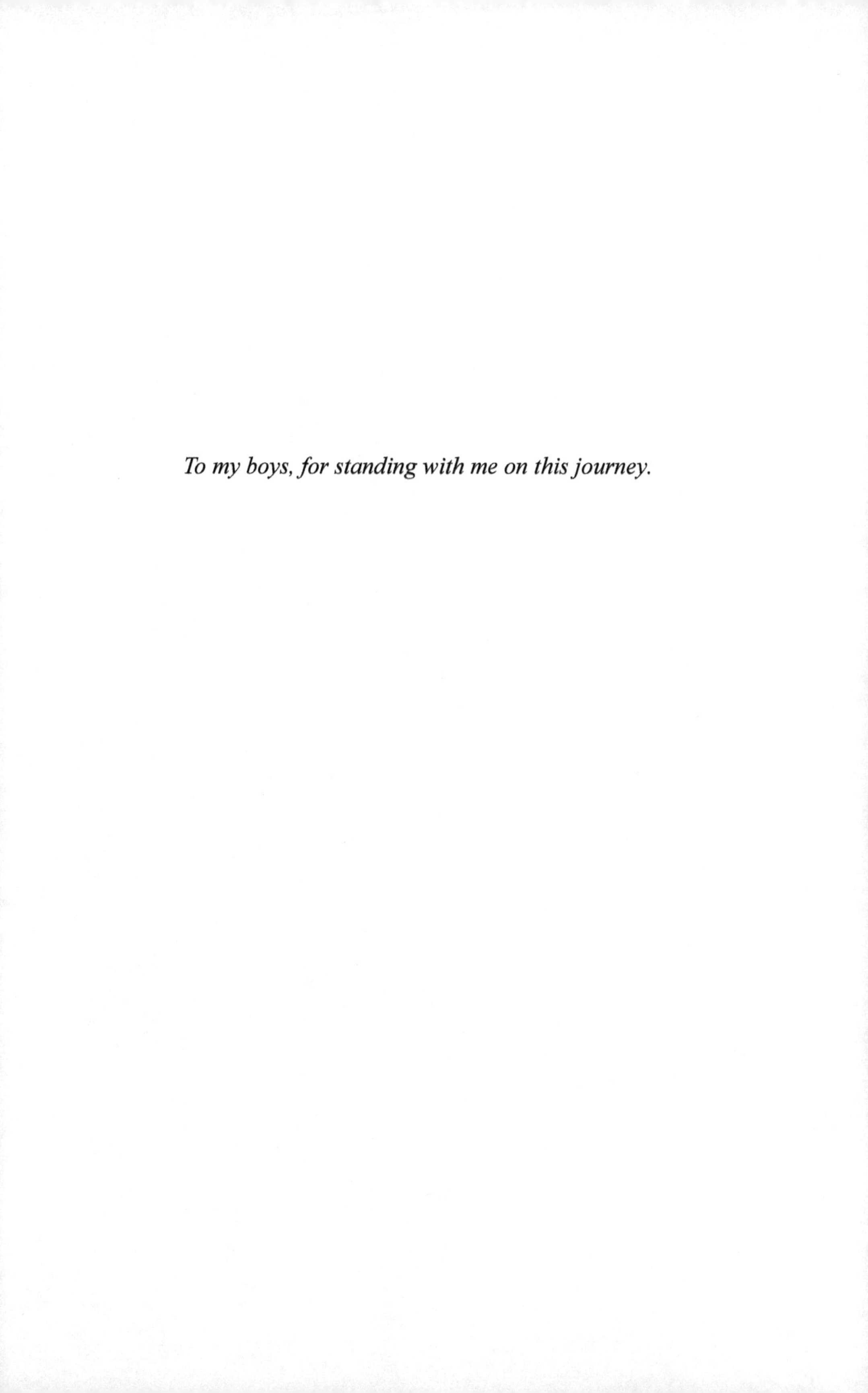

To my boys, for standing with me on this journey.

"You think we can get through this one without anything going wrong?" Deacon asked, his golden gaze sparking with the same combination of frustration and heat that Cary felt.

This was their fourth attempt at a real date.

Attempt being the operative word.

The first had gone… Well, it had started well. But then she'd been forced out of the movie theater to deal with a pissed off werewolf caught in mid-shift. That had taken the rest of the night. And while she'd enjoyed meeting Deacon's sister for the first time, she didn't think the evening qualified as a successful first date. Shame because she'd really wanted to see that movie.

The second date, they'd only gotten as far as the parking lot downtown before Cary got called away by her bosses to protect a young wizard from an irate vampire. That had been interesting. Two powerful adversaries facing off and Cary standing there in her pretty black date night dress trying to stop a fight.

Fun!

And then to add insult to injury there'd been the mugger afterward. Poor guy would likely never recover from the shock of having Cary jump between him and his intended target so fast he grabbed Cary's arm instead of the woman's purse. The fact that his hand got an electric shock after touching her had been interesting. She'd never had that happen before with a mundane human. But she'd stopped questioning the ways of her Protector powers a long time ago.

On their third attempt at a date, they'd made it into the restaurant and started their first course before disaster struck. She was still having nightmares about that night.

She sighed and nibbled at a breadstick. "So long as we get through dinner this time, I'll be good."

Because while she really wanted to see this latest superhero movie —research!—she mostly just wanted to eat. She'd spent the day with Lucy, one of her best friends and her personal martial arts trainer, working on her self defense skills. And Lucy was a brutal teacher. Cary needed the training, now more than ever. She'd entered her seventh year as a Protector and that meant she was cut off from all the support she'd had during her first six years of on-the-job training.

Fortunately, that "support" didn't count her friends or Deacon.

And Lucy was taking her responsibilities for making sure Cary could defend herself even without her powers very seriously.

Deacon grinned. "Soreness gone away yet?"

"Nearly." Cary made a face. She healed fast—which was good since, like any good Kevlar vest, she took the occasional hit while jumping between bad guys and good guys. But Lucy had worked her so hard at the dojo that Cary's muscles were *still* recovering. That had been one hell of a workout.

"I think I could officially throw someone over my head now, though," she said brightly.

Being a perfectly ordinary human woman who'd gotten tricked into this particular job as a Protector left her short a few skills. She was a purely defensive superhero. She could jump between bad guys and good guys and keep the good guys safe from pretty much anything— guns, demon fire, magic and mayhem, walking dead (that had been a gross assignment), rushing cars, knives, vampires, shapeshifters... Anything or anyone that wanted to hurt, maim, or kill another, would run up against Cary's shields and stop right there, no passing Go, no collecting two hundred dollars.

But that was all she could do. She had *no* offensive skills.

Well, there was that one time she'd managed to level a supernatural army with her powers, but she still didn't know how she'd done that, so it didn't count.

She'd gone to college with the intentions of becoming a veterinary technician, maybe eventually a vet. She'd never learned how to fight, taken martial arts, or so much as tried to shoot a gun. She was wholly unprepared for the job she'd ended up in. In fact, she hadn't even known the magical world existed before becoming a Protector. The only really good thing she had going for her was the ability to put herself in the middle of danger and then just stubbornly stand there.

That stubbornness had annoyed more than one bad guy in the past.

"I'm glad Lucy's increased your training," Deacon said.

"I've survived six years without being able to do all this," she pointed out. Much to Lucy's chagrin since she'd been trying to train Cary in self defense skills for five years. "My powers help when I need them."

"I wasn't thinking of your normal job," he said darkly, his gaze narrowed.

"Oh, yeah, that."

Turned out there was a wizard out to get her for reasons that were still unclear. But whoever he was, he wanted her dead and knew how to get around her powers to kill her. He just had to be aiming for her with no interest in hurting anyone else around her. And the bastard had gotten close twice now. It was a little nerve-wracking if she were to be honest. But she wasn't about to admit that to Deacon.

"I still think you should consider—"

"No," she said firmly. "I have to stay here and work. I can't run away and hide." Especially not to Deacon's mother.

Especially given who Deacon's mother was!

"It wouldn't be running away," he insisted. "We have this charity event every January. It would just be a week away. That should give Jaxer more than enough time to track down the wizard."

Jaxer was Cary's former mentor and someone who wasn't supposed to be helping her this year. But he'd been sneaking around trying to uncover more information about this wizard threat for her, under the excuse that it had to do with something that happened right before she was cut loose.

"The Nags won't let me go into hiding," she pointed out. "Or on a holiday or however you want to spin this."

Her bosses were the North American Fae who made Protectors. They infused them with magic and through a series of premonitions and old-fashioned research, sent Protectors out to save the day. They couldn't stop all the bad things in the world from happening. No one could. But they did their best to stop some of it, and Cary respected that.

She wasn't thrilled with how they'd tricked her into becoming a Protector, but still, what they did try to do for this world deserved some consideration. Although she would never admit that out loud to them, ever ever. And they were kind of a pain in her ass. Which was why she called them Nags—mostly to annoy them but also because they were.

"They've had no compunction about interrupting our dates," she said, "what makes you think taking me off to Eugene will stop them?"

She sighed as their food arrived. Pizza. A large pizza she felt perfectly justified in eating half of because of all the work she'd done with Lucy. Deacon would eat his half of the pizza plus his calzone and pasta dishes because he had a shapeshifter metabolism. She really really envied him that metabolism.

She was halfway through her first slice—authentic New York style cheese and pepperoni, *yum*—before she finished her reasoning. "The Nags will still demand I do something while I'm away. I'll either have to protect someone there, or I'll be called back to Portland. And I don't dare try to avoid my job."

If she did, the Nags would cut off all their support. They paid her, which was useful, but more importantly, they had a protective glamour on her house that kept anyone she didn't want to find her home from finding it. Her house was one of the few places she could be certain she was safe. And with a wizard out to kill her, she needed that safety more than ever. But it wasn't just the wizard that wanted her dead. She'd built up a lot of enemies in six years of stopping bad guys from doing exactly what they wanted. If they ever discovered where she lived, she'd never be safe again.

Deacon didn't know about the glamour. No one beyond the Nags and Jaxer knew. Not even her best friends. She was still deciding whether to tell Deacon or not.

They'd only known each other for two and a half months. They hadn't even exchanged presents at the holidays because the thought of it had wigged her out. She was still adjusting to the idea of this mate-boyfriend thing.

He'd claimed they were mates on the first night they'd met. At this stage she believed him. But the permanence of it was intimidating.

Though it turned out that, technically, because she was a human, she could break the bond at any time. Deacon couldn't walk away that easily, not now that they'd slept together. For him, the permanence of the thing was a lot more real and it would cost him to break their bond —if he even could anymore.

She had the freedom to walk away from their relationship, even now, if she wanted to.

Thing was, she really didn't want to.

"They can leave you alone for a week," Deacon insisted. "You still get to have a life outside of protecting people."

"Right," she said with no little sarcasm. The Nags had never taken her life into consideration when it came to doing her job.

She finished off her first slice and moved on to a second. The one truly lovely thing about eating with Deacon was she never felt self-conscious about how much pizza she could eat—especially when he could always eat so much more than she could. He was used to shapeshifters and all shapeshifters with their super high metabolisms ate a lot. There was something relaxing in knowing she wouldn't be judged if she decided to eat this entire pizza by herself.

"Let's change subjects," she said, because she didn't want to think about her job anymore. "Your control..." A delicate topic. "How are you doing?"

"Better."

She narrowed her eyes. "You nearly ripped that werewolves arm off," she pointed out. All the wolf had done was make a snide comment to her—which was pretty typical bad guy behavior when she was thwarting their attempts to hurt people.

"I only broke it a little," he said, almost defensively. "And it healed."

"It was over the top and unnecessary. He was already restrained."

"He threatened you."

"Deacon, they *all* threaten me. You know that. You've been there. Why isn't your control coming back?"

That was the million dollar question. Leopard shifters lost their minds a little right after finding their mates, and it apparently took a lot of sex to make them feel settled and secure in the bond. At which point, their control supposedly returned. At least that was according to Deacon's mother.

Cary was still traumatized that this information came from his *mother*.

Deacon shrugged. "We haven't been together long enough I suppose."

"We have been having sex all the time."

"Are you complaining?"

"Ha! You should know better than that."

"Guess my leopard needs more of you still."

She scowled, not sure whether to take that as a compliment or not. She lowered her voice. "How much more? I mean, every spare moment hasn't been enough?"

"That's how it is with mates," he said, in that terrifyingly matter-of-fact way that left her a little breathless.

"Really? All the time? They don't have other things to do? Like jobs and laundry and walking the dogs and stuff. How do other mates do it?"

He smiled a little. "Eventually the frequency slows. But never the intensity."

Her heart thumped harder at that thought. Because so far the intensity had been…intense. One thing still bothered her though. "Our current frequency is about as much as we can work in around everything else in life, and yet you're still not yourself. What happens if—" She cut herself off, afraid to say more aloud.

Since she was human, their bond was different. And since Deacon's control hadn't returned yet, despite them following his mother's advice (*ahhhh*!) and having sex a lot—and it had really been a lot over the last three weeks—Cary was starting to worry. More than she'd wanted to let on.

He reached across the table and squeezed her hand. "I'll be fine. *We'll* be fine. It just takes time." He dropped his gaze to the table. "Unless you're rethinking us being together."

"Stop." She tightened her grip on his hand. "That's not what I was talking about."

He met her gaze again and nodded. But the uncertainty was there, in his eyes and her gut. She wanted him in her life. She was pretty sure she'd fallen in love with him somewhere in the last few months. But there was a lot still that scared her about this relationship. A lot of things that apparently still scared him too.

Which was weirdly reassuring.

"I just want your control back so you can stop feeling so edgy," she said. "And maybe go back to work."

"Getting tired of my company?" he said, only half joking.

"Yeah, you're tough to take." She rolled her eyes. "No. You just do good work, and I don't like that you haven't been able to do your job."

He and his family ran animal shelters around the country, taking in both ordinary animals as well as the more exotic species. They were no-kill shelters and the family ensured those animals who couldn't be adopted were sent to appropriate sanctuaries. Cary loved that his work involved rescuing animals, and she'd felt a little guilty that their mate situation, and his slipping control over his leopard side, meant he'd had to take a hiatus from that work.

"Caitlin is handling things fine in my absence. And there's email. I haven't been cut off entirely."

She let out a long breath. "Okay."

"You don't sound sure?"

"I'm worried. I'm worried you might not ever get your control back and that will suck a lot."

"We could talk to my mother about it," he offered. "Another good reason to go stay with my parents for a week."

She suppressed a shudder. "You want me to ask your mother why all the sex I'm having with her son isn't working?"

"Not working?" He contrived to look offended, though she saw his lip twitch with amusement.

"You know what I mean," she said, her cheeks warming. "It's been working just fine for orgasms."

"I'm glad to hear that."

"But not for your control," she finished.

"She's really the best person to talk to for answers."

Cary sighed. She'd only just recently found out his mother was basically the queen of the leopards—at least the west coast leopards. A little fact he'd failed to mention when they'd first met. His mother being the leader of his people was intimidating enough. The thought of discussing their mate issues with her, their *sex* life, was almost more than she could contemplate.

"I'm not sure I need answers enough to face that conversation," she admitted. She ignored Deacon's suppressed smile. "And I did a piss poor job of subject change here. Let's try another topic. Something innocuous."

They went on to debate the various merits of New York style pizza versus Chicago style—she only threatened to leave him once when he defended Chicago style—and that led into other food related topics which were safe and easy date conversation.

The complications of her job and their relationship could wait. At least until after the movie.

Or so she'd thought. But when they stepped out of the restaurant, a tingle crawled down her spine. A too-familiar sensation. One she'd been learning to interpret for the last six years.

Danger.

Someone was in need of her particular brand of help.

2

The small square outside the restaurant, across from the Max platform looked innocuous enough. Like nothing much was happening, just people coming and going on a Friday night in January when the weather in Portland was actually pleasant and not raining.

Then Cary spotted the girl jerking out of the hold of a grown man. She was short and from the glimpse Cary got of her face, she looked maybe fourteen or fifteen years old. She was wearing a head scarf, a hajib, which the man pulled at. The girl stepped away again, holding her hajib in place. And then she gasped.

Cary was already running through the throngs of moving people, but despite her Protector powers kicking in, giving her a speed she couldn't normally achieve, she realized with a shock of pain and fear that she wasn't moving fast enough. Too many people in the way. Things happening too fast.

Shit! She wasn't going to get there in time.

She couldn't even see what the man was doing, but she knew in her gut she was going to be too slow.

In the next instant, the world around her blurred. She had a moment to gasp. And then she was between the girl and the man, and she realized the man was holding a gun...

That had just gone off.

The bullet hit Cary in the shoulder, square and true. She took the impact with as little backward movement as she could manage against the momentum of the moving bullet. It still hurt like hell. And she wasn't looking forward to the bruise this would cause.

But like any good Kevlar vest, the bullet crumbled against her skin without penetrating, flattening into a useless lump of metal and collapsing onto the sidewalk with a little chinking noise.

Cary put her hands on her hips and glared at the man who'd just shot her—though he'd been aiming for the girl. A teenager! Cary was outraged. The man was easily six foot tall, a good half a foot or more taller than the teenager, and thickly muscled. His brown hair was cut short and streaked with gray. His fatigues didn't fit him properly, too tight across his stomach, too loose in other places. Between his five o'clock shadow, the faint stench of alcohol and sweat clinging to him, and the slightly greasy look of his pale skin, he was a wholly unappealing excuse for humanity.

"That was very rude," Cary said to him. "Do you mind telling me why you just shot me while attempting to shoot a *teenager*?" She was fairly vibrating with her anger. She hated bullies. And she hated people who attacked kids even more. It was one of the reasons she'd kept doing this job over the years.

He snarled some curses at her and some offensive racial slurs at the teenager, which just pissed Cary off even more. She was tempted to try out some of the new things Lucy had been teaching her. Then he raised his gun again and pointed it at her chest.

She lowered her chin, holding his gaze, and said, "No."

He blinked. The gun wavered.

And before he could straighten his arm, Deacon was beside him, gripping his wrist hard enough to break bones.

The man cried out and dropped the weapon. Deacon, eyes slightly glowing, didn't release his wrist, forcing the man to fold to his knees. The man started sweating profusely.

"You're breaking my wrist, man. You're hurting me!"

"Shut up," Cary said. "You were just holding a gun on me and a *kid.* Just because she had a head scarf? You deserve to have your hand ripped off and it's only because he's a nice man that he hasn't done that yet."

"No," Deacon said, the growl of his leopard clear in his tone. "I haven't ripped his arm off yet because the police are coming and I don't want to deal with the paperwork."

"Ah," Cary said with a nod. "Well, that's fair enough. Paperwork can be a real pain." She showed her teeth to the still whimpering asshole, then turned to face the girl. She was several yards behind Cary, her arms crossed over her chest, her dark eyes wide in her way-too-young face.

Cary stepped closer to draw her gaze away from the man who'd been threatening her. "Hi," she said to the girl. "I'm Cary. Are you okay?"

The girl nodded.

"Did he hurt you when he grabbed you?" Cary asked gently. "Do you need a doctor?"

The girl shook her head.

"Do you have people somewhere nearby to help you get home, friends or family? Or do you need a ride?" Cary wasn't about to leave her alone now. Looking at her closer, she realized she wasn't fourteen or fifteen. If she was twelve, Cary would be amazed. And she looked traumatized. It was all Cary could do not to pull the girl into a hug to comfort as much as to continue protecting.

The girl swallowed a few times, then said, very quietly, "My father's store is just there." She pointed to the opposite side of the road to a small sundries shop.

"I'll walk you there, just to make sure you're okay," Cary said. She glanced back at Deacon just as the police were walking up to him. Warily, she noted with some worry.

Deacon was smiling broadly at them, though he still had the asshole in a brutal grip. Cary blinked and looked at the cops again. Her shoulders relaxed when she recognized Deacon's cop friend. She'd met him once but his name escaped her. His irritating partner was with him, but both men approached Deacon without their guns out or any other sign of aggression so Cary assumed Deacon could handle the situation.

She took a few seconds to consider the fact that Deacon had raced her through the crowd so she could get in front of the asshole before he shot the girl.

Deacon had used Cary as a shield, ensuring she was between him and the asshole so he didn't get shot either, which might have been offensive to anyone else. But the gesture, his helping her to make sure a child wasn't killed, made her chest swell with tender emotions. That he'd trusted to her skills, that he hadn't tried to take the bullet himself and had instead pulled the girl out of range…

Cary fell a little more for her mate in that moment.

To the girl, Cary said, "Let's just take you to your family. If the police need to take your statement, they can do that there."

Also, Cary didn't want to talk to the police officers, even if one was a good friend of Deacon's. She'd been shot. And she wasn't bleeding. That wasn't easy to explain. There were witnesses too, but she kind of hoped it had all happened so fast no one realized the bullet had actually hit her.

Human brains had a hard time accepting what they didn't know was possible. In the past, if there had been witnesses to her Protector skills, the witnesses typically made up plausible sounding excuses to explain what they'd seen—the bullet missed and hit a light pole; the knife obviously missed her completely; the fall wasn't as hard as it looked; that guy looked drugged up, she was lucky to avoid him; obviously the car hadn't been going as fast as it looked.

In fact, Cary had found that the occasional witness made up better excuses and justifications for what happened than Cary usually did. So she'd leave it to them to explain away how she'd been shot without getting hurt and concentrate on getting the girl back to her family.

She caught Deacon's eye first, nodding toward the shop so he'd know where she'd gone. He gave her a barely perceptible nod and a little smile.

She grinned back. Their fourth date and another interesting end to it. Ah well. At least she'd gotten her dinner this time.

3

"Tell me again what happened to this coat?" Marianne said, scowling at the jagged tear through the sleeve.

Marianne, one of Cary's best friends in the whole world, was also her go-to woman for all things clothing. Marianne was a seamstress by day, secret magical weaver by night. Or really any time. And she was very good at keeping Cary in clothing that could handle the abuse Cary put it through.

Cary blanched. "I was just a little late getting there so the bullet caught me." She pulled a face. "I'd just eaten dinner. I was full."

"You go on hella weird dates, girlfriend."

"I saved Jasmine from getting shot," Cary said. "I'll take that over an uninterrupted date any day."

"Which is why you got roped into your current job," Marianne said with a fond smile. The look turned to a fierce frown in the next instant. "Why weren't you wearing something I'd made for you? You wouldn't have this rip if you had."

"My only coat from you is the leather one and I wanted to wear something a little fancier for dinner. I was hopeful we'd get a quiet night." She shrugged and ducked her head.

"Then just ask me to make you a fancier coat," Marianne said.

"I've been itching to make you proper dress up clothes, but you keep telling me there's no point. I had to make and then send you the little black dress before you'd wear it."

Cary had actually worn that dress on her second date with Deacon. It had survived the wizard-vampire thing, but her high heels hadn't. Which was why she'd stuck to slacks and flats for their last two attempts at dates.

"There hasn't been a point before now," Cary said with a sigh. Her romantic life had been sorely lacking since becoming a Protector. It hadn't exactly been hopping before that, but she'd at least had the occasional date. Since becoming a Protector she'd been with exactly two men and neither had last long because she kept disappearing on them to go do her job.

Frankly, the fact that Deacon was still around two and a half months later was pretty amazing.

"Well now you have a mate," Marianne said. She waggled her eyebrows. "A gorgeous one at that. You need date clothes. I will make you the best date clothes your ass has ever been in."

"Will they show off my ass?" Cary said with a cheeky grin.

"Of course!"

She laughed as Marianne disappeared into a back room where she kept additional bolts of material.

Marianne was a seamstress bar none. She could create the most gorgeous clothing from her imagination without a pattern—which impressed the hell out of Cary—and design outfits that suited their wearers impeccably. The fact that she could also slip a little magic into her creations only magnified her genius.

Technically, Marianne was a weaver, the kind from myths and legends that could weave flax into gold. She found that boring, though, and much preferred designing women clothing with the best pockets every created by anyone ever.

Cary had met Marianne before becoming a Protector, when she'd still been working as a vet tech. Marianne had volunteered on the weekends at the veterinary office. They'd gotten along well then, bonding over 80s music and the no-fruit-on-pizza ethos. But they'd become best friends after Cary became a Protector, when she'd gone to Marianne for help. Cary had lost her car and house keys five times and her wallet twice before acknowledging she needed that help. At the very least, she needed pockets with zippers and reinforcements because diving between bad guys and good guys had a tendency to make ordinary pockets ineffective for holding stuff inside.

Marianne had taken one look at the shredded denim jacket Cary had brought her, and—after Cary had helped prevent Marianne from being kidnapped by the imp messenger of a goblin king—created a range of jeans, shirts, and a leather jacket specifically designed to prevent rips and tears and to keep things in. Reinforced-with-magic material that didn't tear easily at the swipe of a shifter's claws. Pockets that sealed closed with a touch, or if Cary forgot to close them, automatically kept their contents from falling out. Hidden spaces in her outfits that could hold a lot more than seemed possible from the outside. One of the pockets in her leather jacket could hide all kinds of weapons safely without worrying about them going off, or piercing the leather, or in the case of magical objects, accidentally getting triggered.

All these years later, Cary had no idea how she'd lived her life without Marianne in it. And not just for the perfect work clothes. They still bonded over no-pineapple-on-pizza and 80s music. As well as the struggles of leading a life that intersected with the mystical when so many of their loved ones were mundane.

Marianne's two sisters were also weavers, so she had family that understood. Cary's younger sister, Valerie, knew what she did, in an abstract hadn't-seen-it-in-practice kind of way, but no one else in her family had a clue. And Marianne's girlfriend, the partner she'd been with for ten years, was an ordinary woman, a nightclub owner, and completely unaware of Marianne's magical ancestry. Marianne couldn't bring herself to reveal that side of her life to Gina. Cary couldn't really blame her.

Balancing the mundane world with the magic world wasn't ever easy. And Cary was grateful every day for her friends, because they at least understood.

Marianne came out from the back room with a huge skein of white wool. "This is for a new winter coat," she explained. "A fancy one."

"Do you think white is a good idea for me? Cause, you know, it's harder to hide…stuff on white."

"It'll be perfect. Very classy. Trust me. I'll be back."

"Wait, what else do you need?" Cary called, leaning sideways where she was sitting on one of the huge staging tables in Marianne's storefront.

As it was after regular shop hours and Marianne didn't have any private appointments, the shop's glass front door was locked and the shades had been lowered over the glass front walls. The lights in the main room were set at a comfortable illumination that didn't glare or make Cary feel like she was in an office, but gave Marianne enough light to see well. One of Marianne's two assistants had swept the wooden floor of the main room before clocking out, giving the pale wood a lovely glow. The whole place smelled of cinnamon from Marianne's favorite air freshener and the faintly musky undertone of piles of material.

"Lining for the coat," Marianne called from the backroom. "And some pretty material for a dress…" Her voice trailed off. Then as she came back into the work room. "And some fancy shirts and slacks since all that diving around in front of bad guys that you do makes the skirts trickier."

"Yeah, I'd rather not flash my underwear to all of Portland on a regular basis," Cary said, wincing and laughing at the thought. "I'd love a pretty dress," she continued, eyeing the skeins of jewel-colored material Marianne had brought out with a sigh of longing, "but I'm not sure I'll get the chance to wear it very often. That skirt I wore to the girls' night when the wizard tried to kill me is one of the very few skirts I own."

"I am aware." Marianne shook her head at Cary's reminder of the wizard attack outside Angie's house back in November. Marianne and Lucy hadn't arrived yet, but Cary and Angie had told them all about it. It had been one of the main topics of that night. Also Deacon. And Jaxer, Cary's erstwhile former mentor. And Gina. And Lucy's latest crush. And Lucy's dojo. And Angie's psychic readings business. And retirement investments. And a pretty long ramble about the mating behaviors of different shapeshifter species, but that was after the entire bottle of tequila was empty and Cary barely remembered that part.

"The silhouette of that skirt really suited your shape," Marianne said, tapping a blue tipped finger against her plum-colored lips. Marianne's favorite accessory these days was lipstick, and this particular shade really complimented her dark brown skin. "But I think I'll give you a flip shape on the dress skirt," she said with a sharp nod. "Something more fitted to your hips, flaring around your knees…"

"I'm still not sure a dress is necessary," Cary said, though inside she was doing a little happy dance at the idea of one.

"Stop arguing. You know I'm putting in the good magic. The skirt won't fly up at inopportune times, it'll flow around you like ordinary material, but will stretch and adjust to any movements you need to make, just like good yoga pants. And best of all…" She held Cary's gaze, a twinkle in her dark eyes, drawing out the suspense.

"What, what?" Cary said, leaning closer.

Marianne lowered her voice, leaned in to Cary and said, "Pockets."

Cary whooped.

Marianne laughed and snapped out her tape measure. "Let's get some numbers," she said. "You look like you've lost weight."

"Hardly," Cary said. "Deacon feeds me too well. I've probably gained."

"Whatever. It looks good on you." She grinned wickedly. "So does Deacon."

"Ha, ha." Cary pretended to scowl.

An hour, many measurements, and a few debates over color later, Cary left Marianne's shop with a promise to return in two days for the new clothes.

She was almost to her car parked on the street not far from Marianne's boutique when a dark shape stepped from the shadows of a nearby tattoo parlor, looming over her and blocking her path.

4

Cary gasped and stepped back, a jolt of fear and adrenaline surging through her blood, before she recognized the shape.

"Jaxer, damn it, you scared me." She put a hand on her heart, and not just for show.

Not only did she have a wizard out to kill her, but she didn't have anyone nearby to protect. Which meant she was as vulnerable to muggings and attacks as anyone else. And while she was more confident of her self defense skills these days, she hadn't had to put Lucy's training to the test in a real-life situation yet.

"I thought you'd been training more with Lucy," Jaxer said, his comment echoing her thoughts and making her scowl deeper. "You should be able to kick my ass easily now."

She snorted. "Right."

Since Jaxer was one of the Fae, she doubted her rudimentary self defense skills would do her any good if they ever actually fought, even if the idea of kicking his ass was *extremely* tempting just then. He'd been around long enough—although how long he refused to tell her—to learn a bit more about fighting than she had or likely ever would. And combat wasn't even Jaxer's greatest talent.

That was glamour, the ability to make other people see and feel what he wanted them to, a type of illusionary magic that went way beyond what ordinary witches or wizards could do. Jaxer's magic made his illusions *feel* like reality. Even people who could normally see through glamours, like other Fae, or Angie if she was wearing the right charm, couldn't sense Jaxer's illusions. Cary didn't know the full extent of that particular power, but she'd seen him do some pretty impressive things, like somehow convincing ordinary humans that they didn't want to wander down a particular street while Cary was busy keeping nasty bad guys from doing bad things.

Jaxer even disguised his own appearance with a constant glamour that Cary suspected actually made him slightly less beautiful that he was in real life. But only slightly. Jaxer was a gorgeous man and too vain not to flaunt it.

"What are you doing here?" she asked as he fell into step next to her on her way to her car. She'd parked on the street about two blocks from Marianne's shop, but since it wasn't raining, the walk was pleasant.

"Getting new outfits?" Jaxer asked, ignoring her question.

"Jaxer…" She put a warning note in her tone.

He raised his hands in mock defense. "I just wanted to make sure you were okay," he said. "No more wizard attacks?"

She shook her head. It was like waiting for the other shoe to drop. She was on a constant edge of anticipation, which was frankly exhausting. "Have you found out anything?"

Technically, he wasn't supposed to be helping her anymore. But he claimed that his searching for the wizard wasn't a violation of the Seventh Year rules since he thought this threat had to do with a case that had happened before the start of her test year. She didn't argue the point very hard because she needed all the help she could get.

He dropped a casual arm across her shoulders, pulling her closer to his side.

She frowned at him. "Are you about to deliver bad news?"

"What makes you say that?" He pretended an innocent expression, but she wasn't buying it.

"Spill" she said.

He sighed dramatically. "Can't I just enjoy an evening stroll with my favorite protégée?"

"No. What have you found?"

"Fine. I haven't found much. But I have found a link back to Sheldon."

"I knew it," Cary growled.

Sheldon was a teenage wizard who'd kidnapped Deacon at Halloween in order to swap bodies—Sheldon intended to send his essence into Deacon's body, send Deacon's essence into his own body, and then kill his old body—and Deacon along with it!—so he could keep a shapeshifter's body. It was a pretty skeevy plan, and Jaxer and Deacon had apparently been working together to uncover it, but then Deacon got trapped and Jaxer sent Cary in to save him.

To this day, Cary was pretty sure Jaxer regretted everything to do with that night.

She and Deacon had assumed the teenage wizard, an evil little bastard, had been killed when his own power backlashed on him off of Cary's shields. But when Jaxer had gone in to clean up the mess she'd left behind...no body.

"I told you I saw him in the middle of Holland's army, didn't I?" she said, feeling vindicated. That had been a busy night and she still wasn't entirely sure what had happened, but knowing she hadn't been seeing things helped her piece of mind.

"You did, and you were right and very smart to make the link." He kissed her cheek. "Good instincts."

She scowled at the kiss and the condescension, and made a show of wiping her cheek. He grinned.

"So who's the old wizard and what does he have to do with Sheldon?" she asked. She'd gotten a look at the wizard the second time he'd attacked her. He wasn't anyone she knew, which was why all this had been so frustrating. She was used to knowing the people who wanted to kill her.

"I don't know for sure who he is yet," Jaxer said. "But Sheldon had a master...a mentor of sorts who was training him. I haven't been able to identify the master. I'm pretty sure he's the one after you, though."

"But why?" She huffed. "Sheldon is apparently not dead. If he didn't kill himself on my shields, and if he's still alive, why would his master want me dead? Sheldon I could understand. I interrupted his disgusting plan to steal Deacon's gorgeous body."

Jaxer snorted at her description, and she tossed him a smug grin.

"So I can see Sheldon wanting me dead," she finished. "And Sheldon knew I was a Protector. He didn't seem to know how to kill me, though. He just wanted me as a bodyguard. Do you suppose he told his master and it's his master who figured out how to kill me?"

"Apparently, since he's nearly got to you twice now."

She shivered and Jaxer's arm on her shoulders tightened. She leaned into him for just a moment before realizing that she wasn't supposed to be relying on him anymore.

"Okay, so maybe the master is just helping Sheldon get revenge?" she continued. "I suppose that makes some kind of evil sense. And Sheldon had that evil glint in his eye so I doubt he's hanging with a good and benevolent mentor."

"While I couldn't get a name, the hints of information I've gathered agree with you," Jaxer said. "The master is not a nice man."

She barked a laugh heavy with irony. "Ya think?" She sighed. "So… What do I do about him? I can't hide in my house and hope he forgets about me. The Nags won't let me." If they would let her, she'd probably have been spending a lot more time at home in bed with Deacon. Which sounded like a great way to hide out from a vengeful wizard.

"If I can figure out who he is," Jaxer said, "we can always negotiate with him to get him off your back."

"Yeah, he seems like the negotiating type." They reached her car and stopped beside the passenger side door. Cary slid out from under Jaxer's arm to face him. "But that counts as helping me," she pointed out. "If you try to negotiate with him, you're helping me."

"Not with your job," Jaxer said with a casual shrug.

She frowned a little at the movement. How could one being be so damned graceful without even trying. "I'm not sure the Nags would see the distinction."

"If you negotiate," Jaxer said, "I'll just be there to keep you safe. You can protect me and I'll have your back."

"I can take Angie to do that. She's a witch and knows how to shield against magic."

Jaxer tucked his chin, looking offended. "And I don't?"

"How would I know?" she countered. "You never have told me everything you can do. Outside of the glamour and a few skills with a sword, you've been very tight-lipped about your talents all these years. Which is a little strange given how vain you are."

"I'm not sure whether that's a compliment or an insult," he said, leaning in close so his face was right in hers.

"Your choice." She grinned at him, a part of her relieved. Since the weeks before her seventh year started, Jaxer had been acting really strange. Their banter tonight felt a lot more like the old Jaxer, and she'd missed that. She'd missed her friend.

He lowered his voice. "I have a lot of talents you don't know about," he said. "Yet."

She snorted. But her amusement died along with her relief when he leaned in even closer, pressing his body up against hers, his gaze dropping to her lips. Jaxer was a touchy-feely kind of guy and always had been. This was different. The intensity in his gaze set her heartbeat thumping hard in what she suspected was…fear.

"Jaxer?" she asked, her voice quiet. "What the hell are you doing?"

"Trying *not* to do something I've wanted to do for years," he murmured.

"Huh?"

His lips lifted in a faint smile. "I adore you, Cary Redmond."

"Okay."

"I love you," he said quietly, brushing a finger down her cheek.

"You better mean that in a friendship kind of way," she said, though her voice sounded choked and breathless.

"I don't. And I've been trying to tell you that for two months."

"No, you haven't."

"Stop telling me what I feel and what I've been doing."

"Stop talking nonsense. You've never shown any signs of interest in me before."

"Because I couldn't," he growled. "I was your mentor. It wasn't allowed." He cupped her face between his palms. "I'm not your mentor anymore."

"Don't you dare kiss me," she said.

"I kiss you all the time," he pointed out.

"Not like this." She let out a shaky breath and gripped his wrists, not pushing him away but holding him in place. "Jaxer, you can't mean this. You're just feeling weird about having to abandon me to the seventh year."

"No. I've done that with Protector protégés for two centuries. You're different."

She shook her head, not wanting to hear this. It broke her heart in a way she couldn't quite explain to herself. "Jaxer… Deacon."

He snarled. "Yes. Deacon."

"Hey, it's your fault I even know him."

"Mores the pity. But you know you have a choice now. You aren't bound by this mate bond the way he is. And he will get over it."

Jaxer had been the one to point out to her that because she was human and not a leopard shifter, the bond between her and Deacon wasn't as binding as Deacon had led her to believe. They could both get out of the relationship if they wanted to. At least, they could have before they started sleeping together. Now…

But she'd made her choice to go to bed with Deacon after learning about the option to end their bond, after having confronted Deacon with the information. They'd talked, and she'd decided she wanted Deacon in her life—even though the idea of permanent and long term scared the ever-loving shit out of her. She wasn't good with commitment as it turned out. But she had made the choice to try things with Deacon. And she wasn't changing her mind about that now.

"Jaxer, I'm not still with Deacon because I have to be," she said gently.

"Do you know about his family?"

"Are you trying to make me suspicious and distrust him?"

"Yes."

"Well, at least you're being honest. Yes, I know his mother is like the queen of the leopards or something. And yes, we talked about him hiding that little fact from me." She winced. "At the same time as we talked about me hiding the fact that a wizard was trying to kill me. So I wasn't exactly super honest with him either."

Jaxer held her gaze, his blue-green eyes faintly sparkling under the streetlight. His blond hair glowed. Shadows cut into the sharp lines of his ethereally handsome features. He didn't comment for a long moment, just stared at her.

Finally, he dropped his hands from her face and took a step away. "I'm not giving up on us," he said. "I've loved you for a long time now. And Deacon isn't who you think he is. I'll be here for you when he breaks your heart. I'll always be here for you."

She wanted to cry and she wasn't even sure why. "Jaxer, please. I don't want to hurt you, but I don't want you pretending there will be something between us eventually either."

"Are you saying if Deacon hadn't come into your life, and I'd told you I loved you, you'd have still refused me?"

She raised her hands in a helpless gesture. "I can't honestly say, one way or the other. I never even considered that you saw me that way. You never even hinted…"

"I told you why."

"Still, from my perspective, it never occurred to me to consider a romantic relationship with you. I have no idea what I might have done, what I would have felt, if you'd told me this before Deacon. And that really doesn't matter now. We can't go back and change time."

He didn't comment and for just a moment Cary wondered if Jaxer could change time. But then, she realized if he could have, he probably would have already.

Silence settled heavily between them for a long, painful moment. She wanted to say more and yet didn't know what to say. She really just wanted things back to the way they'd always been between her and Jaxer.

Now, she was afraid that would never happen.

Finally, Jaxer broke the stalemate. "I can't give up on you yet," he said quietly. "I've been…hoping and loving you for a long time." He raised a hand to stop her when she opened her mouth to speak. "But I won't push you."

"I don't want to hurt you," she said quietly.

"Too late," he said, but he smiled when he said it. "I'm a big boy. I can take it."

She shook her head. "This sucks you know. Why the hell did you have to go and think you'd fallen in love with me, you dumbass?"

"That's why." He brushed his knuckles over her cheek again. Then he took another step away from her and pulled in a deep breath. "When I know more about this master wizard, I'll be in touch. Stay safe."

She nodded, not sure what to say anymore. She slid into her car as Jaxer disappeared around a corner, going to wherever it was he went when she wasn't with him. She stared at her steering wheel for a moment before starting the Prius. What a weird and sad end to her evening. She adored Jaxer, loved him as a friend, but…

She would never have guessed her heart would break over someone else's misplaced love.

5

"What did Jaxer want?" Deacon asked as soon as she opened the door for him and he stepped into her house.

She rolled her eyes. "Your sense of smell is disturbing." She gestured to the couch and the two glasses of wine she'd already set out on her coffee table. "You'd better sit."

"I'm not going to like this, am I?"

"No. Although, I do have to admit you were right about something and I was wrong, so you get to say 'I told you so' and that might help." She raised her brows hopefully.

Deacon did not look so hopeful.

She shrugged. She generally liked to get in a good "I told you so," so she just assumed other people did too. Maybe not this time.

They sat on the couch and Cary took a long sip of her wine before starting. "So, you were right about Jaxer, and all your jealousy is justified."

"What happened?" Deacon's voice had dropped to a growl and his entire body was still and coiled, as if ready to pounce.

"I really wish your control was back," she said.

"I will always get emotional over someone else hitting on my mate."

She didn't know what to say to that, so she just said, "Apparently, Jaxer's been in love with me for years. Or so he thinks."

"He finally told you."

"You knew?" Cary fairly screeched. "What the hell? He *told* you?"

"He didn't have to." Deacon tapped his nose. "But," he added with a shrug, "he admitted it out loud, too."

"And he's still alive? That's a testament to your control." She blinked. "Wow, what were you like before meeting me?"

"An iceman," he said.

She wasn't sure if that was a joke, an exaggeration, or not.

"And I came close to throttling him when he admitted his feelings for you, but I didn't. Frankly, I can't blame him."

She smiled a little at that. "If this wasn't such a sad situation, that would be sweet."

"You're an amazing woman, Cary. I can't blame Jaxer for seeing that." He glanced down at the couch. "What did you say when he told you?"

She shrugged. "What could I say?"

"Do you… Are you considering his offer?"

"His offer?"

"That's what a declaration of love is," Deacon said. "An offer. Of a certain kind of future."

She'd never thought of it that way before. She and Deacon had different views of love, and what it meant to say I love you to someone, and she still wasn't entirely sure if his way was reassuring or not. But one thing she was certain of—she and Deacon hadn't said those words to each other. Not yet.

"I said no," she answered his question. "Of course I did. I don't love Jaxer that way."

"You could have."

He was stating, not asking.

"I don't know," she admitted. "But I don't have those feelings for him now."

Deacon didn't exactly relax but she noticed the tension in his shoulders eased and he took a small sip of his wine.

"How did he take the news?" he asked.

"Hard to tell with Jaxer, but he wasn't happy." She hesitated to say this. "And he's not giving up just yet."

Deacon growled.

"Hey, rein in your jealousy. You can't expect him to just switch off feelings. Any more than he can expect me to switch feelings on and off. He'll need time. I'm giving it to him because he's been my friend for years. And you're going to have to deal with that."

"He'll still be around?"

"Yes. He's still helping with that vengeful wizard issue I'm having." She told him the little bit of information Jaxer had uncovered so far.

The news that Sheldon was definitely part of this made Deacon snarl. "I hate that little shit. If he shows up again…"

"I know he's evil, but he's a teenager. Maybe we can help him."

Deacon lowered his chin. "Seriously?"

"Okay, maybe not. But since we're the adults, we're not going to hurt him if we can help it."

"And if he tries to kill you? He's likely already trying to kill you through his master."

She sighed and rubbed a hand over her face. "I don't know. I'll deal with that when it happens." She let out a tired groan. "This was a very weird evening."

"Did anything go wrong at Marianne's?"

"No, that was fun. She's making me another date night dress." Cary grinned. This was a much easier topic and she was thrilled to change the subject.

But the time she'd finished describing the dress and the way it would hug her body, Deacon's snarly jealousy had changed to purring seduction. She liked that a lot better and was leaning in for a kiss that would take them back to the bedroom when his cellphone rang.

He cursed, looked at the screen, then cursed again. "It's my mother."

"Well, that was a nice splash of cold water," Cary said. "I'll go get more wine while you talk to her."

She hurried into the kitchen, trying hard not to think about what his *mother* had almost interrupted. She greeted her small dog pack as they came in through the mudroom. They'd all been hanging in the backyard before Deacon had arrived, enjoying the cold night air, and the dogs had remained outside when she'd gone to let Deacon in.

"You guys doing okay? Ready for a bedtime treat?"

Since her Labrador/demon dog Buck had helped fight off a demon god not too long ago, she'd gotten very lax with handing out treats. Her dogs deserved those treats, and she wasn't going to deny them a few extra calories, because life was short. Pickles, the outwardly basset hound, inwardly foo lion, was never one to turn down a snack. Like Cary, Pickles was a girl who enjoyed her food. The single mundane dog in the pack, Fred, a mixed breed terrier, was also thrilled with this change in treat policy. It seemed to be Fred's mission in life to consume as many treats as possible so that he could one day bounce off the ceiling and not just the walls.

She scratched Buck's head as he devoured his nightly bone. His temperature felt normal and he was acting like himself. She kept watching for signs of the moodiness and irritability he'd displayed not that long ago, but so far, nothing. She was starting to think his episode had been the result of the demon god's activity. All the demon magic pounding Portland must have triggered something in her poor dog and brought out his demon side.

Normally, Buck went about his life as a perfectly ordinary Labrador, all blond fur and lazy demeanor punctuated by some fun antics at the park when pressed into play by Fred. His return to his demon dog form... Well really, his first full blown foray into his demon dog nature had been more than a little scary for her. Not because she was afraid of his demon half for her sake, but because she was afraid for him and what that might have done to him.

So far, though, her beloved dog was doing well. Her whole pack seemed to be doing well. Even the stray cat Scratchy that she fed when he deigned to show up seemed to be doing well. The tom was fit and healthy for a mostly feral beast, and seemed to have even put on weight recently.

The fact that the animals in her life were healthy gave her one less thing to worry about and that was a relief given how many things she was currently worried about.

Deacon walked into the kitchen frowning at his phone.

Speaking of worries. "What did your mother want at this time of night?" she asked, even though she wasn't sure she wanted to know.

"I have to go back sooner than I was planning," he said, still frowning. "There were some issues with our usual venue for the fundraiser."

"Issues?"

"She didn't go into detail."

"You're scowling and your voice is doing that growly-leopard-is-close-to-the-surface thing. What's wrong?" She wanted to reach out to him, with an instinct she still couldn't quite fathom, to comfort and reassure even if she didn't know what she was comforting him for. But he didn't look like he'd do well with touch just then. He was holding his phone so tight his knuckles were turning white and she wasn't certain the little rectangle of plastic and circuitry would survive. So she kept her place by the counter, leaning back and crossing her arms.

"She didn't say outright, but she implied the cougars were behind the trouble," he said.

Ah. There were issues between the cougar shifters and the leopard shifters—a fight over territory as far as Cary could make out. Those tensions had escalated in recent months. The cougars had even kidnapped some of the leopard kids in order to force a negotiation. Cary had helped rescue the kids, but then things with the necromancer and her brother had come up and she'd gotten distracted.

"Can you talk about what's been happening yet?" she asked. She knew the cougars had still been harassing Deacon's people, but he'd been very tight-lipped about the details. Just saying the issues were being handled and he couldn't discuss it.

She'd been very reluctant to let that go. Especially now that she knew Deacon wasn't just an ordinary leopard shifter. He would one day take over from his mother, leading all the leopards in the Pacific Northwest. If Cary's relationship continued with him, one day she'd also have to deal with being the mate of the leader of all those shifters.

She wasn't particularly happy with being kept in the dark about what was happening with them now. It didn't bode well for her and Deacon's future communication skills.

He remained silent, not answering her question, but he stopped gripping his phone so hard and physically shook off his anger. "It'll be fine," he said. "I just need to get back and help arrange a new venue last minute. The person my mother has in charge of the event asked for help. It used to be my job, even though Caitlin is better at these things," he explained.

"Why didn't your mother ask Caitlin to help this time, then?"

"She's too busy with the shelters themselves."

Cary frowned. "Because you haven't been able to work." She shook her head. "Damn it, Deacon. I told you it wasn't good your control hadn't come back. You need to get back to work. This…this mate stuff is throwing your life and your family business all out of whack."

"It is what it is," he said with a shrug. "I can't change it."

She didn't comment. But she didn't meet his gaze either.

Not even when he gripped her shoulders and tried to get her to look at him. "Don't even think about it?" he said, his voice deep.

"Think about what?"

"You know what I'm talking about. I don't want out of our relationship. Stop trying to find excuses to end it."

"That's not what I'm doing." She finally met his gaze. "I don't want to end things with you. I…" Nope. Couldn't say it yet. "I want you in my life. I just hate what being with me is doing to you."

"I don't."

"Right." She knew he was frustrated with his fluctuating control. He worked really hard at hiding that frustration from her. Sometimes, he even seemed easy going about it, like it didn't really matter to him. But times like this, when his family needed the old Deacon and he couldn't be that person, she knew it upset him.

"It'll work out," he insisted. "I'll be fine, we'll be fine. This is just the early stages."

She let out a long breath. This wasn't a topic that was going away any time soon, but they also didn't have any answers for it just then. So better to concentrate on what they could actually solve. "When do you have to leave?"

"Tomorrow," he said. "And I want you to come with me."

"Tomorrow? I can't. I can't just…leave."

He pulled her into a hug. "I can't go without you," he murmured into her hair. "Not and still be useful to my family."

She groaned. Shit. She'd almost forgotten that little hiccup. It wasn't just that his control hadn't come back yet. He had a lot of trouble staying away from her. He *had* to spend as much time as possible in her presence or his leopard got a little crazy. They managed short chunks of time apart, but the one period where he'd been away for over a week, he'd spent most of the time in his leopard form. It was another complication of the mate thing. Another thing to worry about.

Frankly, if this part didn't sort itself out soon, she could see it feeling very stifling. She adored being with Deacon, but she didn't want to be attached at the hip with anyone, even someone she…

She almost laughed. She couldn't even say the words to herself yet. Either she was terrified or this relationship was a lot more serious than any previous one she'd been in.

She suspected both things were at play here.

"I forgot about that part," she admitted. "You've been better about not spending every second with me since…"

"Since I've been spending every night with you?" he asked, that sexy purr back in his voice.

Her stomach danced. Boy, he could turn her on quickly, with just his voice, even when she should be thinking about other things.

"Yes," she said. "I forgot you still aren't able to be away from me for long periods."

"I probably won't ever like that," he said.

He stroked one hand down her back, a long caress that made her tingle everywhere.

"But," he said, "once my animal side is secure in our bond, I'll be able to go away for a week on business without losing my mind."

"That'll be helpful," she said dryly.

He chuckled and nuzzled her hair aside, dropping a kiss onto her neck. She shivered.

"Come with me," he said, his breath hot against her skin. "Please."

She groaned. She would never admit this out loud, but she wanted to go. Oh, she wasn't even close to ready to meet his mother yet. That part terrified the crap out of her. But she wasn't crazy about being away from him for a week either. She wouldn't lose her mind or anything so dramatic. But she would miss him.

And really, getting out of Portland while there was a wizard gunning for her did seem prudent.

"Fine," she said, trying to feign reluctance but failing because he was kissing her neck. "I'll go. But you have to deal with the Nags if they get mad."

"I can do that," he said, his voice deep. "But right now…" He kissed his way up to her ear, nibbling her lobe. "Right now, I'd rather deal with you."

She really *really* loved the way Deacon dealt with her.

6

---

*C*ary stared into her closet. What the hell did you wear to meet your boyfriend's mother who was also a kind of queen?

Most of her wardrobe consisted of jeans and t-shirts because she spent most of her time either throwing herself in front of disaster or playing with dogs. Neither activity required fancy queen-meeting clothing.

She sighed.

"Wear what you always wear," Deacon said.

She glared at him over her shoulder. "You better not be laughing at me. This is your *mother*." She waved a hand in a vague gesture. "The leader of your people. I can't show up in ratty jeans and a torn t-shirt."

"What about the new stuff Marianne is making for you?"

"She's a genius and a miracle worker, but even she can't create a whole new wardrobe for me over night." Well, actually, given Marianne's particular magical weaver skills, she might be able to do that. But it would take time and Marianne was a busy woman. Cary didn't like to take advantage of her friends if she could help it.

"I could do with the new coat, though," she muttered under her breath. The one fancy coat she'd had now had a bullet hole in it.

"My mother won't care what you're wearing," Deacon insisted. "And we can buy something for the event down there."

Cary dropped her head back and closed her eyes. She'd forgotten all about needing dress-up clothes for the charity ball. "I really needed more than a few hours to get ready for this trip," she said.

"I've been asking you to come with me for three weeks," he pointed out.

She scowled at him but didn't comment. He might be right but she didn't have to admit it aloud.

"Angie is good with house sitting?" he asked, wisely changing the subject.

"Yup. She loves the dogs, and she claims she needs time off from reading other people's futures."

One of Cary's best friends since her early days as a Protector, Angie ran a psychic readings business from her home, selling charms and ready-made "spells" on the side. Given that Angie was an authentic psychic and actual witch, despite most of her clients not having a tie with the magical world, she did really well in her business.

"Good." Deacon paused. "Cary, we have to leave soon."

"Argh! Fine." She started pulling things out of the closet and tossing them into her small suitcase. It was only a week and a half, and only Deacon's family, and really no big deal. If his mother didn't like her in jeans and t-shirts, she wasn't going to like her period.

Cary paused mid-motion to catch her breath, her pulse pounding hard in her ears. What if Deacon's mother hated her?

"She's not going to hate you," Deacon said.

"Stop reading my mind," she snapped.

"Your scent is so full of fear I'm surprised the dogs aren't in here checking on you to see what's wrong," he said.

She snarled at him. "I can be scared if I want." Yes, that was a childish response. But the panic rushing through her bloodstream justified it. "This isn't like meeting some ordinary boyfriend's mother. Your mother is the fricking *queen* of your people. I don't meet the leaders of entire preternatural populations on a regular basis."

"What about the Master vampire of Portland. You met her."

"That was different. And she's been deposed. And… Vampires shouldn't suck kitten blood," she said when she ran out of other excuses.

His lips twitched.

"Don't you laugh," she warned.

"Never," he said, before pressing his lips together.

She glared, but returned to packing, desperately trying not to let the panic take hold again. She faced off against dangerous bad guys every day. Maria Jones wasn't out to kill her or get past her to kill someone else. This would be fine. Just two grown women meeting each other.

"My dad will be there, too," Deacon reminded her. "He's a good calming influence on my mother."

Cary's eyes widened. "Your mother needs a calming influence?" Her voice squeaked.

Deacon shook his head and rose from her bed, crossing to take her shoulders in his hands. "It'll be fine," he said. "And…if worse comes to worse, we're only a couple hour's drive back to Portland. We can always leave."

She blinked up at him a few times as that settled in. "Hey, we can leave. You're right. If your mother hates me, I can run away." She met his gaze. "But…what happens if your mother hates me?"

"She's not going to hate you," he said. Then shrugged. "But if she does, we'll deal with it."

"Oh good." She wasn't even close to being reassured, but at least she could run home if she needed to. And she'd sort out the rest from the safety of her own house—literally since thanks to the Nags' glamour, if she didn't want Maria to find her house, Maria and her leopards wouldn't find it.

Deacon kissed her gently, the brief contact further settling her nerves. She never ceased to be amazed out how simple physical contact with him had such a profound effect on her. She was more seriously caught in this mate business than she liked to admit. While she might not be permanently bound the way Deacon potentially was, she was definitely in deep.

She opened her mouth to tell him she felt better when a warning tingle along her spine made her groan. She closed her eyes for a moment, then tapped him on the shoulders and motioned to the living room. He dropped his head back and sighed before following her out.

"What?" she asked the two beings standing in her living room. She'd given up the pretense of politeness when they sprang this seventh year trial on her without warning.

As they were Fae, there was no mistaking the otherworldliness of her bosses. They were beautiful but in a strange and unique way. Liruk, the one who most earned Cary's Nag nickname, was all white and gold, with pale flowing hair, golden brown skin, and two little gold horns coming out from the top of her head. Wisat, the one Cary managed to get along with, was black and red to Liruk's white and gold. Through his black hair sprang two red velvet-covered antlers that twisted in a halo over the top of his head. Both had startlingly green eyes, a green so bright it reminded Cary of sunlight glowing through thick tree leaves.

"What?" she repeated when they just stood there, their eyes narrowed at her.

"Where are you going, Protector?" Liruk asked. "You are in the middle of your trial year."

"Yeah, that's not something I can forget," she said. "I'm going to Eugene. For a week and a half. Deacon has to go and I need to go with him. I'm less than two hours away from Portland, depending on traffic, if you need me. And I'm allowed to have a life. Get over it."

"If we need you urgently?" Wisat asked, with a lot less accusation than Liruk, but still with a mildly censoring tone.

"Only two hours away, remember? And if you can't figure out that you need me farther out than that, you need to work on your premonitions."

Truthfully, they did sometimes only realize they needed her at the last minute. They sent her on missions based on premonitions and research. But sometimes, they simply didn't realize a problem was about to happen very long before the problem happened. That was the nature of premonitions. They came and went at their own whims, even for beings like the Nags.

But she wasn't going to let a little honesty and reality intrude on her point. "I need to take this trip. I'll still be available to come back and do protecting if you need me."

"Who will look after the dogs?" Wisat asked, sounding more interested than accusing now.

"Angie."

"Ah. That's acceptable."

Cary raised her brows. Wisat cared who looked after her dog pack?

"The demon dog likes your witch friend," Wisat said. "He will be content."

Oh. Yeah. Buck's approval of his sitter probably would be a concern for the Nags, given Buck was now capable of opening rifts between demon realms and this one. Wouldn't want him randomly doing that and accidentally letting loose a host of demons on Portland while Cary was out of town.

"Buck will be fine," she assured. "They all will be. And so will Portland for a week." Although, she couldn't remember the last time she'd had even a full week without *something* going wrong. But again, no reason to let reality stop her plans. "So, wait, are you just here to nag me about my travel plans, or did you actually have a job for me?" She couldn't refuse a job during her seventh year without risking the glamour on her home.

"No," Wisat said. "All is currently quiet."

"We are…monitoring two situations, though," Liruk said sharply. "Do not get comfortable on your vacation."

She said vacation like it was a bad word.

"Fine," Cary said. Wasn't like she would be relaxing around Deacon's mother anyway. "Are we done here? I need to finish packing."

They glanced at each other. Wisat smiled faintly at her. Then they both vanished.

Cary blinked. And sighed. "Well, at least they know. Probably be worse if they popped in here and discovered Angie instead of me."

Deacon gripped her shoulders from behind, pulling her back against his chest. She went willingly.

"Everything will be fine," he assured.

But she heard the hesitance in his voice. The Nags were monitoring two situations.

"I better bring my own car," she said.

7

*C*ary swallowed, hard. "This is your mother's house?"

"This is home," Deacon said.

Cary stared up at the mansion.

A mansion.

She shook her head.

She knew Deacon and his family had money, though it never really came up in conversation between them. She hadn't even been to his house in Portland yet. And she'd been so busy getting used to the idea of being cut off from her sources of support—and fighting demons and gods and saving kids and necromancers and innocent teenagers—that it was only just occurring to her that there was an *awful* lot she didn't know about Deacon.

"I should have asked to see your house in Portland before this," she muttered.

"You're welcome anytime," he said, as if this wasn't a big deal. "Your place is cozier, though. And I figured you wouldn't want to leave the dogs overnight."

She glanced at him from the corner of her eye. He was absolutely right about that. Which showed he might likely know her better than she knew him. She consoled herself with the knowledge that he had an unfair advantage. If she had a sense of smell that allowed her to read his mind, she'd know him better at this stage, too.

"So, we should probably go inside now, huh?" she asked as she wiped a wet palm over her jeans.

The place was huge and calling it a house was a misnomer. Even calling it a mansion seemed a little small, though palace didn't quite work either. Because for all its size and grandeur it wasn't outrageously ostentatious. It was just…roomy. From the front, it looked to have about three stories, but it was sitting at the top of a hill and she got the impression there might be more to it around the back—or maybe she was just imagining that since what she saw out front was so huge.

The wings of the stone building stretched out on either side of the front door, at least thirty windows on the ground floor going in each direction. And not narrow, arrow slit windows either, but big, airy, let-in-the-light sort of windows with clean glass that sparkled in the sunlight creeping in past the gray overcast.

Looking at all those windows reminded her she should probably get around to cleaning her own house windows soon—a job so much easier than it must be at this place it was pathetic if she couldn't manage it.

The building was made from pale, gray stone bricks—a little surprising for the area—and there were the occasional carved bricks, bearing the faces of animals in bas relief scattered over the façade. But they blended into the overall stonework and she had to really look to see them. The front door was a solid oak, left natural. The stairs leading up to it were also pale stone, sweeping upward in a wide arch. The tree-lined road up to the house opened on a gravel circular driveway, which led back into the trees at one side, she presumed to a garage. But there were no fancy fountains or elaborate landscaping otherwise. Just open grass directly around the house, and woods beyond that as far as she could see.

They were outside Eugene by a few miles, in an isolated area with few houses nearby. The mansion dominated the landscape, looking out over the valley beyond, like a castle surveying its territory.

"I so do not belong here," Cary muttered.

"You'll be fine. It's just a house."

"Said the prince who grew up here."

He chuckled under his breath. "Gird your loins, then, princess because the queen is about to arrive."

"You are not funny," she said just as the front door opened.

"Just don't curtsey," Deacon said near her ear. "That's exposing your neck to a leopard."

She snarled at him, then focused on the open door. A woman strolled out, elegantly but simply dressed in wide black pants and a white button up shirt that fit her perfectly. She wasn't particularly tall, but not short either, with generous curves. Her black hair was thick and hung around her shoulders in gentle waves.

Her golden eyes were familiar.

"Your sister?" Cary asked.

"My mother," Deacon corrected.

Cary blinked. The woman standing at the top of the stairs as they walked up to meet her looked to be *maybe* forty-five years old. Her light brown skin was smooth but for a few creases around her eyes and a soft furrow between her brows that no doubt deepened when she scowled. Since Deacon was fifty-four—because leopard shifters lived a long time and didn't age like humans, he only looked about thirty-five —she knew his mother was a lot older than that.

Damn but his family had good genes.

Cary tried to smile in greeting but was pretty sure the expression looked pained and terrified.

His mother managed a much more gracious smile that still none-theless carried a weight of hauteur. Deacon made the introductions while Cary discretely wiped her sweaty palms on her jeans so she could shake hands without embarrassing herself. Knowing his mother smelled her fear and hesitance did *not* help.

"It's a pleasure to finally meet you, Cary," Maria Jones said. "This meeting is long overdue."

Cary smiled and made some noises of agreement while thinking,

Not long enough. Not nearly long enough. "Thank you for having me," she managed.

"Please, come inside." Maria gestured into the house. "This is my mate, Deacon's father Evan."

Cary glanced past Maria to the man standing just behind her, a man Cary hadn't even noticed until Maria brought her attention to him.

Evan's smile was a lot softer and more friendly than his mate's. "Welcome, Ms. Redmond. It's truly a pleasure to meet you."

"Thank you. You too." Cary shook his hand with a lot less terror.

Which was a nice trick considering he *should* have been as intimidating as his wife, the queen. He was the queen's consort, he was as big as Deacon, and equally handsome in his own way. There was as much of the father in Deacon as there was the mother. Evan had blue eyes, a beautiful contrast to dark lashes and hair, his features were a little narrower and sharper than Deacon's. But the family resemblance was unmistakable. She would have known this man was Deacon's father without being told.

He should have scared her as much as Maria. Whatever he'd done to set her at ease, it worked, though. Or at least, it mostly worked. Her heartbeat was still pounding like she'd run a race. Since she didn't run unless necessary, the feeling wasn't pleasant.

She followed Evan and Maria inside, trying not to trip over her own feet. Only to find herself gaping at the entryway.

It was huge, going up all three stories with light cascading in from the surrounding windows, including a set of stained-glass windows overhead that spilled colored light across the pale wood floors. One of the stained-glass images was a mosaic of the jungle and large cats sitting on tree limbs, another of leopards in a more desert-like environment, staring down at the viewer as if ready to pounce.

"Wow," she murmured.

"You like them," Maria said. "They were made by my brother, many years ago in Guyana."

Cary looked back at her.

"Where I grew up," she clarified.

"Is your brother still there?" Cary asked.

"He was killed, more than seventy years ago," Maria said bluntly. "So no."

Oops. Cary felt her cheeks heating as Maria studied her. Yeah, she needed to change the topic.

Except in her embarrassment and discomfort, not a single new subject came to mind. She did not want to ask how Maria's brother had been killed—even though frankly she was really curious—but she didn't know how to switch to a lighter topic—any topic!—without sounding like an unfeeling ass.

By some miraculous turn of events, she was saved from her own foot-in-the-mouth situation by the screaming greetings of…children.

She blinked as a pack of kids rushed up and circled her.

"Cary, Cary! You're here."

"Daddy said you were coming to visit."

"Mine says you fought off a demon."

"Cary's a superhero."

"Yay!"

Cary held up her hands, laughing at the enthusiasm. "Hi, everyone! It's so good to see you all. How have you been?"

The group of six kids were some of the leopard shifter children Cary had helped Deacon and his people rescue from the cougar shifters who'd kidnapped them.

One of the little boys tugged at her sleeve. She recognized him immediately. Miguel was the son of a shifter named Lucas who'd been with her and Deacon during the whole demon god fight.

Miguel leaned into her and whispered loudly, "Daddy said you saved him too. Thank you."

"No, your daddy was a hero," she told the boy. "He helped *me* save all of Portland."

The boy preened. "Daddy helped a superhero," he told another boy standing next to him.

Cary chuckled. While she sometimes liked to think of herself that way, she technically wasn't a superhero in the classical sense of the word. Kevlar vest really was the more accurate description.

"I'm not exactly—" she started but was interrupted by another friendly voice, an adult this time.

Sherri hurried forward and took Cary's hands, kissing her on both cheeks. Another shifter whose daughter had been among the kids kidnapped, Sherri had also helped Cary a lot during the demon god fight, including providing equipment from her construction company so the leopards could cordon off a section of Portland's underground, preventing humans from stumbling into danger.

"I'm so happy to see you," Sherri said. "I was so relieved when Deacon let us know you'd survived the demon god."

"Thanks," Cary said with a shrug. "I was pretty pleased and surprised I survived, too."

Lucas appeared from behind Sherri, surprising Cary. She hadn't noticed him in all the chaos created by the kids. He shook her hand.

"It's so good to see you," Cary said. "I'm glad I get the chance to thank you both, again, for all your help. Really, thank you."

"If you ever need us," Lucas said, "don't hesitate to ask. Seriously. You helped save our babies. There's nothing we wouldn't do for you."

"Even if all you need is some wine and pizza," Sherri said with a wink.

"Now you're talking my language." Cary grinned.

"If we're finished with the reunion," Maria said into the melee, her tone quiet but firm. "Perhaps you could take the children back to the playroom now," she said to Sherri and Lucas. It didn't sound like a request.

Sherri met Cary's gaze and squeezed her arm. "We'll talk more later." With her back angled away from Maria, she mouthed, *Good luck*, before taking hold of her daughter, Angelina's hand and ushering the rest of the kids ahead of her, back into the depths of the mansion.

Lucas lingered just long enough to give her a reassuring wink, then he followed the kids. His son Miguel glanced over his shoulder to grin at Cary and wave goodbye before his father urged him on. Cary waved back.

Maria cleared her throat. Cary pressed her lips together and tried not to visibly wince. The annoyance in the other woman's tone was clear even if subtle.

"Sorry about the interruption," Cary said.

"They haven't stopped talking about you," Maria said. "The children. They were very impressed with…whatever it is you do."

Cary tried for a casual dismissal of her skills because she had no idea how much Deacon had told his mother about her. "Just glad I could help and none of the kids got hurt."

Maria narrowed her eyes, but her mate stepped in before she could say more.

"I'm sure you're tired after the long drive," Evan said. "Would you like a drink? I'm sure we can find someplace more comfortable than a huge drafty hallway to get acquainted."

There was a slight, sing-songy tone to his accent that charmed Cary. Deacon said he was originally from Wales, but she'd never heard a Welsh accent in person before. She gave him a grateful nod, then glanced at Deacon who'd remained silent during most of the exchange.

He didn't comment then either, just gestured his parents to lead the way, falling into step next to Cary as they left the massive entryway and entered a side corridor. He seemed a little distant, a little contained, but she wrote that off to the fact that he was introducing his mate to his parents for the first time.

As they walked through the mansion, Cary gaped at everything. The place felt and looked like a palace even more on the inside than it had on the outside. The hardwood, inlaid floors were polished to within an inch of their lives, the pale walls were spotless. A scattering of antique tables lined the corridors in between what seemed like a never-ending line of closed doors.

For reason's she couldn't quite pinpoint, the house felt cold. There was nothing obvious to create that impression. The colors were warm. The temperature was pleasant—which must cost a fortune in heating and cooling bills given the size of the place. The oil paintings on the walls were landscapes and nature scenes, nothing warlike or unpleasant. No martyred saints. The occasional object d'art on the tables tended toward glass bowls or ceramic vases painted in beautiful colors.

Still, it all felt very cold and impersonal. Like a museum. Someplace you passed through to admire the art, not someplace you lived.

Cary realized it hadn't felt so cold when the children had surrounded her, so maybe her reaction was purely down to her company.

She glanced at Deacon. He seemed to grow more distant the farther they moved into the house. He usually kept some sort of physical contact between them when they walked, a palm at her lower back, his fingers brushing hers. At the moment, he strolled next to her as if she were any other person, no physical contact between them at all.

Was he more worried about this first meeting than he'd let on? Was he afraid of his mother's reaction to her?

In any other circumstance, that would have been reassuring to Cary. His confidence and certainty in this mate business were disconcerting most of the time. It made her feel better when he was as nervous about things as she was. In this particular case, though, his worry was not comforting.

Maria and Evan led them to a large room behind one of the many doors, this one facing the back of the house. Floor to ceiling windows let in huge amounts of light, making the room bright to the point of almost glowing. More polished wooden floors, more soft colored walls in pale blue here, a fire place at one side of the room that was large enough for Cary to stand up in, chandeliers hanging from a ceiling that looked like it belonged in a French chateau. And four huge tables in the center of the room, all filled with…

Pizza?

8

The smell was heavenly, permeating the air with a glorious cheesy, garlicy scent that made Cary's stomach growl. She glanced nervously at Maria.

"My son tells me you like pizza," she said, her tone neutral and impossible to read. "Please enjoy a meal while I speak privately with Deacon."

Cary frantically looked at Deacon. His attention was on his mother as she motioned him across the room, a distance that meant they could speak without Cary overhearing.

She was left standing by the tables of pizza with Deacon's father.

She turned to him, not even a little sure what to say.

He smiled at her, his gaze softening. "She's very keen on hospitality," he said. "And ensuring guests here are given every possible comfort. But we may have forgotten you eat like a human and not a shifter when we set out lunch."

Cary snorted at that, glancing at the sizable spread. "I can eat a lot, especially of pizza, but this is well beyond even my appetite. This is enough to feed a party. Of teenage boys."

He chuckled. "She won't be offended if you don't eat it all, don't worry."

"Oh good." That was more of a relief than she realized it would be. She was *pretty* sure she wasn't expected to eat all that pizza, but since she couldn't read Maria at all, she wasn't *certain* about that either.

"You're nervous," Evan said.

"Well, yeah. She's… You're both Deacon's parents. She's the leader of your people. And her son and I have only known each other a few months."

"You're his mate. You're welcome here."

"Mm hm," she murmured as neutrally as she could.

"Don't let Maria's aloofness bother you," he said.

He gestured to the tables and a stack of *fine china* plates. No paper plates or chipped ceramic from the local discount store here.

She gently took the plate Evan handed her and surveyed the selection. She wrinkled her nose at the pineapple-covered pizza before she realized she might be offending someone and quickly moved on to pepperoni. The pizza's looked handmade, not store bought or even delivery. And her first bite confirmed they were glorious. She groaned without meaning to.

Evan smiled. "I'm glad they're to your liking. I made them."

She widened her eyes. "Really? Deacon didn't tell me you were a chef."

He chuckled. "I'm not. Officially. Just a cook." He shrugged. "But a very good one."

"Yeah, you are. These are delicious."

"Thank you." He gestured to a couch. The wood was gold embossed and the thin cushions were covered in damask silk.

She balked. "I'm comfortable standing."

"It can be cleaned," Evan said with a grin, guessing at her hesitance.

She sat, but at the edge of the couch, and kept her plate close to her chin while she ate so she wouldn't drip. "You're not having any? I feel a little weird eating alone."

"I've already eaten about three of those pies while I was cooking. I'll be hungry again in a few minutes, and then I'll join you."

She grinned at that. Obviously Deacon came by his appetite honestly.

"Back to Maria," Evan said.

Cary swallowed her bite and tried not to wince. She glanced at Maria and Deacon across the room, talking quietly. Neither moved much. Deacon stood at an angle to his mother so he could lean down a little to listen. She was a good foot shorter than him, Cary realized. Not that size seemed to make any difference to Maria's intimidation factor. Both their facial expressions were controlled and serious, neutral and impossible to read. They didn't look upset, but they didn't look particularly happy either.

They did, however, look a lot alike just then.

"She has to be very controlled," Evan said quietly. "She's extraordinarily strong. If she isn't in full control of herself and her emotions, she could hurt people. The other leopards here are especially vulnerable to her, so she's extremely careful."

Cary looked at Evan.

"Deacon is the same," he said. "Without full control of his leopard, he's dangerous."

"So he's told me." Though not in detail, not in the way Evan seemed to be implying. Something she and Deacon would have to discuss more, she thought. "Is it dangerous for us to be here, then? He hasn't really regained his full control since we met."

Evan raised his brows and glanced at his wife and son. "Maria said that, but he seems his usual self to me."

"He does?" she asked. She'd been thinking he seemed distant and was acting strangely.

"Yes, even his scent is measured—only the very strongest of our people have any control whatsoever over their scents. Deacon, Maria. I can a little because of my birth order, but I'm not like them."

In leopard shifters, birth order played a huge roll in the power of an individual. Birth order of parents factored in too. Deacon was the firstborn of two firstborn parents. From what he'd told her, Maria was also the firstborn of firstborn parents going back generations. His father was apparently as well. It wasn't typical to have that sort of chain, but when it did happen, the shifter at the end of the chain was strong as all hell.

"He'll be fine here," Evan continued. "He's always been very careful of his power."

"He hasn't been able to go back to work," Cary said.

Evan shrugged. "Probably just his sister giving him time with his mate and using his control as the excuse."

Cary wasn't so sure about that. Not being able to return to work, his control still tentative… She knew Deacon was uncomfortable with those issues even if he did try to hide it.

Though now, seeing him here, distant and neutral, perfectly in control, maybe she'd been reading him wrong. Maybe he'd been feigning his lack of control to spend more time with her?

She wasn't sure if that was flattering or infuriating.

But she leaned toward infuriating because it meant he'd been lying to her. He knew she'd been worried about him. She narrowed her eyes and glanced down at her pizza.

"Full already?" Evan asked.

She blinked and looked up. "No. I can see why you ate three of these. If I could manage it without exploding, I'd probably do the same."

He smiled. "I'm really pleased you're enjoying them. I can officially add pizza to my repertoire now."

"They weren't already part of it?"

"I learned to make them for you."

"Oh." That was sweet and intimidating all at once. "You've don't a great job." And because the food was yummy and he'd gone to all this trouble, she finished off her second piece and went back for two more.

Her gaze kept darting to Deacon and Maria, though. They were deep in discussion, but she couldn't tell if they were talking about the venue, the cougars, or lunch menus. There was really no expression of emotion in either of their body language, and frankly she found that fascinating. How did one maintain that level of neutrality? Especially knowing Deacon as she did, and how rarely he appeared neutral…

She paused at that thought.

She didn't actually know Deacon that well. Not really. There was still an awful lot he kept to himself.

"You're worried again," Evan said. He glanced at his mate and son. "They're discussing the venue issues, if that helps."

She smiled a little. "I was wondering." She glanced around the magnificent—and large—sitting room, and asked, "Why not just have the event here? Your home is definitely large enough."

"Most of our donors are ordinary, mundane humans. They're rich, often spoiled, and clueless about the world beyond their lives." He dipped his head in a shrug. "And that's fine because they give a lot of money to our organization so we can save as many animal lives as possible. But we don't dare bring them here, were they might encounter a leopard child too young to know better than to shift in front of strangers. Or a shifter fight that moved at speeds they could barely see. No, this place is for our clan, for our people, and for the more unique aspects of our lives. Not for the mundane people we deal with for business."

"I can understand that." Her home was a bastion of supernatural craziness too, and it was always a bit complicated when her parents came to stay for a visit, making sure none of that bled into their world. She kept her research library and work computer up in her attic so they wouldn't encounter random volumes of "Current Thinking on Demon Phylogenies" or "Best Practices for Handling Rouge Spells." And fortunately, her two non-standard dog breeds were good about appearing as ordinary dogs almost all the time. But she could imagine that balance would get infinitely more complicated with a whole house full of shifters—especially children.

"So where will you hold the event now?" she asked, mostly to keep distracted from her own worries.

"There's a hotel farther outside of town that should be large enough. But we'll need the entire thing, and they have bookings already for that night." He made a face. "Also, the room where we'd hold the main event isn't quite as… Well, not to put too fine a point on it, not as classy as our usual venue. Sasha has been having trouble convincing the manager to let us redecorate as extensively as we'd like."

"Sasha?"

"Maria's assistant and the one who's been working on all this mess."

"The one who asked for Deacon's help?"

"Everyone knows Deacon can get things done when he puts his mind to it. My son is very good at getting his way."

Said with pride, Cary noted. She tried not to make a face. Having a relationship with someone who always got their way seemed distinctly unfair.

Evan chuckled. "Don't worry. Mates tend to bow to their partner's needs above their own. He'll always take your feelings into consideration."

She made another non-committal sound around a bite of pizza.

Evan studied her quietly for a moment before saying, "You're worried about your relationship with him."

She gulped her food, trying not to choke. "What makes you say that?"

"It's okay to be nervous," he said. "It's still very early days. And I imagine being claimed as the mate of a shifter wasn't something you were prepared for."

"No. Most definitely not."

"It's normal to worry," he said, again all reassurance and wisdom. "Settling into a mate bond can take months. Some couples take years."

She swallowed hard again. Years? That didn't sound good.

Evan glanced fondly at Maria. "Beginnings can be volatile, but that adds to the ultimate bonding."

Cary realized she could read his emotions easily, especially in that moment when he was looking at his mate with such love. She smiled at that. It was sweet.

But the difference was stark between what she could plainly see in Evan and the lack of those obvious emotions in either Maria or Deacon. She thought about what Evan had said, about them both having to exert such control over themselves for the safety of others. It must be exhausting, having to always be that controlled. And that made her wonder if Deacon weren't, on some unconscious level, resisting the full return of his control.

So many questions.

So much uncertainty still.

She sighed. At least the pizza was good.

9

ary was just starting her fifth slice—and not feeling at all guilty about it because Evan was so pleased with her appreciation—when the door to the sitting room opened and one of the most stunning women Cary had ever seen walked in.

She was tall, and as slim as Angie but still generously curved—how was that possible? She had dark, thick brown hair falling just below her shoulders and styled to look effortlessly chic and silky. She wore tan, wide-legged pants and a fitted white button up shirt with thick cuffs. Her jewelry was minimal—small winking diamond earrings and a simple gold chain necklace. Her pale complexion was flawless, her makeup impeccable, her features elegantly feline. And her blue eyes were a stunning contrast to her long dark lashes.

Cary watched the woman smile at Deacon and every part of her growled with a jealousy that surprised even her. She was well used to women smiling and ogling Deacon. It was impossible not to. He was like a Greek god walking around in the real world. Her own friends had been stunned by him the first time they'd seen him. She was amused by, and sometimes annoyed by, the attention other women paid him. But something about this woman, something about her smile and the glow in her greeting…

Whether it was because of the mate bond with Deacon or just ordinary human jealousy, Cary's hackles rose, her nostrils flared, and her eyes narrowed. Instinctively, she disliked this newcomer. A lot.

She was so startled by that reaction, so embarrassed by it, that it took a full minute for her to realize Evan had spoken.

"Sorry," she said, her cheeks heating. "What was that?"

He nodded to the newcomer. "That's Maria's assistant."

"*That's* Sasha?" That was the person who'd *specifically* requested Deacon's help?

Cary felt her lips twitch with a snarl and pressed them together. Holy shit her reaction to the woman was extreme. She'd never felt this level of instinctive, full blown jealousy. So intense she literally wanted to stomp over and place herself between Sasha and Deacon. The sensation was very disconcerting.

And really really weird.

Evan let out a huge sigh. "This is going take them some time," he said. "Since you're finished eating, maybe we should leave them to it. Would you like to meet more of the family?"

What Cary wanted was to smash Sasha's prefect face with her fist. But since she was mortified by that impulse, she nodded and quickly set aside her remaining pizza crust. She tried to catch Deacon's eye on the way out, but his full attention was on whatever Sasha was saying. In fact, none of them even acknowledged Cary's presence now, or the fact that she was leaving the room.

She made a face at that, but since she couldn't tell if her annoyance was real or because of the instinctive reaction Sasha had caused, she followed Evan out wordlessly.

The instant she was in the corridor, away from Sasha and Deacon, she pulled in a deep breath. The internal rage that hadn't felt like her own eased, dropping away like it had never been there. Now she just felt silly. And embarrassed.

She glanced at Evan, whose expression was carefully composed and pleasant, and realized he no doubt smelled her reaction to Sasha. She closed her eyes briefly. That was just so humiliating. No wonder he'd hurried her out of the room.

"Deacon tells me you were a veterinary technician at one point," Evan said. "Perhaps you'd like to meet Michael."

"Michael is a vet?" Deacon hadn't mentioned his twin brother, younger by two whole minutes, was a vet. She wondered at that, but since he'd shown signs of jealousy whenever she brought up his brothers, she'd avoided the topic.

"He is," Evan said. "We have a clinic at the bottom of the road, for the public. Would you like to visit it?"

"I'd love to." Getting out of this palace and away from her confused emotions seemed an incredibly wise idea at the moment.

It was a chilly winter day, but dry and sunny, the gray overcast having burned away sometime over lunch. The walk down the road gave her pause, though. It was a steady downgrade, surrounded by trees, and absolutely lovely, but still downhill. Which meant she'd have to walk back uphill at some point. She sighed. The fresh air was worth it. And probably the hike would do her no harm after eating almost an entire pizza by herself.

She had vague memories of the building they'd driven past on the way up to Deacon's family home, but she'd been so nervous about meeting his mother she hadn't really given the clinic much attention. Now she took in the lovely building. Large, built of wood, and painted a soft blue color that was bright but not in a gaudy way. The front door was painted bright white with an open sign on it. Beneath the open sign hung another with a cartoon kitty on it that said, "The Vet Is In." She grinned when she noticed the leopard spots on the kitty. That wasn't very subtle. But she imagined most ordinary humans missed the connection since they wouldn't know about leopard shifters.

There was a paved parking lot at the side of the rectangular building. And a smaller lot and emergency entrance on the other side. A set of wooden stairs led up to the small porch in front of the main door, natural wood that gave the whole place a very homey, country vibe.

"It's fantastic," she commented as Evan held the door open for her to enter.

"We get a lot of business here," he said. "Michael offers lower rates and some free services to people who can't pay. And he's really good with both people and pets. The locals love him."

A small reception area with seating took up the front of the main room, a reception desk and office to the rear. Behind the high counter, a woman dressed in purple scrubs was discussing medications with another older woman clutching a small, yippy terrier.

"That's Joanna Huang," Evan said, nodding to the woman in purple scrubs. "She's the other on-staff vet."

Behind Dr. Huang, another woman sat behind a computer entering something and printing it up for the woman with the terrier. From Cary's time working at a veterinary office, she assumed it was instructions and the bill. When the woman and terrier walked out, a man with a scruffy looking cat moved up to the counter. Dr. Huang gave Evan a nod of greeting, but otherwise ignored him.

The receptionist waved to him and mouthed, "He's in back."

Evan led Cary through an inner door to the long hall bracketed by exam rooms. The scents of disinfectant and nervous animal filled the place, a very familiar smell from all those years ago. She wondered how the leopards dealt with that scared animal smell, and decided she'd ask later if she got the chance.

At the very back of the hall, a room opened up to kennels for overnight patients, a glass enclosed side room for operations, and the various supplies and rows of medicines that a vet might need. A man sat at a desk filling in something on a chart, ignoring them until he'd finished.

When he finally looked up, he was grinning. "Finally, I get to meet the famous Cary Redmond who's claimed my difficult brother."

She was too bemused by that greeting to do more than smile. And more than a little bemused by Michael's resemblance to Deacon. He was as gorgeous, though with blue eyes like his father rather than Deacon's golden eyes. His hair was a lighter brown, his features a little narrower, and when he stood he was maybe an inch or two taller than Deacon. But those were really the only differences.

She had to give herself a little internal shake before she took

Michael's pro-offered hand. "Nice to meet you," she said. "Deacon hasn't wanted me to before this."

Michael laughed. "I'm not surprised. We can be pretty jealous of our partners."

She noticed how careful he was with his language, even though it was just the three of them in the back room. But she imagined since he worked here with mundane humans and colleagues, he'd had to establish that habit to keep from slipping. Especially being so close to home and the leader of his people.

Who was also his mother.

"Where is the prince?" Michael asked, glancing between her and his father.

"Discussing the venue with your mother and Sasha."

Michael sighed. "I hope they can get it sorted out." He looked back at Cary. "We make enough money at this one fundraiser every year to make up about half our annual operating costs. That's a lot of money we can't afford to lose and still offer so many free services."

"I really admire what your family does," she said. "I thought at one stage I'd be a vet, but I didn't have a stomach for some aspects."

"Putting animals down?" Michael asked.

"Yes! How did you guess?"

"That's always the part that gets animal lovers. Even the ones who can handle the surgeries can have trouble with knowing they have to put an animal to sleep." He shrugged. "But what is it you do now? Deacon's been very tight-lipped about it all."

She hedged. Technically, she didn't tell people what she did because it kept her safer. If they didn't know, they couldn't figure out how to kill her. But she didn't think her cover story of assisting a former professor who wrote popular science books would be appropriate either.

She settled on, "I help people who need it. I'm pretty good at keeping people safe if they're in trouble."

Michael's eyebrows rose high and he glanced at his father. Evan shrugged. Michael gave Cary a narrowed-eyed look. She shrugged.

He laughed. "Fair enough. We're a family of careful words. I don't suppose I could expect anything less from my big brother's girlfriend."

She grinned back. "So tell me more about this place." She gestured to the clinic.

Michael gave her a tour, introduced her to the staff and the three clinic cats who lived in the reception area. Two were quite friendly and let her pet them. One gave her a sniff and then showed her his tail in a dismissive cut that would have made any aristocrat proud.

They were near the emergency entrance, where Michael was pointing out some of their new equipment, when Evan lifted his head and frowned.

A tingling of unease dropped down Cary's back, a sense that danger was approaching, just as Sasha turned the corner and came into view.

Cary's hackles rose almost instantly, even as her Protector instincts kicked in.

That couldn't be good. What the hell? She couldn't imagine what threat Sasha would pose here.

Deacon followed her, but he was on the phone and didn't look up at any of them as he approached. Sasha smiled, a beautiful and insincere expression that made Cary want to snarl.

The jealousy, as intense and weird as it was, Cary could understand. But the fact that her Protector senses were jumping with warning... *That* she couldn't quite figure out.

Sasha reached them before Deacon and put her hand out to Cary. "You must be Ms. Redmond. I'm sorry I didn't introduce myself earlier. As you might have heard, we're under some time pressure."

Cary forced a smile, trying to be as pleasant as possible since the jealousy reaction was all hers and she couldn't blame Sasha for it. She didn't like the woman's smile, but then again, a lot of people looked at her in that condescending way. Really, Cary should be used to it by now.

"Nice to meet you," Cary said.

Sasha reached back and put a hand on Deacon's shoulder. He didn't look up from his phone but did grunt an acknowledgement. "We're very pleased Deacon could come home to help," Sasha said. "I don't know what I'd do without him."

"You'd manage," Michael said.

Cary frowned a little. His own tone was surprisingly neutral. Not as vibrant and happy as he'd been just a moment earlier.

"Where's Maria?" Evan asked Sasha.

"She's on a call. The bank."

To Evan, Sasha was deferential and polite. Everything in her attitude respectful, right down to her posture.

When she faced Cary again, her posture changed. And, Cary noted, she still hadn't removed her hand from Deacon. A part of Cary she didn't recognize in herself wanted to snatch that woman's hand away from him. And maybe break her pretty little fingers.

Whoa. That was a lot of violence for a first introduction. She only got this pissed off when bad guys were hurting innocent animals. If she'd been able to do more than kick that kitten-blood-drinking vampire, she would have. But that had been justified rage. Her reaction to Sasha was way over the top.

"What brings you down to the clinic?" Michael asked, again very neutrally.

"Maria needs some numbers for one of our patrons. And she wondered if you would speak to Dr. Greelins about the menagerie he's bringing to the fundraiser. She'd like him to leave the poisonous snakes at home this year." Sasha shrugged elegantly, without removing her hand from Deacon, and smiled at Cary. "Insurance," she said, as if that clarified things.

Cary gave her a fake smile and nodded, as if she understood any of this.

"I'll have Jolene send the numbers you need up to the house," Michael said. "I can call Dr. Greelins after lunch."

They continued to discuss the fundraiser, Deacon looking up from his call to grunt something at Michael that Cary could only barely decipher as words. Michael apparently understood, though, because he answered. Cary let the conversation wash over her. Her Protector nerves were still jumping, big time. With the imperative to get between some innocent bystander and danger.

Now.

She hunted their surroundings, looking for the source of her unease, her heartbeat pounding. The breeze was blowing away from them, down the hill toward the front of the clinic and into the trees across the road, so she could only smell the clinic at her back—not that she had the sense of smell the others surrounding her did.

She glanced at the group, still deep in conversation, Deacon typing something into his phone now. None of them seemed to be reacting as if there was danger near, either. And they were shapeshifters with heightened senses.

What the hell?

"I suppose this is all pretty boring for you." Sasha's mildly condescending comment broke through Cary's concern.

"No, it's not that." She frowned at the trees across the road again. "Just…" She opened her senses as much as she was able, the full spectrum of her Protector instincts on high now. She edged away from the group, which earned her a little offended gasp from Sasha.

"Cary?" Michael asked.

Hearing Michael say her name brought Deacon's head up. They exchanged a look and he frowned slightly.

"What's wrong?" he asked.

"I'm not sure." She faced the trees again. Except for the soft, chilly breeze making shushing noises through the leaves, the area was eerily silent. No cars on the road. No random bird song.

Another shiver raced down her back. Those things had been part of the background just ten minutes ago, though she hadn't been as aware of the noises before they were gone.

Then one sound did disturb the silence. In the parking lot on the opposite side of the building, she heard a car door close and the laughing rhythm of a woman talking to a child while a dog barked. Cary's heartbeat picked up speed.

She started edging toward the front of the clinic, keeping her eyes on the trees across the road.

"Is she always this rude?" Sasha asked the group in general.

Cary glanced back, ignoring Sasha to meet Deacon's gaze again. Deacon made a move toward her, but then his phone rang. He answered the call, his attention diverted. Damn it.

But if he wasn't sensing danger, maybe this was just her imagination. She never got "false signals," or at least hadn't before this. Maybe this was part of the seventh year challenge? Or maybe it was because she didn't like Sasha and was looking for an excuse to be away from her?

That didn't make sense. Cary ended up around a lot of people she didn't like and hadn't had this kind of reaction before.

One thing she was certain of now, though, her Protector senses weren't raised by Sasha. This was something else.

Her gut tightened and a kind of panic started to set in as the mother, daughter, and yapping dog circled the building, heading toward the front door of the clinic from the parking lot. Her gaze snapped to the trees just across the road, in time to catch the flicker of light off metal.

And then she was running, diving between the small family and the hail of bullets.

Cary wrapped the mother and girl in her arms, feeling one stinging hit from a bullet on the back of her shoulder before the rest were stopped by her shields.

The frantically barking dog pulled at its leash, so Cary wrapped her arm around the nylon rope, tightening the slack and keeping the dog close, inside her protection.

Which turned out to be good because the mother dropped the leash when she wrapped her arms around her daughter. The little girl and mother both screamed, their shrieks loud enough to almost overwhelm the *putputput* noise of gunfire.

A window at the far end of the clinic exploded, and Cary panicked. Shit, she was protecting the family this way, but not the whole clinic. She edged her small group toward the front door.

"Get inside," she shouted. "Take cover."

She ushered them in, then turned to face the source of the gunfire. Taking a few steps forward, she made herself an obvious target, hoping to draw the shooter's full attention. The hail of bullets turned to her, focusing on her.

Relief made her smile. Yay, for predictable bad guys.

A small pile of flattened bullets dropped into the grass at her feet as she leaned into her shields, mentally extending them to circle the clinic's entire building. She was never entirely sure if that worked, but it did help to visualize what she was protecting. And no more windows exploded even as more shots shifted from her to other parts of the building—a second gunman, she realized.

The gunfire paused suddenly, the silence deafening. Then a black leopard raced from the side of the building where Cary had left Deacon and his family. Behind the black leopard, another spotted leopard followed, keeping pace with the black as they both dove into the trees.

Giving chase, she realized. The fact that they were in leopard form surprised her a little. She'd assumed they wouldn't shift anywhere near their business where a human might see them. Especially when Michael had been so very careful with his language.

But extreme circumstances…

She turned to head back into the clinic and check on everyone inside just as Evan and Sasha came around the corner, still in human form. Evan blinked at her, glanced at the flattened bullets littering the grass, then met her gaze again.

She shrugged and sort of smiled and then hurried inside so she wouldn't have to try explaining right away.

"Anyone hurt?" she asked, as people started poking out from the back of the clinic where they'd obviously run to take cover.

Dr. Huang glanced around. "I think we're all okay." She put a hand on the arm of the mother Cary had hurried inside.

The woman nodded, but she was clenching her daughter tight to her side, her eyes wide.

"The animals in back?" Cary asked Dr. Huang.

"I'll check now," she said and moved off as Evan and Sasha came into the reception area.

The next few minutes were a stream of questions and reassurances and a call placed to the police—by the receptionist, Jolene, who'd dialed 911 from the cover of her desk during the gunfire. Brave woman, Cary thought.

Evan was quick to settle everyone down and keep the group calm. Sasha held back for the first few chaotic moments, frowning at Cary, then she also went to work settling and comforting the humans. Dr. Huang confirmed all the animals in the back were fine, and after a brief tour of the clinic confirmed that only that one window had taken any damage.

That news earned Cary another couple of narrow-eyed speculative looks from Evan and Sasha.

"Must have been really bad shots," Cary said, attempting to make her tone amazed and innocent. "That was lucky."

Evan and Sasha's expressions said they didn't buy her excuse even a little bit, but the humans seemed relieved by her comment. The mother hadn't apparently noticed that Cary directly blocked bullets, which was good.

But her daughter kept glancing at Cary. The girl was maybe six or seven years old, a beautiful black-haired child with huge dark eyes, she clutched a doll dressed in bright shorts and t-shirt, its normally blond hair striped with blue and pink.

When her mother was distracted talking to Dr. Huang, the little girl edged up to Cary and tugged at her jacket sleeve. Cary leaned down so the girl could whisper in her ear, "You stopped those bullets. I saw you. You're a superhero, huh?"

Cary made a face and glanced around at the other grownups, then put a finger to her lips. "Shh."

The girl grinned. "I knew it. Thank you."

"You're welcome," Cary whispered, then ushered her back to her mother, shaking her head. Leave it to a kid to notice.

By the time Deacon and Michael reappeared—in human form and fully dressed in the clothes they'd been wearing earlier—the people and animals in the clinic were calmed. The police arrived just moments after the brothers, so Cary didn't have a chance to talk to Deacon. He took charge the moment he walked in, speaking with the cops, adding an authoritative air, even more than Evan. His mere presence calmed the atmosphere further.

That was pretty impressive. He didn't even seem to notice what he was doing, just took charge and handled things, calm and in control. She'd expected to see signs of his rage—she was enraged by the attack and this wasn't one of her businesses. But he showed no outward sign of his anger. Michael was a little more visually upset, and kept reassuring himself that Dr. Huang and the others were okay before he went into the back to calm the noisy animals.

It took another half hour of answering police questions and getting the various humans away safely before Cary could speak with Deacon. He'd somehow managed to convince them that a forensic team wasn't necessary—how, she had no idea—and this was written off as a crazy person attacking completely at random. The police would look out for him, but otherwise there was nothing more to be done here.

That bit of manipulation truly impressed Cary. She was going to have to ask Deacon how he did that. She normally tried to avoid interactions with the police because explaining her survival was often so difficult. But if she could learn how to divert their attention that well, she could worry less about having run-ins with the law.

When she had a moment alone with Deacon, she said, "You okay?"

He nodded, still not showing the rage she'd been expecting. "No one was injured. Thank you for what you did."

He sounded like he was talking to a random passerby. She frowned. "You're welcome," she said with a little snark in her tone. He didn't seem to notice. "Did you see who was shooting? Did you catch them? There were at least two."

He did look at her with more interest then. "How did you know there were two?"

"The way the gunfire happened." She'd had a firsthand view. "Did you catch them?"

He shook his head. "It was the cougars, though."

"What?" She lowered her voice when her comment drew Sasha's attention. "What the hell were they doing trying to shoot up the clinic with innocent humans inside?"

"Upping the stakes," Deacon said. "Escalating the conflict."

"As if kidnapping kids wasn't enough," Cary said with a snarl.

"Yes." His tone was still amazingly controlled, but he did finally show a crack in that control, when he said, "Were you hurt?"

She shrugged and then winced. "Just one bruise on my shoulder.

You know, this is the second time I've been shot in less than a week. I think too many people are walking around with guns." She raised her brows. "Hey, isn't shifters using guns a trick your mother taught you. Since preternatural types don't tend to protect against mundane weapons. You suppose that's why the cougars used guns?"

His shoulders straightened and he frowned a little. "I need to talk with my mother. Are you okay from here?"

"Yeah, sure, great." She scowled. He hadn't reacted at all to the news that she'd been *shot*. Again. He usually got upset when she was injured doing her job.

Something in her tone must have gotten through, because he finally looked at her, really looked. "Thank you for helping," he said. He brushed a finger across her cheek. "I'm sorry you got hurt."

Mollified, she shrugged. "It'll heal. Go talk with your mother. If the cougars are escalating again, she needs to know."

He nodded and bent to give her a brief kiss on the cheek. It wasn't exactly a passionate, relieved gesture, but at least it was physical contact.

She was still faintly frowning at his back as he left with Evan when Michael joined her.

"You're okay?" he asked.

"Fine. Just one bruise that will heal."

"I saw the bullets in the grass," he said, his voice quiet. "Flattened like they'd hit something. The cougars weren't bad shots."

Cary shrugged. "I did mention being good at keeping people safe, right?"

"Yeah, you are," he said with feeling. "Thank you. I can't ever thank you enough."

She waved that away, a little embarrassed now. "Anytime."

"You told Deacon this was the second time you've been shot in a week."

Damned shifter hearing. "Yeah, well…" she muttered.

"You can get shot without any more damage than a bruise, huh?"

"It's complicated," she hedged.

"I bet." He gave her a little hug that surprised her. "I'm glad my brother found such a wonderfully complicated mate," he murmured for her ears only.

She was smiling when he walked away. Until she caught Sasha staring at her, a speculative look in her stunning eyes. She raised her brows at Cary. Cary returned the gesture. Sasha smirked for reasons Cary couldn't fathom and turned her back on Cary, walking out of the clinic.

Well, that was weird. She didn't trust Sasha, not even a little bit. What the hell had that exchange even been about?

With a sigh, she realized she'd have to make her way back up to the house on her own since everyone but Michael had left and he was staying at the clinic to handle the aftermath of the attack. A quiet walk on her own seemed like a good idea, though. She was more than a little confused by the way Deacon was acting, the way she was reacting to Sasha, and the general undercurrent here. The fact that the cougars were attacking them was the least confusing part of her afternoon.

Which did not bode well for this being a relaxing vacation.

Oh boy.

11

The mansion was in uproar by the time Cary reached the entryway. She stood for a minute watching people come and go, a lot of shouting information, a lot of questions being asked with no answers forthcoming.

Finally, she spotted a familiar face. "Lucas," she called.

Lucas hurried to her, three kids in tow. "Cary. You were there? What happened? We can't get a straight story. We've been told to keep the children inside the security of the building and away from the windows."

She told him what had happened as best she could, including that Deacon and Michael had given chase but the cougars had gotten away.

"They used guns?" Lucas asked. "I thought only Maria used that trick."

"Apparently, they've learned from their enemy," Cary said. "No one up here was hurt?"

"No, we didn't even know anything had happened until Deacon called Maria and she started ordering the children inside and everyone to remain under cover. She's increased the guards patrolling the grounds."

"That's good." Cary glanced at the still chaotic back and forth of a mansion full of people with exceptionally good hearing and lowered her voice. "Do you have a few minutes to talk?"

He frowned a little, but nodded and motioned to someone nearby. "Can you take the kids to Diana?" After he'd kissed and reassured his children, watching them hurry off with the woman he'd entrusted them too, he turned back to Cary. "Diana is my mate. She's with a friend who's pregnant and in the early stages of labor."

"Will she be okay?" Cary asked, a new worry lodging in her throat. "Do you need to get her to a hospital? I can go with her and make sure she's safe from the cougars."

Lucas smiled. "We have an infirmary here that can safely accommodate births. Most of our people give birth with a shifter doctor anyway. Complications and the reaction of a shifter in labor can be a little too out of the ordinary for the average human doctor."

"That's a relief." She edged Lucas closer to a wall, out of the way, almost in a corner. "Deacon hasn't told me much about the tension between your people and the cougars. He's skimmed over the issue, but won't give me many details. Just says it's being taken care of."

"If he doesn't want you to know, maybe there's a reason?"

"Whatever the reason, I think it's moot now. I was front and center, the focus of those cougars' guns. They know me. Someone from the tunnels could have escaped and told the others about me. They probably don't know what I am—"

"Which makes a lot of us," Lucas said with his brows raised.

She grinned but didn't answer his unspoken question. "I'm in this now whether Deacon likes it or not. And I can't do my job, if I'm completely in the dark. They were lucky I was there today."

"They were," Lucas acknowledged. "And we're lucky the cougars haven't tried this before."

"So what the hell is the problem between your people and theirs?"

Lucas pressed his lips together, his gaze jumping around the huge entryway. "We tend to keep the inner workings of our people pretty close to the vest, but since you're our prince's mate…"

She tried not to wince at that. She wasn't sure why she wanted to. Mostly the idea that they thought of her that way.

"The leopards and the local cougars have been at odds for the last seventy-five years."

She let out a low whistle. "Not the Hatfields and the McCoys but still a long feud."

Lucas nodded. "There was tension before Maria moved to the US, but the feud got infinitely worse after she arrived."

"She was in South America before, right? She mentioned Guyana."

"That's where she was born. Her people came to South America from India a long time ago. Her great grandparents made peace with the local shifters in the area so they could live quietly there. I don't know why her family left India, but it had to do with conflict and hunting or something."

Since most shifter species bore a strong resemblance in their animal forms to their mundane animal counterparts, they were as likely to get caught up in human hunting and territory decimation as mundane animals. There were a few species that could never be confused with their animal namesakes—like werewolves—but for many shifters, the encroachment of humans across their territories had caused them a lot of difficulties.

"So what brought her from peacefully living in Guyana to the US?" Cary asked. "Or is that a mystery, too?"

"Not really peaceful by the time she left. And I don't know all the details. But..." Lucas frowned. "You know birth order matters to the strength of leopard shifters, right?"

She nodded. That information had been in the books she'd studied over the years, although she was only just now starting to really understand the difference it made.

"Maria was the firstborn of firstborn parents on both sides of her family for six generations. That rarely happens. Once in a millennia. Maybe."

Cary had gotten some of that from Deacon already, but not what it signified. "Which means..." She frowned. "She's got to be super strong and powerful right?"

"Incredibly so," Lucas confirmed. "Not just standard shifter strength and speed. Well beyond what any other leopard shifter on the planet can currently claim." He paused. "Except for Deacon."

Cary straightened to stare hard at Lucas. "Meaning?"

"Deacon is the seventh. The firstborn of firstborn parents for seven generations. It's almost unprecedented. The fact that Maria's mate also happened to be firstborn…" He held his hands up. "These are statistically small odds."

Seventh firstborn, a near unprecedented birth, her mate, whom she met going into her seventh year as a Protector, which turned out to be a test year. She might just have to hate the number seven soon.

"Okay," she said, "this means Deacon and Maria are unparalleled among leopards in strength, right?"

Lucas's frown deepened the crease between his eyebrows. "It's more than just the usual shifter strength and speed. More than their ability to shift in a blink—which isn't typical with most shifters, except for maybe dragon shifters. And dragons can do it because they have actual magic."

Most shifter species didn't technically have *magic*. Their uniqueness was biological, not magical even though most humans considered it unnatural. But there were a few who possessed magic. Dragon shifters being one. She'd had to face a dragon shifter before—a young one still coming into his powers from what she could tell. That had been interesting.

It took her another beat before what Lucas had said sunk in. "Wait, are you saying Maria and Deacon have magic? Like real magic?"

"It's very specific and not like a witch's magic where they can cast spells and things, but yeah. They have magical abilities that are beyond what the average shifter can command."

Whoa. "Does Evan?" she asked.

"No. He's the firstborn of firstborns going back about three generations, which happens more often. It's still not commonplace, but statistically speaking, it's probable. He's super strong, a powerful shifter in his own right. But not the way his mate and son are."

"What about Deacon's twins? Michael and Jocelyn?" Cary hadn't met Jocelyn Jones. According to Deacon, Jocelyn spent most of her time on the east coast, handling their business there. She was due in for this event, though, and after meeting Michael, Cary was super curious what the female version of the triplets would be like.

"They're both more like Evan since they weren't firstborn," Lucas said. "Just Deacon's luck he was the first out by two minutes. He got the power."

She couldn't help but wonder if his siblings were jealous of that or relieved.

Her brain was starting to hurt from all this new information. She needed a lot more time than she currently had to process the fact that Deacon had *magic*. Since she didn't have that time yet, she got back to the original topic.

"Okay, what does all this have to do with the cougars?"

"Maria had to leave Guyana. She's never said why to most of us. I'm not sure if her family knows. But she had to leave."

"Sounds ominous."

Lucas shrugged. "Whatever the reason, she came here, to the Pacific Northwest. The area was cougar territory at that point, but in a loose collection of ranges. They weren't a strong group. The leopards in this part of the US were the same, not a cohesive clan. Just individuals with territories that may or may not bump up against each other."

"Was that a bad thing?" She rubbed her temples, trying to remember her shifter history. She had a vague memory of reading that the shifters along the west coast of the US and Canada were a mixed bag, and that fifty to a hundred years ago there had been a lot of territorial disputes.

Something else about that period… She dug into her memory and recalled something about those fights increasing to dangerous levels. When was that? She wasn't good with dates—which was why she hadn't become a historian. Maybe the mid-twentieth century? Or even a little earlier. World War Two era?

"The cougars didn't think their way of doing things was bad," Lucas said in answer to her question. "They were the dominant species, in charge of the whole of the Pacific Northwest range at that time.

Other species lived here, quite a lot actually. This is a good place for shifters."

Cary nodded at Lucas's aside because he looked like he expected it.

"There were even—still are actually—a few tigers living throughout this region and they're really rare."

Tiger shifters were a mysterious group that tended to keep to themselves and not interact much with other shifters. There was very little written about them in the current literature. Most of what was known was at least two centuries old. Cary knew there was a tiger shifter living in the Portland area—or had been up to five years ago—but she'd never met them, or heard from anyone else who'd met them either.

Lucas turned his gaze to the still flowing movement of people past the entryway. The chaos was starting to die down some, as people got to where they needed to go. A small group of children, circled by four adults moved past and Cary recognized one of the little girls from a month ago, one of the kids who'd been kidnapped by the cougars.

The girl spotted her and waved. Cary waved back. The exchange earned a slight frown from one of the adults until the girl whispered something up at her. Then the adult's eyes widened and she stared at Cary, almost tripping before turning away.

"What have the kids been telling everyone?" Cary asked, nodding toward the passing group.

Lucas grinned. "They've been saying you're a superhero who can throw shifters around with your mind."

Cary raised her brows. "You've been setting the record straight, right?"

Lucas's grin grew. "I have no explanation for what you can do other than that you're a superhero."

"That's not funny," she said sternly.

Although, she did have a secret attic with all her research material in it. And she did like to think of it as her bat-attic—as opposed to a bat cave. And she did occasionally think of herself as a superhero.

Frankly, it was a nice change from being confused for a witch.

But still, to be a superhero you needed skills beyond the innate ability to freeze like a deer in headlights when faced with danger.

Lucas laughed, then said, "We're going to start drawing attention here."

"And you don't want to get caught explaining the cougar situation to me," she guessed, "but you haven't told me anything significant about that yet."

The revelation that Deacon had magic, on the other hand, was extremely significant.

Lucas shrugged. "All of this background is important to what came after Maria got here." He gestured Cary to follow him.

They walked down a corridor to the left, following a slight bend that took them into a wing that wasn't obvious from the front of the mansion. The crowds were almost non-existent here.

"Where are we going?" she asked.

"The infirmary. I can check on Diana and the kids, and finish telling you the rest of this before we get there."

"Cool." She wouldn't mind getting reassurances that the pregnant shifter Lucas had mentioned was doing okay anyway.

"Where Maria came from," Lucas said, "the kind of loose and disorganized groupings that made up the shifters of the Pacific Northwest had led to conflict, among the shifters and the humans. There were a lot of deaths." Lucas glanced around before saying, "Even the truce between the resident jaguar populations and the leopards who'd immigrated to South America broke down. War among the shifters of South America broke out."

"When was this?" Cary asked.

"Not too long before Maria came to the US, so about eighty years ago. She was young at the time, but still an adult in leopard terms, and her powers had come in."

Cary did some calculating. That would have been around the time of World War II. Same general period when she'd read the fights among shifters in the US and Canada were getting worse.

"Geez," she said, "there was a lot of conflict going on all at the same time during that era."

Lucas shrugged. "There's always a lot of conflict going on somewhere."

She couldn't argue with that. "Okay, so war broke out and Maria left for mysterious reasons?"

Lucas gestured down another corridor and Cary followed, so fascinated by his story she barely noticed where they were going.

"The shifters here were on the verge of war, too," Lucas continued. "And the cougars were apparently encouraging that for some reason."

"After just getting out of a war zone, Maria probably wasn't happy to find another one brewing in her new home," Cary said. "What did she do?"

"She took over," Lucas said simply. "No one here, of any species, knew what to make of her power because no one in this area had powers like she did. She decided that the leopards would govern a large territory throughout Oregon, where they would be safe and protected. And that within that territory, other shifters would also be safe, so long as they adhere to the rules that she established."

"What rules?" Cary narrowed her eyes a bit.

"Mostly things like no in-fighting, especially around humans. No picking fights with humans and drawing attention to us. No aligning with other supernatural beings against shifters. That kind of thing. Rules that let us thrive for the last half century living among and alongside humans. She was so successful, the shifters from farther north, in Washington and into Canada, all instituted her rules among their own groups. The species who live in packs got stricter about fighting and conflict around humans. Shifters that are naturally more individualistic came together to form loose groups that could help and monitor others."

"Okay," Cary said, "all this sounds good, especially if groups beyond her influence were adopting her rules. So…what's the problem with the cougars?"

"There's been tension between them and our people since Maria took over but nothing like what's been happening." Lucas stopped walking and faced her, lowering his voice so it was almost impossible to hear. "We don't know for sure what's changed, and that's part of the problem. From the cougars we captured after the kidnapping, we know they're determined to 'take back' their territory. But they won't tell us why this is suddenly a thing."

"How did Maria take over the area in the first place?"

Lucas shrugged. "She fought the strongest members of each shifter species for the right to establish the territorial laws."

Cary raised her brows. "How many?"

"There were five different species who put forward champions," Lucas said. "Cougars, bears, werewolves, jaguars, and leopards. The rest of the shifters either shrugged off her challenge and went about their business—like the tigers—or were more passive species and happy to let the predators establish some kind of cohesive rule."

"I take it she won," Cary said.

"With amazing ease," Lucas confirmed. "From the stories I've heard, the grizzly was the most surprised he got his ass kicked by a little cat."

Cary smiled at that. "Who was the leopard? Are they still around?"

Lucas grinned. "Evan was the leopards' chosen champion."

Cary gaped at him. "Wait, what? How did they end up mated?"

"They realized the instant they got close for the fight, of course." Lucas tapped his nose.

Cary almost rolled her eyes. Of course. That shifter sense of smell, always causing trouble.

"They still fought," Lucas continued, "but it was more like flirting. And when Maria won because Evan decided to stop, the leopards acting as witnesses accepted her leadership."

"Just like that? They didn't argue to send in another challenger?"

"My father was there at the time," Lucas said. "Apparently, there was no one in all of Oregon as strong as Evan. And while he was holding his own with Maria, it was obvious from her other fights that she could have beaten him if she'd wanted to. They decided collectively that they wanted someone that strong on their side rather than working against them. She was one of them, another leopard, so there were less issues with having her bring them together."

Lucas started walking again.

Cary hurried to keep up. "So she took over, brought peace to the region, spread peace past her own borders, and now the cougars are… mad about it? Do I have that right?"

"That's as much as I know," Lucas said with an apologetic shrug. "That's probably why Deacon hasn't told you more."

"What am I supposed to have told her?" Deacon asked.

Cary and Lucas froze. Deacon's voice came from directly behind them, so close the hairs on Cary's arms rose.

She winced as she slowly turned to face her mate.

"on't be mad at Lucas," Cary said, holding her hands up, palms out to keep Deacon calm.

She was somewhat surprised to realize he *was* calm.

Deacon glanced at Lucas and Lucas hurried away silently, without even a backward glance.

Cary narrowed her eyes. "You're not going to do anything to him are you?"

"What would I do to him?" He sounded genuinely confused.

"I don't know. Punish him or something for telling me what you wouldn't."

"What was he telling you?"

"Background on the cougar issue."

Deacon nodded. "I haven't told you much because we don't know much. We don't know why they're doing what they're doing."

She sighed. "So Lucas just said." She bit her tongue before she continued, so she wouldn't inadvertently get Lucas into any more trouble by revealing what he'd told her about Maria and Deacon's magic.

"I'm sorry if you thought I was keeping things from you. I'm not used to talking about leopard business with—" He cut himself off.

"With non-leopards?" she guessed.

"Habit," he said as if it were no big deal.

She wasn't sure herself whether this should be a big deal or not. She still hadn't told him about the glamour on her house. So maybe she didn't have a lot of moral ground to stand on when it came to complete open honesty in their relationship.

"Anyway," she said, trying to wave away the whole thing since she didn't know how to deal with it. "What's happening? Is everyone okay?"

He nodded, then glanced in the direction Lucas had gone. "Hannah's labor is progressing."

Cary glanced back over her shoulder. "How can you tell?"

He tapped his ears and for the first time since they'd walked into the mansion, smiled a little.

She snorted. Of course, he could hear that with his super shifter hearing. "She's okay?"

"We have good doctors and nurses on hand. She was due a few days ago so no one was caught unaware with an early birth. She's in good hands."

Cary let out a sigh. "I was worrying. Thanks for that."

He brushed a finger along her cheekbone. Her skin tingled in the wake of his touch and for several moments she could only stare up at him.

He blinked a few times and looked away first. "You're okay? After the attack, I didn't have a chance to really check on you."

She narrowed her eyes a little. He'd forgotten? "Yeah, I'm fine. Just that one bruise. Remember?"

He looked at her closer, as if startled. But it was subtly done, not a grand double-take. A very slight narrowing of his eyes, his mouth turning down just a bit. The change was there, but very very controlled.

Cary had known he felt out of control before this, but seeing him exert the kind of control he was doing here was very disconcerting. It was like he wasn't the same man. His joke about being an iceman before he met her no longer seemed like such a joke.

"That's right," he said. "Sorry. It's been a long day. Already."

And it was only one o'clock. "Well that's true enough."

A faint smile. "Is the bruise healed?"

"Getting there."

"Do you need one of our doctors to look at it? I know how you feel about hospitals."

She let out a small chuckle. She really hated having to go to the ER, even though she did all the time. Mostly, because she hated having to explain her weird injuries in ways that ordinary people might understand.

"I'll be fine, thanks." She glanced back toward the direction Lucas had gone.

"Do you want to leave?" Deacon asked.

That comment surprised her for some reason. "I'm just worrying about the pregnant woman," she said. "What did Maria say about the guns?"

"She's taking care of it."

Cary waited for more. When he didn't explain further, she frowned. "Are you not telling me what's happening on purpose? Cause, you know, it's easier for me to do my job when I can plan a little for it."

"You rarely have time to plan."

She scowled. He was right, but that didn't mean she had to like it. "You're not answering my question. Also, you're acting weird since we got here."

His brows raised high. "I'm not avoiding your question, necessarily. And how am I acting weird?"

"I'm starting to believe that iceman joke you made the other night."

He did another one of those super subtle double-takes, the skin around his eyes crinkling just slightly. Then he nodded. "I'm feeling more myself, I suppose."

"This is how you were before me, huh?"

He shrugged. "I'm in more control right now. That's a good sign, right?"

She grunted a non-committal comment. She'd wanted him to get back what he'd felt he lost after meeting her. But this man who didn't even remember she'd been hurt seemed so completely different to the

Deacon she'd been getting to know, she wasn't sure what to think anymore.

And unfortunately, she couldn't question him about it more because the stunningly gorgeous Sasha chose that moment to interrupt them.

"Deacon," she said, her voice smooth and coaxing. "We need to get back to work if you're finished here." Sasha gave Cary a faint, dismissive smile.

Cary's lip started to lift in a snarl. She forced the snarl into a smile. The expression felt so strained she thought her face might break. "I'll go check on Hannah," Cary said. "Don't worry about me. I'm good at entertaining myself."

Deacon nodded and moved off with Sasha without a backward glance, his phone already in his hand.

"You're upset," a female voice said from behind Cary.

She closed her eyes briefly before turning to face Deacon's mother. "You shifters move too damned quietly," she said.

Maria shrugged. "I came to thank you for your help at the clinic."

"You're welcome." Cary tried to sound gracious.

"You're worried about Deacon, though."

"You can smell it?" Cary asked, pointlessly since she knew the answer. "He hasn't seemed to have noticed."

Maria glanced back over her shoulder. "We have two new additions to our community now."

Cary blinked at the non sequitur, before the realization hit. "Hannah, she gave birth already? That was fast. And twins. Congratulations. That's wonderful. Everyone is healthy?"

Maria faced her again. "You care?"

"Of course! What kind of monster doesn't care about that kind of thing?" She almost bit her tongue when she realized that humans often called shifters monsters—they weren't, not even close. There were actual real monsters in the world. Fortunately for Cary, those were handled by other people.

Maria didn't appear to take offense. "Mother and babies are all healthy."

"Is that what you were just doing?" Cary wasn't sure why, but the idea of the queen of the leopard shifters helping one of her people give birth seemed out of character.

"Among other things," Maria said.

"Ah, yeah, making sure the mansion is secured."

Maria nodded. "Lucas told you about our magic."

Cary winced. "He's not in trouble for that, is he?"

"Deacon didn't tell you." Maria wasn't asking.

"Apparently, there's a lot he hasn't told me." Cary glanced over her shoulder in the direction Deacon had gone. Then she faced Maria again. "Well, since everyone seems to be happy and settled, I'll just—"

"Walk with me. Outside. We need to talk."

Not a request, Cary noted. But, "Is that safe? The cougars are probably gunning for you—no pun intended."

Maria's mouth twitched. "You'll be with me. You can keep me safe. Right?"

Cary dipped her head in a nod. "I suppose I can. All right. You lead the way."

She wasn't particularly keen on talking to Maria alone. But her day had already been so much confusion and chaos and uncertainty, this hardly seemed the time to dial things back to normal. Might as well get this conversation over with.

Maria led her down a hall that branched off from the one they'd been in but still angled toward the rear of the house.

"This place is massive," Cary commented. "Larger than it looks even from the outside."

"We live in a Tardis," Maria said with a straight face.

Cary raised her brows. She hadn't been expecting a pop culture reference from Maria, especially not a Dr. Who reference. "You are joking, right?" she asked.

A very slight smile, then, "There's a back door this way."

Still not sure what to make of Maria's comment, Cary followed her down a set of narrow, highly polished stairs to a solid oak door that opened onto a large swath of open grassland and a thickly wooded area about eight hundred yards beyond that.

"The open space around the mansion allows us to see an enemy approaching," Maria said. "A trick Evan taught me."

"Cool." What else could she say? It hadn't occurred to Cary that the mansion might be fortified like an actual castle, but maybe it was since it was the home of a queen.

"Even with the speeds shifters can move, the distance gives us time to react," Maria continued. "We have security cameras and alarms in place as well."

Cary nodded. She had nothing to contribute but felt like she should respond in some way.

"You're not well versed in defensive fortifications?" Maria asked.

Cary shrugged. "It's not my primary field of study, no." She didn't really need to know that kind of thing. If an army of bad guys approached in that moment, all Cary had to do was stand her ground and she could hold them off.

"You're a Protector," Maria said when they were halfway between the house and the woods.

Cary stopped in her tracks. "Did Deacon tell you that?"

Maria paused and faced her. "No. He knows?"

"Yes."

"Does he know how you can be killed?"

Cary winced. "I accidentally told him." She made a face. "The night we met." She *never* slipped up that way. But meeting Deacon had thrown her off her game completely. She only later realized it was probably because of the whole mate thing. At the time, she'd written it off to having found him naked and chained to a bed.

"It was the mate bond," Maria said. "It will cause you to behave in ways that aren't necessarily normal for you. Like admitting something to Deacon you hadn't intended to confess."

Cary narrowed her eyes. "Do you mind read?"

"No." She tapped her nose, a gesture that reminded Cary sharply of Deacon. "But I can smell a lot that a human wouldn't be able to decipher."

"Yeah, I've heard. How did you know I was a Protector?"

"I met another one, once, a long time ago." Maria started walking toward the woods again.

Cary glanced back at the house that was getting farther away, suddenly worried this was a bad idea.

"I'm not taking you out here to hurt you," Maria said, a faint hint of humor in her voice.

"You know what I am and how to kill me," Cary pointed out even as her pulse jumped with the realization. "I think staying in the open might be a good idea."

Maria turned to face her again, several yards of space between them now. "You don't want to be my son's mate."

"I never said that."

"You're unsure."

"Yes," Cary said.

"Why?"

"I'm bad with relationships," Cary said flippantly. At Maria's hard stare, she shrugged. "We've only known each other a short time. And frankly, I barely recognize the man I'm seeing since we arrived. That Deacon I was talking to before you snuck up on me, I don't know him at all. That doesn't bode well for our future."

"I didn't sneak up on you," Maria said. "You were distracted."

"Not really the point to what I just said."

"It was its own point. Lucas told you about our magic."

"Just that you and Deacon have it," Cary said.

Maria glanced up at the house. "We're being watched."

"From the house?"

"From the woods."

Cary frowned and glanced over Maria's shoulder. "The cougars?" She made a move to get between Maria and the forest, but Maria held up a stilling hand.

"No. There's no danger from the watchers. We'll get to them in a moment. We need to finish our discussion first."

Cary frowned. "You don't want me to see your son anymore," she guessed. "You don't think I'm a worthy mate."

"I never said that."

"Then what do we have to discuss?"

"You're worried about Sasha?" Maria asked. "You're jealous of her?"

Cary's head spun. "Yes. Absurdly so. Which is completely unlike me and it's really weird."

Maria lifted her brows in a very mild type of shrug. "They have slept together before, so I supposed there might be call for jealousy."

"That's not helping," Cary growled. "And also, it's a little gross to hear about that kind of thing from his *mother*."

Maria smiled. A full and genuine smile.

Cary was instantly on alert for danger.

"If he can keep you," Maria said, "you'll make him a good mate."

"You make no sense to me at all," Cary admitted. "I don't even know what we're talking about anymore."

"The reason Deacon is so controlled right now," Maria said, her voice even and quiet, "is because the house is full of leopards. And if he loses control, he could kill them all in an instant."

1 3

ary blinked. A few times. Her brain worked through several moments of stunned silence before she could finally muster, "Huh?"

Maria started back toward the woods again. "His magic," she said by way of explanation. "There hasn't been a leopard with Deacon's pedigree in…two millennia, maybe longer. He's extraordinarily powerful."

Cary hurried to follow Maria, less concerned with her own safety now because this information seemed like something she should have known about *before* this moment. "What, exactly, does his magic do? Lucas said it was different to a witch's magic."

"It is. It's specific to his people. Other leopards. And occasionally he can influence other shapeshifters." Maria glanced at Cary. "That's something I can't even do."

"So… I still don't understand. What can he *do*?"

"He can control another leopard with just his thoughts. He can make them do whatever he wants them to do. He can break them and rip them apart with a thought."

Cary swallowed hard. "That's terrifying."

"Fortunately, most of our people only know he's strong. They don't know that last part. His father and I, Michael, and Jocelyn are the only ones who know the full extent. His twins only because they witnessed the one and only time Deacon lost control. When he was seven."

Cary wasn't sure she wanted to know, but she asked anyway. "What did he do?"

"He nearly killed a young leopard, a boy only just into his twenties, because the boy had pushed Jocelyn over and swatted Michael to one side."

"Why?"

Maria shrugged. "The boy was going through a dangerous time for a leopard, equivalent to puberty in humans, and this particular young man wasn't a very nice person before his puberty hit. He was a bully and he thought bullying seven-year-olds—especially these seven-year-olds who were the children of the queen—would make him feel powerful. He was wrong and he almost died for it."

"Geezus," Cary muttered. "What happened?"

"Evan and I reached them before Deacon could do more than make the boy bleed a bit. At the time, I was still strong enough to control my son and contain his powers."

Cary heard the underlying meaning to those words. "You can't contain him anymore."

"Not since he finished his own period of puberty," Maria confirmed. "I can help him, when he needs it. When he lets me. But if he let go completely, there's nothing I could do to stop him."

She sounded remarkably easy-going about it all. Cary's heart was thumping hard as she worked to process the news.

They stepped just inside the treeline before Maria stopped again and faced her. "Deacon is very aware of his strengths and the danger he poses to our people. And we've all been very careful to keep the full extent of his powers a secret. Our people don't need to know how dangerous he is."

"Yeah, I can see that," Cary said. "Why are you telling me all this?"

"So you know why he's acting the way he is. The house is full of leopards. If he can't maintain his control here, he risks hurting someone. He wouldn't be able to live with himself if he did that."

Now that sounded like the Deacon Cary had known for the last few months. The tension in her shoulders loosened a little. She could deal with his weird behavior for a few days if it meant his people were safe. But...

"What happened when he was here at Thanksgiving?" she asked, her eyes narrowing. "He came to you because he wasn't able to be with me for a few days and he was worried about his control."

"He stayed in the woods as a leopard most of the time," Maria said, confirming what Deacon had already told her.

"But," Cary said, "if his control was so tenuous then, why come here where there were leopards he might hurt?"

"I sent everyone away," Maria said bluntly. "Only a few of the family were in the house by the time he arrived. I can protect a limited number of people from his strength if needs be."

Cary let out a long breath, puffing her cheeks up. "So. So meeting me has been a lot more dangerous even than he let on. Why didn't he tell me?"

"You were already balking at the requirements of being a mate," Maria said, still not pulling punches. "He didn't want to scare you off."

"Yeah, that probably would have. Being responsible for keeping him from killing people is not exactly a little thing."

"You're a dangerous person for him to be mated to. You're disrupting a long and powerful genetic line. You could be killed in your job at any point. And being human, you can walk away from him whenever you like."

Cary narrowed her eyes at Maria. "I thought you said I'd make him a good mate."

"You're the perfect mate for him."

That was such a surprising compliment, Cary straightened, almost like she'd been slapped.

"You're a firstborn?" Maria asked.

"I'm the oldest, yes."

"But human. Which means, if you and Deacon have children, even the firstborn won't carry Deacon's level of power. They might not have any magic at all."

"And this is good or bad?"

"Good. Very good." Maria glanced back toward the house. "I love my son. I love him fiercely. And if there was never another leopard born with his power that would be the best of all imaginable worlds." She faced Cary again. "He can't kill you on accident because you're not a shifter. You won't produce a child even more dangerous than Deacon is. And you don't come to him easily. As far as I'm concerned, these are ideal traits for his mate." She sighed. "But your job…"

The words were barely out of Maria's mouth when Liruk and Wisat appeared not two feet away. Cary groaned. She hadn't even felt their approach or presence. She'd been too caught up in what Maria was telling her to notice the warning signs.

Damn. She glared at them, putting her hands on her hips. "I've only been here for, what, three hours? At the most. What could possibly bring you here already?"

"There is a girl you need to protect," Liruk said.

"Here? Or Portland?"

"Here," Wisat said. "Soon."

"She can't leave," Maria put in. "You know that. If she leaves him here alone…"

"It is necessary, your majesty," Liruk said, her tone haughty and not at all deferential despite the honorific. "It is her job. She must do it."

Cary looked between her bosses and Deacon's mother, then snarled at her bosses. "You knew? This whole time you knew about Deacon?"

"If you don't go now, Protector, a child will die horribly," Liruk said. "Do you want that?"

"Fuck you," Cary snapped. Liruk knew exactly what buttons to push. She hung her head, grumbling more curses under her breath. Then she looked up at Maria. "I have to go," she said.

"You can control him for a few hours," Wisat said to Maria, his tone that bit kinder than Liruk's.

"Only for a few hours, though," Maria said. "What if she's killed?"

"Thanks for the faith in my skills," Cary grumbled to no one in particular. "I'll be back before dinner," she said to Maria. "And if Evan wanted to make me more pizza, I wouldn't object."

That earned Cary a slight smile from Maria.

"If Deacon asks," Cary said, "tell him I had a job to do. He'll understand." *If* he asked, she thought.

"He'll notice when you leave," Maria said.

Cary wasn't so sure about that, but she didn't argue. Instead, she faced her bosses and focused on the job she had to do. The complications with her mate would have to wait. "Okay, where am I going and who am I looking for?"

14

Cary pulled her car to the side of the road and climbed out scanning the area as she zipped up her leather jacket. The weather had turned colder as the day progressed, but mostly Cary wanted to make sure her wallet and car keys were sealed into the right magic pockets.

The drive had taken her the better part of a half hour to get here and her nerves were jumping as she scanned her surroundings. She'd turned off the I5 onto a small slip road and into the outskirts of one of the many small towns that circled Eugene. This particular area had seen better days, the few buildings and single gas station within view all abandoned or beat up. Distant car noise from the highway hummed in the background, but no other signs of people or traffic moved along the slip road.

The sound of shouting caught her attention. She jogged toward the noise, coming from the lot behind a battered old wooden building that had once been a bakery. In the scrub dappled parking lot, Cary spotted two women in each other's faces, one tugging on the other. She ran forward and insinuated herself between them.

Glancing between the two, she pointed to one and ask, "Are you Becky Hall?"

The older woman glowered, dark eyes narrowed, pale skin pulled tight over her bones.

Cary pointed to the other woman, girl actually. She looked *maybe* seventeen, maybe even younger. "Becky Hall?"

The girl nodded, her blue eyes huge in her pretty oval-shaped face.

"Okay." Cary turned to face the older woman, putting Becky Hall at her back. "Good guy." She gestured behind herself. "Bad guy." She pointed at the woman in front of her. "All set. So. What seems to be the problem here?"

The dark-eyed woman snarled. "She's mine. I won her fair and square."

"Uh," Cary said, "first, no. You can't own a person or win them. Second, she's just a child." Over her shoulder she asked, "How old are you, Becky?"

"Fifteen."

"Fifteen." Cary shook her head. "See, a kid."

"She's old enough for what I want from her," the woman spit.

"Which would be?" Cary asked. It was always nice to figure out what was going on as she kept bad guys from hurting good guys.

Also, it helped to know *why* the Nags sent her on this particular mission. Sometimes it was just a random "save someone's life" kind of thing. But these two women seemed like perfectly ordinary, mundane humans. While Cary got between mundane humans all the time, and sometimes even at the Nags' urgings, she had a gut instinct there was something more here.

Huh, maybe she had learned something in the last six years.

"None of your business," the dark-eyed woman said.

Which didn't help with the whole figuring-this-out part of the job. "Okay, maybe you might tell me *why* you think a teenager who isn't yours…" She glanced back at Becky. "She's not a relative, right?"

Becky shook her head. Some of the color had returned to her face, and she was looking angry now. "She was gambling with my father. He put me in the pot."

"Well, that's not good," Cary said with feeling. "What the hell is wrong with your father?"

"He's a drunk. He probably didn't even know what he was doing." Becky sniffled a little, but wiped the single tear on her cheek away with a vicious swipe.

Cary couldn't tell if those were angry tears or heartbroken tears or some combination of both, but it didn't really matter, because the sight of fifteen-year-old Becky Hall trying not to cry hurt Cary's heart.

She faced the other woman again. "You can't win a child in a poker game and everyone with sense knows that. Either you have no sense in your head, or you want her for something nefarious. And I'm not allowing that. If it's a lack of sense, go get some."

"She's mine," the woman snarled.

"No," Cary said, shaking her head. "And if you don't leave her alone, I'm going to call the cops and have you arrested for kidnapping."

Not that she actually wanted to call the police if she didn't have to. But dealing with this kind of situation between two mundane humans was easier to explain to the cops than some of her more unusual protections, so she could call them if she really needed to.

"I *need* her," the woman said, her voice dropping to a weird register.

Cary frowned. "What the hell do you need a teenager for?"

She was sorry she'd ask the minute the words were out of her mouth. She honestly didn't want to know what this woman wanted Becky for because with this kind of intensity, it couldn't possibly be good.

But while Cary's mind went to dark places like child and sex slavery, the woman before her apparently went to even darker places. She pulled a long, dagger-like knife from the back of her tight-fitting jeans. Cary couldn't even imagine how she'd had that thing in her pants and it hadn't cut her.

Or maybe it had because the blade glinted with something red. Before Cary could analyze what that red was, the woman lunged at her, knife thrusting for Cary's throat.

Under ordinary circumstances, Cary just stood still and made a face at someone trying to stab her. When she was protecting, the stupid knife wouldn't get anywhere near her anyway. And after getting shot twice in the last few days, a knife was supposed to scare her?

But she'd been training with Lucy *a lot* lately. Every day for hours —after several years of sporadic training. And she reacted without even thinking about it.

She reached across her body and grabbed the woman by the wrist, twisted her wrist around and to one side, throwing the woman off balance so she folded over and her arm was wrenched at an awkward angle. Cary pressed a hand to the back of the woman's shoulder with her free hand while pulling the woman's arm straight and back. At this point, with very little effort, she could easily dislocate the woman's shoulder. The realization made her eyes widen.

And she grinned.

"Hey! I did that on my own." She glanced back at Becky. "That was all me!"

Becky nodded but her brow furrowed deeply. And now she looked as nervous of Cary as she was of the woman trying to kidnap her.

Cary shrugged. "Usually I just stand still while people try to stab me," she said by way of explanation. Then to the bent over woman, who was cursing up a storm, she tsked. "I've been shot twice this week. A little knife is hardly going to bother me."

"No," the woman screamed. "I have to kill her. I have to. It demands it."

That finally got through Cary's pride in having used her own skills. She took a better look at the dagger still clutched in the woman's hand. The blade was pointed upward, and the woman's knuckles were white where she gripped the hilt tight, despite the awkward and painful bend in her wrist. Technically, a little more twist and if the woman didn't drop the knife, Cary could break her wrist.

"You should drop the knife," Cary said, watching the woman closely. Her Protector instincts were humming now. Not just a couple of mundane humans after all.

Or at least the situation wasn't just mundane.

"I can't drop it," the woman cried. "I have to kill her. Don't you understand? I have to."

Cary watched the dagger vibrate. "What happens if you don't?" She studied the red on the dagger closer now that the thing wasn't plunging toward her neck. Yeah, that definitely looked like blood. Fresh blood still dripping down the blade. Dripping toward the woman's hand and absorbing into her skin.

Oh, that couldn't be good.

"Drop the knife," Cary said, frantically now. "Drop it."

"I can't!" The woman's cry was desperate.

And Cary realized she had two people to protect.

"Don't move," Cary warned.

She released her hold on the woman's shoulder but kept her wrist twisted and her arm stretched tight. Very carefully, she took the base of the hilt where it met the blade in her fingers and tugged gently upward. When she had more room, she gripped the hilt better, wincing when the dripping blood reached her hand where it was now between the blade and the woman's hand.

Thanks to her Protector powers, the blood didn't actually touch her skin. It seemed to hover over her, defying basic physics.

Cary could feel the things malevolence now, the evil emanating from it like a physical presence. She tugged upward again, pulling it very slowly from the woman's tight grip. The woman's wrist tendons stuck out sharply from strain, and she whimpered as Cary worked. But not in resistance, Cary realized. In fact, the noise reminded Cary of the sounds people made when they were anticipating severe pain.

"Don't worry," she murmured to the woman. "I've got you. Just a few more seconds and I'll have it."

"It'll take you too," the woman said, whispering now. Her voice sounded harsh and strained, gravely and...different than it had sounded a moment ago.

"I'll be fine," Cary assured. "Don't worry." She gave one final, gentle tug and the dagger came away from of the woman's fingers with a popping sound.

Cary's eyes widened as the blood dripping down the blade sucked back into the metal. A sound like a growl of hate actually seemed to emanate from the dagger, although it was so deep it was something she felt in her bones more than heard with her ears.

"Holy hell," she murmured.

The woman whose wrist she still held started to cry. Cary loosened her hold and let the woman rise back up but she didn't release her wrist completely.

"You're okay now?" Cary asked. "No more urges to stab me or Becky here?"

The woman shook her head. Cary could feel her trembling.

"It wasn't me," she said, her voice softer and a lot less astringent and mean now. "It was that thing. I don't know what it was doing to me. I... I..."

Cary blinked and the woman folded forward into a faint. Cary barely caught her one armed and wasn't strong enough to hold her up that way, not while clenching a cursed knife in her other hand. She knelt awkwardly, lowering the woman as gently as possible to the ground. The broken paving wasn't the best place to lay someone down, but it would have to do for now.

Over her shoulder, she said to Becky, "Don't get near the knife. Can you keep an eye on her for a minute?"

"She just tried to kidnap me," Becky said. "Kill me."

"Yeah, but I don't think she was doing all that on purpose."

Cary lifted the dagger, studying it more closely now that she was holding it. As she angled it in the dim winter light, she caught the faintest flashes of blue writing in the metal along the short, wide blade. The stunningly sharp edges winked wickedly.

"Boy, that would hurt if it cut you," she murmured.

"How can you hold it?" Becky asked. She was kneeling down next to the woman now, feeling for her pulse.

Cary waved away the question with her free hand. "I just have a knack for these kinds of things." She couldn't read the runes on the blade, they moved like liquid, but she'd seen something like this before. In the headboard Deacon had been chained to when they first met. A wizard's headboard.

So... Magic for sure. Very evil magic.

"Where the hell did you get a magic dagger?" Cary asked the unconscious woman. The dagger was obviously cursed to make its barer kill. "Must need a particular type of sacrifice, though," Cary murmured aloud.

She glanced at Becky, and thought probably virgin sacrifice, but didn't want to embarrass the poor girl by asking out loud. That just seemed rude after someone had tried to kill her.

The woman on the ground started to rouse and Becky quickly stood and took several steps away from her, edging behind Cary again.

Smart girl with good instincts. Cary smiled at her approvingly—which felt a little condescending, but hey, they'd both had a tough day.

The woman groaned and put a hand to her forehead. "What happened?"

"You fainted," Cary said. "After you tried to kill Becky and I got the cursed knife out of your hand. Where the hell did you pick up a cursed knife?"

The woman's eyes rounded and she glanced in panic at the dagger Cary was holding. "Don't touch it!" she said pointlessly.

"I'll be fine." Cary held the thing up a little higher. "See? No urge to kill. Where did you get it?"

"In an antique shop," the woman said. "In Vegas."

"Las Vegas? Are you even from Oregon?"

"I live in Olympia," she murmured.

Washington State. So at least the same coast. But… "What are you doing here?" Cary asked.

The woman swallowed, her gaze on the dagger. "It's not talking to me anymore," she said.

"It was talking to you?" Cary asked.

She nodded. "It…called to me in the shop. I couldn't take my eyes off it. I had to have it."

Cary noticed the woman couldn't look away now either. Very carefully, using an interior pocket specially designed by Marianne to contain sharp and sometimes magical things safely, Cary slipped the dagger out of sight. She pressed her fingers to the pocket's opening to ensure it sealed closed. Then she lowered the edge of her jacket back into place. She couldn't even feel the dagger there now, not even the outline of it against her ribs.

When she got home, she was going to have to buy Marianne a drink. Maybe four. She always appreciated the magicked clothing Marianne made for her, but in this particular case, she was extra special grateful for this pocket's ability to block and contain magic.

"Better?" Cary asked.

The woman blinked a few times, then met Cary's gaze. "What happened to me?"

"Do you know where you are?"

"Vegas?"

Oh boy. "Nope. And I think you need to get home and maybe visit a doctor."

"Huh?"

"You've had a long few days. I don't suppose you remember the name of the antique shop in Vegas that sold you the dagger?"

"What dagger?" the woman said, frowning slightly.

Cary blinked. Well hell.

Becky muttered something under her breath, but Cary couldn't hear her clearly. The words sounded a bit like a prayer though.

"Okay," Cary said with a deep breath. "Here's what we're going to do. You—" she pointed to the woman who was just starting to pull herself back to her feet, "—are going to go home and never go back to Vegas ever again because obviously gambling and antique shops aren't good for you."

"Huh?"

"Just do what I say," Cary ordered.

The woman nodded, even though she looked confused.

Cary hoped she didn't forget all this and head back down to Vegas and the mysterious antique shop again. Cary glanced back at Becky. "Your father sounds like an asshole. Do you have somewhere to go that isn't the streets? A safe relative? A friend's house?"

"My mom's aunt lets me stay with her. She's a good woman."

"Will she keep you away from your father until he gets help for whatever makes him an asshole?" Cary asked.

"There's no help for his brand of asshole," Becky muttered.

Cary pressed her lips together so she wouldn't smile inappropriately. She liked Becky.

"But my aunt will keep me safe," Becky said.

"Good. Do you want me to take you to her house?"

Becky glanced around. "My bike is just there." She pointed.

Cary shook her head. "It'll fit in the back of my car. I'll give you a ride to your aunt's. Make sure you get there safely." She turned back to the woman. "I take it that sideways parked Lexus is yours?" She nodded to the expensive black car half parked on the sidewalk, half in the lot. The thing sported a few dents and a lot of dust that Cary suspected hadn't been there before the trip to Vegas.

The woman blinked at the car. "A rental," she said, still sounding a little befuddled. "But... I was supposed to return it on my way to the airport in Vegas. I flew there and was flying home. My own car is parked at SeaTac."

"Why were you in Vegas?" Cary asked, more curious than thinking it meant anything.

"Work. A conference. I'm in finance."

"Okay," Cary said, "well, you're just outside Eugene, Oregon now. And you can't go back to Vegas to return the car. Was it a national rental place?"

The woman nodded, but her frown deepened.

"Drive back up to Seattle and return the car to one of the outlets there," Cary said. When the woman nodded but didn't look like she was really listening, Cary touched her arm. She flinched and jumped away. Cary held a hand up, palm out to calm her. "Are you listening to me?" she asked gently.

The woman nodded.

"Drive to the Seattle airport," Cary said. "Can you do that safely?"

"Of course," the woman said.

"You're sure?"

"Yes," the woman said, now looking a little offended. And less and less confused.

"Drive back, drop this car off there, get your car, and go home.

Never go to Las Vegas again, even for work." Cary said every word slowly and distinctly, holding the woman's gaze so she understood. "You had a very bad experience there. You have to avoid putting yourself in that situation again. Do you understand?"

"Sure." The woman shrugged and headed back to her car. "I have to get back for work tomorrow."

She climbed into the Lexus and after some unhealthy sounding metal grinding against concrete, managed to get the car back onto the street.

Cary watched her drive away, hoping she'd remember enough of what had happened to avoid Vegas in the future. And antique shops.

Cary faced Becky again. "Grab your bike. I'll get you to your aunts."

"Who are you?" Becky asked. "How can you hold that knife without...anything happening?"

"Just a concerned citizen," Cary said. "Go get your bike."

Becky nodded, but her brow was still deeply furrowed as she hurried to collect her cheap bicycle from the opposite side of the lot.

Cary was used to people looking at her that way. In fact, she frequently generated confusion in people.

All in a day's work.

Between seeing Becky safely to her aunt's house and getting stuck on the I5 behind a traffic accident, it was full dark by the time Cary returned to the mansion, and well past dinner time. Deacon met her in the entryway, his presence surprising her.

"Everything okay?" he asked, coming to her and pulling her close into a hug.

She frowned up at him. "Fine. Just had to sort out a cursed dagger that was making a woman try to kill a teenager. How was your day?"

He grinned. And kissed her. And her frown deepened.

"All right," she said, pushing a little at his shoulders. "What's going on? You've been distant and *controlled*," she snarled the word, "all day. So much so, you forgot I got shot this morning. And you said that was you feeling more like yourself. Now you're all huggy and kissy and touchy again. What gives?"

He brushed a hand up into her hair, tugging gently and loosening her ponytail. "The house is virtually empty at the moment."

Ah. "So, what your mother said was true?"

He met her gaze. "What did my mother say?"

Before she could answer, a larger than typical leopard strolled into the entryway from deeper in the house, emerging from the shadows like a ghost. And a ghost was a fantastic analogy because the leopard was white. White fir covered in pale brown rosetta spots and golden eyes that looked very familiar.

Except for the fur color, the familial resemblance in this form was strong.

"Maria," Cary greeted.

Deacon glanced back and nodded at his mother. Then frowned a little at Cary. "You can tell? You've never seen her in her leopard form, have you?"

Cary shrugged. "You have her eyes."

In a blink, Maria shifted to her a human form. She was smiling, a genuine and full smile that surprised Cary.

But not as much as the fact that when she shifted to her human form, she wasn't naked. In fact, she was fully dressed in an elegant pair of cream-colored pants and a fitted, button down shirt in a burnt orange color that complimented her skin tone beautifully.

Cary raised her brows. Woah. "That part of the magic," she said, gesturing at Maria's clothes.

Maria tipped her head down slightly.

Then the implications hit Cary. She glared at Deacon. "You can do that too, can't you? You don't have to be naked when you shift back to human form."

He shrugged, not looking the least bit guilty. "Sure."

"Then why do you keep shifting around me without making clothes?"

His grin was too wicked for his mother to witness. Cary's cheeks heated, and she felt like she might combust.

Aloud, he said, "I don't use my magic. Ever if I can avoid it."

"He thinks it helps," Maria said.

"It does," he said. "The less I use it, the less control it has over me."

"The truth is the opposite," Maria said, sounding tired. As if this was an argument they'd had many times before.

"Not for me," Deacon said.

Cary glanced between the two equally stubborn expressions. Like mother like son. She wondered in passing if Evan was also that stubborn. It would make for some interesting family dinners.

Her stomach chose that moment to disrupt the standoff by grumbling loudly. Speaking of dinner. She winced and felt her cheeks warming again. "Guess I need to get some food."

Deacon smiled. "Dad left some dinner in the kitchen for you."

"He is obsessed with making pizzas now," Maria said, shaking her head. "I blame you."

Cary grinned, not feeling even a little guilty about that.

"Are you well after your…outing?" Maria asked.

"Yes." Except for the cursed dagger in her pocket, she was dandy. "But I'd like to talk with you more when you have time."

"Of course." She glanced at Deacon. "You're okay now? I can call the others back?"

He nodded. "Thank you."

She blinked slowly, in what Cary took as acknowledgement of his thanks, though it was subtly done. "I'll see you both in the morning." She disappeared soundless back into the shadows.

Cary shook her head. "You definitely get your quiet movements from your mother, too."

"Let's get you fed," he said. "I suspect we need to talk."

"Yeah, we do," she said with feeling. "You can start by explaining how you have magic and neglected to tell me this fact."

"I didn't want to scare you."

"You say that a lot. It keeps backfiring on you."

His mouth lifted in a rueful expression that wasn't quite a smile. "Will you tell me more about what happened this evening?"

"Sure, if you want to know. Just Protector business as usual, though. By the way, did you know your mother knows what Protectors are? She knew who the Nags were when they showed up to send me on this mission."

"I need to hear more about that, too."

Cary tilted her head to one side, studying him as they walked toward the rear of the house. "You didn't know. She didn't tell you."

"She didn't have reason to," he said, but he sounded irritated. "I haven't told her what you are. She must have figured it out when you saved the clinic."

"She's met another Protector," Cary said. "I haven't even met other Protectors yet. But I keep meeting people who have. It's weird." She frowned a little. That was weird, wasn't it? Could she asked Jaxer about that, or would that violate the seventh year rules?

A question for later. "First, before we go much farther into this conversation and I get sidetracked, I want to know about this magic of yours. Your mother told me…some of it. But I need to hear more about it from you because you've been acting weird since we got here."

He sighed as he held the kitchen door open for her. "It's complicated."

"Humor me," she said. Then stopped in her tracks. The kitchen was huge, and modern, all shiny silver appliances and warm recessed lighting. The cabinets were white, the countertop was a pale gray stone. The island in the center of the room was topped with that wooden cutting board material. There were two stacked ovens, a separate stove top on the island, a lot of shelf space…and a pizza oven against one wall.

Cary blinked a few times at the pizza oven. The heat from its dying fire still warmed the room. "An actual pizza oven?" She looked up at Deacon.

He shrugged. "Once my dad started making pizzas, he had to go all the way."

"I'm not sure whether to be flattered or appalled," she murmured.

"My mother is taking care of the appalled for you," he said. "You can be flattered."

"Gee, thanks." Her eyes widened when she spotted the giant pepperoni pizza sitting on the counter waiting for them. It was under a clear dome, keeping it warm, the cheese gooey and browned just a little on the top. She groaned and her stomach growled again.

"I wish I could get you to look at me the way you look at pizza," Deacon commented, only partially joking.

"I do," she said, making a beeline for the chairs around the island. "When there's no pizza around." She grinned at him, relieved when he smiled back.

He sat next to her and dished them both out two slices. "Do you need coffee?" he asked.

Proving just how well he knew her, she thought. But, "It's too late and I'm tired. I'd better not."

She savored her first few yummy bites before launching into their much needed conversation.

"We have a lot to talk about here," she said. "First, I'd like to know where your mother sent everyone. Are they safe? What about the leopard that just gave birth?"

"Everyone is safe, sent to their various homes. The new mother and her mate are still here."

"But you're okay?"

"I'm fine around a limited number of my people. When my mother is here to ensure they're safe."

"And the cougars aren't a threat to any of the leopards when they're scattered around? I got the impression this place was a sanctuary."

"It is." He shrugged. "It's a lot of things really. Government offices. A safe house. My childhood home. The main offices for our various businesses. A hospital for my people when necessary."

"So why not keep everyone here after the attack?"

"They're all on guard and will be able to return tomorrow." He was looking at his pizza when he said, "It was safer for them not to be here while you were gone."

"Got that part. I think. Your mother told me your magic can…affect the other leopards."

"One of the reasons I don't use it."

Did she mention his mother had told her about the time he was seven and almost killed another leopard or not? Maybe later. She didn't want to get diverted.

"And that's why you have to be so controlled here?" she said instead.

"Exactly."

"Okay, then why are…were there so many leopards here when we arrived this morning? They haven't all been here since the kidnapping?"

"No. They're here for the charity ball. I said it was a big event. Most of our people come every year."

"That big, huh?" She might not have the right clothes for this thing. She'd better ring Marianne tomorrow. Maybe she could sneak back to Portland really quick for that dress Marianne was making her.

Except that apparently left Deacon too dangerous.

"There are a lot of the kids here," she said, trying to stay on topic. "The ones I helped."

"The kids have their own event during the ball. Separate, but special for them."

"Ah." She smiled around another bite of pizza. "That's really thoughtful of you all to throw the kids a party too." She munched a bit more before finally saying, "So. You have magic and when you're not controlled, that can endanger your people. Since meeting me, your control has been dodgy at best. But you were around your people for a few days without me when the kids were kidnapped. How did you manage that? Your control was even worse then because we hadn't slept together yet."

Saying that out loud in his family home made her cheeks warm, but she really needed to understand all this so she pressed on. Hopefully no one with super shifter hearing was near enough to eavesdrop.

"My mother helped augment my control when I was here, like she did this afternoon after you left. But it was difficult and it drained her, which was why she couldn't help recover the children. Once I was back in Portland, and especially once we were near each other again, I had enough control to focus on what needed to be done. It helped that I got to unleash some of my animal side's short temper on the cougars, too. That gave me enough control to be safe for the leopards."

"How does your mother help?" Cary found all this fascinating, and might even have enjoyed the conversation if it wasn't all information she should have known weeks ago.

He frowned a little as he stared off to one side, thinking. She waited him out.

"It has to do with our magic. She told you it's not like Angie's? It's not spells and scrying and premonitions. It's not like wizards or faeries or even the Nags. It's very specific and really only affects us and our people."

"That's the thing there, isn't it?" Cary said, setting her slice down for a minute to focus fully on him. "Your mother said you can control your people."

"Against their will," he said with a faint shrug. He didn't meet her gaze, instead picking at a piece of pepperoni on what remained of his second slice.

Cary paused. "You can make them do anything?"

"Anything. I can make them take a gun and shoot themselves in the head. I can make them calm down and focus. I can take away their pain by making them no longer feel it. I can also make them feel excruciating pain where none should be. I can force them to move or shift or freeze in place."

And according to his mother, he could kill them with a thought. "That's terrifying, Deacon."

"Exactly," he said with feeling. "And it's not something I want. I don't use my magic. In any way. Ever. Even without it, I can sense my people easily, no matter where they are, so long as they're within a certain range. I can communicate with them through thoughts, not telepathy but a kind of nudging that makes my intentions clear, even when we're not in scenting range. I did do that while we were rescuing the kids, but even that I rarely use. Too close to the controlling magic for my taste."

"And this is why your control is so important to you," she said quietly. "Without it, you might use your magic in a fit of anger. Against one of your own who might be innocent."

He nodded, but still wouldn't look at her.

"Which is why you don't use your magic to make clothes when you shift? Why you keep ending up naked around me," she said in an attempt to get him to look at her.

It worked. "I have different reasons for that," he said, his gaze turning all sexy and seductive. "And they have nothing to do with innocence."

She huffed out a laugh. But at least the mood had lightened a little. Or at least picked up a different kind of tension. She found herself leaning toward him and realized if she followed through they'd get sidetracked. There was more she needed to know first. So she returned to the subject at hand.

"So your mother controls you with her magic when you need her to? Is that what happens when you're here and I'm not, when she's helping you?"

He shrugged. "I'm stronger than she is now, but because she's my mother she seems to have a more calming influence than another shifter might. So she can do enough to keep me from lashing out or…" He trailed off.

She didn't need him to finish. "What about your sister in Portland? You were working with Caitlin in the beginning, right after we met, before she made you take a leave of absence."

"I'm less likely to hurt any of my own family," he said. "And to be honest, I thought I could work without hurting her. I didn't really understand how compromised my control was at first. But my nearly shifting in front of our human employees wasn't the only reason she sent me away. We both thought the precaution necessary."

"That's why you haven't gone back yet," Cary guessed. "Not because you're worried about shifting in front of humans. But because you're worried about your sister, being near her if I'm not around."

"My twins seem to be mostly immune," he said, in a very slight subject change. "More so even than my mother. Which means they're more likely to give me grief." He smiled a little when he said that.

But the sister he worked with in Portland wasn't one of his twins. According to Maria, Caitlin didn't know the extent of Deacon's full powers either. But she obviously knew he wasn't your run-of-the-mill shifter.

"I suppose Michael and Jocelyn used that against you when you were kids?" she said. "My sister would have."

He flashed a genuine smile then. "Yeah, they did." He looked at her closer. "Did you get along with Michael?"

"He's great. You two do look shockingly alike. It's a little terrifying that two people who are as gorgeous as you walk the earth. If Jocelyn shares that trait, the human race is doomed."

"I'm not sure whether to be complimented by that or jealous that you think my brother is handsome."

"He looks just like you but for the eyes. If I didn't think he was handsome, you should worry."

Deacon didn't look convinced. But seeing that edge of jealousy in his expression, the fact that he seemed to *care* was a relief for reasons she was embarrassed to admit. So she decided to admit something else embarrassing.

"If it helps," she said, "I finally got a taste of why you act the way you do around Jaxer." She ducked her head. "Through no effort of my own, I keep snarling and growling every time Sasha walks into the room."

His eyebrows rose. "Sasha? Why?"

"Don't pretend you didn't used to have a thing with her. Your mother already told me."

"A long time ago," he said with a shrug. "I'm surprised it would affect you now."

"Well, it does. And I have no control over it. It's kind of irritating actually. I get overwhelmed by jealousy every time she's around, and I don't even know the woman."

"Is it wrong that I'm a little pleased with your reaction to her?"

"Yes," she said with a scowl. "It's very rude of you."

But again, his faint smile and the wicked look in his eyes was a relief. That was the Deacon she knew. Or had thought she'd known. And seeing him again made something tight and ugly in her gut relax.

She titled her head to study him. "You don't have to answer this if you don't want to, because it's nosey and probably none of my business, but... How did you have sex with other leopard shifters and maintain your control?"

In her experience, limited as it had been over the years, sex was not a place where control asserted itself. In fact, she tended to let go of it all together, especially in those lovely climactic moments. Did he? Could he with another shifter?

And did she *really* want to know?

Too late to retract the question. She'd have to leave it up to him to decide if he wanted to answer or not.

"Mostly, I haven't had affairs with other leopard shifters," he said, matter-of-factly. "But the few times I have, it was only after I was certain my control was solid. My control has been solid since I was a teenager." He held her gaze. "Until I met you."

She narrowed her eyes at him. "Insult or compliment?"

"Fact of nature."

She snorted. "Fine. But you did have a thing with Sasha." It wasn't a question. "And somehow she survived it. Mores the pity."

He smiled a little at her snarky comment.

"Don't be happy about me saying that," she said. "It doesn't make me feel very good to be acting like such an ass about her. Is this how you feel whenever Jaxer is around?"

"Yes." Said without any hesitation.

"But I've never slept with Jaxer."

"Even considering the possibility makes me want to tear him apart."

"That's terrifying."

"I don't have any more control over it than you have over your reaction to Sasha. Jaxer is in love with you. Sasha and I haven't been together for years. Jaxer is more of a threat, as far as I'm concerned."

"He's not. And you might think things with you and Sasha have been over for a while, but she doesn't. So don't get all high and mighty on me." She huffed out a breath. "I don't like this jealousy thing. It's weird and feels shitty of me to want to rip someone's hair out just because she touched you."

He raised his eyebrows at her last comment.

"Don't you dare look smug and pleased with that," she warned, pointing a finger at him.

"Wouldn't dream of it."

"I do have more sympathy for your reactions to Jaxer now, though," she admitted. "So I'll try to stop nagging you to get over it."

"Thank you. Because I can't."

She so so wanted to mumble that he could at least try. Being the bigger person was sometimes hard.

She held his gaze for a long moment. "It's nice having you back."

He startled at that. "What do you mean?"

"You as the 'iceman' Prince Deacon isn't someone I know." She shrugged. "I've missed you this way."

"Both ways of being are me. I have to maintain that control when there are so many other leopards around. I can't afford not to."

"I'm realizing that. I just have to get used to you when you're all controlled and distant." She stared at her now empty plate when she said, "It kind of hurt, not having you remember I got injured this morning." She felt her cheeks heating and rolled her eyes at her own sentimentality. Geez, she was turning into a sap.

"I don't want to hurt you," he said quietly, taking her hands in his. "I'm sorry about that."

She waved away his apology, embarrassed by her own hurt feelings because she was supposed to be a grown woman, not a teenager girl in the throes of her first love affair. "It's fine. Let's change the subject. Are the others coming back or will they stay away until the ball?"

"They're back in the morning. We have a lot to do in the next few days."

"Do you have a new venue yet?" With everything else going on, she'd nearly forgotten that hiccup.

"We're nearly at a deal for one. I had to call in a few favors."

"So like her or not, Sasha's idea to bring you in was a good one." She lifted her lip in a snarl. "I hate admitting that."

He leaned in and kissed her. A surprise that made her freeze for just an instant. Then she kissed him back, taking in his heat and scent and the lovely warmth of having him near. The tingling of desire traveling over her skin, settled low, starting a slow burn that was just a few breaths away from being a full-fledged fire. She wrapped her arms around his neck and pulled him closer, so he was standing between her spread legs, pressing into her with an intent that made her hum even as he deepened the kiss. And she forgot all about being jealous of that other woman.

Until a feminine throat-clearing broke the moment.

"Sorry to interrupt," Sasha said, not sounding the least bit sorry.

Cary leaned back and narrowed her eyes at Deacon. "You knew she was on her way here," she accused in a quiet voice. Though why she bothered being quiet when Sasha could hear her, she didn't know.

He nodded and brushed his fingers through the loose hairs at her temple where they'd escaped her ponytail. "I wanted to get in a kiss before I had to go back to work," he said. "Did anyone ever show you to our room?"

"No." She'd forgotten that too. Wow, it had been a weird day.

"I can show her," Sasha offered, her voice a purr of helpfulness that Cary didn't buy for an instant.

Being alone with Sasha didn't seem like such a great idea, since just having her in the same room made Cary crazy. But at least Sasha wouldn't be alone with Deacon. That was something.

Deacon kissed Cary on the cheek before stepping out of her arms. "I'll see you later. Don't worry about waiting up."

She watched him leave the kitchen, the way his control and that icy exterior took over his movements as he walked past Sasha. He didn't even seem aware that he was changing his physical demeanor. His control just rolled back into place and turned him into this other Deacon.

That was going to take some getting used to.

Sasha brushed a hand over his shoulder in passing, making a comment so quiet Cary couldn't hear it. Cary's eyes narrowed at Sasha's hand on Deacon, a part of her considering how best to break Sasha's wrist.

She blinked at that and wanted to curse but was afraid Sasha would misunderstand. This was a horrible feeling and the thoughts sparked by her jealousy were embarrassingly awful. She wasn't this person. And she didn't like that the chemistry between her and Deacon, the bond that brought them together, was doing this to her.

She was more impressed now than she'd admit to Deacon with his ability to control this around Jaxer.

Sasha watched Deacon leave, then faced Cary. Her smile was extremely feline—sexy and sly and mean all at the same time.

Maybe Cary's instinctively wanting to rip her hair out wasn't so far off the mark.

She mentally shook that thought off and forced a smile. "Lead the way," she said in what she hoped sounded like a friendly tone.

Given Sasha's smirk, Cary was pretty sure she'd failed at friendly.

Because Cary had barely exchanged more than a few words with Sasha since meeting her that morning, she acknowledged that she should maybe make more of an effort. This woman was Maria's assistant, which meant she'd be in their lives for a while, as long as Cary and Deacon were together, probably. Trying to get along with her on some level seemed prudent.

In an attempt to do that, and also so she could ignore the way Sasha moved over the polished wood floor with such elegant, silent grace it made Cary feel like a plodding ogre, Cary said, "Deacon tells me you're close to a deal on a new venue. That's good news."

"Deacon can work miracles," Sasha said. "He'll make an excellent leader when he takes over from Maria."

Cary kept forgetting that was out there in the future. A terrifying thing to contemplate. "I'm sure Maria will be around for a long time, so he won't have to worry about it for years."

Sasha shrugged. "Of course, our queen is in excellent health. But you never know, with the cougars and all. It's good to know our people are in good hands no matter what happens."

"This issue with the cougars, any thoughts on it?" Okay, a little deeper than small talk, but she didn't want to talk about Deacon with this woman anymore.

Sasha shrugged, a ridiculously urbane gesture the way she did it. "They're a loose group of renegades. They won't be a threat to our people for long."

"Any idea why they've suddenly started coming after you guys. I mean, it's been, what, half a century since Maria established peace here."

Sasha narrowed her gaze a little as she looked at Cary. "No idea," she said after a pause.

The pause left Cary wondering what she was missing.

"It'll all work out though," Sasha said. "And in the meantime, we have a huge event to pull off in a few short days."

"Are you worried the cougars might try to interfere with the ball? Or even attack during it?"

"No."

She was so firm about that Cary raised her brows. "Really? Not even a little worried? I mean… They shot at you guys in front of humans today. What's to stop them from using all the humans at the event as fodder in their war?"

"We'll have sufficient security in place," Sasha said. She gave Cary a pitying look. "We have considered the threat, you know."

"Uh huh." Cary worked very hard not to snarl at the woman's tone.

They were in a fairly dark hallway at the back of the house, on the ground floor, which for some reason surprised Cary. She'd have assumed the bedrooms were all on higher floors. The walls in this section of the house were painted a soft gray that nicely complimented the light wood floors. An occasional bronze wall sconce provided the only real illumination as the overhead recessed lights were off. No pictures hung on the walls to break up the space, and there were no tables or knickknacks anywhere here. Just a series of closed doors with antique bronze knobs.

Cary's footsteps echoed in the empty corridor as they moved farther into the west wing. Sasha's didn't even though she wore spiked high heels. That was just irritating.

Sasha finally stopped in front of a door, seemingly at random, and pushed it open. "Here you are." She glanced inside. "I wouldn't expect Deacon tonight, though. We have a lot of work to do, moving things to the new venue."

"Won't everyone you work with be asleep?" Cary clutch her hands together behind her back.

"Logistics wait for no man," Sasha said with a slight smile. "Don't worry. I'll make sure Deacon gets some rest."

It was on the tip of Cary's tongue to say that wasn't what she was worried about, but she clenched her jaw so she didn't let the words out. The response seemed to be exactly what Sasha was expecting or hoping for, and Cary didn't want to give her the satisfaction.

When Cary didn't say anything, Sasha added, "I'm used to looking after him."

Yeah, the woman was definitely trying to get a rise out of Cary. And damned if Cary didn't want to take the bait. She smiled—with more teeth than was strictly polite—and said, "Thank you for showing me to our room." Emphasis on the "our."

"You're welcome." Sasha looked her over, from Cary's hiking boots to her t-shirt and beat-up leather jacket. "Do you need any help with an appropriate outfit for the ball? Maria mentioned you might."

Okay, now that wasn't even a *subtle* dig. Cary might not like that she'd reacted with anger and jealous to Sasha without getting to know her first. But as it turned out, Sasha was a bitch. An oddly comforting realization. Her reaction wasn't all chemistry and irrational jealousy after all. Yay!

"I'll be fine, thanks," Cary said. "I'm having a lovely dress made special."

"Really? Do I know the designer?"

"I doubt it. She's very exclusive. Almost impossible to book." A lie but Sasha didn't know that. Cary was only a little embarrassed that she was playing this game. And maybe not even a little, she thought, when Sasha narrowed her eyes in irritation. Yes, Cary was being petty, but what the hell?

Although, she was going to have to panic-call Marianne as soon as Sasha left.

"Thank you for showing me the room," Cary said again. "I'm sure I can find my way back in the morning."

"Of course." Sasha looked her over again. "You might want to skip the pizza tomorrow, though. If you still want to fit into that dress you're having made special."

Cary snarled at the woman's back. If Sasha wasn't going to pretend at polite anymore, Cary didn't have to either.

She closed the bedroom door, a little too hard, and looked around.

It was a lovely open space with a huge four poster bed, an antique dresser against one wall, and ceiling-to-floor sage green curtains pulled closed over the windows. To one side, a door opened onto a bathroom that was bigger than her bedroom at home. And when she pushed the curtains aside, she discovered they hid French doors leading out onto a stone porch surrounded by a scrolled wrought iron railing.

She stepped outside, breathing in the cold night air to help cool off her temper.

"Met one of Deacon's exes, huh?"

Jaxer's voice coming unexpectedly from the dark next to her startled a screech out of her. "Sonofabitch. Jaxer, you ass. Don't do that."

He grinned from his perch on the wrought iron railing. He looked a bit like the Cheshire cat there in the dark, his teeth very white, his smile full of mischievousness. He was dressed elegantly as always, his silk shirt gaping open to reveal his perfectly sculpted chest muscles. His blond hair fluttered lightly in the cold breeze.

Cary shivered just looking at him. How could he not be cold?

"Sorry for startling you," he said.

"No, you're not," she said.

"No, I'm not."

He dropped off the railing and leaned in to kiss her cheek, but she ducked away.

"None of that anymore," she said, pointing him back toward the rail. "Not now that I know it's not a harmless you-being-you gesture."

He shrugged as if it didn't matter and settled against the railing. "So which of Deacon's exes has you all jealous and pissed off?"

"How on earth do you know that?" She stopped, put her hands on her hips, and huffed when she realized, even if he'd been guessing, she'd just give herself away.

"I've known you long enough to read your body language," he said. "And I know there are at least three of Deacon's exes among the crowds expected for this event. I've been once. Did he tell you?"

"No. Did he know you were there?" Since Jaxer could use his glamour magic to look like anyone, it wasn't an idle question.

"He knew." Jaxer grinned. "After the fact. So which ex has you all hot and bothered?"

"Why do you care?" And three exes? She was going to have to deal with this reaction to three different women while she was here? That sucked a lot.

"I care about you," Jaxer said. "You're upset. You can talk to me."

"Stop. I know what you're doing."

"Just being a friend. Like you wanted."

She snorted. "Right. Why are you really here?"

Something she couldn't quite read moved through his expression but then he shrugged and said, "The Bathsheba dagger you got today."

"That's what it's called?" She reached carefully into the inner pocket of her jacket where she'd stored the knife. "This puppy is dangerous. The poor woman under its spell didn't even realize she was trying to kill a kid."

"It is dangerous. Thank you for recovering it."

He reached out for the dagger and she automatically started to hand it to him. Then stopped.

"Wait, you're not supposed to be helping me. Isn't it my responsibility to find a safe place for this now?" she asked in all seriousness.

For the last six years, Jaxer had handled all the cleanup for her—getting rid of recovered weapons, destroying evidence of a supernatural fight, disposing of dead bad guys if they accidentally killed themselves on her shields, calming hysterical witnesses. But now he wasn't supposed to be helping her. She just assumed that meant she was supposed to handle the cleanup from now on. Even if she didn't know how to.

"Special case," Jaxer said. "The Nags sent me to get the dagger. They've been aware this resurfaced and have been monitoring the situation, hoping they'd be able to pinpoint its location and get it back."

Cary wondered if that was one of the two situations they'd been monitoring before she left on this trip.

Geez, was that only this morning that they'd told her that? This had been a very very long day.

"It has a habit of…attaching itself to people," Jaxer continued. "Especially when they're upset." He raised his brows. "You're upset. It's safer for everyone if you don't have it anymore."

She scowled. "This thing could affect me?"

She wasn't protecting anyone from it at the moment, so she probably should have thought of that. But she hadn't considered she might get sucked in by the curse. Even without a direct target, the thing was still a threat to others. Her Protector magic should keep the curse from affecting her so she could keep other people safe from the dagger.

Right?

"Will it affect you?" she asked suddenly. He might be hiding it, but she knew him pretty well after all these years too, and he was upset at the turn in their relationship. Jealousy was one of those emotions that called to curses a lot in the literature.

He pulled something from the air just over the top of the railing at his hip. Or at least made it look like he'd produced something from thin air, though she suspected it had been sitting on the railing this whole time and he'd just hidden it with his glamour magic. The object looked innocuous enough—a loop of unadorned leather attached to a ring of metal. Not iron or Jaxer wouldn't want to hold it. He had the typical Fae allergy to iron, though his was mild and allowed him to move in the modern world without much trouble, as evidenced by the fact that he could lean against wrought iron without breaking out in hives. He did avoid cars though. And he didn't tend to touch iron or iron alloys with his bare hands if he could avoid it.

"Brass," he said, nudging the metal ring with one finger. "And this spelled bit of leather should contain the dagger's curse."

She got close enough to touch the leather. "Cool," she murmured as the faintest of tingles tickled her fingertip.

She wasn't a magical person, so she didn't really feel magic that often, unless she needed to while protecting someone. The fact that she reacted to the spell in the leather loop must mean it was extremely strong. Which was a good thing give what the dagger could do. As she watched, a scrawl of runes in a faint blue color crawled along the leather, as liquid as the runes on the dagger had been, and just as impossible for her to read. A moment later the runes melted back into the leather, leaving it looking like a normal bit of brown hide.

Very carefully, she slipped the blade through the loop, settling the edges of the hilt gently into place. When she released her hold on the thing, her fingers stuck to it for just a split second and then she was able to let go completely.

"Whoa." She shivered and took a step away from it. "I'm glad you're taking that. You're sure you're safe?" she asked, meeting his gaze.

"I'll be fine," he said, his tone gentle and reassuring.

"Don't give me that look," she said.

"I can't help it. I like that you're worried about me. Proves you still care."

"I never stopped caring," she said, letting her irritation show. "I just don't care the way you want me to."

"Because of Deacon."

"Yeah."

"You know I'm still hoping he'll fuck up and you'll kick him to the curb, right?" He glanced back at the house through the opened French doors. "And given the setting, it looks like a prime opportunity for him to fuck up."

"Shut up."

He grinned. "How do you like him as he is here? All cold and detached and distant."

"Do you know why he has to be that way?" she asked, genuinely wondering if he did.

"I have a pretty good idea."

"Then you know why I'll have to accept it."

"Ah," he said sounding much too pleased with her answer. "So you don't like it, then."

"Go away."

He leaned toward her but didn't attempt his usual touchy-feely hugs or cheek kisses. "I'm delighted by this turn of events."

"You're a real ass, you know that. Even if Deacon and I don't work out," and the thought of that hurt more than she was willing to admit to Jaxer just then, "that doesn't mean you get to just step into the hole he'll leave in my romantic life. It doesn't work that way."

"But with him out of the picture, I can at least try to—to use an old-fashioned phrase—court you. To see if you might, one day have feelings for me. As long as he's in your life, that's not possible."

"Even if he's not in my life, it'll be a fool's errand," she insisted.

"Then at that stage, I'll let you go. But I'm not going to stop hoping until I know it's me you're turning down, not just the mate bond with Deacon interfering."

She shook her head. "Pointless and stupid. Why do you have to be here irritating me tonight when I'm already annoyed?"

He held up the dagger.

"That doesn't count," she said. "You could have just collected it and left."

"I like your company too much to resist this."

"You really are an ass," she said again.

"And that attitude is why I'm in love with you."

She snarled. "I don't need this tonight. Go away. Take that dangerous dagger with you and leave me to the shifter war building around me." She suddenly glared at him. "Did you know there was a shifter war building around me?"

"I might have heard a rumor or two," he said with feigned innocence.

"And you didn't think to warn me?"

"You were already in your seventh year. I couldn't."

She dropped her chin to give him a look. "That's a very convenient excuse when you want to use it."

He grinned.

She flicked her hand in a dismissive gesture. "Go away."

"I'll call around again when I've got news about your wizard problem. Or if you just need me."

She snorted but didn't look at him. "Goodnight."

"Goodnight, love."

She turned to tell him not to use that particular term of endearment but he was already gone. She huffed out an irritated breath, scrubbed her hands over her face, and went back inside. So much for fresh air. What she needed was a good night's sleep. Everything would look less annoying in the morning. In the sunshine. With coffee.

Lots and lots of coffee.

Cary woke to the sound of rain and the dull gray light of a stormy morning. Of course.

"If there's no coffee in this house, I'm going back to Portland," she told the empty room. Glancing at the other side of the bed, she confirmed there was no Deacon-shaped dent or mussed covers. She couldn't even smell his scent around her, and at home, she almost always did.

He hadn't come to bed all night. At least not to her bed.

She dropped back against the mattress and considered hiding from the world. No one would miss her. She could stay right here, under the covers, and maybe read a book. For fun. She hadn't had a lot of time for that in the last…six years.

But the lure of possible coffee, and maybe cold pizza for breakfast had her tossing off the covers and stumbling into the bathroom.

She emerged clean and dressed, made the bed because her mother had raised her to be polite in other people's homes—even if Maria and Evan likely had people to keep this place clean—then headed out the door, turning back the direction Sasha had brought her. She had a vague sense she was heading in the right direction, confirmed when she heard voices and smelled the best, most perfect smell ever wafting through the hall.

Freshly brewed coffee.

To her surprise, the kitchen was relatively quiet but for a handful of people, all gathered around a long table taking up one end of the room, opposite the pizza oven. The table hadn't been there last night.

She smiled when she recognized two of the people at the table. "Good morning, Lucas. Miguel."

"Cary!" Miguel jumped away from the table in a very non-human leap that took him halfway to her before he charged her at a run and plowed into her for a hug.

She laughed as his enthusiasm knocked her back a few steps. "Well, it's good to see you too," she said.

Lucas stood and gestured to the lovely red-head sitting next to him. "Cary, this is my mate Diana. Diana, the infamous Cary Redmond."

Cary snorted at that. "You probably mean notorious at this stage." She ruffled Miguel's hair then went to the table to shake Diana's hand. "How's your friend doing? Hannah, right? Has she been able to sleep at all?"

Diana's smile was gentle and pleased. "She's doing well, but of course exhausted. Nursing twins is a never-ending process." She shrugged. "You learn to nap and nurse at the same time."

Cary grinned, but a part of her was pretty grateful she wasn't looking to become a parent any time soon. Her sister had gone for nearly two years without sleeping more than a couple of hours at a time with her third baby. Cary enjoyed her sleep so much, she wasn't sure she could do that.

She glanced around at the various coffee mugs and the pot sitting on a metal trivet in the middle of the table. "I could really use a caffeine shot," she said. "Do you mind?" She nodded to the carafe.

"Of course!" Diana handed her an empty mug. "It's for everyone. There's only a few of us back so far, and most who made it in for breakfast finished already." She gestured to herself, Lucas, and the four kids around the table, ranging from about sixteen down to Miguel who was only six. "We just arrived less than hour ago and were too tired to hurry our meal."

Lucas introduced the other two adults at the table, Jillian and Nicky, mates who lived a little south of Astoria. Both women shook her hand gently, as if afraid of using too much pressure.

"We're still sipping our coffees because we don't like the crowds," Jillian said, pushing aside the swath of hair hanging over one dark brown eye. The lower half of her brown hair was buzzed short, but the top made a wave along one side of her head which framed her face beautifully. "And there are about to be a lot of people here again. Very soon."

The other woman, Nicky, nodded and groaned. Her blond hair hung in a short bob around a wide, heart-shaped face. There were very faint circles under her blue eyes. "We do this every year since the Joneses started these charity balls," she said, "and every year I say I won't come back the next year."

Jillian smiled. "She loves the ball itself."

"I love the dresses," Nicky corrected. "I adore the dresses."

That reminded Cary, she still needed to call Marianne. Eek.

"Deacon didn't exactly explain what *kind* of dress I should wear," she admitted. "I could use some advice. He just said it was formal."

"Men are hopeless," Nicky sighed.

Diana and Jillian nodded in agreement. Lucas grinned and shrugged.

"It is formal," Nicky told Cary. "Think Oscars kind of dresses."

"Oh boy." Even the dress Marianne was making for her wouldn't fit that bill.

"Don't worry," Jillian said with a friendly smile. "A few of us—" she grinned at her mate, "—bring extra outfits just in case. I'm sure we can find you something beautiful that will fit without needing to be altered."

"A chance to dress someone up?" Nicky said, all signs of fatigue leaving her expression. "Yay!"

Cary chuckled. "Should I be worried?"

"Oh, yeah," Jillian said. She leaned over and kissed Nicky's cheek. Nicky grinned and patted her hand.

Relieved she wasn't going to have to pull an Oscar-worthy dress out of thin air, or have to ask Marianne to do that—which, given her skills, she might be able to pull off, but it still seemed like Cary would be taking advantage of her friend to ask—Cary let the conversation roll around her, sipping her coffee and enjoying the easy company.

When she felt sufficiently caffeinated and had eaten enough eggs and bacon to keep her going for a few days, she asked Lucas, "Is there anywhere I can make a phone call without being overheard by every shifter in the house?"

Lucas laughed. "If you take a walk outside, you should be fine. There are a few patrols." He glanced at his son, and Cary nodded, understanding the heightened security was due to the cougar attack yesterday. "But," he continued, "you should still have plenty of privacy."

"Thanks." She promised to find Nicky and Jillian later that afternoon to peruse dresses, then returned to her room for her leather jacket before hunting up a door that led out to the grassy expanse behind the house.

The rain had stopped, but the clouds were still low and threatening. The air was cold, thickly damp, and scented by the recent rain, muddy earth, and wet grass. The ground underfoot squelched as she moved away from the house. She zipped up her jacket before pulling out her cellphone.

Glancing in the direction of the trees, she frowned. The open space seemed narrower today, the woods closer this morning than she remembered them being yesterday, and a little shiver danced along her spine.

Keeping her gaze on the treeline, she dialed Angie.

"Buck is just fine," Angie said the instant she answered.

"How did you know that's why I was calling?" Cary asked. "Wait, don't answer that. Silly question." Outside of her witchy skills, Angie was an extremely skilled psychic, so asking her to explain her instincts seemed rude.

Angie laughed. "I don't need that talent to know you'd be worrying about your little pack. Especially Buck. But he's just fine. No rising temperatures or weird behavior. We've been sitting on the couch reading romance novels since yesterday afternoon."

Cary grinned. "Any other news to report?"

"Not much. The house is in good shape. You're so lucky you don't get any weird visitors."

Cary hummed agreement. That was because of the glamour on her house. But Angie didn't know about the magical shield that kept Cary's house hidden from people Cary didn't want to find it. That was one little secret about her life she'd kept from her friends over the years and sometimes it felt disloyal to not tell them.

"Oh," Angie said, "you got a note and a small present from Jasmine Hashemi. Remember the girl you saved from getting shot by that asshole racist a few days ago?"

"Of course. How did she find my address, though?"

After much badgering by Jasmine's father, who was so grateful Cary had saved his daughter he'd been in tears, Cary had given them her full name. She'd been so overwhelmed by his gratitude she'd forgotten to only give her first name. She tried not to give out more than her first name to the people she saved, although she slipped up more often than she liked to admit. Old politeness habits instilled by her mother kept getting in the way. But she was pretty sure she hadn't given the family her home address.

"The card didn't come in the mail actually. I…might have bumped into them the day after you rescued her," Angie admitted. Sounding a little guilty.

"What did you do?" Cary started pacing toward the woods, but a tingling of unease in her gut had her moving back toward the house. She didn't mind woods and trees. She liked forests. But for some reason, she felt exposed out here today.

"It was an accident, honest," Angie said. "I was in that part of town and went into the shop to get a drink, and I brushed up against a young girl in a narrow isle and… Well, that was all it took for me to know who she was."

"How you live with that particular skill, I will never know," Cary said.

"I'm used to it," Angie said, matter-of-factly. "Not even close to the most inconvenient skill I have. Anyway, I know I should have ignored it, but she still looked pretty haunted, and I just started talking to her, mentioned I was your friend, before I knew it, they'd invited me to lunch. I couldn't say no."

"Of course not," Cary said.

Angie might have the physical frame of an underweight supermodel, but she adored food and ate a lot, which was one of the many reasons Cary loved her. They often bonded over food. Except for fish. Cary hated fish, and Angie loved anything with fish in it.

"The food was delicious, too," Angie said with feeling. "So, Jasmine asked me to come back when I could. I stopped in yesterday when I ran a quick errand, just to make sure she was doing better, and she gave me the card and gift for you."

"Any idea what the gift is? I hope she didn't spend much money." Cary would feel really guilty about that.

"She said it was a small thing."

Something in Angie's tone made Cary narrow her eyes. "Did you peek?"

Angie sighed loud enough for Cary to hear. "I just wanted to make sure she hadn't done anything extravagant. I didn't actually open the present. But I might have put a little energy into *feeling* it."

"And?"

"And it's actually magic, though I don't think Jasmine knew that. It feels very protective and generous, though. Probably a lucky charm of some kind that actually has a touch of magic in it."

"Ah, that's so sweet." Cary felt all melty at the gesture. "She shouldn't have done that, but that's really really sweet. I'll have to go visit her and say thanks when I'm back in town."

"If her family invites you to a meal, go," Angie said. "Her father and mother are both superb cooks. And her aunt has a wicked sense of humor."

Cary chuckled.

"So how's your visit so far?" Angie asked.

"Delightful," Cary said, maybe a little too sarcastically. She told Angie everything that had happened in the last twenty-four hours.

"Wow," Angie said. "You should probably practice taking vacations more often cause you're not very good at them. The ex sounds like a bitch."

"According to Jaxer there are two more here too."

"Fun."

Cary snorted. "It wouldn't be so bad if I didn't have this irrational reaction to Sasha. I don't like her, but the uncontrolled jealousy and anger I feel toward her for no good reason doesn't feel particularly pleasant. And it makes me feel petty."

"You talked to Deacon's mother about it yet?"

Cary winced. "I will later today. If she has time. They're all really busy getting ready for this ball. Which is formal Oscar-type dress, by the way. A fact Deacon forgot to mention."

"Oops," Angie said, laughing a little. "What will you do?"

She told her about Nicky and her kind offer. "With luck the next couple of days will be a lot less eventful and all I'll have to worry about is the dress," Cary said.

"But you're not holding out much hope for that, are you?" Angie asked.

Cary sighed, her gaze moving toward the treeline. "Not really."

"Stay safe. You're not there to get in the middle of their war with the cougars."

"Too late. Already there."

"But you don't have to get invested. Do your thing, but otherwise, stay safe."

"I will." Or at least she'd try.

"And if you need me, just text. I can be there in a few hours to help."

Cary grinned at that. "I love you."

"I love you, too. Now Fred is telling me it's time to eat."

"It's always time to eat in Fred's world." Her mundane mutt terrier-collie cross would eat as much as Deacon if Cary gave him the chance.

Angie chuckled. "Call if you need me or just want to bitch about Deacon's ex-girlfriends."

Cary was still smiling when they disconnected. She opened her contact's list to dial Marianne next, but a shot of nervous energy and a too-familiar tingling along her spine had her pausing.

And looking up at the treeline again.

Movement just inside the darkness under the cedars caught her attention. Shifting shadows. Her heartrate jumped.

Before she fully knew what she was seeing, she started to run.

1 8

ary reached a spot in the open ground that put her between the threat and the mansion just seconds after the five cougars cleared the woods—four in human form, one in animal form. They loped toward the house, moving just short of full shifter speed. Or maybe Cary's senses had sped up with her Protector magic. Either way, she got between them and the house an instant before they would have gotten past her.

They rushed to run over the top of her, but came up against her shields and were thrown backward. Two landed gracefully on their feet, including the one in animal form. The other three got tossed on their asses.

"Nope," Cary said. "Not allowed here. No fighting today." She mentally encompassed the entire mansion in her powers, though now that she was protecting it, she was pretty sure it was safe without that extra step. Still, better safe than sorry.

The cougar in animal form growled and launched at her. The other four tried to run around her. She shook her head when they got bounced back a few feet. Although she noticed all except one landed more gracefully on their feet this time. The last, well another drop on the ass probably served him right.

A cougar in human form snarled. "I don't know who you are, witch," she said, "but this is none of your concern."

"Yeah, well, first, not a witch. Second, yes, it is because you all kidnapped kids and tried to shoot up a vet's office with humans inside." And outside. "And that's exactly the kind of thing that's my concern."

Another cougar hissed. "We'll rip your skin from your hide for interfering."

"Do you know," Cary said, "that's not the first time I've heard that threat. In fact, it seems to be a favorite of shifters." She made a face. "That's pretty gross, now that I think about it."

The two cougars in human form not threatening her verbally launched at her again, their hands reaching for her. She shook her head when they were stopped in mid-leap and just hung in the air for a moment before dropping to the ground.

"So, as you can see, you're not getting around me." She frowned a little. "And yeah, I felt that from the front of the house. They aren't getting in either. Can't just sneak up behind me."

Must have been a pretty decent sized group of cougars there trying to get in for her to actually feel it, though.

No matter how often she'd asked Jaxer, he'd never actually explained how some of this worked. He'd just said, "Visualize what you're protecting and you'll be good." So she did, and it worked. But the *how* still escaped her, even after all these years.

Actual physical locations were a bit easier for her to do that with, too, because visualizing a shield around a building with walls was simpler than thinking about protecting, say, an entire woodland area without definitive boundaries—which, fortunately, she'd never had to do because she wasn't sure she could. At least she didn't want to test the theory that she couldn't.

She'd had to protect an entire hidden city once, and no one had gotten around her then. But since there'd only been one entrance to the city in this realm, she'd only had to guard that one limited space, so really that wasn't as impressive as it sounded.

In this case, her powers did extend to include the entire house. So those shifters trying to sneak into the front weren't having any luck either.

She frowned a little. "Small group of you here." At least in the back. "There were more in Portland. What are you trying to do?"

She didn't say it out loud, because bad people didn't need to know all the details, but there weren't that many leopards inside yet either. They'd all arrive over the course of the day. Some obviously had started returning before breakfast, but the house wasn't nearly as full now as it would be later this afternoon. Why attack now? Why not then?

A beat later, she answered her own question when she realized they wouldn't know there weren't many leopards in the house. Not unless they had spies watching the place, and probably Maria would notice that. Or her patrols would.

And speaking of which...

Cary frowned toward the woods, wishing she could feel the presence of the leopards the way Deacon could. Where were the guards Lucas had mentioned? Shouldn't they be helping to stop this?

While she was considering the patrols, the cougars in front of her tried to attack again, a blur of movement in front of her that she mostly ignored while they wore themselves out. It did give her a chance to wonder why four of the five were in human form. Maybe the house doors made shifting *before* getting in impractical? That made sense.

Satisfied with that explanation, she crossed her arms and counted to ten. Bad guys could be very persistent and stubborn. When she reached ten and they were still snarling and throwing themselves at her, she counted to ten again.

Glancing toward the woods, she narrowed her eyes. Movement inside the shadows caught her attention. More cougars or the leopard patrols?

There was a pause in all the cougar growls. As a group they turned to look toward the woods.

An instant later, another group in human form charged toward the house. They put on a burst of speed that turned their forms into streaks of color, and then they were on the cougars, attacking in a flurry of shouts, curses, and large cat hisses.

The leopard patrol it was then.

Watching a shifter fight was both awesome and terrifying. They moved so fast it was impossible to tell who was winning. All the growls, howls, and snarling noises didn't help. She instinctively wanted to move in and stop things, get between the leopards and the cougars, but she was supposed to be protecting the house, and really the leopards were doing their job trying to chase off the cougars.

Still, she bounced on the balls of her feet, torn between her job of keeping the house—and the innocent kids inside—shielded from danger and her need to protect the leopards in the fight. This was one of those moments when her job got complicated and her fear of failing and someone getting killed raised its head.

That had happened once in the last six years. Once was enough.

Just as the tension of not helping the leopards in the fight started to get to her, a streak of black and a second of white shot past her from the direction of the house. In leopard form, Deacon and Maria roared into the middle of the fight. More human and leopard shapes charged out of the house. And within minutes, two of the attacking cougars were fleeing toward the woods with leopards hot on their heels, while three where being restrained by leopards in human form.

Cary raised her brows when Deacon shifted—naked, she noticed with annoyance—and joined her.

"What happened?" he asked, his tone perfunctory and neutral. Like he was talking to a fellow soldier and not his supposed mate.

She was not going to get used to that. And since he *hadn't* been that way in Portland, she half wondered if it was for show in front of his mother, to prove he could control himself better here.

She scowled up at him. "I'm fine, thanks." She waited for him to glance at her. When he did, some of the distance in his tone and expression lightened and she was looking up at the Deacon she knew again. "That's better," she muttered. Then, "I was out here making phone calls when I spotted something in the woods. Lucas had mentioned leopard patrols, but then these jokers charged the house and I did my thing. There are more out front. Did you get them, too?"

"My father and Michael are taking care of that group," Deacon said. He didn't touch her, but he did search her face. "No injuries?"

"No. I'm fine. Not even a bruise this time."

"Good."

"What took you so long?"

"We only heard there was trouble when Lucas spotted you holding them off and came to get us." Deacon gestured toward one of the shifters in leopard form.

Cary smiled and waved at Lucas. "Thanks," she called to him.

He was busy hovering over one of the prone cougars but lifted his head in acknowledgment of her comment.

She faced Deacon again, lowering her voice even though she was pretty sure everyone would hear her anyway. "The patrol took a few minutes to get here. The cougars obviously found some holes in your guard. Might want to increase the numbers of shifters out here."

Deacon narrowed his eyes at her, then looked toward his mother. She was still in leopard form, but she held her son's gaze for a long moment before nodding.

"Can you two talk mentally?" Cary whispered.

"No," Deacon said with a slight smile. "But I know how she thinks and she knows how I think."

"Terrifying," Cary muttered.

From several yards away, Maria made a grunting noise that sounded suspiciously like a laugh.

"So what are you going to do with these guys?" Cary gestured to the three captured cougars.

"Ask them a few questions," Deacon said, his tone very neutral.

"No torture, right?" she asked suspiciously.

"No torture. Just questions."

"Whatever happened to the cougars from the kidnapping?" Some had been captured by the leopards but she'd avoided asking what they'd done with them. A pretty large part of her didn't want to know.

"They're in the basement," Deacon said. "We have cells there."

She raised her brows. "They're still here?" She supposed they couldn't turn them over to the cops, so she wasn't sure why she was surprised. It wasn't like the leopards would have just let them go. She glanced at the three newly captured cougars. "Think that's what they were trying to do? Free the others?"

"Wouldn't be the first time," Deacon said. "They know our terms for the release of our prisoners. Attacking our clinic wasn't among them."

Cary swallowed hard at the deadly tone in Deacon's voice. Cold and deadly.

"So, okay," she murmured. "If you all have this handled…" She trailed off. She wasn't entirely sure what to do now, but she felt awkwardly in the way. At the same time, she was a little afraid to leave the cougars alone. They might be the bad guys, and she really hated when she had to protect bad guys, but she couldn't abandon them to potentially being slaughtered just because they were bad guys.

Deacon touched her shoulder. "They'll be fine," he said, as if sensing her hesitance. "We're going to lock them up, and ask them questions. They probably won't answer, but you never know."

She made a face. "Yeah, bad guys do like to talk about their evil plans sometimes."

His lips twitched, an almost smile that made her heart lighter.

She looked around the crowd. "What are you doing after you lock them all up? You were working all night." That last wasn't a question. She didn't want to ask the question—was Sasha there all night? She didn't want to know. Even thinking about the woman set that weird and extreme jealousy instinct off.

"I'll finish our contracts for the new venue," he said. "And the insurance is almost hammered out. I can take a break for some sleep then." He glanced down at her. "Will you be okay on your own today?"

The fact that he didn't invite her to take a nap with him was unusual enough to raise the tension in her gut again. Once they'd given in to the chemistry between them, they'd been pretty much insatiable ever since. Frankly, that had worried her. Because there were other things to do in life besides *just* have sex constantly with your boyfriend. But still, it was a bit early for the "honeymoon" phase to be over. Wasn't it?

Since he'd been up all night and was probably exhausted, she felt petty for her concern, so she just said, "I'll be fine. I actually met some lovely women who are going to help dress me for this charity do. You failed to mention the requirements for Oscar-level attire."

He shrugged. "I didn't think about it. Anything you wear will be fine."

"Right." Sometimes he was such a man. She wanted to say more, try to draw him out a bit, but his mother joined them, shifting to her human form as she moved—clothes and all—in such an effortlessly graceful transition Cary shook her head. "That is truly impressive," she told Maria.

Maria smiled and gave a regal nod. "Thank you, Cary. For once again helping to keep my people safe." She held Cary's gaze, her dark eyes impossible to read. "I'm very grateful that you've come into our lives." Without even flicking a glance toward her son, she said, "I do hope you'll stay."

She moved toward the house with a trail of leopards and the captive cougars following her. Cary noticed Maria didn't even have to give a verbal order. The rest just fell into line.

Lucas paused in front of Cary and Deacon and gave a grunt of acknowledgment, a kind of leopard "I'll see you later" before following the rest.

"Well, that was fun," Cary said watching the procession. "I suppose you have things to do." She faced Deacon. "Cougars to questions. Charity events to fix. Clothes to put on."

He was watching the other's leave, but her last sentence earned her one of his small, sexy smiled.

She raised her brows at that. "You know, I'm still having issues with your transition between iceman-Deacon and the Deacon I'm used to."

"I know," he said. He tapped his nose. "I can smell it. So can everyone else."

"Well hell. That's not good." Although now Maria's comment

made more sense. She wasn't just sensing the tension between Cary and Deacon. She could actually smell it.

When they were finally alone, Deacon cupped her cheek in his hand. "I'm sorry I can't be as relaxed as you'd like with everyone around. It's more difficult this time than it's ever been to…just be a shifter. When we were rescuing the kids, or fighting the demon-god, adrenaline and a few uses of my magic were helpful in the moment. I was balanced and in control." He shook his head and sighed, looking out toward the woods. "I'm not here. Despite you being with me. I'm edgy and it feels like I could drop into using my magic much too easily." He met her gaze again. "I don't know why. But it's scary."

She hugged him, sighing when he wrapped his arms around her in return. "Okay, I will try to keep my annoyance to myself. At least about the way you have to be here. I'm sure everyone knowing our business isn't helping."

He shrugged. "They'd know anyway. It's hard to keep secrets among shifters. At least when it comes to the things that create scents, like emotions."

She grunted a non-committal response. Sometimes she envied Deacon his speed. And his metabolism. But she would find it very claustrophobic living among her own people and knowing she couldn't keep her feelings to herself even if she wanted to.

It was hard enough having a boyfriend she couldn't hide her feelings from.

She squeezed him a little tighter, then pushed away. "You're too naked for us to be hugging in public. Go get dressed and do what you need to do."

"We're not in public at the moment," he murmured with a wicked glint in his eyes.

She grinned. "But we have people watching from the windows," she said, her voice low.

He chuckled and kissed her, a slow lingering kiss that left her a little more than breathless by the time he lifted his head.

"That should do for now," he murmured.

"Do what?" she asked.

"Settle my leopard, and satisfy our audience," he said.

"Ha!" She pushed him away, but was smiling as she did. "I have a phone call to make. Get back to work."

She was grinning, and unabashedly watching his ass as he returned to the house, while she pulled out her cell to call Marianne.

She might have a hard time getting used to his personality switches, but she was pretty sure she'd never get tired of staring at Deacon's ass.

"**G**irl, you do not know how to take a vacation," Marianne said with a chuckle. "What did Angie say?"

"Same thing," Cary said. "Also, she was kind enough to call Sasha a bitch so I didn't have to."

"Jealousy is a deadly thing, isn't it?"

"Tell me about it. I really hate the feeling."

"I was talking about this Sasha woman's jealousy, not yours," Marianne said. "Watch her. Those sorts of emotions have a way of making people do stupid things, and this woman is a shapeshifter. Her stupid things can rip your throat out."

Cary swallowed hard. "Thanks for the reminder."

"Okay, for a more in-my-wheelhouse conversation—the pocket worked for a cursed dagger?"

"Yeah, it did," Cary said with feeling. "Thankfully. That was the creepiest feeling piece of cutlery I've ever had to touch."

"When you get back into town, stop by with your jacket. I have another two spells I want to add to it."

"What and why?" Cary asked. She was still eyeing the woods, but that sense of being watched and the nervous energy she'd had earlier had evaporated. All was well in the area. At least for now.

"I want to strengthen some of the deflection properties in the leather itself. And I want to add something to the cuffs, a little spell to help with any injuries you take."

"Cool," Cary said. "But…why?"

"Because you don't know how to stay out of trouble," Marianne said. "As evidenced by your current vacation." She said the word like it was a joke. "Your job is dangerous, you piss people off more than is healthy, and I worry about you."

Cary sniffed, surprised at the scratchy feeling in her eyes and the tightening in her chest. "Thanks," she said, wiping her fingers over her eyes. "I mean that."

"I know you do." Marianne's voice softened. "Now, since we want you to be all glamourous and shut down this Sasha bitch's snide remarks, are you sure you don't want me to whip you up a dress for this event? What I'm already making you won't do for this level of fancy, but I've got this new material that would make a gorgeous gown."

Cary chuckled. "I think Nicky will be able to help. If she doesn't have anything that fits, I'll know by this afternoon. At which point I'll be calling in a panic for your help. But hopefully, it won't come to that. And we really should stop calling Sasha a bitch. Seems a bit petty. Plus, she can probably hear us."

"I don't care if she hears," Marianne said firmly. "She's being rude to one of my best friends. I don't have to be diplomatic about that."

"You're the best ever, you know that, right?"

"I do," Marianne said. "Now, you're sure about the dress? At least for now?"

"Yeah, I don't want to put you under pressure."

"I don't mind that at all."

Cary could practically see Marianne waving away her concerns. Frankly, when Marianne wanted to, she could create spectacular outfits out of thin air in only a few hours. But Cary didn't like to push her to that point. Draining her best friend just so Cary could show up a romantic rival didn't seem like a very healthy use of Marianne's gifts.

"Okay," Marianne said, "but since there won't be any magic in that dress, be careful. And stay safe. And only get in the middle of something dangerous if you have someone to protect."

"Will do." She gave a little salute even though Marianne couldn't see her over the phone. "Thanks for understanding."

"Love you, sweetie. Stay safe."

"You too."

Cary sighed as she hung up, feeling more settled now. She pulled in a deep breath, full of the scents of cedar, pine, damp grass, and a coming rain, then turned back toward the house.

Lucas met her just inside the door. He was in human form again, and fully dressed, but his forehead was creased with concern.

"What's up?" she asked, instantly on alert for trouble.

He frowned and glanced over his shoulder. "I need to warn you about something..." He trailed off, still frowning. "I think. I'm not entirely sure about this, but..."

She waited until her nerves were stretched, then as calmly as possible given that fact, said, "But?"

"I think Sasha saw you holding off the cougars," he said in a near soundless whisper. "And she ignored it."

"What?" Cary snapped, her voice rising. She pressed her lips together and closed her eyes for a moment. Then in a quieter tone, said, "Tell me what you saw."

"Sasha was looking out a back window from one of the second floor sitting rooms. I was looking for our oldest daughter when I came into the room and saw Sasha. She turned, smiled at me, and walked out. Casual and slow, like she wasn't in a hurry or anything." He glanced behind him again, the nervous gesture telling. "I'm not sure why I even went to the window to look out. Something about her smile. Some instinct. I don't know. I saw you standing in front of the cougars and raced to get Deacon. Maybe... Maybe that happened after she turned away?"

Cary didn't believe that excuse for one minute, but she also knew her perspective on Sasha was tainted, so she tried to give the woman some credit. Really, Cary had no way to be certain. The attack *had* been sudden.

"Maybe," she said. "I mean, it did all happen pretty fast. It's possible she just saw me out there on the phone and left just before the cougars charged the house."

Lucas nodded but his expression didn't change. He still looked worried. "She was with Deacon when I found him to tell him about the attack. She didn't look surprised."

"Could be with all the cougar harassment, she wasn't?" Cary was stretching her benefit-of-the-doubt muscles big time here. But Sasha was Maria's assistant. She'd hardly want the cougars to get into the mansion. Right?

Lucas's expression was not particularly reassuring. "It's possible," he said. "It's possible I was so worried about you I misread her expression."

"You were worried about me?" Cary said. "Ah, that's sweet. But I was fine. Just doing my thing."

Lucas smiled then. "I know. I realized that as soon as we reached the grass. You weren't even a little bit worried, were you?"

"Well, I had no idea how I was going to get them to go away," she admitted. That was always the most complicated part of being a magical Kevlar vest with no offensive powers beyond her self defense training with Lucy. How to get the bad guys to give up and leave. "But holding them off was no issue," she finished. "I'm good at that part."

"Yeah, I've seen that a time or two."

She grinned, but her levity didn't last long. "Tell me more about Sasha," she said. "She's been around for years, I presume? How long has she been Maria's assistant?" It was on the tip of her tongue to ask how long ago Deacon had been sleeping with Sasha, but she bit the inside of her cheek to keep from asking. That would not be helpful information.

"She grew up under the queen's care," Lucas said, references Maria's status in a way the leopards didn't always do aloud.

She noticed Lucas slipped into using the honorifics more often, though, especially when he was under stress or worried. He'd almost slipped and called Deacon "my prince" when they'd been rescuing the kids in the Portland tunnels. It had been Cary's first hint that Deacon had left something significant out of his history.

"She was orphaned," Lucas continued. "Her father killed before she was born by human hunters. Her mother not too long after she was born in an accident. She was only a few months old when the queen took her in."

Cary's sympathies spiked. She didn't particularly want to, but the story did make her feel a bit sad for Sasha. "So Maria is like a mother to her?"

"I'm not sure she's ever felt exactly that way about the queen. While Evan is very open with us, Maria can be more standoffish. She has to be," he said matter-of-factly. "But Sasha was safe and well cared for. And loyal enough to Maria to work as her personal assistant."

"Is she generally loyal to all the leopards?" Cary asked because she had to. Given Sasha's position with Maria, Cary would have assumed loyalty. But something was bothering her, a disconcerting possibility that she was hoping to disprove.

"She always has been. Very." Lucas frowned. "You know she and Deacon had a thing in the past?"

"Yes," Cary said, her tone flat.

Lucas's mouth lifted at the corner but he suppressed his smile. "Well, this is just a rumor so don't give it too much credit. It could just be the gossip of jealous shifters."

"What?" Cary asked.

"There were whispers that Sasha assumed she'd be the next queen," Lucas said quietly. "That she and Deacon would rule together."

"She's not Deacon's mate, though," Cary said. "If she was, they would have bonded years ago. Right?"

Cary's hands curled into fists without her realizing she was angry. The information about Sasha's supposed ambitions was so engrossing, Cary wasn't consciously aware of her instinctive jealousy until her palms started to hurt from the press of her nails. She scowled and rubbed her hands on her jeans.

"We don't always find our mates," Lucas said. "Sometimes, we just settle down with an acceptable lover."

Cary searched her memory. "But… From what I remember, having children is more difficult if the couple aren't mates. Or is that wrong?" It wouldn't be the first time her more academic collection of books and information had gotten some detail wrong.

"I don't know that Sasha cares about having kids." Lucas winced a little when he said, "I don't know if she really did think she and Deacon would rule together, but I am certain she assumed she and Deacon would end up together."

"How certain?"

"She said so to Diana," he said. "Years ago. Before Diana and I met." Lucas gave her a side-eyed look. "You know Diana had an affair with Deacon, right?"

"No," Cary said, annoyed. Until she realized she hadn't had any of the knee-jerk jealousy reactions to Diana that she'd had to Sasha. She liked Diana and had enjoyed meeting her that morning. "That doesn't bother you?" she asked Lucas curiously.

Lucas shrugged. "That was before we met. And since we're mates, it wasn't a thing after we met."

"Maybe that's why I'm not having these weird reactions to Diana," Cary murmured.

Lucas raised his brows in question. Cary shrugged and admitted to the jealousy thing that kept biting her in the ass. She felt her face heating as she made the confession, but Lucas kept his expression carefully neutral, showing no signs of judgment. Though, Cary was glad in the moment she couldn't smell his emotions and know what he really felt.

"It's possible that since Diana is mated, you're not seeing her as a threat to your bond," Lucas said with a shrug. "Once a couple is well and truly mated, the bond solid and tight, most of the jealousies go away."

"That's good to know," Cary said, also thinking of Deacon's reactions to Jaxer.

"Are you reacting with jealousy to Alisha?" Lucas asked. "She and Deacon also had an affair. And she's not mated."

Cary made a face. "I haven't met her yet. We'll have to see. In the meantime, tell me what Sasha said to Diana."

Lucas sighed. "Diana told me the relationship between her and Deacon was brief and really just physical. All of Deacon's relationships with women have been strictly physical. Before you."

Cary wasn't sure whether to be pleased or not with that bit of information, so she forced a little smile and waved her hand for Lucas to continue.

"Diana had no illusions. According to her." He smirked. "But she told me Sasha had threatened her. Told her that a fling with Deacon was allowed, but Diana wasn't to get any ideas about making the relationship permanent. Deacon was destined to be Sasha's—Diana said those were her words—and no other woman would get in the way." He pressed his lips together before finishing. "Diana said Sasha threatened to kill her if she didn't end things with Deacon."

"Geez," Cary said. "That's…serious."

"It's not entirely unusual for shifters to be more aggressive in their threats than humans," Lucas said. "But, yeah, Diana felt Sasha meant what she said. Diana ended things with Deacon the next day."

"Does Deacon know about all this?" Cary asked. "Does he know Sasha's this…convinced they'll be together?" She almost used the word "obsessed" but thought that might be unfair.

It was getting harder to give Sasha the benefit of the doubt, though.

"I'm not sure. Diana says he doesn't. But he's so distant most of the time, so controlled, it's impossible to judge what he feels or thinks, what he knows and doesn't." Lucas shrugged. "He has to be distant, like Maria. So we've always assumed even if he found his mate, he'd remain aloof and hard to read. Frankly, I wasn't the only one surprised by how easy and open he was with you in Portland." Lucas smiled. "It was nice to see him happy. Like a weight had been lifted."

"Happy, you mean, like when we had a demon god attacking us and ghouls rising from the ground all around us?"

Lucas laughed. "To be fair, most of the ghouls were on our side."

Cary would give him that. She was trying not to be pleased with Lucas's comment on her effect on Deacon, even though she was.

"I don't want to cause trouble," Lucas said. "For you, for the prince, for Sasha. But given the way she threatened Diana, and then today… I just thought you should know."

That she couldn't trust Sasha, Cary finished Lucas's unspoken end to that last sentence. But he didn't need to worry. She'd distrusted Sasha from the start.

"Thanks, Lucas. I appreciate the information." She frowned. "Did you ever find your daughter?"

He chuckled. "Yeah, she was with one of her friends trying out some makeup tips they'd seen on YouTube. They hadn't even noticed the house was under attack." He sighed. "Teenagers. Just wait until you have them."

Cary shuddered, which made Lucas laugh again.

They parted ways and Cary went back to her room to mull over what she'd just learned. Did it change anything? Was it something she could talk to Maria about now? She'd intended to ask Maria about the knee-jerk jealousy—even though she still hated the thought of discussing her romantic life with her boyfriend's *mother*. But now she wasn't so sure. If Maria saw Sasha as a loyal assistant, Cary risked insulting them both with her questions.

And she really wasn't certain there was any reason to be worried. Sasha might have missed the initial cougar charge. Sasha could have exaggerated her threat to Diana all those years ago. It was entirely possible that Cary, and Lucas for that matter, were concerned over nothing.

But if Sasha had seen the cougars charging the house and chosen not to warn the others, that made matters a lot more complicated.

Because it meant, either Sasha was hoping Cary got killed. Or Sasha had betrayed her own people.

Or both.

2 0

---

ary stood in the door of the bedroom she and Deacon were supposed to be sharing and stared at the bed, too stunned to move into the room. Slowly, silently, she stepped backward and closed the door, pressing her palm to the wood when it stood between her and the room inside.

"What's wrong?"

Deacon's voice from behind her made her jump and screech.

"You need bells or something strapped to your feet so I can hear you," she hissed.

"Cary." He took her shoulders and gently turned her to face him. "What's wrong?"

She swallowed. "So, remember that cursed dagger I told you about?"

"Vaguely. You had it sealed into your jacket pocket." He ran his hands down her arms, putting his fingers near the inside pocket without actually touching it.

"Yeah, well, Jaxer showed up last night to take the dagger."

"Jaxer?"

The growl of jealousy in his voice shouldn't have pleased her. In fact, it should have annoyed her. But given what she'd been going

150

through with Sasha, and the fact that Deacon's moods were so hard to read here, it was nice to have a predictable reaction from him. And also nice she wasn't the only one experiencing the stupid jealousy.

"The Nags sent him," she said. "To take the dagger into safe-keeping."

Deacon grunted, and she took that as a cue to continue.

"We put the dagger into a spelled leather loop—so Jaxer wouldn't have to touch it—and when I slipped it into the leather, it sort of pulled at my fingers, as if reluctant to be released, but then it let go. Jaxer took it away. All was well."

Deacon frowned. Glanced at the bedroom door. And putting Cary behind him, slowly opened it. She smiled a little at his protective gesture.

The dagger gleamed in the murky winter light coming in from the opened curtains, centered in the middle of the big king bed Cary had slept in last night. It wasn't contained in the spelled leather anymore. The way the light danced along the sharp blade made it look like the thing was winking at her.

"That's not good, is it?" Deacon asked.

"Nope. Not good." She shivered. "I have no idea why it's here, how it got here, and what to do about it. I don't dare touch it since I'm not protecting anyone from it at present. But no one else can touch it either."

"We'll contact Jaxer."

She raised her brows at Deacon's back. He finally looked away from the blade to face her.

"I don't like doing it," he confirmed. "But he's the one who supposedly took it to be stored safely and now it's here. Either he fucked up, or that blade is more trouble that you thought."

"I thought it was dangerous." She shivered again. "Guess I was right. Only thing is, the previous user was trying to kill a virgin." She grinned up at him. "No problem with that here."

He chuckled. But neither of their humor lasted long. There was a house full of people, with more people arriving by the hour, many of them children. If the dagger wanted a victim, there were plenty of options right inside the mansion.

Cary forced another hard swallow. Her throat was thick with fear, and she could feel her pulse beating at her neck.

"Why here?" she whispered. "Why our bed?"

"Good question," Deacon said. He eased Cary back out of the room, then closed the door. "I need to make sure no one goes in there." He took her hand, the gesture extremely comforting, and they hurried to find Maria.

They found her with her head tilted toward her mate, the two deep in conversation over a steaming pot of tea in a library full of books and beat up, overstuffed furniture.

Cary's eyes widened. The room was perfect!

Floor-to-ceiling, wall-to-wall books—except for a few windows to let in the natural light. But no stuffy formal furniture or leather bound books lining the cases. No, there were mounds of battered paperbacks, some hard covers, all of various sizes and shapes, piled some in order, some haphazardly across the many shelves. At a glance, Cary spotted authors from the thriller and romance genres. And against the far wall, it looked like the lower shelves were filled with kids' books.

The carpets were covered with rugs, all of it randomly arranged. There was no design to any of it, no obvious plan. Just a lot of comfortable furniture around a comfortable room filled with books and light.

Cary sighed. "This is the most perfect room I've ever seen," she said to no one in particular.

Maria glanced up from her conversation with Evan and smiled faintly.

Evan grinned. "Thanks," he said. "It's one of our favorites, too."

"What's wrong?" Maria asked, making it clear that Cary's delight in the room hadn't covered the scent of her worry and fear. "Not the cougars this time."

Cary sighed. "Them I could deal with."

"We need to ensure no one goes into mine and Cary's room," Deacon told his mother. "There's an issue, and it's dangerous."

Maria motioned to the couch across from her and Evan. "Tell me."

Cary told the story—since Maria already knew she was a Protector it made the details a lot easier to explain—including the fact that she'd felt a tug from the blade before handing it over to her former mentor.

Maria's gaze flicked to Deacon at the mention of Jaxer, but she didn't comment.

When Cary reached the part about discovering the blade, unsheathed and gleaming, on her bed, Evan sucked in a breath and cursed roundly.

"What does it mean?" Maria asked Cary.

"Got me," Cary said. "But it's not good."

"No," Maria agreed. She glanced away and a moment later Sasha walked into the room.

Cary pressed her lips together and sat on her hands to keep her reactions to the woman at bay. Sasha was Maria's assistant. Of course she was the one Maria called.

Cary blinked when she considered that Maria had called Sasha without words, even though they couldn't actually talk mentally to one another. Deacon had said he could do that by giving the others a mental nudge. Was that what Maria had just done?

"What do you need, ma'am?" Sasha asked smoothly, as if there was no tension in the room and no issue between her and Cary.

"Order everyone in the house to stay away from Deacon and Cary's room," Maria said. "No exceptions. No cleaning crews. Nothing. Until I say otherwise."

Sasha raised her brows. Elegant and beautifully, Cary noted sourly.

"May I ask why?" Sasha said. "There will be questions." She glanced at Cary, then back to Maria. "The children seem to enjoy Ms. Redmond's company. They'll want to know why they're avoiding her."

"Not her," Maria clarified, her eyes narrowing. "The room. Only the room. I expect everyone in this house to follow that order. Am I clear, Sasha?"

"Crystal, ma'am. I'll spread the word."

She smiled at Evan, her smile warmed when it passed to Deacon, and iced over when she looked at Cary, her lip twitching in what looked to Cary like the beginning of a snarl. Cary was more than prepared to answer that snarl in kind, but she forced something resembling a smile instead.

"How will you get this cursed weapon out of our home?" Maria asked once Sasha had left.

Given Sasha had only just closed the door, Cary realized Maria had just told her—thanks to shifter hearing—why people needed to stay out of the room. Cary wondered at that. If she'd intended to tell Sasha anyway, why not just say so while she was in the room?

"We'll contact Jaxer to come get it," Deacon said.

"He failed to keep it before," Maria said to her son. "Maybe you should contact your bosses," she said to Cary.

"They haven't given me a way to contact them," Cary said, a touch of sour in her mouth. "They just show up when they need me to hop to."

Maria raised her brows but didn't comment. "Are you sure Jaxer is the best option?" She glanced at her son again, the unspoken question clear. Will that set off Deacon's jealousy and cause issues?

"I'll be fine," Deacon said, not even a hint of a growl in his voice. "The dagger needs handling. Then I'll get back to working on the event."

"You haven't slept," Evan pointed out. "You are allowed to rest. There are other people here who can take care of some of the logistics." There was both humor and reprimand in Evan's tone, but Cary couldn't tell if that was directed toward his son or his mate.

"I'll sleep," Deacon said, with a very slight smile for his father. "Then get back to work."

"The venue is arranged," Maria said and asked.

"Everything including the insurance is settled," Deacon said. "We'll have the paperwork today to finalize."

"Then you have time to rest properly," Maria said.

"Thank you," he said.

Cary watched the exchange, too fascinated to step into the middle of it. Seeing the way Deacon was with his parents, the way they were with each other, was enlightening. And the nosey part of her was enjoying getting to see this aspect of Deacon's life uncensored.

Or maybe less censored, she thought, since she suspected there were things she wasn't picking up on in this conversation.

She and Deacon left the perfect room to his parents and Deacon led her out the front door to the winding driveway bracketed by trees.

"Wouldn't this be better done from the bedroom?" she asked. "So Jaxer can collect the dagger immediately?"

"It would. But I can't be in our room with your scent all over it, and have Jaxer in the same space."

"You do that in my house all the time."

"Things are different in Portland than they are here."

"I've noticed," she said sourly. Then bit her lip. She'd promised to stop getting so annoyed over his need to remain aloof and in control. That promise had lasted a full hour. Maybe.

He paused to look at her. "You're upset."

It wasn't a question. She rolled her eyes. "Sorry. I'm still adjusting to the way you have to be here and how that seems to change depending on who's around." Her mind flashed a taunting image of Sasha before her and she ruthlessly pushed it aside. But her snarl was too obvious for him to miss.

Fortunately for her, he misunderstood it. "If I'm around both my parents and you, I'm more settled," he admitted. "But the house is almost full again. I can't afford to relax my control."

He wasn't touching her now. Back to the distant, iceman Deacon. But his tone was less irritatingly cold. That was something she guessed.

"Does this go away when we get back to Portland?" she asked.

"I won't require this much control," he said.

But would he go back to that state of very little control that had kept him from going back to work? Or would he fall somewhere between that and what he had to be like here?

Since they were only likely to get answers to those questions after they got home, she instead asked, "So how did you plan on contacting Jaxer?"

Jaxer didn't exactly walk around with a cellphone. She rarely needed to contact him because he was always around, sometimes even when she didn't want him around. The only time it had been an issue was when he'd started pulling back, right before her seventh year began but before he'd bothered to mention she was going into a test year. Frankly, it was the first time she'd even noticed that she didn't have a way to contact him.

She blinked when Deacon led her into a copse of trees next to the driveway. It wasn't a thick clumping of trees. She could still see the road clearly through the trunks. But apparently it was enough. Deacon paused seemingly at random. And a moment later, Jaxer stepped out from behind a tree.

"Okay," she snapped, hands on her hips. "How the hell do you two do that? Why can't I do that with Jaxer? Explain that now or I'm gonna be really really pissed."

Jaxer grinned at her, and despite Deacon's looming glower, cupped her cheek in the palm of his hand. The touch was light and brief but too personal given the circumstances. Her scowl deepened.

"If you need me, come to a wild place," Jaxer said. "I'll know."

"And why haven't you told me this before?" she asked.

"Before you were my protégée, my student. I don't tell my students how to contact me. It's part of the training."

"So what am I now?" she snapped, then wanted to take the words back. They tempted comment and conversation none of them had time for at the moment.

After a pause, his expression gentle, he said, "You're my friend."

She snorted to hide her pleasure in that assessment. She was afraid both men would misinterpret her feelings. "Well, friend," she said, "we have a problem."

Jaxer glanced between her and Deacon, his expression turning more serious. "What's happened?"

"That dagger you collected from me last night," Cary said. "It's baaack."

He frowned at her sing-songy tone, obviously not recognizing the movie reference. Then the news hit him. "What? It's here? Where? How?"

"Good questions," Deacon said, his voice very tight but very controlled.

"I found it just lying on my bed after the cougars attacked," Cary said.

"Wait, the cougars attacked?" Jaxer asked.

Cary sighed. "It's a long story." But she gave him a brief rundown before returning to the main topic. "Why the hell is that blade on my bed, Jaxer? What did you do with it after you took it back to the Nags."

"I gave it to them to store," he said, very seriously. "And they are usually good at that kind of thing." He turned back toward the trees.

"Wait! Where are you going?" Cary felt an edge of panic. "You need to take the dagger again. It's too dangerous to have in this house. There are kids everywhere."

"I need to talk to the Nags," Jaxer said. "They must have thought it was a different Bathsheba dagger."

"What?" Cary squeaked. "How many are there?"

"Seven," Jaxer said.

"Of course." She hung her head. "I really really hate the number seven now," she said.

"Huh?" Jaxer asked.

"Nothing." She waved away her comment. "What do we do about it?"

"I'll be back soon with more information." He returned to her long enough to run a finger down her nose, which made her frown and Deacon growl. Then he disappeared into the trees.

She wasn't sure how, but she knew he was gone a moment later, with no idea how he'd left. "You going to explain how he does that?" Cary asked, facing Deacon. "Or will I have to grill him at some future date?"

"He moves through the earth," Deacon said. "Through Faery." When she continued to frown at him, he frowned back. "The Fae realm that abuts ours but isn't in ours?"

"I know what Faery is," she snapped. "I have been studying."

Although she did intent to refresh her memory at her earliest opportunity because she'd had no idea Jaxer traveled through Faery. She wasn't sure why this hadn't occurred to her. The Nags were Fae, obviously they moved in and out of Faery. Of course Jaxer would, too. It was a little embarrassing to realize she hadn't figured that out on her own.

"I got the impression he wasn't welcome there anymore," she said to cover her embarrassment. To be fair, he'd told her only vaguely that he had a complicated relationship with both the English and Irish Fae courts. She'd just assumed he wasn't welcome. But complicated didn't necessarily have to mean bad, she realized. "Have you always found him just by going into a 'wild place'?"

"It's easiest," Deacon said with a shrug. "Mostly he's come to me over the years, though."

Cary stared back at the tree where Jaxer had disappeared. There was a lot about his and Deacon's relationship before she'd met Deacon that Cary didn't know. A lot Jaxer hadn't told her about his life outside of working for the Nags.

Which begged the question, what else did she *not* know about her former mentor? And how much trouble would that ignorance create?

21

"You can't sleep in the room with the dagger," Cary said on the way back up to the mansion. "Where will you rest?"

"My old room, I suppose," Deacon said.

Cary gave him a look. "Why weren't we staying in your old room this whole time?"

"First," he said, "I'm glad we weren't because then I'd have a cursed dagger in my old bed."

She twisted her mouth in a sour look. Like that was *her* fault. She'd tried to get rid of the thing. It was Jaxer's fault. And the Nags for apparently thinking it was the wrong dagger—something she needed to know more about after Jaxer returned.

Deacon's mouth twitched with a hint of a smile and she knew he'd been teasing her. That was nice.

"Second," he went on, "I thought you'd be more comfortable in a more neutral room while we were here."

"You stay in my non-neutral bedroom all the time," she pointed out.

"Fair enough. We'll move to my old room. It's nothing particularly special. I promise. Just a couple of rooms. A living room and a bedroom, but both pretty ordinary."

"So…a small apartment then?" she asked, trying not to laugh. She couldn't wait to see it. If it was *ordinary*, she'd be surprised.

As it turned out, though, it was relatively ordinary. In fact, she couldn't believe the rooms they went to were truly Deacon's childhood rooms because they were so…basic.

The place wasn't all that much different to the guest room they'd been staying in. Not a lot of art on the walls, or old teenage posters, or anything personal. The closet had a few shirts and a tuxedo hanging in it. She assumed the tux was for the charity ball. The bed was king-sized but no four-poster monstrosity or anything so grand like they'd had in the guest room. For being a technical prince, his bedroom reflected no outward grandiosity.

It *was* big, though. High ceilings, pale walls that gave the room spaciousness, a hard wood floor with only a few scattered rugs. The living room area had a huge couch that was nonetheless dwarfed by the general size of the space. A big-screen tv looked like a more recent addition against the wall opposite the couch. And a wall of windows looked out onto the south side of the house, into a thicker section of woods across from the requisite expanse of wild grass.

She wandered around the room, flicking at the thick blue curtains, and noticed the windows opened sideways. In fact, because of the sheer size of the windows, they almost looked like small doors. She supposed since this room was on the second floor, that was Deacon's way in and out when he wanted to spend time in his animal form.

There wasn't any obvious childhood memorabilia anywhere. She didn't know why that surprised her. Her parents had downsized after she and her sister had gone to college. Her own childhood memorabilia was in a storage unit now. But then again, the house with the room she'd grown up in had also been sold. She didn't have access to that room anymore. These were supposedly the rooms Deacon had spent his childhood in. And even though he'd been a grown man for a very long time now, the fact that there was nothing personal, nothing that really spoke to Deacon's past was disconcerting.

"How long have you lived in Portland?" she asked, realizing as she looked at the relative blankness of this room that she had no idea how long he'd been out on his own.

"Portland, about twenty years."

She faced him. "You say that like you lived somewhere else before."

"I did. A few places on this coast—Seattle for a couple of years, San Diego for a few months. And I traveled some."

"So it has been a long time since you lived here," she said, turning back to explore the room.

"A while," he murmured.

Something in his tone… "You don't like this room?" she asked, facing him again.

"Not so much that I don't like it." He shrugged, his gaze traveling over the space. "It just reminds me too much of my youth. The one or two times during my early years when control was difficult and…"

She waited for him to finish, patiently despite not feeling particularly patient.

"Puberty was a volatile time," he said, "as it is for most kids, but the control I'd had solidly in place slipped a couple of times during that period. My mother was able to help and keep the chaos in check. It didn't affect anyone but me. But there were some dark months in there." He shrugged. "I still associate this room with that period of time even though it's been forty years."

She was suddenly glad she couldn't revisit her old childhood bedroom. She'd gone through a period of time where she'd had a lot of really vivid and disturbing nightmares. If she re-experienced that every time she walked into her old bedroom, she wouldn't want to go into the room all that often either.

"We can stay somewhere else," she said. "We don't need to stay here."

He glanced around, pulling in a deep breath. "It's fine. I still stay here off and on when I'm home." He met her gaze. "I guess I didn't want to mix this memory with you."

"Was that a compliment or insult?"

His lips twitched into a full smile. "Compliment. You're—mostly —good memories for me."

"Mostly?" she asked, pretending to be offended even as she softened against him when he took her in his arms.

"Well, the memories of you almost dying as you held off a supernatural army aren't my favorite," he said dryly.

She winced. "Well, yeah, there was that."

"And watching you face down a demon god when you were cursed to become a ghoul after death wasn't exactly fun." He kissed her forehead.

"Okay, okay. Enough. I get it."

He chuckled and pulled her closer. His deep breath expanded his chest against her, which felt delicious. He smelled delicious too. So she leaned in and nuzzled his neck.

"How tired are you?" she murmured, letting her lips drag over his throat. When he shivered, she smiled against his skin.

"Not nearly as tired as I should be anymore." His voice dropped to a deeper note, the rasp of his faint growl danced down her spine and lit up all her nerves.

"How about we put some good memories into this room?" she said.

"Best idea I've heard all day," he said.

She melted into his kiss, feeling the heat curling low in her stomach even as the relief left her weak. His arms tightened around her, carefully because he worried about hurting her with his shifter strength, and he tugged her backward toward the bedroom. She really wasn't in the mood for gentle today, though. Not after the last forty-eight hours. She wanted him hard, and fast, and rough.

And then maybe a little gentler. But right now, she wanted rough.

She shoved him at the bed, letting her lust rise up and fill her, knowing he'd catch the scent, taste her need. His low sound, a cross between a growl and a groan, made her smile. And she wanted to taste his need too.

With a jerk, she pulled his shirt off his head, tossing it aside before putting her hands on him, stroking his chest, the rough patches of hair over his abdomen and lower, watching his muscles contract and flex.

She never got tired of Deacon at her mercy. Weeks of this and she still couldn't seem to satisfy her need to feel him, touch him. She settled her lips against the pulse in his throat. Taste him.

And then it was all touch, all taste, all passion and heat. He ripped her shirt—not the first time—and she broke the button on his pants— also not the first time. She pushed him backward onto the bed and he surprised a gasp from her by taking her with him so that they tumbled onto the large mattress together.

She landed on top of him, settled against him, kissed him like she hadn't tasted him in weeks. Hunger and need and the residuals of her fear feed her passion. She filled her hands with him, filled her mouth with him. And when she finally filled her body with him, she took flight.

There was nothing better than having Deacon under her, inside her. Not pizza. Not coffee. Everything felt perfect, in that moment, right. And so for the moment, she forgot all the fears and worries and just let go, taking him all the way into blissful togetherness with her.

2 2

After taking a shower together, Cary left Deacon to sleep—finally—and went in search of Nicky and Jillian so they could get started on finding her a dress. The big ball was only two days away. Having nothing appropriate to wear was stressful. And if they couldn't find something that fit her, she wanted to give Marianne as much time as possible to do her magical thing.

She got directions from a few of the people she passed in the corridors, and eventually she found her way to Nicky and Jillian's room. Nicky answered her knock.

"Dress up time?" Nicky asked hopefully.

"Yes, please," Cary said.

"Yay!"

The next hour was a whirlwind of dresses, wine, and a lot of giggling. Within minutes of Cary walking into Nicky's living room, Jillian had marshaled the troops, including Diana and her oldest daughter, Lily the makeup expert, and two other leopard shifters Cary hadn't met before—one of which was Deacon's other, as-of-yet-unmated ex.

"A test," Jillian said when she finally admitted Alisha was the third former lover in the house. "To see if your mate jealousy is Sasha-focused or just generalized."

"Gee, thanks," Cary said.

But she hadn't had any reaction to Alisha. In fact, Cary found Alisha hilarious and friendly. She'd enjoyed having her as part of the group and hadn't noticed even a hint of the jealousy reaction. And that despite the fact that Alisha was stunning, with hip length black hair so thick it made Cary sigh and the most perfect complexion any woman had a right to have.

Cary let out a resigned huff. "I guess it's Sasha-focused, for some reason."

Alisha snorted. "Sasha is very possessive of Deacon." She glanced at Diana. "Did I ever tell you she threatened to kill me?"

"She did the same to me," Diana said. "The woman has issues."

"Maybe we shouldn't be talking about this in front of Cary?" one of the new people, Vivica, said. She was a lovely older woman who treated all the people in the room like her kids. Her soft voice and maternal attitude didn't disguise the note of warning in her tone, though.

Cary waved that away. "It's fine. I have been worried about my reaction to Sasha. Not being a shifter has made all this a bit strange. To say the least."

Jillian snorted. "I'll bet. But if it makes you feel better, for the most part, until we find our mate, *all* our relationships are casual."

Nicky grinned at her from where she was adjusting a strap over Cary's shoulder. "And then when we find our mate, if we're lucky enough to find our mate, we're all growly and jealous and possessive."

Jillian smiled back, the two women exchanging a look that conveyed a lot of unspoken memories. Cary grinned.

"Sasha always took her flings with Deacon seriously, though," Alisha said, as she stood back and studied the cut of the dress Cary was wearing—a ball gown style that flared around her legs and reminded Cary of something Cinderella would wear.

"It was strange," Diana said. "They were obviously not mates. Deacon never showed the same sort of intensity toward her as she did toward him. He's completely different about you, Cary."

"You've seen that?" Cary asked. "Because here, he's like a different person to me."

"The fact that we have to leave the house if you're not around is a very good sign," Jillian said with a snort. Alisha laughed.

Obviously, no one cared that Deacon was dangerous right now. Except, of course, Deacon. And Cary wasn't too thrilled with it either. Although, if she'd understood Maria right, no one realized just how dangerous Deacon was, so maybe they didn't know they should be worried?

Cary had to hold her lips still while Diana's daughter applied a new color of lip tint as a test. When she was allowed to speak again, she said, "Do many leopard shifters have long term romantic relationships with people that aren't their mates, if they can't find their mates?"

"They can," Vivica said gently. "Sometimes they do. But it's a kind of consolation prize that no one really wants."

"I understand from a friend that not all mate bonds...go well," Cary said.

She wasn't sure she could trust Jaxer when it came to his information about shifter relationships. Or any of the books she'd read on leopard shifters. Or even Deacon's answers for that matter. So she was curious what these women would tell her when they didn't have a stake in the outcome of her relationship with Deacon.

"Some don't," Alisha confirmed. She frowned. "No, she needs a slimmer cut through the hips," she told Nicky. "Something that accentuates her curves and her smaller waist."

Cary tried not to wince at the implication of big hips that Alisha carefully didn't mention. Or maybe that was just Cary projecting.

As Nicky started to unzip the dress, Alisha continued, "There have been some disastrous mate pairings. People who just could not stand each other personally but were chemically compelled to be around each other. That's never a good thing."

"It's really rare, though," Vivica assured with a soft touch on Cary's shoulder. "So rare, we can name most of the couples that's happened to for the last hundred years. And I wouldn't have to use both hands to count them."

Cary wasn't sure if Vivica's statement was comforting or not, so she glossed over her confusion with another question. "How often do leopards end up with non-leopard mates?"

All six shifters in the room exchanged a look. Even Diana's daughter seemed to understand the unspoken exchange.

"What?" Cary said, her hands on her hips—a gesture which kept her dress from falling off.

"It's rarer than the mates that don't like each other," Jillian admitted, her tone quiet.

"But it *does* happen," Nicky assured as she ushered Cary behind a screen to remove the rejected dress.

Shifters didn't have any issues or hang ups about nudity, and often stripped in front of each other without even thinking about it. Because Cary was human—and personally a lot more reticent about being half naked in front of strangers—they'd set up a pretty wood and painted silk screen for her to change behind. They'd set it up without her even having to ask, and Cary had been extremely grateful for their thoughtfulness.

Nicky handed her another gown around the edge of the screen. "Step into the neck of this one instead of pulling it over your head," she instructed. "It's too tight in the hips to get over your shoulders."

Cary did as she was told, but she was too deep in thought to consider the dress closely. When she stepped back from behind the screen, adjusting the straps of the form fitting gown over her arms, Diana's daughter whistled. Cary glanced up.

Lily grinned. "That's the one."

Cary raised her brows and glanced down, finally taking a moment to actually look at the dress. It was a deep shade of blue, dark but shimmery like a jewel. The cut skimmed her body over her hips and down her thighs before flaring out gently from just above her knees. The dress was fitted but Cary found she could walk in it without her knees feeling tied together, which was nice, and the way it hugged her waist and hips was surprisingly perfect.

Once Nicky had the zip up, Cary turned to look in the tri-set of floor length mirrors.

"Wow," she said. "I think Lily is right. This is the one."

Nicky clapped her hands together and squealed. The reaction made Cary laugh.

"Yes, yes, yes," Nicky said. "It's the prefect cut. And look! It fits so well you won't need alterations anywhere. I *knew* I'd have something perfect for you."

"Thank you so much," Cary said, still looking in the mirror. "This is amazing."

The satiny material looked rich, luxuriant, and simple all at once. She skimmed her palm over the center of the dress along her stomach. The only thing it was missing was pockets—though Cary figured only Marianne would be able to manage pockets in this type of cut without the pockets making the wearer's hips look bigger, which Cary did not need. Other than that, though, it was ideal.

She turned to grin at the room. "Now, we need to decide hair and makeup."

That earned her a delighted crow from Lily and Alisha. She was surrounded by them all then as they tugged and combed at her hair, trying out different updos. Lily murmured something about a new makeup technique she'd just learned and started turning Cary's face this way and that as she brushed on various things.

Cary let them do their worst, content for this moment of peace and girl fun. She realized that if not for her encounters with and reaction to Sasha, she'd feel perfectly comfortable here with all these shifters. She'd felt very protective—no pun intended—of the shifters who'd helped her with the demon god last month. She was starting to realize that protective feeling extended to all of Deacon's people. And she couldn't help but wonder if that was *her* reaction and nature, or if it had something to do with their bond and the fact that he would one day be their leader.

She was still mulling that thought over when someone knocked at the door. Lily dashed across the room to open it.

Cary heard Jaxer before she saw him.

"Hello," he greeted Lily, his lovely voice deep and laced with just a touch of the Irish he used sometimes when he was trying to be endearing. "I understand you're harboring a Cary Redmond?"

Lily giggled, charmed, and opened the door wide.

Cary was trying not to roll her eyes as Jaxer walked in. He smiled at the crowded room, then looked at her.

And froze.

He just stared for a full thirty seconds before quietly murmuring, "Wow."

Lily giggled again.

"Thanks," Cary said, no longer resisting the urge to roll her eyes even as her cheeks heated. "We're playing dress up."

He nodded. "You look lovely."

She narrowed her eyes, extremely uncomfortable with all this—especially in front of witnesses—because now she knew how Jaxer thought he felt about her, which made his stunned appreciation of her current appearance more than a little awkward.

"And you would be?" Jillian asked.

"Sorry," Cary said. "This is my former mentor Jaxer." Cary went around the room introducing everyone. Then to Jaxer, "Are you ready to get that thing taken care of?"

He nodded, but he hadn't stopped staring at her, even as he'd said hello to each person she introduced. His stare made her want to squirm in discomfort. If she didn't know what she knew, she might be flattered and pleased that Jaxer thought she looked good this way. But now his reaction was offset by complications and feelings she didn't want him to have.

To avoid thinking about it, she said, "I need to change, so I don't get the dress messed up, then we'll go…take care of that thing."

"What thing?" Alisha asked.

Cary sighed and waved a hand. "It's a work thing."

"Yeah, we still don't know very much about what you do," Diana pointed out. "Lucas has told me all about Portland. And Miguel still claims you're a superhero."

Cary chuckled. "Nope, not a superhero. Although that would be cool."

"She's definitely a hero though," Jaxer said. His tone should have been playful and light. Instead, he sounded sincere.

That was really weird and unsettling.

"A stunning hero," he continued. "Really. Very beautiful."

"Stop that," she hissed. "You're surrounded by shifters—*Deacon's* shifters. They can smell you."

"Don't worry," Nicky said, patting her arm. She leaned in close and very quietly assured, "We can smell you, too."

When Cary met her gaze, she looked both sympathetic and sad. Cary gave her a little hug of thanks and went behind the screen to change.

"Jaxer," she called, "you can wait outside."

The door closed quietly without comment.

Cary came back out from behind the screen in her jeans and t-shirt, which still had a tear in the hem from her earlier time with Deacon— she tucked it in so it wasn't obvious—then sat on a chair to put on her boots.

"Well, that's an interesting twist," Jillian said. "Does Deacon know about him?"

"Yes," Cary said. "In fact, the only reason I know Deacon is because of Jaxer."

"Whoops," Diana said.

Cary snorted.

"Deacon's not likely to tell us, and I was hesitant to ask…" Nicky raised her brows.

"You want to know how we met?" Cary asked.

Everyone in the room edged a little closer.

She chuckled. "I rescued him from a demented teenage wizard who'd chained him to a bed and was going to try stealing his body." She shrugged. "You know, just a typical blind date."

Lily glanced at all the laughing adults. "What?" she asked.

"You'll understand soon enough, I'm afraid," her mother said, pulling her in for a hug.

"Anyway," Cary said, standing and facing the door. "Jaxer and

Deacon were friends, and Jaxer is the one who asked me to go rescue Deacon. So really this is all his own fault."

"Bet that hasn't gone over well," Jillian said. She tucked her arm around Nicky's waist and pulled her close.

"Not even a little bit," Cary confirmed. She put her hands on her hips and sighed. "I wish Jaxer and I could go back to just being friends."

"Give it time," Alisha said. She gave Cary a hug that touched Cary's heart.

"Thanks." Cary looked at all the women in the room. "For everything. This was fun. And thanks so much for helping me find my look."

"The day of the ball, meet us all here," Nicky said. "We'll have a getting dressed party." She waggled her eyebrows, and Jillian groaned.

"We'd better have plenty of wine on hand for that," Alisha said. Then she pushed Cary gently toward the door. "I believe you have work to attend to. And a former mentor's heart to break."

Cary groaned. With a wave, she headed out into the corridor to find Jaxer patiently leaning against the wall a few yards away.

"Ready?" he asked.

"As I'll ever be." She led the way, ignoring the silence and tension hanging heavily between them.

*C*ary set her hand on the doorknob to her previous room and hesitated. "How the hell are we going to get this dagger secured this time?"

It was the first thing either her or Jaxer had said and the sound of her own voice startled her a little. She shook off all the tension as the reality of their current dangerous situation returned. She didn't have time to mope, she had a pretty serious issue to take care of.

"What did the Nags say about the thing coming back here?" She faced Jaxer fully, all business now.

"They exchanged a look then pulled the leather loop from thin air—"

"As you do," Cary couldn't resist inserting.

Jaxer smiled at that. It was an Irish phrase he'd taught her years ago. "It was empty of the dagger I'd brought them. They told me to come back and get it again."

"But you said there were seven of these Bathsheba daggers. That they'd likely mistaken which one I'd found. Did they say anything about that?"

"They don't like to admit mistakes." His faint scowl would have amused her under different circumstances.

"It was *their* mistake, though? Nothing I did?"

"Nothing you did," he said. "They had assumed this one was the greed dagger and sent the spelled scabbard for it. Each blade can only be contained by a very specific scabbard. If the wrong one is used…"

He shrugged but she got the point. The stupid thing just got out again and returned to cause havoc in the world.

"What did you mean by greed dagger?" she asked.

"All seven feed off of blood, sacrifice, and intense, negative emotions. Each dagger is drawn to a specific emotion."

Since the one she'd recovered had turned up in Las Vegas, and the woman using it had found a sacrifice for it through a poker game, Cary might have assumed it was the greed dagger too. "Did the Nags say which one this one was, then?"

He held up another leather scabbard, a full one this time, not just a bit of leather and metal, and this one fairly glowed with a blue light.

"Whoa," Cary said. "I've never seen leather do that." Just like on the blade, the blue light danced over the scabbard making shapes that almost resembled words.

"This contains the blade that feeds off jealousy," he said.

"Do the Nags have all seven scabbards?" She glanced up at Jaxer, her eyes wide. "Are there still six of these things floating around the world?"

"Four, beyond the one you found. Two are contained."

"Contained how?" she asked.

"The English Faery court has one supposedly in safe keeping."

He was so careful of his phrasing she knew there was a story there. "Supposedly?"

"The Irish and German courts aren't convinced the safest place for that particular weapon is with the English Fae. But it's been safe and out of this realm for three centuries so the grumblings have died down."

"Which one do they have? Or do you know?"

"They have the Lust dagger."

"Lust?" She frowned a little. "I'm assuming it feeds off bad lust and not the good lust?"

He grinned at that. "You would be right. Good lust isn't its thing."

"What other one is contained and who has it?" she asked, a little embarrassed to be talking about lust with Jaxer now.

"The Fear dagger is safely with the wolf branch of the Seven Families," he said.

"The Seven Families?"

She didn't come across them very often. They hunted actual, honest-to-god monsters—not vampires and shapeshifters, not even demons, but the things that came out of nightmares and could drive an ordinary human brain into mush. There was very little written about them, and they kept to themselves, but they reliably kept the monster population in check. And she for one was very grateful that they did. Demons and vampires were enough stress in her life.

Except there was that stupid number seven again. She shouldn't be surprised. Seven did show up a lot in the supernatural world. But really, this was starting to get ridiculous.

"Okay, so that's Fear and Lust contained. We're pretty sure I've got Jealousy hanging out inside this room?" She raised her brows in question, and Jaxer nodded. "The Nags thought it was Greed, though, which means Greed is still out in the world. What are the last three?"

"Rage, which hasn't surfaced since the mid-twentieth century. Ignorance, which comes and goes but no one seems to be able to confine it. And Hate is the last one. That disappeared about twenty years ago and no one has been able to locate it since."

"So these things just pop up every now and then and then disappear again?"

He shrugged. "Magical blades will do that."

"Well that's nice," she said sarcastically. She touched the blue lines of runes dancing along the worn leather of the scabbard Jaxer held. A very faint zing of energy, like the bite of static electricity, tingled along her finger tips. "Do the Nags have the scabbards for all five remaining daggers?"

"They didn't deign to tell me," Jaxer said.

"So they were just guessing when they sent this scabbard this time? What if this isn't the Jealousy dagger?"

"Given how you've been feeling since arriving, Jealousy was a good guess."

She flashed him a scowl, but her gaze dropped back to the scabbard. "That's a wizard thing, isn't it? The way the words keep shifting and I can't quite read them." She squinted and leaned a little closer. "When I rescued Deacon from Sheldon, the headboard Deacon was chained to did that."

"It is a wizard thing," Jaxer confirmed, sounding amused by her wording.

She gave him a look.

He grinned, then said more seriously, "Bespelled with some pretty powerful magic."

"Who made these Bathsheba daggers?" She raised her brows. "Obviously, not Bathsheba."

"They're ancient," he said. "The wizard who created them is long dead. They have so much evil worked into them, though, they've just continued feeding through the centuries, taking on a life of their own."

"And sacrificing innocent lives," she muttered.

"Exactly. But Wisat and Liruk were pretty confident this scabbard would work for this particular blade. At least in this case, we can ensure the Jealousy blade stops feeding for good."

"Groovy," Cary said. She faced the door again. "Now, how do we get the dagger into the scabbard without either one of us turning into murderous mad people?"

She was still reluctant to open the door. The fact that it had returned *to her* gave her the creeps. Especially since it likely fed off jealousy.

"Maybe we can slide the scabbard over it without actually touching it," Jaxer suggested.

She faced him. "You mean you don't know how to do this?"

He shrugged. "Every cursed blade works differently. I wouldn't want to guess."

"*Every* cursed blade?" She frowned. "Wait, how many cursed blades are there beyond these seven?"

"Lots." He waved a hand in the air. "There's an entire field of study dedicated to the things. What do you think Excalibur was?"

She blinked at him. "I have more reading to do, don't it?"

He patted her cheek, the gesture so reminiscent of their relationship before he'd had to go and insert *feelings* into it, she almost sighed.

"You're not expected to know everything," he said.

"Right. Tell that to Liruk who keeps expecting me to know everything."

He nodded at the door. "Shall we?"

She wrinkled her nose, then pushed the door open.

She and Jaxer stared at the bed.

"Shit," Cary said.

"This isn't good," Jaxer said.

"I swear," she said walking slowing into the room. "I swear it was here. On the bed. Deacon saw it." She eased around the room, carefully hunting for the now missing deadly dangerous cursed blade. Under her breath, she kept up a constant stream of "shit shit shit" because it helped keep her from screaming in frustrated fear.

"I believe you," Jaxer said. "The scabbard for the greed dagger was empty. Whichever weapon you recovered, it definitely escaped the Nags."

"No one was supposed to come in here," Cary said. "Damn it. I should have camped out in front of the door. I shouldn't have been off playing dress up and—" She cut herself off before mentioning what she and Deacon had been doing earlier, before the dress up. "I thought everyone would follow Maria's orders. I mean, she's the queen right."

Cary straightened from looking under the bed—while remaining about six feet away just in case—and shook her head. "My fault," she muttered. "I should have stayed here."

"You blame yourself too much for things that are beyond your control," Jaxer said. "I would have assumed all the shifters here would follow Maria's orders too. Even if not of their own will, then at least because of hers."

"I don't think she used her magic to compel everyone to follow the order," Cary said, turning in a slow circle as she continued to study the room.

"Then you underestimate her," Jaxer said bluntly. He disappeared into the attached bathroom, reemerging with a shake of his head.

"Do you suppose the *dagger* took itself off somewhere else?" Cary asked. "I mean, it managed to get here own its own. It could have gone somewhere else without anyone having to come in and take it."

Although, that was probably the worst possibility because it meant the damned thing could be anywhere. In the world. It meant they'd lost the chance to take something truly dangerous out of the world for good.

She let loose another string of obscenities.

"It could have," Jaxer said, not helping her guilt or her mood. "But I doubt it."

"Why?" She wasn't sure whether to be relieved or not.

"It returned to *you* for a reason. It found something here it wanted to feed off of."

She winced. If Jaxer and the Nags were right, and this was the dagger that fed off jealousy, then she knew exactly what it had found that brought it here. Some Protector she turned out to be, her emotions so horrible they actually called to a cursed blade.

But she wasn't the only one in the mansion wrestling with the green-eyed monster. "Why me?" she asked. "Why not someone else experiencing jealousy? The world is full of people struggling with envy."

"It touched you," Jaxer said. "It had already established a connection to you."

"Then shouldn't it still be here?"

"Actually," Jaxer said, with a scowl. "Yes, it should. The only explanation is someone in the house took it."

"But who would disobey Maria? Especially if you're right and she did add some magic compulsion to her order."

"Someone she can't compel?" Jaxer suggested. "Someone not a leopard shifter?"

"The only non-leopards here are me and the cougar shifter prisoners they have locked up in the basement. Maria doesn't have any human staff. Not even day staff."

"But they're getting ready for a big event. She might have people coming in for meetings?"

"Not here," Cary said. "Not that I've seen. Evan told me they're very careful about keeping the humans they work with separate from the mansion. That's why they wouldn't have the charity ball here even though the place is big enough."

She faced the bed again, scowling at the spot where the dagger had been. "I didn't touch it," she said, under her breath and talking mostly to herself. "The cougars are safely locked up. And if there'd been another assault on the house, someone would have found me and mentioned it." She was thinking about Lucas and the fact that she'd been with his mate and oldest daughter all afternoon. He would have come to check on them if there'd been another cougar attack. "I'll double check with Maria but not likely to be other humans in the mansion that I don't know about."

She rubbed her hands over her face and then up through her hair, belated remembering she still had makeup on and her hair had been twisted into an updo she hadn't bothered to take down yet. Hairpins dropped to the rug at her feet soundlessly. She sighed.

"Either the thing moved itself," she said, facing Jaxer. "Or a leopard came in here and took it, despite Maria's orders."

Jaxer didn't agree with her, but he didn't contradict her assessment either.

"I need to talk to Maria," she said.

"Yes, you do," Jaxer said. He handed her the scabbard. "In case you find it while I'm gone."

"Where are you going?" She swallowed the squeak in her voice, the hint of panic that was a little too embarrassing.

"To talk to Liruk and Wisat. Find out what they haven't told me." He sounded annoyed with them again. "I'll be back in a few hours."

Instead of heading into the hallway, he went to the French doors that led out onto the small patio. She watched him test the locks, realizing she hadn't thought to do that. Someone could have snuck in that way without alerting the house. Another stupid mistake on her part, she thought. Fortunately, the doors were securely locked, so despite her mistake, no one had gotten in that way.

Jaxer let himself outside, then turned to face her. "Lock these again." He gestured to the doors. "I set off a silent alarm opening them but I'm sure they'll see it's me and turn the alarm off."

"How do you know there's an alarm?" she asked, wondering if she'd set it off the other night as well. And where were the cameras to show it was Jaxer?

He grinned and gestured to a small white box just above the doors. A little red light on the box was blinking. "Alarm," he said.

She winced at having missed something so obvious. She glanced up at the box and hoped that wasn't were the camera was as well. That could be embarrassing having a security camera overlooking your bedroom.

"Remember," Jaxer said, pulling her attention back to him, "if you do come across the dagger, be very careful."

"That part I can remember," she said. "Don't take too long."

She was more than a little freaked out about a cursed weapon just appearing and disappearing around her. And she couldn't afford to go back to Portland and her research attic to look up the information she needed herself. She was trusting Jaxer, relying on him—as she'd been doing for the last six years. The fact that she wasn't supposed to be doing that anymore didn't escape her. But given the potential harm the dagger could do, she hoped the Nags would give her a break.

Jaxer gave her a little salute before disappearing over the patio's wrought iron railing. By the time Cary got to the doors to close and lock them, Jaxer had disappeared.

She faced the room again, studying it through narrow eyes. Then she tucked the scabbard into her back pocket and left to find Maria, carefully closing the door to the room behind her.

24

Instead of Maria, Cary found Evan. In the kitchen, trying out yet another pizza recipe. She grinned. If she and Deacon did end up working out, and Evan became her father-in-law, she could see herself spending a lot of time in this house being the guinea pig for his pizza experiments. She'd be good with that.

"Is Maria around?" Cary asked. "I have a problem."

"She's out at the venue with Deacon and Sasha."

"Deacon left?"

Evan misinterpreted her reaction and said, "Maria is with him to keep him steady while he's not around you. And there are no other shifters at the venue right now. He's fine."

That was good to know but wasn't the reason for her surprise. She wasn't sure why she was so surprised. But she'd left him sleeping, or so she'd thought, and that had only been about four hours ago. She'd just assumed he was still asleep. The fact that he hadn't left her a message or sent her a text to let her know he was leaving didn't thrill her. In fact, it hurt. More than she had time to think about just then.

"That dagger I told you about?" she said. "It's not where we left it."

Evan stopped mid-cheese grating to stare at her.

She explained Jaxer's return with the scabbard and their search of the room. "He's gone to find out more for me, but in the meantime, I need to find that dagger. Would any of your people ignored Maria's order?"

"No," Evan said with absolute certainty. "No one disobeys Maria's orders. Not without risking her censure."

Cary narrowed her eyes. "Do I want to know what that might entail?"

"Nothing permanent," he said.

Yeah, that wasn't particularly reassuring.

"But in this house," he said, "in this territory, my mate's word is law. No one here would disobey her."

"Did she…?" Cary hesitated to ask, but after Jaxer's comment, she had to. "Does she use her magic to compel them to follow an order like this? Would it be physically impossible for a leopard to have gone into that room?"

Evan slowly set aside the cheese and scowled at her, hard, his expression as tense as she'd ever seen it—even following the attack on the clinic. She straightened a little against the counter, recognizing too late she'd asked the wrong question.

"I realize you don't know much about her magic," Evan said, his tone cold and controlled. "Or Deacon's. I'll have a talk with my son about that. But just know that while Maria could do that if necessary— and during coordinated battles, it has been—she doesn't use her magic lightly. Frankly, she doesn't have to. The others wouldn't follow her or allow her to lead them if she took away their free will at the drop of a hat."

Cary nodded and swallowed the lump in her throat. Insulting her hosts had not been part of her plan. "I'm sorry if I offended you. I did need to know though. It means someone could have gone in, despite the threat of her punishments. That the possibility exists. And I need to know that if I'm going to find this weapon."

He turned to remove a pizza from the brick oven, giving the process of sliding the now hot circle of dough and sauce onto the flat wooden, long-handled peel his full attention. She waited him out.

"One of our people wouldn't risk the safety of the others out of mere curiosity," he finally said, without looking at her. "Especially after Maria has given an order."

"This dagger, it's not your run of the mill blade. It's possible the cursed part of it called to someone. It feeds off emotion." She left out the part about it also needing blood. "We think this one's drawn to jealousy."

Evan carefully set the steaming pizza on the kitchen island. The cheese was bubbling and just a little brown. She leaned in, without meaning too, pulling in a deep breath to absorb the scent of well-cooked cheese.

When she glanced up, Evan's expression had softened a little. "I'm glad you approve. I'm working on the basics so it's just cheese."

"I'm always good with basic pizza," she said. Then, more seriously, "I'll need to search the mansion. Even if no one disobeyed Maria, it's possible the dagger itself found a new target to tempt and went wherever that person is. And I'll have to ask questions. How much is this going to upset everyone?"

"Depends on how you ask," Evan said. The softness had left his expression again. In fact, now she couldn't read his mood at all. "But I wouldn't piss anyone off unnecessarily. You are still a human in a house full of shifters. Despite being Deacon's mate, you're not invulnerable."

Cary wasn't sure what to make of that warning. She'd been comfortable here—at least when she wasn't around Sasha—and no one had given her the impression they might hurt her. Given she'd saved their asses twice in her first twenty-four hours here, she thought it might afford her a little security.

Maybe she'd been wrong. Maybe a house full of shapeshifters hadn't been a very safe idea.

Evan must have scented her concern, because he said, "I'm not trying to chase you away or dissuade you from doing what you have to do. You brought that dagger into our home. You've endangered our people, allowing that thing out of your sight. It's your responsibility to fix this."

Ouch. "Which is why I'm clearing the search and questioning with you," she pointed out, defensively because her fear of failing clenched around her gut.

And she didn't appreciate the guilt trip one bit. She'd already rescued someone from the dagger. Two people technically. And she'd saved the leopards from attack. Twice. Yes, she'd made a mistake. But she didn't need Evan to remind her of it. She could take care of the guilt for her mistakes on her own, thank you very much.

"You're angry now," Evan said. He didn't have to ask. He also didn't show any regrets about making her angry.

"A little," she said.

"The others will scent that too. Be sure they know why or they'll misinterpret your questions."

"Thanks for the advice. I'll start searching the mansion now." She pushed away from the counter and left the kitchen without looking back. Even the lure of the pizza didn't cut the sting of both threat and guilt trip.

She'd liked Evan quite a lot before this moment. And maybe it was her own sense of failure that was making this feel worse. Or maybe it was the fact that she had to face all this on her own because Deacon was always gone. Or maybe it was because she didn't want to be here in the first place.

Or maybe she was just upset and tired and overwhelmed and Evan could have said her hair needed a comb and she would have gotten pissed off. Sometimes it was hard to tell.

All she knew was that her stomach was tight and her mood was bad and she didn't have anyone to discuss all this with because the man she'd come here with had disappeared on her—again—without bothering to tell her where he'd gone and when he'd be back.

She decided the only way to cover the entire mansion was to begin at one end, third floor first, and work her way through, top to bottom, wing to wing. She knocked on doors, poked her head into empty rooms, asked anyone she came across if they'd happened to see this decorative dagger she'd had in her old room. She made up a story about it being a present for a friend but she'd left it in the old room and now it was misplaced. Shifters could smell lies, so the first few people she spoke too looked at her through narrowed eyes, but by the time she'd told the story for the tenth time, it was so rote they no longer picked up that it wasn't true.

She did not go into any of the private apartments or occupied rooms—especially not any of the family's rooms—because Evan hadn't explicitly told her she could. But she did search the more public places and any space unoccupied.

This left a huge gap in her search, of course, but she could at least eliminate a few areas.

She sighed when she reached the end of the first floor in the west wing. She was looking for something that was easy to conceal and move around. Something that could move itself if it wanted to. In a mansion that was huge and had rooms she couldn't enter. A needle in a fucking haystack.

This was a waste of time. Her Protector instincts hadn't gone off once during the entire search either. Which meant, at the moment, no one was in danger from the stupid weapon. That, at least, was good news.

A glance out a window confirmed it was full dark now. Her stomach growled but she didn't want to face Evan again. There was no word from Deacon, whether he was even in the house or not. And she hadn't heard back from Jaxer yet.

For reasons she couldn't quite understand, a wave of loneliness washed over her. She felt very isolated and distant from all the people around her just then. And she didn't even have her dogs to hug.

She was considering just getting in her car and going somewhere else for dinner when Diana spotted her and hurried toward her. "I've been looking all over for you! You have visitors."

"Visitors?" Cary followed, wondering if it was Jaxer. Or maybe the Nags in disguise.

When they reached the entryway, Cary almost burst into tears when she saw Marianne, Lucy, and Angie standing there, gawking at the building.

"What are you all doing here?" She went in for a group hug, relieved beyond words and so grateful she couldn't talk for a moment.

"We were worrying about you," Angie said quietly.

"And since you keep getting in the middle of shifter fights, I wanted to get you a new shirt I made for you," Marianne said. "Along with a few other useful accessories."

"And I brought the present from Jasmine," Angie added. "Because I thought you could use a little luck."

"And I brought wine," Lucy said. "Because wine."

"You are the best friends a woman could possibly have," Cary said, "and I love you all so much I might just cry."

"Wait till we open the wine before we get to the tears," Lucy said.

Cary grinned. She introduced them to Diana. Then asked, "Where do you think we could go to talk?" Cary was more than usually aware of the fact that her friends were all human, and given her conversation with Evan, she wasn't even sure they'd be welcome here. But fuck it, she needed her friends.

"I'm sure no one will bother you in the yellow room," Diana said. "I'll show you."

"Thanks," Cary said. At least Diana wasn't showing any signs of being offended by the human invasion.

The yellow room turned out to be a large living room with an open fireplace that wasn't lit, two groupings of cozy couches all in various shades of cream or yellow, and walls painted in a pale yellow color over a light wood wainscoting. Even the thick rugs over the wooden floors were tones of cream and yellow.

"I see where the room gets its name," Lucy whispered to Cary.

"What color wine did you bring?" Cary asked.

"Red," Lucy said.

"Oh oh." Cary glanced at Diana. "You're sure this will be okay? Maybe someplace a little less…" She glanced around. "Stainable."

Diana waved that away. "Don't worry. We turn the kids loose in this room a lot." She motioned to a couple of trunks against the wall near the fireplace. "Those are filled with board games and building blocks. A wine stain won't be any more difficult to clean than some of the stuff the kids have dropped in here."

Cary wanted to laugh that Diana had brought her and her friends to the "kids' room." Probably a smart move. "Thanks again. You want to stay for a glass of wine?"

"Thanks," Diana said with a smile, "but I promised Lily I'd help her with her hair. She's trying some styles for the ball." She waved on her way out the door, closing it gently behind her.

"So," Lucy said the minute the door closed, "tell us everything. Leave out no details."

Cary sighed, settling onto one of the overstuffed couches. "Open that wine. This might take a while."

"First," Marianne said, "I have a present for you."

From the depths of a bag that looked like an ordinary large purse, she pulled out a small silver clutch purse, a package wrapped in tissue paper, a shoe box, what looked like a large jewelry box, and four wine glasses. Cary was just starting to think that was it when Marianne pulled out one last thing—a bottle of non-alcoholic sparkling cider.

At Cary's raised brows, Marianne said, "I'm driving us home later so no real wine for me."

"Fair enough. I'm very glad you're being safe." The reminder that they were all here and it was two hours back to Portland only made her more emotional. To distract herself, she asked Angie, "The dogs were good when you left?" They'd be perfectly content for hours without any humans in the house—Cary had had to stay out all night before when working, so her dogs were pretty flexible—but given what Buck had gone through just last month, she wanted to check.

"Everyone is doing wonderfully," Angie confirmed. "Still. And Scratchy showed up today to torment Fred and steal some of the food I left out for him."

Cary grinned. Scratchy was the resident stray tomcat that Cary fed when he deigned to show up. Scratchy was way too independent to become a pet, but he'd adopted Cary and her home as part of his territory. He also liked to sit around just out of Fred's reach while her terrier attempted to attack. Not that Fred would know what to do if he caught the cat. Fred was all about the chase.

Knowing her little pack was doing well, Cary turned her attention to the stack of boxes Marianne had pulled from a purse that was much too small to carry it all. "That's the coolest purse I've ever seen," Cary said. "What is all this?"

"First, the shirt," Marianne said. She opened the tissue paper wrapped package and pulled out a simple, long sleeved, button up black shirt. "This material is the good stuff," she said as she handed the shirt to Cary. "You get cut or anything starts to bleed, press that material against it. It'll seal the wound. Keep you from infection. Or bleeding out."

Cary's eyes widened. "Wow. That's super amazing. Does it just work on me?"

"Nope. Anyone needs a wound sealed, you can manage it with that. It won't show the blood stains. And its machine washable. But I'd hang it dry, just to keep the shape."

Cary laughed. "You're a genius."

"I know. Now, did you find a dress that will work for this ball or do I need to make you something?"

Cary told her all about the dress that they'd settled on.

"Perfect," Marianne said. "Then you'll need this." She handed Cary the clutch. "It'll adjust its color to fit the color tone of the dress. I brought some nice jewelry to choose from and a pair of heels. Figured all you'd have were that black standard pair of yours."

"You know me so well."

Marianne handed her the shoe box. "Those will adapt to the color of the dress too, if the silver tone isn't right."

Cary opened the box. The beautiful strappy heels sparkled with clear-colored beads like diamonds. Cary noticed the height of the heel wasn't beyond her skill-set either. And another wave of gratitude filled her.

"Best thing about those," Marianne said. "They'll turn into flats if you need to run for some reason. Just stomp on the heel and it'll retract."

Cary set everything aside and gave Marianne a bone squeezing hug.

While she'd been going through Marianne's loot, Lucy had opened the bottle of wine and the sparkling cider and was filling the glasses Marianne had pulled from her purse.

As Lucy handed the drinks out, Cary shuffled Marianne's gifts to one side of the couch and told them everything that had been happening. Including her unsettling conversation with Evan and the loss of a super deadly cursed blade.

"To cap it all off," Cary finished, "I'm still not sure what to do about Deacon."

"You didn't have the reaction to Diana or Alisha that you did to Sasha?" Angie asked.

"Not even a hint," Cary said. "It's all Sasha. But the jealousy isn't even the worst part. It's like Deacon is two different people here. Sometimes he's the man I know. Sometimes he's a stranger. I told him I'd accept it. But I'm having a hell of a time getting used to it. And things like him not letting me know he was leaving the house today... That's really getting to me." She groaned and leaned into the couch. "It feels weird to be worrying about that when there's a cursed weapon missing. That really is a bigger problem at the moment."

"Want us to help you look for it?" Lucy asked as she refilled everyone's glass.

"I've searched where I could," Cary said. "But the thing could be anywhere."

"I hate to say it," Angie said, "but you might just have to wait until someone tries to use it. At least then your own powers will work and you'll be able to handle it to get it into the scabbard."

"I really really hate the idea of that," Cary said. "Especially if someone gets hurt before I can reach them."

"The thing feeds off jealousy, right," Marianne said.

"So the Nags and Jaxer assume," Cary said. "At least, that's their current guess. But they were wrong once already."

"But it came to you," Lucy said, a look passing between her and Marianne. "You're experiencing some pretty serious jealousy at the moment."

When said in Lucy's high, sweet little girl voice, that sounded almost harmless. Except if it was Cary's jealousy that had called the dagger back here, it wasn't harmless at all.

"Plus, you're the target of jealousy," Angie pointed out. "Sasha's. Jaxer's jealousy of Deacon because of you."

"You are surrounded by that nasty green monster at the moment," Marianne said. "From every possible angle. If that's what the dagger is feeding off, why would it go anywhere else? You've got more than enough to satisfy it."

"And the blade did try to hold you when you passed it to Jaxer that first time," Angie said. "It centered on you then."

Cary winced. "Jaxer and I had a tiff over his feelings in that conversation too."

"More jealousy," Lucy said.

"But it wasn't mine. It was Jaxer's. Why the hell did the dagger have to come to *me*? I don't even want to feel the jealousy I'm feeling."

"You're the center of it all," Angie said. "Cursed weapons like that."

"Gee, now I feel special," Cary said.

Marianne snorted at her sarcasm.

"The good news," Angie said, "is that if it is centered on you, it's not likely to be in someone else's hands. It probably just hid when you went in with the scabbard that could contain it. It'll show up again as soon as you don't have that on you."

"You think?" Cary raised her brows. That made a weird kind of sense.

Although why Jaxer didn't think of it she didn't know. But five of the seven daggers had been on the loose for centuries without anyone being able to contain them. It made sense they'd know how to hide from the one thing that could capture and secure them permanently.

"I'm not sure that's a good thing," Cary continued aloud, "but it would make my life easier if it wasn't off causing trouble for anyone else." She frowned. "Is it weird we're talking about an inanimate object like it's a living thing?"

"Cursed weapons are living things," Angie said. "They take on their own essence, and their own objectives, far beyond what the person who spelled them ever intended." She shook her head. "I swear wizards never learn. They just keep creating these things that *always* get out of their control and end up floating around the world causing trouble."

"Lovely," Cary said, lifting her glass in a toast full of sarcasm. The other three followed suit.

"Here here," Lucy said.

"So…" Cary frowned as she worked through this new possibility. "If the blade is just hiding from the scabbard, how do I contain it? If I leave the scabbard behind, go into the room and the dagger is there, I'm vulnerable to it—no one to protect. And without the scabbard, I have no way to contain it."

"We could try with you," Angie suggested. "At least see if the theory works." She glanced around. "Anyone here feeling particularly beset by envy or jealousy at the moment? Besides Cary?"

Cary wrinkled her nose.

"I've got some envy going," Lucy said.

"Of who?" Cary asked, leaning forward.

"The dojo across town that keeps stealing my regular students," she said.

"What?" Cary said. "You didn't tell me that was happening."

"Me neither," Marianne said.

Lucy sighed and they spent the next fifteen minutes finishing off the bottle of wine and discussing Lucy's problem. It was so nice to think about someone else and something else, to be a support for her friend instead of being the one in need of support, that Cary eagerly set aside her worry for a few minutes.

She might have remained distracted by the new topic if Angie hadn't brought the conversation back to the Jealousy dagger.

"Since Lucy's got the jealousy, and it's directed at someone who is *not* in the vicinity," Angie said, "she should go into that room with Cary. That way, if the blade tries to tempt Lucy, Cary can protect her, get the blade into her leather coat, where we already know it'll be safe-ish. And then Marianne and I can come in with the scabbard to seal it up."

Cary pointed a finger at Angie. "You are a genius and this is a good idea." Cary turned to Lucy. "So long as you don't mind being the bait, so to speak."

"I will dial up my envy to epic levels if it will help you, sweetie," Lucy said.

"You guys really are the best. I owe you big time." She stood. "Wait here. I have to go get my jacket from Deacon's room. Oh, I haven't told you about that yet! After we test this theory for recovering the dagger, remind me to tell you about his childhood bedroom."

"Like we could forget after you dangle that hint," Marianne said. "Hurry. The bottle of wine is empty and our bravery will never be higher than this."

Cary snorted, especially because Marianne hadn't had any alcohol. But she did hurry, jogging through the corridors and up the stairs. Deacon's room was empty when she arrived, no sign that he'd been there in the time Cary had been gone. The bed was neatly made again, which gave it the appearance of having not been used at all.

She quickly searched the room, just in case the dagger had followed her here. There was no sign of it, but she did have the scabbard in her back pocket still. If Angie's theory was right, the weapon wasn't likely to appear until she wasn't in possession of that anymore.

She grabbed her jacket and hurried back to her friends, forcing her feelings about the empty room and the silence from Deacon all afternoon out of her head. She could continue to worry about her personal life later.

Right now, she had a dangerous weapon to find. And she finally had some help she could rely on.

2 5

Angie and Marianne waited around a corner farther up the hall, well away from the room Cary had slept in her first night in the mansion. Angie tucked the scabbard into the courier bag she always carried in place of a purse, where it would be safe and hopefully magically hidden since Angie's courier bag was a present from Marianne. Like Marianne's purse, Angie's bag held a lot more than it looked like it should from the outside. It also had a pocket that blocked magic leakage.

"A constant problem when I have to carry my witchy gear around," Angie had said.

Cary stood outside the guestroom door with Lucy. "Are you sure you want to try this?" she asked. "If it's there and it calls to you..." Cary let the rest trail off. She wasn't entirely sure what that would mean for Lucy, but she didn't want her friend going in blind.

"I got this," Lucy assured, patting Cary on the arm. "I've got more than enough envy right now to catch the things attention. And I've got my best friend who's a Protector here to keep me safe from it."

Cary gave her a quick shoulder hug. Then they opened the door.

The room was dark except for the light from behind them in the

192

hallway that cast hers and Lucy's shadows into the room. Cary's gaze went immediately to the bed.

No dagger.

Her shoulders dropped. Damn. A part of her had really hoped this would work.

Then Lucy tapped her arm. Cary glanced at her over her shoulder. Lucy nodded toward the dresser opposite the bed. A faint blue glow made Cary blink. She hadn't even taken a step toward the glow, hadn't fully realized what she was seeing, when Lucy moved around her, heading right toward the dagger.

Cary got to her just as she was reaching out to touch the thing, her fingers hovering over the blade, her brown eyes wide as she stared at it. Catching her by the wrist, Cary held her gently, preventing her from making physical contact with the dagger.

"Did you know," Lucy said, her little girl's voice sing-songy in the quiet, "it can help me? It can help me get my students back. I can have the best dojo in Portland."

"Lucy," Cary said. "You already do. And I'm very very sorry we used you as bait. And also, damn woman, you do have a lot of jealousy. We'll have to discuss that more after we're done here."

In answer, Lucy strained toward the blade. Cary's Protector magic worked and she was able to hold Lucy back. But because of their positions, she couldn't slip between Lucy and the blade easily. Not without shoving Lucy away which seemed like a bad idea given that Lucy was a highly trained martial artist who might take the shove in the wrong way.

Even as Cary thought that, she watched Lucy narrow her eyes and adjusted her stance a little. Each move subtle and easy to miss. But Cary had been training with her for years. She recognized the signs just seconds before Lucy swept her hand up to grip Cary's arm and turned gently to one side in a move that, had it not been for Cary's magic, would have easily sent Cary flying over Lucy's ducked head and into the far wall.

Despite her powers, Cary still felt the tug of the momentum in

Lucy's move, rising onto her toes slightly before her powers fixed her firmly back on the ground.

"Wow," Cary commented. "You have some serious skills. I knew that already, but still." From her position, with her arm over Lucy's shoulder but Lucy's back to her, Cary gently wrapped her free arm around Lucy's waist and took a step forward, moving them both a few inches from the blade.

Lucy cursed. "Stop that. It will help me. I need it."

"Oh sweetie," Cary murmured, very sorry they'd done this now. But obviously her Protector magic was working, which meant she could get that stupid blade into the safety of her pocket.

She used her full body, and superior size, to keep Lucy blocked from the blade, then reached back with the hand Lucy wasn't still holding—and trying to use to toss Cary over her head—to lift the dagger. Cary felt a little frizzle along her nerves, but as she edged open her jacket with the hand holding the blade and used the point of the weapon to slide open the pocket that would hold the thing, she didn't get the tugging on her fingers she dreaded. The dagger dropped into the magic pocket with a slight hiss of metal against material. Cary pressed her fingers against the opening to seal it.

Almost as soon as she had, Lucy dropped her hold on Cary's arm and faced her, her brow crinkled. "What the hell just happened?"

"You were right about the levels of your envy," Cary said, "and we need to talk a lot more about that and what's happening."

Lucy shrugged. "Told you."

"You're taking the fact that a cursed dagger almost took over your free will in stride," Cary said.

"But it worked, right? You got the dagger into a safe pocket. You kept me protected." Lucy grinned. "All is well in the world."

Cary shook her head and pulled Lucy in for a hug. "We're not doing that again, though, okay."

Lucy chuckled. "Fair enough. That was a very weird sensation, feeling like I wasn't quite here and yet sort of vaguely aware even though I didn't know what I was doing." She pulled back and met

Cary's gaze. "Think I'll stick to meditation for that kind of high going forward."

"Good," Cary said.

Angie and Marianne poked their heads around the door. "What happened?" Marianne asked.

Cary patted her jacket, over the pocket holding the dagger. "It worked. Lucy needs some counseling though."

Lucy snorted in response.

Angie came in carrying the scabbard. "You want to risk putting it in here or do you want to leave it in your jacket?"

"It'll be safe enough in that pocket," Marianne said. "Not forever, but for a while. It can't get out and run amok from there."

"You're sure?" Cary asked. She'd never had to test the pocket in quite this way.

"Do not insult my work," Marianne said, her chin lowered. "Of course it'll hold that thing." She glanced at the scabbard. The words on the leather were churning harder now, as if it sensed its blade nearby. "Although, it appears this thing is designed to contain it so maybe that would be better."

"Question," Lucy said. "Once it's in there, and the blade is under control, what's to stop someone from just taking the dagger back out of the scabbard?"

"The fact that it'll be safely stored wherever the Nags want to hide it," Cary said. "The instant Jaxer gets back, I'll hand it over and be done with it." She looked between her coat and the scabbard. "Yeah, let's get it in there. And then I'll put the whole lot back in my pocket. That should keep the stupid thing contained." She stared hard at Lucy. "As soon as I pull this out, it may start to affect you again." She scowled and looked at the others. "It could affect any of you."

Angie said, "I have an idea." She placed the scabbard on the bed. "We'll wait on the opposite side of the room. None of us move like shifters. Even if it calls to us, you'll have time to get it into the scabbard before we reach you."

"I don't know," Cary said. "Lucy can move pretty damned fast when motivated."

Lucy grinned.

"I'll stand in her way," Marianne said. "Give you a few extra seconds while she has to get around me." She stared hard at Lucy. "But if you throw me on my ass, we will have words when this is over."

Lucy held up her hands, palms facing Marianne. "I cannot be held accountable for my instincts if that cursed weapon is motivating me."

Marianne grunted but gave a look that said she'd still hold Lucy responsible if she ended up thrown across the room.

Angie gestured them all back to the far wall as Cary went to the bed and stared at the scabbard. She glanced at her friends, waited for their thumbs-up-ready signal, then unsealed her pocket.

The minute the blade cleared the edge of the opening with another hiss of metal against material, Lucy started toward her.

Cary watched them all from the corner of her eye as she picked up the scabbard. Angie held Lucy back, but Marianne's eyes had taken on that slightly glazed look, narrowing in a calculated way that resembled the look Lucy was giving Angie.

Shit.

Cary hurried to put the dagger into the spelled leather. Only the tip kept jumping away from the opening, straining against her hold and jerking back toward her friends.

The blade's erratic thrashing made Cary's pulse jump. And when it nearly pulled out of her grasp, she cursed.

Tightening her hold, keeping her back to her friends so she could protect them, she snarled and muttered every bad word she knew, forcing the tip of the blade closer to the scabbard.

"Get that thing secured," Angie barked.

"I'm trying damn it," Cary said. "It's fighting me."

Cary heard Angie start to murmur something under her breath.

She didn't waste focus to figure out what spell Angie was building. Panic made her pulse race and her muscles tremble.

She shoved the tip forward, nearly slicing her own finger on the sharp edge twice before she finally got the very point of the blade inside the opening of the scabbard. As soon as the leather surrounded that small section of metal, the dagger started to slide home of its own volition, as if the scabbard itself was pulling it in.

Once the hilt hit the edge of the scabbard, a sound like a click and a deep moan vibrated through Cary's bones.

She held still for a long moment, watching for any sign of the dagger escaping the scabbard's hold. Everything seemed secure. But just in case… She opened the inner pocket of her leather jacket and carefully put the full scabbard and blade inside, sealing the material closed with a press of her fingers.

Finally, she faced her friends.

Angie was scowling at Lucy and rubbing her side. Marianne was blinking, a hint of red creeping across her dark skin. She pressed her hands to her cheeks and muttered something Cary couldn't here.

"Everyone okay?" Cary asked.

Angie grunted. Lucy winced. "Sorry about that," she said, motioning to Angie's side.

"You're lucky my spell kept me in place," Angie said.

"I'd be better if that thing hadn't been whispering at me," Marianne admitted.

"Yeah," Lucy said, "I think you have some things you haven't told us."

"Uh huh. But I'm going to need another drink after this," Marianne said, ignoring the fact that her "drink" was non-alcoholic tonight.

Cary sighed and let her shoulders relax. "This has got to be the weirdest girls' night yet," she said. "And that includes the wizard attack and that time the goblin king crashed our party."

"I was so disappointed he didn't look like David Bowie," Lucy said with a sigh.

"I tried to tell you," Marianne said. "If he looked like David Bowie, you think I'd have been resisting going to work for him all those years?"

"Still," Lucy said, "a girl can hope."

They all took a moment of silence in honor of the beauty that was David Bowie as the goblin king in the movie *Labyrinth*.

Then Angie said, "We definitely need more wine."

Cary pointed at her jacket. "Do I just leave it there until Jaxer shows up?"

"Yes," all three of her friends answered at once.

"Let's get some more wine while we wait," Angie said.

"I thought we drank it all," Cary said.

"You need to double check that clutch I brought you," Marianne said with a smirk.

Cary's eyes widened. "If that bag produces wine whenever we want some, it is my new favorite accessory."

Marianne just grinned.

2 6

They retrieved all their belongings then returned to the room where they'd recaptured the dagger. Cary figured it would be the easiest place for Jaxer to find them, and they'd have privacy as they discovered just how many bottles of wine—and sparkling cider—Cary's new clutch could hold.

Jaxer appeared at the French doors not long after they'd opened their third—fourth?—bottle, looking bemused as Cary stumbled over to unlock the door and let him in.

"How much have you had to drink?" he asked quietly.

"Not nearly enough," she grunted. "We got the blade back." She reached toward her inner pocket, but before she pulled it out, she said, "It is definitely the Jealousy dagger."

He sighed. "At least we know that much. The thing is so old there are a lot of myths about it, and I had to dig to get to the real stuff."

"You sound funny when you say 'stuff' like a normal person," she said with a laugh.

Jaxer raised his brows.

"He's so pretty," Lucy murmured—in a voice not nearly quiet enough to actually be a murmur.

Jaxer pressed his lips together, which Cary suspected meant he was trying not to laugh, so she glared at him. "No laughing," she said.

"I'm not laughing," he assured.

"Now, he could make a sexy goblin king," Marianne said matter-of-factly.

At Jaxer's raised brows, Cary waved a hand in the air. "Long story."

"Good story," Angie said.

Jaxer glanced at her. "Et tu, Angie."

"Bet your faery ass," Angie said.

He did chuckle at that.

Though Angie didn't bother trying to stand from her sprawl across the bed—where they'd all gathered to drink and gossip—she said more seriously, "That blade reacts to jealousy and there's apparently more than enough of that to go around here." She gave him a pointed look. "So maybe the Nags should come and get the thing. You know, cause…jealousy and all that."

Jaxer's relaxed expression didn't seem to change at Angie's not-so-thinly-veiled point, but Cary couldn't be sure because the room was spinning a little bit and Jaxer kept coming in and out of focus. Maybe they'd had five bottles of wine?

"It's safe in my magic pocket," Cary said. She blinked. "That almost sounds like innuendo." She burst into giggles. "Magic pocket," she said again.

Lucy and Marianne laughed.

Angie raised her brows and shrugged. "Well, that works for that too."

"Ha!" Cary chuckled. "So, yeah, anyway, it's safe for now. We've been hanging with it all night and no more weirdness." She made a vague swirling hand gesture toward her pocket. "All is well in the world. Or, well, no, but…" She frowned because she'd lost her train of thought.

Jaxer touched her shoulder until she focused on him, blinking a few times.

"You okay?" he asked.

"Fine. Happily drunk. Needed it," she added very seriously.

"You're still mad at Deacon?" he asked, not sounding particularly upset about that.

"And you. And everyone in this house that's not a woman in this room right now."

"Damn straight," Lucy said, lifting her mostly empty wine glass.

"Your voice is so cute when you're drunk," Marianne said.

"You owe me a refill for that crack." Lucy waved her glass under Marianne's nose. Marianne obliged by refilling with a generous pour from their most recent bottle.

Six down now maybe? Cary blinked and tried to count the bottles she could see on the floor near the bed, but they kept swimming around.

"To be fair," Cary said, still trying to count wine bottles, "I'm not mad at the kids, or the lovely women who helped me pick a dress this afternoon either."

"You looked stunning in that dress," Jaxer commented.

"Thank you but you're not supposed to be noticing," Cary said without looking at him.

"It was very hard not to."

"Shut up," she said pleasantly. "What should we do about this blade? How much wine have we had?" she asked without waiting for an answer from Jaxer.

"Lost count," Angie said. "A lot."

"That purse is the *best*," Lucy said to Marianne. "Can I have one?"

"Of course," Marianne said.

"Where is the wine coming from?" Angie asked.

Marianne grinned. "Somewhere no one will miss it."

Angie barked out a laugh. "I thought this stuff tasted better than our usual fair. You've tapped into someone's wine cellar haven't you?"

Jaxer tugged Cary around to face him as her friends continued to discuss the brilliant Tardis clutch. It really should be blue, Cary thought, before blinking to focus on Jaxer.

"Angie is right," Jaxer said quietly. "It might be better for the Nags to take the blade back."

Cary scowled as she tried to figure out what he was talking about. She noticed he still had his hands on her and he was stroking her shoulders. The sensation would have been nice if she wasn't certain on some level that he shouldn't be doing that. Not now.

She batted his touch away. "Stop that."

"Habit," he said with a casual shrug she didn't buy for a minute.

"Right." She huffed out a breath and glanced at the French doors. "I really would like to be rid of this thing, but I guess it's my job to keep it safe and I failed that once already and Deacon's dad was sure quick to let me know that was my fault and now I feel icky and guilty and sad and I just want to go home and hug my dogs."

Her friends had heard her sad little monologue because all three of them left the bed and hurried to embrace her.

"We will take you home now if you want," Marianne said.

"Absolutely," Angie said, slurring the S sound.

At that moment, the main bedroom door opened. Cary squinted around the mass hugs of her friends to see Deacon standing in the doorway.

With Sasha, she noticed with a snarl.

Deacon's brows were raised, but Cary couldn't begin to read his expression. Too much of the iceman, she thought sourly.

"This is going to need an explanation," he said, his voice deep.

The sound gave Cary a little shiver—not fear but lust. He really was pretty and sexy even if he was acting like an ass the last couple of days.

"As well as why there are so many humans in the house," Sasha said in an aside to Deacon that was more than loud enough for everyone to hear.

Before Cary could answer, Lucy said, "I'm the only real human." She waved expansively to encompass everyone in the group hug. "They're all magic. Have magic?" She frowned a little.

"You have magic," Cary defended. "You're a superhero ninja. Better than Batman, even, cause you don't have all that money and those gadgets. Just a bucket ton of training."

"Yeah," Angie said.

"Yeah," Marianne echoed.

Lucy grinned. "I like being a superhero ninja."

"I think we've gone off topic a bit," Sasha said.

"That's Sasha," Cary said, nodding to the woman in question.

"Oh," Lucy said. "Well, that explains it."

"Explains what?" Sasha asked.

"None of your business," Lucy said primly in her little girl voice.

Cary jerked her chin down in a nod, patting Lucy's arm in support of her comment.

"I'm still waiting for an explanation," Deacon said quietly. He was staring at Jaxer, who was smirking at him.

Cary rolled her eyes. "What the hell time is it?"

"About four in the morning," Deacon said.

"Oh wow, where did that night go?" Cary looked at her friends. "You guys can't leave now. It's too late and not safe driving home, even if Marianne is sober as a… What's that phrase? Church mouse."

Marianne chuckled. "Something like that. I'm good to drive."

"No." Cary shook her head. "Too late, too dangerous. You have to stay here." She looked at Deacon and raised her brows. "Right?" she said pointedly.

He blinked and looked at her, dropping the staring contest he'd been having with Jaxer. "Right," he said. "Of course, they're welcome to stay."

"Deacon," Sasha said in a quiet voice, a warning note in the single word.

He turned a look on Sasha that would have frozen Cary's gut had he turned it on her.

Sasha ducked her head. "I'm sorry, sir."

"Wow," Marianne murmured.

Angie leaned in close and whispered in Cary's ear, "She's turned on by that."

"Huh?" Cary tried to whisper back but wasn't sure she managed.

Angie's breath hot against the side of her face, she said, "Sasha likes when Deacon is cold like that with her. It turns her on."

"How can you tell?" Cary asked.

"I'm reading her aura," Angie said matter-of-factly.

"You do that? I thought it was just touch psychic stuff."

"I'm a woman of many talents," Angie said.

"Yeah, you are," Cary said with an emphatic nod.

"Arrange two more rooms for them," Deacon said to Sasha, pulling Cary's attention back to them. He glanced at their group. "I assume one of you can stay in this room?"

There was a note in his question Cary wasn't sure she liked, but she also wasn't sure why. She glanced at the wine bottles again. Was that seven empty bottles?

"We can share," Lucy said. "We don't need a lot of space."

"Speak for yourself," Marianne said. "I'm not sharing a bed with Angie again. She kicks."

"Sorry," Angie said.

"I forgive you," Marianne said, "but I'm not taking home those bruises again."

"The room across the hall has two beds. Will that do?" Sasha asked, her tone quiet and contrite.

Cary was absolutely positive that was an act. Cause Sasha only ever seemed contrite for real when her queen scolded her. But if Angie was right, and she *liked* being scolded by Deacon…

First, what a thing to be turned on by. Could he smell it? Wow, he probably could. If Angie picked it up then a shapeshifter definitely picked it up.

What the hell did he think about that?

Oh, that was definitely something she was going to ask him about. Like, did he purposefully make his tone all commanding and deep just to turn Sasha on? Cause that was not okay. Especially since he was supposed to be *her* mate.

Wait… What had she been thinking about?

She blinked. "Rooms!" she said aloud. Everyone looked at her. She shrugged. "Are the two rooms going to be good?"

"So long as I don't have to share a bed with Angie, I can sleep anywhere," Marianne assured.

"You're a genius," Cary said.

"I know."

Jaxer leaned in close to Cary which drew a narrow-eyed look from Deacon.

"It might not be a great idea to pull that dagger out any time soon," Jaxer said quietly.

Why he bothered… Of course Deacon would hear him. And Sasha.

"There's a lot of emotion in the room right now," Jaxer finished.

"Tell me," Cary said. Loudly as it turned out. She scowled at the noise. "From a lot of different angles and all feeling a lot of the same things."

Marianne had been drawn to the dagger because she was having issues with her girlfriend Gina. She thought Gina might be cheating on her, which was also not okay if true, but Marianne and Gina had been together for so long Cary found it hard to believe Gina would cheat.

Lucy was definitely into deep jealousy over the rival dojo. Apparently even the facilities and location were better. And he apparently had a small cherry tree garden in the back. It was very Zen, and Lucy was livid that she didn't have room for a cherry tree garden. Or at least, that's what Cary thought was bugging Lucy. They'd probably have to talk about it more when she was sober.

Then there was Cary's jealousy of Sasha. And Deacon's jealousy of Jaxer. Although, Cary noticed with a sniff, he wasn't showing an awful lot of that jealousy with Sasha standing next to him. And Jaxer's feelings. And Sasha's feelings. And…

Cary blinked at everyone in the room.

"Angie," she said, "you are the only person in this room without any big bad envy-jealousy stuff going on. What gives?"

Angie grinned and wrapped her arm around Cary. "I am happy as a cat in cream with my life right now. My business is going well. My investment fund is growing. My house plants are all healthy and thriving. And I haven't had to deal with demon realms in like…years." She emphasized the years with a nod and a lot of emotion.

"You are a witch not a demon hunter. Demon realms?"

Angie waved a hand in the air. "Long story."

"You say that a lot. I'm not sure it means what you think it means."

Angie snorted and started to laugh, which gave Cary, Lucy, and Marianne the giggles. Jaxer looked on amused. Cary noted that Sasha and Deacon did not look amused.

"It's a line from a movie," Cary explained to them patiently, speaking slowly so the words were clear. "*Princess Bride*?"

"You mangled the line a little," Jaxer said.

"Adjusted," Cary corrected him, "because she didn't say inconceivable."

"I think it's time for everyone to go to their separate rooms and sleep this off," Deacon said.

"You know you're not the boss of me, right?" Cary said, hands on her hips. "Sasha may love all that bossy attitude, but I don't."

Deacon focused on her, and for the first time she noticed his eyes were glowing ever-so-slightly yellow. That meant his leopard was close to the surface. She couldn't see it in any other part of him, but oh boy, there were some serious emotions rolling under the surface to bring out that reaction.

She narrowed her gaze. "We need to talk, don't we?" she asked him.

He gave a slight nod, just the barest jerk of his chin.

"Okay." She turned and hugged Angie. "Don't leave in the morning without saying goodbye."

"We won't."

"But we will have to leave early." Marianne looked at her cellphone and groaned. "Too early for the amount of sleep we're gonna get."

"The dogs," Cary said.

"And my shop," Marianne said.

"I don't have my first class until seven p.m.," Lucy said. "I'm going to sleep all day tomorrow."

"Now I'm jealous of someone," Angie said. "I have a reading at eleven a.m."

"I'll be back tomorrow," Jaxer said, his gaze floating briefly to Deacon's before focusing on Cary. "In the meantime, good job recovering the thing. And keeping it safe. I'll see you after the hangover."

She snorted at that.

With a wink, he exited back through the French doors.

"He's so pretty," Lucy hummed as Cary closed the doors and locked them again.

"He's also capital T Trouble," Cary reminded Lucy. "Remember? We've had this conversation before."

"I like trouble," Lucy said.

"Yeah, you do," Marianne said. "Come on, drunk girl. Let's go crash for a few hours. Angie, you good in here?"

Angie waved a hand in the air. "Glorious," she said. "I promise not to turn you into a newt when you wake me up way too early."

"Thanks," Marianne said. She wrapped an arm around Lucy's waist to keep her upright, and they stumbled past Sasha and Deacon who stepped aside to let them pass.

"Show them the room," Deacon ordered Sasha without looking at her.

Sasha ducked her head and obeyed.

Cary scowled. "If she likes that, you shouldn't do it, you know. You're *my* mate."

"I'm not sure what you're talking about, but we'll get to that," he said, his tone emotionless.

"You're in for some serious talk," Angie said, her gaze on Deacon but her head leaning toward Cary.

"Don't know what he's mad about," Cary muttered. "I'm the aggravated party here."

"I think you mean aggrieved," Angie said.

"Also that one." Cary nodded. She hadn't stopped looking at Deacon either. His leopard was still close to the surface, but she noticed the glow had dimmed a little after Jaxer left.

"Fair enough," Angie said. "Oh wait, before you leave, I don't want to forget." She tripped over to the bed and pulled her courier bag up from where she'd left it on the floor, taking a small envelope out.

She dropped the bag unceremoniously—it clattered against the wooden floor, making Cary wonder what was inside—and then walked back to Cary, taking a slightly sideways route.

"The present from Jasmine," Angie said as she handed the envelope to Cary. "Open it." She glanced over her shoulder at Deacon. "I have a feeling you'll need it."

Cary snorted, but tore through the sealed envelope. Inside was a handwritten note, the script so neat and even Cary thought it looked printed. Unfortunately, the words swam before her as she tried to read them, so she tucked the note into her pocket for later. Then she pulled out a pretty little necklace. It was a slim gold chain with a small medallion hanging from it. Cary squinted at the medallion. It was the size of a quarter, but gold plated and shaped vaguely like a hand with three fingers pointing up and two thumbs curving out to the sides. The hand seemed to be decorated, but Cary couldn't see the details because she still couldn't master focusing her vision. But the cool metal felt lovely against her palm, and her throat tightened a little.

"This was a really sweet present," she murmured. "Remind me to thank Jasmine in person." She fingered the clasp, but didn't have the dexterity for it at the moment, so the necklace went into her pocket with the note. She'd put it on tomorrow. "Thanks for bringing this to me here," she said to Angie.

"Figured you could use a lucky charm," Angie said with a smile. "Anyway, I need to sleep before I pass out. I am also now jealous knowing your hangover won't last as long as mine." She hugged Cary. "Goodnight." With a glance at Deacon, she whispered, "Good luck."

Cary grunted and wobbled toward the door. She could hear Sasha across the hall asking Marianne and Lucy if they needed anything else.

"Sasha isn't joining us for this talk is she?" Cary asked Deacon.

"She's done for the night and off to bed," he said. "You and I can talk in our room."

"Your room," Cary pointed out, though why she wasn't sure. "*Our* room was this one but now it's Angie's room."

"You fought with my father?" Deacon asked, changing the subject so fast she nearly fell over. She must have really wobbled, because he reached out and took hold of her arm to steady her.

"Not sure it was technically a fight," she said. "But he managed a guilt trip better than my brother-in-law's mother."

"I'd be happy to eavesdrop on this conversation," Angie called from where she'd sprawled face down on the bed, "but I suspect you'd prefer privacy. Right?"

"Goodnight, Angie," Deacon said quietly and eased Cary from the room. He closed the door gently. His every move was extremely controlled and deliberate.

If she wasn't so annoyed with him, Cary might have been leery of his careful gestures.

If she'd been sober, she would have been.

*D*eacon didn't look at Sasha when she came back into the hall and closed Marianne and Lucy's door behind her. Cary glared at her, though, just because it felt necessary.

Sasha lifted her lip in a snarling grin.

Over his shoulder, Deacon said, "Goodnight, Sasha."

Nothing more. But it was enough. Sasha ducked her head again and murmured, "Goodnight, sir." Before heading back toward the main section of the house.

"Really?" Cary said. "You know that turns her on and you *still* do it. While I'm standing here? That's just rude. You want to dump me for her, you need to get the dumping part over with first. *Then* you can do that weird boss thing with her."

"I'm not dumping you for Sasha," he said quietly. "You're my mate."

Cary snorted. "Sure. Cause that's why you were so concerned with my feelings you let me know you were leaving the mansion all after-noon. Right?"

He frowned. "What do you mean?"

"Not even a fucking text," she said, hands on her hips. She listed to one side, but straightened her legs to stay upright. "Until your father told me, I had no idea you were even awake. Not to mention off galli-vanting with Sasha again. And then there was the dagger going miss-ing. And yeah, I know that's my job and it was my fault, but your dad didn't have to guilt trip me. And I'm sorry I accidentally apparently insulted your mother. I didn't mean to. But I guess I did cause that pissed your dad off big time."

Deacon took her arm and turned her slightly, leading her back down the corridor. "I wasn't gallivanting with Sasha," he said. "I was working. There was another issue."

"Right, right. Always an issue. An issue that requires you to spend inordinate amounts of time with *Sasha*." Cary snarled the woman's name. Then she tripped on nothing and only didn't hit the floor because Deacon still held her arm.

She scowled at the ground, trying to see what she'd tripped on. "Why is everything moving?" she asked.

Deacon sighed, the ground shifted dramatically, and Cary blinked.

It took her about ten seconds to realize Deacon had picked her up. Easily. She pressed her lips together. It was embarrassing to admit, but this was what he did that turned *her* on. The show of ridiculously amazing strength got her motor running. But now was not the time.

"I like that you like when I carry you," Deacon said quietly, his expression still not showing much emotion.

"Stop reading my scent," she huffed.

"No," he said.

"Why do you care how I feel?" she said, leaning into him because her head hadn't stopped spinning yet.

"You're my mate."

She snorted. "Right. That's been *so* obvious since we arrived."

"I can't be away from you for long without losing my mind. So yes, it has been obvious. To everyone but you."

"Bah." She was fading quickly, losing track of the conversation—which wasn't a very good way to win an argument—but she knew there was something important she had to say. She squinted hard at the air, trying to put the words in order.

"It can wait until you've sobered up," Deacon said.

"Don't. Read. My. Mind."

"I'm not. It's your scent, and I can't help it. Especially right now."

"What's different about now?" She sighed as her eyes drifted shut. He smelled really good. That was distracting. Was he doing it on purpose?

"I saw you with Jaxer. Again. And Diana said he came by earlier. He's been here a lot."

Cary snorted. "And you haven't been. You've been off with *Sasha*."

"Diana said they could all tell Jaxer wanted you."

"That was embarrassing," she said. "You all need to stop reading everyone's scents." She opened her eyes and looked up at him. "I like Alisha a lot. And Diana. Don't even care that you've slept with them. Why the hell is Sasha such a bitch?"

"I'm glad you're getting along with so many of my people," he said.

She was not so drunk that she missed how he'd glossed over that Sasha was a bitch. "Sasha wants you still," Cary said. "She threatens to kill the other women in your life. She thought she'd be queen. You need to stay away from her. Even if we break up, you need to stay away from her."

His arms tightened around her. "Why are you talking about us breaking up?"

"Cause, you want to. I can tell."

"You're misreading me."

"Maybe I want to."

His voice went very quiet. "Do you?"

She sighed. "Not really. But I don't like being ignored. Hate it actually. And I don't like the way you don't even think about me or my feelings. That doesn't seem like a great place to be in a relationship."

Hey! Those were the words she'd wanted to get out. And they came out in the right order. At least, she hoped they did because in her head that's exactly what she wanted to say.

"You know why I'm so controlled here," he said, still quietly.

"It's not your control," she said, leaning her head on his shoulder again. Most of her energy drained away, and she drifted for a while, just enjoying the ride in his arms.

"What is it then?" he asked, nudging her back to the conversation.

"I could probably take the iceman act," she said, "if it didn't also involve basically distancing yourself from me and ignoring me. No text to say you'd be gone? No note. No finding me to tell me in person. No consideration for my feelings. I'm in this house full of mostly strangers, and *your* family, and you've basically left me to my own devices since we arrived." Wow, that came out better than she'd expected. She was murmuring, though. Did he hear her?

"I'm sorry," he said.

So, guess he did hear her.

"I haven't meant to ignore you," he said. "I didn't think I was."

"You weren't on purpose," she allowed. "You just weren't thinking about me."

"I have been. All the time. Every moment."

She snorted. "Right. Sorry, bub, but your actions say otherwise."

"What happened with the dagger?"

She barked a laugh. "Changing the subject, huh? Cause you know I'm right."

"No, but you're too drunk to argue the point with right now."

"Uh uh."

"The dagger, Cary?"

"Oh, Jaxer came with a magic scabbard for it. But then it was gone."

"The scabbard or the dagger?"

"The dagger. Not on the bed. Not in the room." She sighed. "Made the mistake of asking your dad if one of the leopards would have taken it. Big big mistake. Got mad at me. No one would ever disobey Maria's orders. She doesn't need to use magic." She mumbled the last as she starting to drift off to sleep.

Deacon's arms tightened around her again. "What else happened?"

"Evan blamed me for the missing dagger. He was right. Shouldn't have left it alone. My job. My responsibility. Probably my jealousy that called it back here to begin with."

"My father wasn't right to make you feel responsible for the dagger," Deacon said. "And I'll be talking with him about that later."

She smiled into his neck. "You smell good. You shouldn't do that."

"Smell good?" A hint of amusement crept into his voice, the first she'd heard in a while.

"That's not fair, the smelling good. But I meant the talk to your dad part. He was just being honest. I got mad cause I felt guilty. Had time to think and can't blame him."

"I'm still going to talk with him. Where did you find the dagger? How did the girls get here and involved?"

"Searched the house, no sigh of it." She waited while he opened the door—while still easily holding her she noticed with a little shiver— then continued. "Girls showed up cause they're my best friends in the whole world, and they knew I needed them. And wine. Cause I definitely needed wine."

"I'm glad they were here for you," he said, kicking the door closed.

"Marianne brought me the *best* purse. Hides *everything* in it."

"What happened with the dagger? You didn't find it in the house?"

"Nope. Needle in a haystack."

"Where did you find it?"

"Angie had a brilliant idea. It was hiding from its scabbard." She sighed. "Great idea. Worked."

"You said your jealousy brought it back to you," he said. He sat on the couch in his living room, keeping her on his lap. "Why did you say that?"

She snuggled closer because he was warm and she was ready to sleep now that they'd stopped moving.

"Cary?" His voice broke into her doze. "Why would your jealousy bring the dagger here?"

"Hmm? Oh. It's the Jealousy one. Feeds on blood, sacrifice, and jealousy according to Jaxer. Lots and lots of jealousy. Lot of it around these days, you know."

"I've noticed. How did you find the dagger?"

"Angie's a genius," she murmured.

"So you said. But not how you found the dagger."

She drifted back toward sleep, only to have him squeeze her awake again. She scowled up at him. "Stop that."

"Why is Angie a genius?" he asked, his tone quiet. "She figured out how to locate the dagger?"

"Yup. She's a genius." Cary started to fall asleep again.

"One last question," he said, adjusting her so she was sitting a little straighter. "The rest can wait until you've slept this off."

"Fine." She nodded.

"You have the dagger back," he said.

"That wasn't a question," she pointed out.

"It's secure?"

"Yup. Safe and sound in my pocket where no one but me can get it and it's in its scabbard that I think was made for it or so the Nags say and now I'm going to sleep we can talk in the morning goodnight."

The last thing she heard was Deacon sighing, but she was too tired to get annoyed.

ary woke, still a little wobbly with the room spinning, long enough to say goodbye to her friends and see them out. Then she stumbled back up to bed and collapsed for the rest of the morning and well into the afternoon. Deacon had taken her clothes off and put her into her jammies, which under different circumstances would have amused her, but given the way her world spun, she was just grateful to be comfortable. He was still in bed with her when she went to say goodbye to the girls but gone by the time she got back. She decided she'd worry about that later. Like, maybe even tomorrow.

When she finally forced her eyes open at three in the afternoon, she was still groggy, but she'd slept off the hangover completely. Yay Protector healing magic! Now it was just the tiredness hangover making her head feel muggy and full of cotton.

A hot shower helped.

Coffee would help more.

She hesitated to go into the kitchen, though. She wasn't sure what to say to Evan if she saw him again. And she dreaded meeting Maria. For reasons she was still working out.

In fact, as she let the hot water in the shower soak away her muscle aches, she realized there were a lot of her feelings she still hadn't worked out. She was out of sorts here, uncomfortable, and until last night with the girls, had been feeling lonely. Spending time with Diana, Nicky, Jillian, and everyone yesterday afternoon had been nice, but they were still Deacon's people. They accepted her, for now. But if it came down to a choice, they would be on the side of their prince and their own kind.

And she wasn't one of them. Even if she was supposedly their prince's mate.

She toweled off, wondering what she'd expected when she came here. Certainly not Sasha. Or the dagger floating around to complicate things. Getting in between the leopards and the cougars hadn't been part of the plan either, although that had—probably—worked in her favor. She had to think at least some of the leopards appreciated her Protector efforts.

Still…

She was lonely here. And she hadn't thought she could be lonely surrounded by so damned many people. Especially after only three, surprisingly busy, days.

Weird. Very weird.

She needed to get home to her dogs, her house, her life. She could figure out the rest from there. And thanks to sleeping all day, she really only had to get through another day and a half before she could get home. She stared at her reflection, at the slight circles under her eyes. She hadn't realized she was this much of a homebody. She didn't feel like this when she went to visit her sister in New York. But then, there she was surrounded by family—and a nephew and two nieces that thought she was the cool aunt.

If she stayed with Deacon, if they somehow got through the revelations of this trip and continued to be a couple, she'd be spending a lot more time here, and with the leopards in general.

Was that the future she wanted?

A noise from outside in the living room jerked her out of her revere. Assuming it had to be Deacon, she wrapped the towel around herself and headed into the bedroom for her clothes. She poked her head into the living room to tell him she'd be out in a sec, but Deacon wasn't the one waiting for her.

"Maria," Cary greeted. "You, uh, caught me off guard."

"I'm sorry to disturb your shower. But I think we need to talk."

She sounded neither sorry no hesitant about what they needed to do. Cary dragged in a deep breath and nodded. Better to get this over with now. They'd been long overdue a talk anyway.

Though, Cary really could have used some coffee first.

She pulled on her jeans and a long-sleeved t-shirt, then wrapped her hair up with a clip since it was still wet and she didn't want it dripping down her back. She might have taken the time to braid it or something equally neat, but she didn't want to keep Maria waiting—despite the temptation to stall and hide in the bedroom.

When she padded, still barefoot, out to the living room, Maria was lounging on the couch, seemingly unconcerned with the upcoming discussion.

Cary sat across from her in a comfy seat. "I owe Evan, and you, an apology," she started.

"I was about to say that Evan owes you an apology."

Cary raised her brows. "You were? Because he doesn't. He was right. I brought something dangerous into this house, and then I didn't guard it properly."

"You trusted my word inside my own home. You should have been able to do that without worry. But you don't know us very well, either. So it's only natural you would question if one of the people here might have disobeyed."

"That really pissed Evan off when I asked," Cary said.

"You hit a sensitive subject with your innocent question. From the beginning, the implication—and accusations—that I use my magic inappropriately with my people, that the only way I can control them is by taking away their free will, has followed us. It's a sore spot for Evan because he knows better. And he tends to overreact to even a hint of the suggestion that I force the leopards to obey me through magic." Maria smiled slightly. "He's my mate. He's very protective. You'll understand that better when you and Deacon get through this…early period."

Cary snorted and thought *if* they got through this period. But she kept that observation to herself.

"You're having more doubts," Maria said.

Didn't ask. Said.

"Of course," Cary said bluntly. "But you knew that. Everyone knows that because you all keep scenting everything I'm feeling."

"Is that what's bothering you? Being here?"

"Being here is just making the fact that I'm not a part of your world very clear." Cary sighed. "I had human friends here last night—"

"Yes," Maria said. "Sasha wasn't happy you'd brought humans into our home."

"Exactly!" Cary sat up a little straighter and pointed at Maria. "Diana didn't seem to mind, but I'm sure Sasha wasn't the only one who found it inappropriate given how guarded you are about this place. And then there's my faery mentor who keeps showing up."

"Who is in love with you and sets off Deacon's jealousy," Maria said.

Again, didn't ask.

Cary groaned. "And everyone now knows that. I haven't been here four days yet. But I keep stepping on toes. And my toes keep getting stepped on."

"It's an adjustment for all of us," Maria said.

Cary held her gaze for a long moment before plunging in. "From the beginning, the fact that I'm a shapeshifter's mate and I'm not a shapeshifter has been a thing. And if you were an ordinary mother, or Deacon was an ordinary shapeshifter, maybe I would be less worried. But the more I learn, the more I worry. I worry that I won't be able to adjust to the way he is here —he's not this way with me at home. He wasn't even this way when we were surrounded by his people in Portland rescuing the kids."

"He explained that? He would have been focused on the battle and that would have calmed his leopard."

Cary waved a hand in the air. "Yes, he explained." She ran her hands up through her still wet hair, loosening it from the clip a little and no doubt making it look weird. But she already felt awkward and inelegant next to Maria, so what the hell. "I've heard all the explanations. I should be over this by now and just getting on with it. But every step I make here seems to complicate things more." She frowned a little and finally met Maria's gaze again. "I don't feel like me."

"The mate bond with Deacon has an effect on you both. Less on you than him, but it's still there. The heightened situation here has probably just highlighted some of those chemical fluctuations."

Despite her hesitance to discuss this with Maria, Cary needed to know for sure. "My irrational jealousy of Sasha isn't me either. I haven't had that reaction to any of Deacon's previous—" She stumbled over a word. Girlfriends seemed wrong after what Alisha and Diana had told her. Lovers seemed too…much for a conversation with his mother. She settled on, "I haven't had that reaction to either Alisha or Diana. I don't like that I'm this way around Sasha for no good reason. Is that one of the chemical fluctuations of the mate bond? Because it kind of sucks."

"Jealousy is common in the early stages." Maria shrugged. "And Sasha has always been attached to Deacon in a way his other women have not. It's natural you want to stake your claim and make clear she's unwelcome."

"She's your assistant," Cary pointed out the obvious. "She will be in my life if Deacon and I get through all this. I do not want to feel this way all the time."

"And you won't, any more than Deacon will continue to rage against your mentor's feelings for you, once the bond between you is satisfactorily secure." She held Cary's gaze. "It's not yet, as evidenced by your doubts and hesitance. Deacon's leopard is aware of that, even if his human side doesn't understand. As long as you doubt your future with him, you'll both have to deal with these side issues."

"Well that's not good," Cary said. "I can't just wave a magic wand and get rid of all my fears and insecurities." Although, if she had that kind of magic wand, she could make a fortune renting it out.

"You're not meant to," Maria said, her tone patient. "This period is necessary to any mate bond among my people. It's just the way it is."

It was on the tip of Cary's tongue to say the way it "is" sucked, but she decided that was a no-win comment. Maria's explanations did help settle Cary's worry about her own reactions and feelings since being here, though. In a way, it was like a weird kind of PMS, all chemistry and chaotic hormones. When that all calmed down, she and Deacon both would be back to normal and all would be well.

Of course, "well" depended on if she survived her job this year.

She gave Maria crooked smile. "It's funny, but I've only felt like myself here in those moments when I've had to do my job. Yet the fact that I've had to *keep* doing my job when I'm on a vacation highlights yet another problem. My life is always like this—mayhem and dangerous."

"You think Deacon's life is not?"

"I think before me, there was a lot more control and routine."

Maria shrugged. "Maybe. But still. He's not unfamiliar with danger, my dear."

Cary snorted. "That's not what I meant really. Frankly, I don't know what I mean."

Maria titled her head, considering Cary for a long moment. "There's a lot you don't understand, and you're confused. Since arriving, you've seen the man you thought you knew in a completely different environment—the environment he grew up in—and he's not acting as you expected. No one else seems to notice the difference. You learn he has magic you didn't know about. You're thrown into our internal conflict. And you're confronted with some of his ex-lovers immediately. It's only natural you'd be feeling off center, Cary. The mate bond, at this stage, is a fragile and volatile thing. It's this period when mates decide if they love or hate each other."

Cary barked out a laugh that didn't feel like humor. "What happens to the ones who hate each other?"

"Do you hate Deacon?"

"No," she said bluntly.

"He doesn't hate you either," Maria said.

"Ah, but can he love me?"

"You don't think he can?"

"I don't honestly know." She shrugged. "And it's too early to worry about that. We haven't been together for very long, and every single date we've been on has gotten interrupted by my job."

"You need a proper holiday."

Cary laughed with more humor this time. "Do you get time off from being queen of the leopards?"

Maria dipped her head to one side, a move at once full of acceptance and resignation.

"Yeah, I don't get time off either," Cary said.

"Are you more concerned with Deacon's impact on your life, or yours on his?"

"Both. But that's always the way with new relationships, isn't it? I just know my life to date has not been very accommodating to romantic relationships. And…" She waved her hand vaguely. "Here, I'm seeing that Deacon's life hasn't been accommodating to relationships either."

"No one's life ever is," Maria said. "Especially in our worlds. But they happen and they are successful. Look at Lucas and Diana."

Cary smiled at that. "And Nicky and Jillian seem very happy."

"They are. But their first year after discovering they were mates was difficult as well. All of us have a complicated first year with our mates. It takes time to adjust to the bond."

"Even more so when one of the mates isn't a shifter?"

Maria gave another nod of acceptance and resignation.

But that was a rabbit hole Cary didn't want to go down just yet. "Let's change direction here for a minute. I'd like to know more about Deacon's magic. Is there anything he's capable of that you two haven't told me about yet?"

"Beyond what I've already said, the rest is for him to tell you."

"Okay, fine," Cary said, narrowing her eyes. "Then tell me more about your magic. I mean, I don't want to risk stepping in it with Evan again."

Maria smiled. "Very clever woman."

That made Cary snort. "You'd be the first to think so. Mostly, I get told I'm not as clever as I think I am."

Maria chuckled, a sound that made Cary blink. She'd seen Maria smile—though in a very controlled way—but she wasn't sure she'd heard her laugh before. The surprise of it made her grin in return.

"I'm very relieved my son found you," Maria said quietly, so quietly Cary almost didn't hear her.

"Don't be so quick to that assessment. Remember, we're still having a *lot* of problems."

"Would you have gotten involved with him if he wasn't your mate?"

"We're supposed to be talking about your magic," Cary said, her cheeks heating.

"We'll get there. This first."

Cary couldn't meet Maria's gaze when she said, "No. I would have run as far and as fast as I could from him."

"Why?"

"He's too... Too. Too gorgeous. Too perfect. He protects animals for a living for gods' sake. He's a shapeshifter and magnificent and..." She sighed. "Every man Jaxer has ever introduced me to in this weird world that's been as stunning as Deacon has been big trouble for me." She winced. "And more often than I'd like to admit, they end up wanting to kill me. So, no, I wouldn't have tried to get involved with Deacon if not for the mate bond. But to be fair—" she raised a hand to stop Maria from commenting, "—he wouldn't have gotten involved with me either. He wouldn't have looked at me twice if not for the scent thing. In fact, when we first met, he thought I was a witch who'd cursed him to be attracted to me." She lowered her chin. "That is not the sentiments of a man who *wants* a relationship with a woman. So it's not just me. We're both in this because of chemistry, not actual choice."

"But you stay in it because of choice. You know you can break the bond."

"So I've been told, although not from Deacon initially."

"That's not surprising."

Cary made a face. "Anyway." She didn't want to talk about this with Deacon's mother anymore. She didn't want to talk about breaking her bond with Deacon while she was sober. "Back to your magic. Is there anything I don't know about it?"

Maria shrugged. "You know I can kill with a thought. You know I can control them, against their wills if I want to. I'm physically stronger and faster. My senses are better. I shift faster than a typical leopard." She smiled slightly and gestured at her outfit. "And I can manifest clothes while I shift. I'm better at reading the scents of my people, and I know where they are at all times."

"Deacon did that when we were rescuing the kids," Cary said. "He could tell where everyone was before we went in. He said he was able to communicate with them then too, although not by scent. He said he could give them a mental nudge to convey what he wanted them to do."

Maria nodded slightly. "I can nudge them with a mental touch, as well, although my range isn't as wide as his. I can't read minds in the traditional sense, or communicate telepathically, but I can pick up enough information from their scents, and pass on enough information in mine, that it can sometimes appear as if we communicate without talking, even without the mental nudges."

"Do you know where your people are because of their scents? Or do you know the way, say, tiger shifters do. You just have a sense of them."

"I have a sense of them. Right now, I can tell you where everyone in the house is. Each child, each adult. I know where the patrols are in the grounds. I know where my Michael is, down at the clinic." She narrowed her eyes. "And my oldest daughter is currently out running in the woods—in her leopard form."

Cary hadn't even known Jocelyn had arrived yet. She still hadn't met any of Deacon's siblings except Michael, and Caitlin back in Portland, and she had to wonder if that was just an accident of timing, or if the bulk of his siblings were avoiding her for some reason. There were six sisters in all and eight brothers. The fact that she hadn't run into *any* of them seemed suspicious.

But she'd have to worry about that later.

"You can tell when they're in human or animal form?" she asked Maria.

"I can," Maria said. "And I often sense their emotions, even without being able to smell them."

"That's got to be hard." Cary had met a few empaths in her time as a Protector. Without barriers and psychic walls built up, an empath could go crazy from absorbing all the emotions of the people around them.

"I've learned how to filter it all," Maria said. "The sounds, the smells, the extra perceptions. Most shifters have to learn how to dampen their senses to live in the modern world. I just have to cut mine back a little more than everyone else."

Which meant Deacon did too. "You help Deacon when I'm not around to keep his control. You control him the same way you can control the others." Deacon hadn't actually answered that question directly. She still didn't know how the process worked between them.

"With Deacon, things are a bit more complicated. Basically, I compel him to maintain some civilized behaviors—or help him to hold his leopard form and not change back to his human form. And I block his magic from reaching the others."

"You can do that?"

"Most of the time." Her gaze flicked away from Cary briefly, which put Cary on alert.

"Most of the time?"

Maria sighed. "It's getting more difficult to protect the others from him. He's a lot stronger than he wants to admit or accept. And the longer he denies his own powers, the longer it takes him to regain his sense of control, the worse it gets. The only thing that truly balances him is you."

"I hate that part, you know," Cary said.

"I know," Maria said. "It's a terrible responsibility. Especially when you're both still so new to each other and your bond. Most couples don't have to worry about that."

"Did you and Evan?"

"Yes." Maria smiled a little, her gaze turning inward before she refocused on Cary. "But I'd already been practicing and using my magic for years by the time I met my mate. I had learned to control it for what it was, rather than suppressing it the way Deacon does. It gave me an advantage. Still, it was a tricky time."

"You want Deacon to use his magic, to train it," Cary said.

"I do. And we've had that argument for years. He's stubborn. He'll do what he will. But it would be safer for him if he just gave in to the inevitable."

Cary mulled that over for a few moments.

Into the silence, Maria said, "I know you still think being a human is a drawback in your relationship with my son, but I really was relieved to hear it."

Maria had said that before, when she'd first told Cary about Deacon's powers. "Because he can't kill me on accident, right?" Cary said. "And our kids won't be too dangerous."

"Important considerations," Maria said. "Mostly, though, I'm pleased you don't give in to him easily. That's good for him. He's so used to getting what he wants from everyone. It's good for his character that you won't roll over and accept his whims."

Cary snorted a very unladylike response.

"Despite the dangers of your job, and from a purely selfish, mother's perspective," Maria continued, "I'm also relieved you're a Protector."

"I don't understand," Cary said.

"So long as he's with you, he'll be safe."

Cary raised her brows. "You've gotten a taste of my life, and I'm sure he's told you some stories about the last few months. He is *not* safe with me."

"Of course he is. At your side, he's protected from anyone who wants to hurt him."

"Only if he lets me protect him," Cary said.

Maria dipped her head to one side in a gentle shrug. "True enough. But in the worst of situations, I know you can keep him alive."

She felt her lips twitch. "You think he'd be annoyed to know his mother was hoping his girlfriend will protect him from danger?"

"He knows me too well to think I'd hope for anything else."

Cary chuckled. "Thank you, for talking with me and telling me more about all of this leopard stuff. And for forgiving all my missteps."

"There haven't been any to forgive," Maria said. She glanced at the door. "Deacon is here. He's waiting. We should relieve his tension."

Cary frowned at the door. "Did he hear all this?"

"No. The rooms are sound dampened or no shifter would be able to sleep in this house. But he can sense me in here with you."

She went to open the door and let Deacon into his own room. He was standing across the hall from the door, his head ducked, hands in his jeans' pockets. A tray rested on the floor next to him. He looked up, just his eyes, and caught her gaze with his. Cary pulled in a sudden breath. Damn but he was sexy. She knew this, but sometimes the reality of it caught her off guard. Her heart thumped a little harder as she stared back. And the fact that his mother was no doubt able to sense and scent her reaction was just embarrassing.

"I brought coffee," he said, his voice deep.

That dropped her right out of awe and into another kind of lust. "You are the absolute best of all possible people to me right now, and I need that inside immediately."

His mouth ticked up in a little smile. He bent and scooped up the tray, brushing past her as he carried it inside. She shivered at the physical contact, but that lusty reaction still didn't beat out her need for coffee.

Maria rose from her place on the couch. "I'll leave you two alone." To Deacon, "Sasha and I can handle the last details." She glanced at Cary then back at her son. "I think you two need some time together."

He didn't comment except to dip his head in a slight nod.

To Cary, she said, "We have a family dinner the night after the ball, just for the family. A kind of celebration. I understand you haven't met all of my children yet. We'd be very pleased if you'd join us."

The fact that Maria was including her in a family event, after everything, after all the things still left hanging, choked Cary up. She nodded her acceptance because she didn't have the words.

Maria closed the door on her way out, leaving Cary and Deacon alone, staring at each other across the coffee table.

After a minute of this, Cary gave in to the rich scent of coffee. "Thanks for thinking of this," she said, sitting on the couch and pouring herself a cup.

"I wasn't about to have a serious conversation with you while you were nursing a hangover without any coffee."

She chuckled. "Actually, the hangover is gone. But the coffee will definitely make me a happier person to talk with." She met his gaze. He was still standing across the coffee table from her. "You better sit or I'm going to get nervous."

He nodded, but didn't sit immediately. And she started to get nervous.

"What?" she asked.

"I'm sorry," he said.

"For what, exactly?"

"That I didn't better prepare you for how I would be here. That I didn't tell you when I left yesterday. That I haven't been around much to help you feel more comfortable in my home."

"That's a good list of things to apologize for. Thank you for that. Now sit down."

He finally complied, with a faint smile. "Do you accept my apology?"

"Probably. I'm still thinking about it. Why didn't you let me know you were going out yesterday?"

"It didn't occur to me." He shrugged and leaned back into the couch. He'd sat next to her but there was still a few feet of space between them. "I don't typically have to tell anyone where I am or where I'm going when I'm here."

"Because your mother always knows where you are?"

He let out a breath. "That too. Also, because I'm not used to accounting for my whereabouts."

"Me neither. But, you know, relationships do require that kind of communication. Or so I'm told."

"I hate that Jaxer keeps showing up here," he said.

"That was a change of topic. Where did it come from?"

"Seeing him with you. Again. Last night."

"And I had to see you with Sasha. Again. Last night. You've been with her a lot more than with me on this trip." She scowled. "Also, stop bossing her around because she likes it way too much. Like in a sexual way. That is not okay."

"You said that while you were drunk. I thought you were making a joke."

"I wasn't joking! Angie read it in her aura. If Angie could see it, you could smell it."

He frowned. "I can't actually. Sasha is…unique among the leopards. She doesn't give off a scent."

"Huh?" Cary stopped with her coffee mug halfway to her mouth.

He shrugged. "She doesn't have a scent. None of her emotions show up that way. She doesn't even have a natural scent. She wears perfume, but otherwise, she doesn't smell like anything at all."

"That's definitely unique. And strange. Everything has a scent, doesn't it? I'm not shifter, but still…"

"Most things, yes. And her disorder is extremely rare in leopards."

"Why disorder? Why not advantage? I mean, she's surrounded by shifters all the time and usually you all can read each other but no one can read her. No one can invade her privacy by knowing her emotions." And now Cary had another reason to be jealous of Sasha because that sounded like a great advantage from where she stood.

"Being able to disguise her thoughts and emotions would be a benefit if that were the only thing scent did for us. But a lot of our interactions, a lot of our social connections, a lot of our ties come about through scent. It's integral to our society in ways that can be hard to explain. But simply put, because the others can't scent her, it's hard for her to form bonds among our people. And because her sense of smell is just fine, she's aware of the distance between her and the rest of us."

Cary took a moment to process the news, not entirely happy that it made her feel some sympathy for the woman.

"Wait." A strange thought occurred to her. "But that means, if she has a mate out there in the wide world, they wouldn't be able to recognize her, right? I mean, without that whole scent thing, you wouldn't have known I was your mate. It's all in the pheromones, isn't it?"

Deacon blinked and glanced away. "Huh. I never really thought about that. You're right, though. Without the chemical signals that we read through scent, her mate wouldn't recognize her."

"Would *she* still know her mate?" Cary asked, a sick sort of suspicion clawing at her. "I mean, you just said she picks up scents and reads other people the way a typical shifter can."

"She can. And I suppose she would know her own mate."

"Deacon," Cary asked very quietly, "can you have more than one mate?"

He opened his mouth to answer, but then his gaze sharpened. "You think I'm Sasha's mate? I'm not. I'm yours."

"Can *you* have more than one?" she asked again.

"No. Cary, no. You're the one."

She searched her memory. "You told me once, that if mates don't like each other enough, they can break the bond. You and your mother, and Jaxer, have all pointed out that our bond is easier to break because I'm human. And everyone has told me that leopards can have relationships with people not their mates. That not everyone even finds their mate."

"That's true. And if Sasha wanted something from me, it would be that. But she's not my mate."

"You're sure? She acts like she is. She threatens any other woman who gets involved with you. She's possessive and clingy to you—even if you don't notice it. And she's made no bones about hating me since I arrived." Cary shrugged. "The feeling is mutual there."

"If she thought she was my mate," Deacon said, "she would have told me. A long time ago."

"You're sure? Because I'm not. Maybe she assumed you knew.

Maybe she assumed you could tell despite the lack of smell because of your magic."

"If she was my mate," he said, "I wouldn't have this bond with you. I wouldn't be so off center and tied up in knots over you. My control wouldn't be hanging by a thread either."

"Yeah," Cary said with a sigh. "That is our issue, isn't it? We wouldn't be together if not for the bond."

"You need to stop using that excuse," Deacon said, a slight edge in his voice. "Maybe we wouldn't have taken the time, maybe we would have run away from our attraction to each other, but it's there and there's more between us than just a chemical bond now." He glanced away, the muscles in his jaw flexing as he clenched his teeth. "I'm still learning how to do this," he said after a moment. "Especially here, where I'm not used to it. But that doesn't mean I want us to end. If you do, you need to tell me now and get it over with. Stop making excuses."

"Me? I'm not the one who's been ignoring *you* on this trip."

He ran a hand through his hair. "I apologized for that already."

She relaxed into the couch, cradling her hot coffee mug. "I know. And I'm sorry I keep throwing it at you. I'm off center and tied up in knots over you, too."

He leaned in and kissed her, the move surprising her into stillness for just a moment. He gently took the coffee cup from her hand and set it aside, then cupped her face in his palms and met her gaze.

"You need to understand," he murmured. "Since we met, you've been the only woman for me. Now and always. Bond or not. The rest of this is noise. Things we can deal with. If you're willing."

She held his wrists, holding his gaze. "Despite all my fears, my insecurities, and my worries, I'm willing. I'm scared," she whispered. "But willing."

He kissed her again, slowly and for a long time.

29

To Cary's surprise, Deacon spent the rest of the evening with her. They ate dinner in the kitchen, with only the occasional interruption from other people passing through. Afterward, they went for a walk outside, taking a path through the surrounding woods at the west side of the house.

"You're sure this is safe?" she asked. The cougars were still out there somewhere, and since they hadn't attacked all day, she'd been feeling that waiting-for-the-other-shoe-to-drop sensation as it got darker.

"You don't think I can kick a few cougar asses?" Deacon asked.

The humor in his tone, the mock offense, made her grin. He'd kept a wall up all through dinner, because there were so many leopards around. But out here, in the fresh cold air, he seemed more relaxed.

"Since I'm here," she said, "you won't have to."

He took her hand, tugging her a little closer as they walked.

The trees were thick around them but the path was clear and easy to manage, despite the darkness. She let him lead, because he could see a lot better than she could, and when he walked her around the muddy spots, she smiled.

"Not exactly the vacation I promised, is it?" he asked.

She snorted. "That hasn't been entirely your fault." She patted her jacket where the dagger was still safely stored. "I can't wait to get rid of this thing."

"That means Jaxer again, doesn't it?"

"Maybe not, since there's a lot of jealousy floating around us all at the moment. I probably need to pass it off to the Nags myself."

"Will they come here for it?"

"I thought they might, but since they haven't shown up yet, I suppose I'll have to wait until we get home."

"What's preventing them from coming here?"

Deacon glanced down at her and she noticed his eyes had a faint golden glow to them, but not the scary his-leopard-was-too-close-to-the-surface glow. Just the natural coloring of his eyes in the faint moonlight spilling through the tree branches.

"Not sure," she said to his question. "Maybe they want me away from the source of my jealousy first? Maybe they're busy and can't be bothered. Who knows? They aren't very good at letting me in on their motives."

He let out a faint chuckle at her dry tone.

"They're waiting for you to get back to Portland," Jaxer said, his voice coming out of the darkness ahead of them and startling a gasp of surprise from Cary.

Deacon cursed. "Why are you here? We're not looking for you."

"You were asking about the dagger," Jaxer said as if that explained it all.

Cary shook her head. "Go away. If the Nags want to wait until I get back to Portland, fine. You could have told me that at another time."

"When?"

"I don't know," she said, her tone harsh.

"I didn't want you to worry."

"Right." She sighed. But since he was here anyway... "Why are they waiting? I'd really like to be rid of this thing."

"Frankly," Jaxer said, "they don't want you taking it out of that magic pocket of yours while you're here. Since it seems to be doing the job of keeping the dagger quiet—"

"I thought that's what the scabbard was supposed to do," she interrupted.

"It does," Jaxer said. "But keeping the whole thing contained in your pocket keeps it from accessing this realm."

"Once the Nags have it, it won't be in this realm. Doesn't that seem even safer?" She was not convinced her *pocket* was the absolute best solution here, even if Marianne's magic was spectacular.

Jaxer glanced at Deacon before answering. "Here, there's more of the emotion that dagger loves. In Portland, there's only a few points of trouble around you. And your jealousy won't be as severe."

"Not as severe? As in, I'll still feel it?" She groaned. "Ugh." She'd been hoping it would just go away since it was primarily a chemical reaction. Obviously, she wasn't going to be that lucky.

Jaxer shrugged. "Sorry about that. Chemistry is a bitch."

He looked like he really meant that last sentence.

"So," she said, "the super dangerous cursed blade stays in my pocket until *I'm* not so overwhelmed by jealousy?" She stared at a tree. "I suppose I could sneak back to Portland tomorrow, before the event. That way the thing is safe and gone well before we have an entire party to worry about."

"I need to be here," Deacon said quietly. "I can't go with you. And I can't send the others away again. There's not enough time."

She dropped her head back and rubbed her hands over her face. "I forgot about that." Resigned, she said, "I guess I'll just have to keep my jacket with me in the meantime. Don't want to take any risks with it." She looked at Jaxer. "I won't be back in Portland for another two days. Are we *sure* the dagger will be safe until then? Maybe I can try and get over my jealousy?"

Jaxer tucked his chin back and gave her a look so disbelieving she winced.

"Fine," she said. "Just trying to find a better answer to all this."

Unfortunately, the only real answer to her jealousy was time for her bond with Deacon to settle. Or not being his mate anymore.

"One last question before you leave," she said to Jaxer. "Did the Nags ever say why the woman who picked this thing up in Vegas caught its attention? I'm pretty sure she didn't know Becky Hall before the poker game with Becky's dad. No real reason for jealousy there."

"Since at the time they assumed the dagger was the Greed blade, they assumed Becky was just a convenient sacrifice to her own father's greed," Jaxer said. "Your guess is as good as mine now. And since the Nags are already out of sorts because they got the details of which blade this one was wrong, they aren't talking about it."

"That's not a helpful way for me to learn," Cary pointed out.

She supposed she might not ever know for sure unless she found the woman and asked—not likely since she didn't even know the woman's name. She hated not knowing, though. It was annoying. But knowing why people did what they did was not absolutely necessary for her job. She was just curious and liked to understand if she could.

"Okay, well, that's all settled then," she said. If a little unsatisfactorily. "So we're done here." When Jaxer didn't move, she said, "You can go away now."

"I have more news," he said, but his gaze was on Deacon.

"The wizard?" Cary asked, stepping between them to get Jaxer to focus on her.

"Still can't find the older one," Jaxer said, "but guess who was spotted lurking around his old apartment building late last night?"

"Sheldon?" She straightened.

Jaxer's smile was not pleasant. "He was gone by the time I got there, but a friend who's been keeping an eye on the place for me confirmed he went in last night around two in the morning. My friend didn't see him leave."

"Well hell," Cary said. "What is he up to?"

"If I find him again, I'll be sure to ask," Jaxer said, his tone serious.

She blinked at him. He didn't often come across as scary, despite the fact that he had the magic and skills to be terrifying if he wanted to be. He preferred playing up his more attractive qualities. But in that moment, he sounded very very serious, and not a little scary. She didn't envy Sheldon if Jaxer ever got to him.

"If you find him," Deacon said, "call me. He and I have some unfinished business."

Well that wouldn't be good. "You two remember he's just a teenager," Cary said, pointing a finger at both of them. "An evil asshole of a teenager, but still… No torturing him and no killing him except in self defense. Right?" She gave them both a look. "I do *not* want to have to protect that shit from you guys. Do not make me do it."

Deacon glanced away but nodded. Jaxer took a few beats longer, then gave a shrug she took as acceptance. She narrowed her eyes at him and he raised his hands, palms facing her.

"I promise," he said. "No torture or killing unless he tries to kill me first."

"Good." She put her hands on her hips and looked between the two men. "So? Are we all settled here? We know Sheldon is alive. We know I have to hold on to the dagger for another couple of days. And we know we're all experiencing way way too much jealousy. Are we good?"

Jaxer snorted at her question.

Deacon took her hand and tugged her a few steps closer so they were almost touching. She raised her brows at the gesture. He shrugged. "You said it. Way way too much jealousy going on right now."

She huffed, but didn't move away from him. To Jaxer, she said, "Thank you for letting me know the Nags aren't going to show up and that my wizard problem is still a problem. I'll talk to you after we get home."

It was a dismissal and they all knew it. Jaxer held her gaze a moment longer than was entirely comfortable. She practically felt him leaning toward her, but he didn't touch her—which was good given the way Deacon was clenching her hand. Instead, Jaxer touched his fingers to his brow and disappeared back into the trees.

A moment later, she knew he was gone.

"This trip isn't working out the way I'd hoped," Deacon said quietly.

She looked at him. "What had you hoped for?"

"Jaxer and your wizard issues to go away," he said bluntly.

She barked out a laugh. "Such wishful thinking."

He pulled her into his arms. Out here, where they weren't surrounded by leopards, he'd reverted to touching her a lot. She preferred this. She liked touched him a lot, too.

"Next trip," he said, "we'll take a real vacation. Somewhere not surrounded by shifters and where your bosses and Jaxer will leave you alone."

"More wishful thinking," she murmured. "At least for this year. But I do like the way you think."

He smiled faintly, just before kissing her. She sighed into the kiss, ignoring the unsettling awareness that they weren't out of the woods—no pun intended—yet.

3 0

The hotel hosting the gala was a relatively new establishment on the outskirts of town, a short drive along the I5 back toward Portland. The entrance to the ballroom, a separate entry from the main lobby of the hotel, was glowing in the dark, clear night. The weather gods were smiling on them all, as there was no rain predicted until sometime tomorrow, which meant all the rich people in their fancy clothing didn't have to worry about getting wet.

According to Deacon, the donors had all originally been placed in the same hotel where the event would be held. Since they'd had to move venues for the gala itself, everyone had to be driven in. Sasha had made a point of telling Cary how Deacon had manifested another miracle by arranging enough limos to accommodate everyone.

Hearing the news from Sasha made it infinitely more difficult for Cary to be proud of Deacon for his miracle working for some reason. And that had just pissed her off.

Fortunately, spending the afternoon with Diana, Jillian, Nicky, Sherri, Alisha and about twelve other leopard women getting dressed up for the gala had put Cary in a significantly better mood by the time she rolled up to the hotel in her own limo. Deacon and his family had gone ahead, to be there when the first guests arrived. Cary had agreed to follow, sharing a ride with Lucas and Diana and their kids. She hadn't even seen Deacon in his tux yet—a sight she was looking forward to more than she cared to admit.

As they all climbed out of the limo, Cary stared up at the building, letting her senses open. Despite Sasha's reassurances that the security here would prevent a cougar attack, Cary still felt a touch edgy. There hadn't been another move by the rival shifters for the last couple of days, and given the recent escalation, Cary didn't trust that quiet.

She smoothed her dress down over her hips and adjusted her hold on her miracle clutch. Because her leather jacket didn't exactly go with her dress, and because they weren't going to be outside for long, she'd wrapped the jacket up and stuffed it into the clutch. The fact that it fit and didn't even make the clutch bulge was a testament to Marianne's skills. Although, given the clutch also linked to someone's wine cellar, Cary kind of hoped she hadn't inadvertently put her jacket in someone else's reach.

Lucas took Diana's arm and they all climbed the short set of stairs to the light covered doorway. To her amusement, Miguel took Cary's arm, imitating his father and walking beside her like he was a grown up, looking extremely proud of himself. The gesture was so sweet, Cary melted inside.

Past the door a short hallway led into the ballroom. Red carpets and warm winter greenery decorated the space. Hotel staff took coats from those wearing them and ushered the adults into the ballroom, while the children had a party in a second, smaller conference room to the right. Lucas and Diana's oldest daughter, Lily, led her siblings to the kids' party, giving Cary a thumbs up as she left.

Cary grinned in return. Lily had done a pretty stellar job on Cary's makeup. Since Cary was too lazy to wear makeup most of the time, and therefore only had the most basic of skills with the stuff, Lily's help had been greatly appreciated.

Once they were sure the kids were safely inside their party, Lucas and Diana went into the main ballroom, and Cary trailed behind, hunting the crowd for sight of Deacon. The room was already full of bejeweled patrons of the animal shelters. The huge, airy space was decorated in soft creams and gold, the wood floor polished to a shine. Crystal chandeliers cast sparkling light over everyone, and an orchestra Cary couldn't see through the crowds played strains of classical music which complimented the clink of wine glasses beautifully. It was all very glamourous and chic.

Cary felt instantly out of place.

Over the softer scents of a lot of very expensive perfume, Cary could just smell the hints of a buffet table not far from where she hovered near the entrance—something she'd have to investigate later. Her appetite had waned the closer they got to the event thanks to nerves and being dressed in clothing she wasn't used to. But the smells of something deliciously spicy tempted her and made her stomach growl.

"Hungry?" a deep voice asked from behind her shoulder.

She smiled as she faced Deacon. "A little." She stepped back so she could take him in.

The man could definitely fill out a tux. He looked stunning. The suit had obviously been cut to fit him because it settled across his broad shoulders and thickly muscled arms and chest without looking strained. The crisp white shirt beneath highlighted his dark hair and the golden light in his eyes.

"Wow," she said.

"Same," he said, his gaze traveling over her. "Nicky outdid herself with that dress."

Cary grinned. "It was a group effort." She patted her hair where it had been swept up into a pretty French twist and smoothed her other hand down over the blue silk of her dress.

Deacon's gaze followed her hand as it moved across her hip. "A very successful one," he said.

He didn't touch her, she noticed, and so she resisted stepping into him, too. Given their surroundings and all the shifters here along with all the humans, she'd anticipated him being distant. He'd warned her that he'd be busy and might not get to spend much time with her. They'd had a whole conversation about that. Still, when they got back to the mansion later, she was really looking forward to stripping him out of that tux. Slowly.

He tapped his nose and leaned in just a little closer to whisper, "You're going to distract me from the work I have to do now."

Which meant he could smell her desire. "I'm only a little sorry about that," she whispered back.

She was about to say more but Sasha stepped up behind Deacon then, interrupting them. Cary sighed. Of course Sasha was here to interrupt them.

And the woman looked stunning, damn it. She was elegantly dressed in a form fitting white gown with an asymmetrical skirt that cut up to her knee on one side and fanned out into a small train on the other. The cut showed off her magnificent legs and strappy heels so high Cary would have toppled from them. The sleeveless top and asymmetrical cut of the dress's neckline showed off Sasha's long neck and perfectly shaped shoulders. She wore her dark hair down, the thick silk of it brushing her collarbone. The only jewelry she wore was a pair of dangling diamond earrings.

Cary forced a smile but inside she cringed, because a part of her felt instantly less attractive next to Sasha's effortless elegance. That was not a pleasant sensation. She wanted to go back to exchanging lusty looks with Deacon, not feeling inferior to a romantic rival.

Sasha returned her smile, her expression smug, her white teeth perfectly even with no stray lipstick marks that might have helped alleviate the woman's perfection. She no doubt smelled Cary's reaction and from the look in her dark eyes, she was enjoying it.

Then she did the unforgivable. She put a hand on Deacon's shoulder. Cary couldn't touch him here but Sasha could? Oh, that was not a good thing.

Deacon didn't even seem to notice the contact with Sasha, or that it was in stark contrast to the fact that he wasn't touching his mate.

"Cary," Sasha greeted. "You look precious."

Cary very nearly rolled her eyes and said something rude. It was right there. On the tip of her tongue. She swallowed the comment and forced a civil, "Good evening, Sasha. You look lovely, too."

Sasha smirked. Then to Deacon said, "Dr. and Mr. Allen have arrived. It would be good for you to speak with them."

He nodded. To Cary he said, "Enjoy the party."

He was all control now, all serious and distant, so she couldn't tell if he was sorry he had to leave her or not. But she pretended he was and said, "Good luck with all the fundraising."

He smiled faintly and let Sasha lead him away into the crowd, their heads together as she pointed subtly to someone Cary couldn't see.

"Would you like some Champaign?" a familiar voice said from behind her.

She turned to Michael with a smile. "You're not busy schmoozing with the money bags too?"

"Already done a lot of schmoozing. I need a break." He gave her a once over and grinned. "You look beautiful. My brother is a lucky man."

Cary snorted—a less than elegant noise—but said, "Thanks. You look very nice too. I have a friend who would be melting for you right about now."

"Be sure to introduce us." He wagged his eyebrows.

Cary laugh and some of the weight of her discomfort lifted.

"So, Champaign?" Michael asked again.

"Yes, please." She couldn't afford to drink too much. She didn't want to have to turn her heels into flats just to walk. But if she was going to be at a fancy party wearing a super fancy gown, she should most certainly have at least one expensive drink.

Michael snatched two glasses from a passing server, handing one to her, then led her around the ballroom, pointing out the really wealthy patrons and giving her all the good gossip on the various people in attendance. It crossed her mind that someone—either Maria or Deacon —had asked Michael to keep her entertained because he stayed with her for the next half hour without showing any signs of having to get back to his schmoozing. And where Deacon had to be distant, Michael was all comfort and easygoing conversation. He even convinced Cary to take a spin on the dance floor with him and proved to be a remarkably good partner, leading her effortlessly despite her lack of dance skills.

By the time Maria and Evan joined them, Cary was feeling settled in her surroundings but was convinced Michael had been assigned to keep her company.

"Dr. Greelins is ready to open the menagerie," Maria said to Michael.

"Ah, that's my cue to get back to work," he said to Cary. "Thank you for a lovely visit."

"And thank you," she said, "for babysitting me while everyone else was busy."

He laughed. "That was my pleasure." He winked, nodded to his mother and father, and walked off into the crowd, pulling the gazes of any number of women with him.

"Whose idea was that?" Cary asked, when she faced Maria again. "Yours or Deacon's?"

"Deacon would not have assigned one of his brothers to entertain you in his absence," Maria said, her tone dry. "One of his sisters…maybe."

"So your idea then?" Cary said.

"Honestly, I hadn't thought about it. It was Sasha's idea." Before Cary could comment on that, Maria raised her hand and said, "And I agreed it was a good idea. I knew Deacon would be busy and you aren't well acquainted with many people here. After our talk yesterday, I thought you'd be more comfortable spending time with someone you at least knew."

The fact that this was Sasha's idea didn't please Cary at all. And it raised her suspicion levels through the roof. But because Maria had meant well—even if Sasha had had ulterior motives—Cary said, "Thank you. It was easier to settle into the party with Michael's company."

Hesitantly, Cary glanced at Evan. They hadn't really spoken since the other night, and she wasn't sure what kind of reception to expect from him. But his expression showed no signs of the tension and anger from their last conversation.

"Are you enjoying the gala?" he asked, his tone pleasant and friendly, as it had been when they'd first met.

"Very much. It's beautiful. And when the animals come out, I intend to visit them as well." She glanced down before meeting his gaze again. "I wanted to apologize for the other night."

He waved her away. "I overreacted and I should be apologizing to you."

"How about we call it even and forget about it?" she said.

"Agreed."

He took her proffered hand, but instead of shaking it, he kissed her knuckles. She grinned, bemused by the chivalrous gesture.

They exchanged a few more minutes of small talk before Maria and Evan were pulled away to talk to more donors. Leaving Cary alone for the first time since she'd come into the ballroom. In an attempt to keep from feeling too awkward, she wandered through the room, searching for familiar faces.

She spotted Lucas and Diana dancing. And Nicky and Jillian in an animated discussion with a couple of people Cary hadn't seen before. Sherri stopped her for a quick chat but she was pulled away by her own mate after only a few minutes. And Deacon's sister Caitlin waved across the room to her.

Though she hadn't met them officially yet, she was pretty sure she spotted a few more of Deacon's siblings in the crowd, too. They all bore a striking resemblance to each other and were perfect crosses of their parents. Cary had a feeling the family-only dinner tomorrow night would be enlightening.

Despite telling herself not to, she still hunted for Deacon in the crowd. And even knowing he'd likely be with Sasha, it still ticked her off to see the two of them on the dance floor together. Cary hadn't thought dancing would be part of his night of convincing rich people to give his organization more money.

"Good evening, beautiful," a deep and very familiar voice said from beside her.

She closed her eyes and shook her head. "Jaxer, what are you doing here?"

She faced him but gasped. He didn't look anything like himself at the moment, and for a split second, she thought she'd mistaken the voice. But then he grinned and the grin was so familiar, she knew she was looking at her former mentor.

He was still gorgeous—which shouldn't have surprised her; he was too vain to show up with all these glamorous people and not look his best—but he had very dark hair now, cut shorter and with a thickly wavy texture. His eyes were several shades bluer surrounded by thick black lashes. His normally angular face was broader, his nose and chin less aquiline, and his mouth wider, his skin tone not so pale, like he'd spent time in the sun. He was still wide through the shoulders, and slimly elegant in his tuxedo. But he was hovering over her an extra couple of inches now.

The entire effect was disconcerting. She *knew* the man was Jaxer, but there was nothing about him besides his smile that looked familiar. She was so astonished by the thoroughness of his glamour, she reached up and touched his cheek. Her fingers brushed against a faint hint of beard stubble.

"That's really freaky," she said.

"And not even the most elaborate disguise in my repertoire," he said.

Hearing Jaxer's voice coming from a stranger's face was beyond weird. "What are you doing here?" she asked, dropping her hand when she realized she was still touching him. She glanced toward the dance floor, but Deacon remained focused on whatever Sasha was saying and hadn't looked in her direction.

"While I hate to alleviate your suspicions," Jaxer said, "they're talking about the various big money contributors Deacon still needs to meet with."

Cary glanced up—farther than usual!—at Jaxer. "How do you know? You can hear them from here?"

"No. I made an excuse to dance near them and eavesdrop."

She sighed. "Why?"

"If they'd been discussing anything that might have pissed you off, I'd have been only too happy to tell you," he said without any guilt whatsoever.

"Will you please stop trying to break us up," she said. "It's rude."

"Dance with me," he said.

"No. Why are you here?"

He pressed a hand to his chest. "I'm just here to enjoy the party."

"Jaxer." She put enough warning into her tone to make her mother proud.

"Fine. I'm making sure you're okay. And keeping an eye on things in case there's a problem. And frankly—" he let his gaze drop, taking her in from head to toe, "—I wanted to see you in this dress again. You look stunning."

"Not as stunning as Sasha," she muttered before she could stop herself. Then she scowled. "Sorry. That was a childish response. Thank you for the compliment. Now go away before Deacon spots you. He can't afford to get angry tonight with all these humans around."

"Deacon won't have any idea I'm here unless I want him to know. If he looks this way, he'll just see you talking to one of the elderly guests."

She blinked. "He won't see what I'm seeing?"

"Not unless I want him to."

"Whoa. That's…"

"Freaky?" he supplied, with raised brows.

"Yes." She narrowed her eyes. "I notice you're showing up handsome to me. You could have been an elderly guest for me, too."

"You know better than that. I want you to think I'm gorgeous."

She huffed, amused despite herself. "Still, you could have toned down the gorgeousness. It's wasted on me."

"Oh, you're not the only one seeing me like this."

When she looked at him from the corner of her eye, he shrugged. "I'm vain, remember?"

That made her laugh.

"You really do look beautiful tonight," he said quietly. "I'm sure Deacon isn't pleased he's had to spend all night away from you."

"That's a very kind thing for you to say considering you keep trying to get between us."

"Well, it's the truth. And I want you to think well of me. Unfortunately, that does get in the way of my nefarious plans to break you and Deacon up."

"You're being very sweet and weirdly charming tonight. Is that part of your plan?"

"Of course. Would you like to dance now?"

"No." She sighed. "But thank you for asking."

"Are you not having fun?"

"Actually, I'm having a very nice night. But I feel a bit fish-out-of-water here."

"You look like you belong," Jaxer assured.

"Ha. Guess I have secret glamour magic, too, then."

"If you dance with me, it will keep you occupied for a full five or ten minutes. Give you something to do."

She dropped her chin to give him a look. "No. Stop asking. Even if Deacon sees me dancing with an old man, *I'll* know it's you."

"I should hope so."

"And we can't do things like share a dance without it meaning something more. Not now. So no, I won't dance with you, even to keep myself from feeling awkward for a full ten minutes."

"You don't need to feel awkward here, you know?" he said quietly.

"Yeah, but I do." She shrugged. "I'll get over it."

"Ah, love," he sighed.

She had no idea what he meant by that and she was afraid to ask. "Are you staying here all night or did you just stop by to pester me?" she asked, keeping her gaze on the crowd so she wouldn't see his expression.

"I'm just here to pester you," he said bluntly. "And to have your back if you need me."

"You're not supposed to be doing that this year," she pointed out the obvious.

"That only applies to your job." He glanced toward where Deacon and Sasha were still dancing. "Not your personal life." With a sigh, he said, "You're about to get more company."

She glanced at him and then past him to where Lucas and Diana were walking through the crowd toward her.

Jaxer's hand on her cheek startled her into looking at him again, even as she moved back from his touch.

"I'll be around if you need me," he said. Then he faded into the crowd, disappearing before Lucas and Diana reached her.

"Hi," Diana said. "We saw you alone and thought you might need familiar faces since Deacon is so busy."

Cary blinked at them, then glanced back to where Jaxer had disappeared. Diana and Lucas hadn't seen him standing there talking to her? That could only be Jaxer's glamour at work.

Seeing the effects of his illusions in this way, the completeness and complexity of them working on so many levels, was eye opening. And a little scary.

Maybe even a lot scary.

What else could Jaxer do? And how far could he go with his illusions?

3 1

—————

*A*fter another hour of small talk, another glass of Champaign, and a few nibbles from the buffet, Cary was in need of some quiet time. She'd spent the night standing in heels, which she wasn't used to, and forcing a cheerful demeanor, which she didn't always feel, having to watch her mate spend all evening with another woman on his arm, which she hated.

When she found herself once again on her own, she decided a strategic retreat to the restrooms for some privacy might be in order.

The restroom was huge, with an actual sitting area with couches and everything just outside the section with the stalls and sinks. She took advantage of the couches to rest her poor feet, groaning a little as she sank onto the firm cushions. A little bowl with cinnamon-scented potpourri decorated a small table in front of her. The walls were papered in a soft pink wallpaper with tiny fleur-de-lis across it. And the sitting area was carpeted, which felt strange in a bathroom to Cary. But since the place was empty and the couch allowed her to sit comfortably, she wasn't going to argue with a little carpet.

She rubbed her ankles and considered taking off the heels, but worried once she did, she wouldn't be able to put them back on again —or even want to. And she had a feeling walking around a fancy gala in bare feet wouldn't go over well. Plus, if she did need to run or do any protecting, doing that barefoot seemed a good way to get hurt.

Fortunately, there'd been no sign of trouble all night. And her Protector senses were quiet. That at least had been a good thing. Also, according to Diana, the kids were having a great time. Cary half wanted to go crash that party because she was pretty sure the kids wouldn't care if she was barefoot.

For reasons surpassing explanation, the bathroom was surprisingly cold, an overhead heating and cooling system pumping out cold air. Maybe that was to help people overheated in the ballroom cool off? After only a minute of resting her sore feet, Cary started to shiver. She forced herself off the couch to check the stalls, just in case someone was lurking in here that she hadn't noticed. Then she returned to the couch and pulled her jacket out of a clutch too small to have realistically held it. Wrapping up in the worn leather, she sighed. Better.

A couple of gorgeously dressed woman walked into the bathroom a minute after Cary had slipped into her jacket, thankfully missing the magic trick of it emerging form the small clutch. She didn't know them, and from their too-loud talking, she assumed they were humans. They smiled at her, pleasantly, before disappearing into the stalls. Cary winced at the loud, tipsy conversation that carried out to her, wondering if the women realized how noisy they were.

"You heard he's engaged now, right?" one woman said, her voice echoing inside the huge bathroom.

"Such a shame. He's so handsome," the other woman gushed.

Bemused, Cary eavesdropped because, really, she didn't have much choice.

"His body in that tux…" the first woman said.

"Your husband would not appreciate you admiring Mr. Jones in a tux."

The first woman snorted. "If my husband filled out a tux that beautifully, I wouldn't have to."

"I still can't believe he's a twin. Two of them! Wouldn't that be a fun party?"

Cary pressed her lips together to keep from chuckling out loud. She assumed the Mr. Joneses in question must be Deacon and Michael. Although, neither was engaged so maybe two of Deacon's younger brothers she hadn't met yet?

"And your husband would probably record that party for posterity," the first woman said.

The second laughed. "Oh, I would enjoy that." She sighed. "But unfortunately, no such luck."

Flushing and running sink water dampened the conversation. Thankfully. Cary was regretting listening in because now she had a picture in her head of one of these women getting it on with two of the Jones brothers while the woman's husband recorded the whole thing. That was more than Cary's poor mind could take tonight.

The woman came back into the sitting room, their heads bent toward each other, laughing at something Cary had—fortunately!—not heard. They nodded to her again.

"Have a good night," one said. "Great shoes, by the way."

Cary grinned. "Thanks."

Just as they were headed out, the woman who'd complimented her shoes said to her friend, "Did you see his fiancée's dress?"

"Oh, stunning. I wish I could wear white like that. Not even a bump or lump out of place."

"It's horribly unfair how stunning Sasha is, isn't it?"

The door closed behind them, cutting off the conversation.

Cary let the quiet surround her, trying very hard not to feel the hurt tightening in her chest.

Idle gossip and speculation. Maybe even a rumor started by Sasha herself. Nothing Deacon would have fostered, assumptions he wouldn't have encouraged.

Still…

That last part stung. People here were assuming Sasha was Deacon's fiancée. Cary couldn't pretend they were talking about Michael and Sasha because Michael didn't like Sasha. Cary had watched him avoid her all evening. Beyond that, Sasha had kept herself draped on Deacon's arm all night.

They'd talked about this, her and Deacon. He'd said he'd have to work, and that work involved spending a lot of time with Sasha because she was the one who knew most of the donors personally. He didn't see or have contact with them often enough to remember them all. Sasha did, and could ensure he always knew who he was talking to, always knew what to say and not say to everyone he met. Cary hadn't liked it, had hated it actually, but she'd agreed not to interfere or get upset because she did understand the pragmatic reasons for why he had to do what he had to do.

She'd been able to keep the "not interfere" part of that agreement at least. But she was most certainly upset now. In a way that made her stomach hurt.

She pushed her hands into the side pockets of her jacket, pulling it closer around her in an attempt at self-comfort. Her fingers brushed against something metal in one, and then the crinkling of paper reminded her—Jasmine's present and note.

Cary had forgotten she'd put them in her pocket. She pulled out the note she hadn't read yet. Jasmine's precise and neat script made Cary smile, mostly because despite that precision, the girl still topped her "I"s with hearts.

The note itself was so sweet, Cary felt tears welling. She was emotional anyway, but reading Jasmine's message at least made her teary in a good way.

Dear Ms. Redmond,

I'm not really sure how to thank you for the other night. The charm on the necklace is a Hand of Fatima, turned upward for good luck. You can turn the fingers to point down if you need to, if you need protection from the evil eye.

Cary chuckled as she read. She loved that Jasmine had sent her a "protective" charm. There was something appropriate about that. And given the looks Sasha always sent her, Cary probably could use some protection from the evil eye. She continued reading.

That's the idea, anyway. My dad doesn't like lucky charms. He thinks they're contrary to the teachings of Islam. But I think the Fatima Hand is pretty. And my grandma has one at her front door, so my dad can't complain too much.

This necklace isn't expensive, so please don't feel like it's too much or you should return it. My auntie sells these in her store, and she let me have this one for free because it's one of the less expensive ones. My mother said you might not want to accept one of the more expensive charms.

"Exactly right," Cary said aloud. Since she had been thinking she might need to return the necklace if it was too expensive, she smiled again at Jasmine's prescient thinking, and Jasmine's mother's advice.

I hope you are well and in good health. Thank you again so much for saving me. I will never forget what you did for me.
~Jasmine Hashemi
P.S. my mother says I should invite you to dinner. If you want to come.

Jasmine had drawn a little smiley face at the end of the P.S. Cary grinned back at the smiley face and put her palm over the letter, her heart tight for good reasons now. She gently folded the note, put it back in her pocket, and pulled out the necklace, letting the little charm swing and catch the overhead light. It was a pretty little necklace, the stylized hand covered with decorative swirls and in the center of the palm part of the hand, an open eye surrounded by long lashes.

"Thank you, Jasmine."

She undid the clasp and slipped the little necklace on, patting the charm into place at the hollow of her throat when she had the clip fastened. It didn't really go with her outfit or the silver accessories she had, but she didn't care. She needed Jasmine's good luck tonight. She needed a sense of goodness to counter the icky sensation that had crawled through her gut after the conversation she'd just overheard.

Although, she probably should turn the hand so the fingers were pointing down, to ward off the evil eye. Especially if she was going to go back into that ballroom.

With a sigh that was more groan, she pushed up from the couch. Time to face the crowds and her own insecurities again. Only a few more hours and they'd be finished with this event. She could go home to Portland soon and wallow in much needed dog hugs.

She was almost to the bathroom door when it burst inward, slamming against the wall. Cary jumped, swallowing a screech when she saw Lucas. Her Protector instincts jumped to life in the same instant.

"Cary," he panted. "The kids. The cougars…"

She didn't wait for him to finish. She stomped her heels down into flats in two quick moves and took off at a run toward the kids' party.

*C*ary came to a stuttering halt in the corridor between the ballroom and the room where the kids' party was happening. There were screams and shouts from inside the ballroom. And a few shouts from the direction of the kids' room. For a split second, she couldn't move, torn between which room to protect. She couldn't handle both, not with the chaos. There was no "between" the bad guys and the good guys just then, not that covered both rooms.

The realization that she wouldn't be able to save everyone left her breathless.

Lucas gave her hand a tug. "Come on!" he shouted. And then moving at shifter speed, blurred toward the kids.

Cary followed, moving faster than a human but still not as fast as the shifter. The grownups would have to fend for themselves—even though it would gut her later if any were killed—because she had kids to save.

She skidded into the room, took the scene in a one sweeping glance. A group of adults, moving fast enough to prove they were shifters, were fighting to one side of the room while another group of adults were circling the kids against one wall of the room. There were cries and shouts. Some of the kids were crying.

And to Cary's horror, the shifters facing the kids all had guns.

Ignoring the shifter fight, Cary raced toward the kids, sliding between the legs of two cougars in a way that wouldn't have been possible without her magic working, and rolled to her feet in a move that Lucy had been practicing with her.

She came up facing the gun-wielding adults, solidly between them and most of the kids. The adults were spread out. The kids were arrayed in a tighter clump.

But some of them still looked into the faces of the bad guys.

Cary was one woman and there were a lot more bad guys in front of her and good guys behind her than she could physically block.

She'd never been so grateful that her powers didn't depend on her physical size.

"Nope," she said and raised a hand when a cougar shifted his gun toward her.

It was a big gun, with a long barrel and stuff on it that made it look scary dangerous. She hated guns. She had no idea what kind of gun that was. She just knew it was ugly and deadly.

She snarled at the group. "Guns? On kids? You all are sick, you know that." Over her shoulder, she said, "Kids, you need to all stay back and behind me. Got it? No one moves in front of me."

There were some murmurs and she heard one little boy say, "She's a superhero. We have to listen to her."

She shrugged when the cougar in front of her raised his brows.

"Superhero?" he asked.

"Suppose it depends on your perspective," Cary said.

"I think you're that witch that keeps getting involved in business you shouldn't," he snarled.

"Not a witch either, but you'd be amazed how often people think that."

"You're all going to die," he said, his voice quiet. "No more leopards in cougar territory. That's the deal. Any that remain will die."

"What deal?" Cary asked. "Last deal I heard of didn't involve lots of kids dying."

Someone down the line of bad guys hissed at the man talking to her, and he stopped talking.

But he did finger the trigger on his big ass ugly gun.

She met his gaze. "Shoot me. I dare you."

"Don't," someone else said, a different someone than the one who'd shut him up. "She said it was pointless."

Cary raised her brows. "I did? I don't remember doing that this time around. It is pointless, by the way. But..." She frowned. "Wait, what 'she' are you talking about?"

There was another hiss from someone, so quiet Cary almost couldn't hear it, but one of the kids behind her whimpered so obviously it was a sound a shifter could hear clearly.

She watched the line of gun wielding cougars and frowned.

Now that she was here, they were just standing there, like they were waiting for something. They weren't helping the cougars in the fight with the leopards across the room, but they weren't trying to shoot her or anyone else for that matter.

They were just...standing there.

That was usually her part in the play. She wasn't quite sure what to do with bad guys that just stood there.

Was this how the bad guys felt about her?

The noise from the main ballroom had reached them and it still sounded chaotic—screaming and shouting and obvious fighting. But no gunfire.

Why just bring guns in for the kids? And then not use them?

"So," she said after another few minutes of just staring at the bad guys. "What are we doing here?"

"Shut up," the man in front of her said.

She chuckled. "No." She had no problem aggravating bad guys once she was in full Protector mode.

Plus, bonus, they sometimes gave away information when they were pissed off at her. Cary was pretty sure the "she said it was pointless" comment was a slip. But could she irritate them enough to reveal who "she" was? Or at the very least, admit why they were all standing around not doing anything but watching each other.

A tug on her jacket had her looking down, though she kept the cougars in her peripheral vision.

Lucas's son, Miguel, whispered up to her, "I have to pee."

"Yeah, me too," she said. "But we're going to have to hold it for a few more minutes. Okay?"

His little face screwed up into a pained expression but he nodded.

She leaned down a bit more and whispered, "It's totally okay if you have an accident. No one will even notice in all this mess. 'Kay."

"'Kay," he murmured back, looking relieved.

She smiled at him, then glanced at the rest of the kids behind her.

They were clumped together, some of the older ones hugging and comforting the younger ones. Her heart hurt seeing them all, so scared and working so hard to be brave. She hated, hated when kids were in danger.

This was one of the reasons she continued to do this job.

Lily met her gaze over the head of a little girl she was holding close, her expression very serious, looking way too mature for a fourteen-year-old.

Cary smiled and tried to convey some reassurance. But while the other little kids might not have realized this yet, Lily would be well aware that both her parents were in the mix, fighting with the cougars. Aware of the dangers of that.

Cary faced the line of waiting bad guys again, looking past them to the fight across the room—the one Lucas had leapt into. It sounded vicious and was moving too fast for her to pick out any one individual except occasionally when someone got thrown and had to pause a moment.

She looked at the cougar in front of her again, frustrated that she couldn't help the others, grateful she could keep these shifters from hurting the scared children behind her, and absolutely certain there was more going on here than just the cougars trying to kill leopards.

"Since we're apparently just going to wait here in our little standoff," she said, making her tone irritatingly pleasant, "why don't you explain the plan? I could use a good bad guy monologue about now."

One of the cougars down the line huffed out a laugh that was hushed by the person next to him.

Cary grinned. "He thinks I'm funny."

"You're not," the man in front of her said.

Her grin widened. "I hear that a lot from bad guys."

"We're not the bad guys here," he muttered.

"Oh contraire," she said. "You have guns pointed at children. There's no definition of the words good guy that includes that."

"They invaded our territory," he hissed.

"No. They were already here. And it's been more than half a century since Maria insisted on peace. Peace is good. All the songs say so. Give peace a chance and all that. So why disrupt it now?"

"We want our rightful place back," he said, leaning into her. "And we intend to get it."

She sighed. "Power? All this is about power and control? I hate that. It's stupid. You were doing just fine, no one fighting too much, no one causing trouble that attracted human attention. And you all had to go and fuck that up." She winced and glanced over her shoulder. "Sorry about the language." To the cougar she amended, "Screw that up. So stupid."

"They've gotten rich on our lands," he said.

"Again, they were here when Maria arrived, so there was no taking over anyone else's land. Just changing the power structure. That's not the same thing as invading. And all Maria did was insist on peace, which was so popular, the concept spread beyond her reach. Cause peace is good." She pointed at him. "Also, I'm pretty sure no one is preventing you from running businesses to make money. Peace helps with all that, too."

He growled at her. She gave him a "what?" look knowing it would further irritate him. He was talking, which was what she wanted, so she kept pushing at him.

"Yeah," she said, "I'm not seeing your argument at all. Nothing that justifies kidnapping kids, nothing that justifies holding them at gunpoint. Definitely nothing that justifies taking pot shots at innocent humans. Whatever this is about, it's stupid and self-defeating. You're gonna end up exterminated if you're not careful."

"By who?" He snarled. "You?"

She laughed. "No. I'm just here to keep the kids safe. But the humans are going to catch on to you soon. Even if they don't see shifter, they're gonna see bad guys. And they're going to come after you."

"I'm not afraid of humans," he said. "They're weak."

"And they outnumber you like a hundred thousand to one. Maybe even more. Even a weak blanket can smother if it's sufficiently big compared to the thing its smothering."

"What the fuck are you talking about?"

"Whoa! Language. There are kids here."

"I'm gonna shoot you if you don't shut the fuck up. Now."

She showed him her teeth. "Do it. Shoot me."

"Stop," the woman next to him said. "She's goading you. Ignore her."

He glared at Cary.

Cary grinned back.

He raised his gun to point it at her head. She waved her hands for him to go ahead.

The woman next to him smacked the barrel of his gun down. "Stop. That one is for her."

Cary glanced at the woman. "Which one's for who?"

The woman turned to look ahead of herself, ignoring Cary. She was much better at it than the man in front of Cary. So Cary faced him again.

"Bored yet?" she said to him.

He lifted his lip in a really impressive snarl. Cary smiled. Unfortunately, he didn't respond and she got distracted by the fight across the room which was angling closer toward them now. Shit.

She motioned the kids to tighten up their group and spread her arms out to the sides a little, mostly for balance if the fight washed past them. The cougar in front of her narrowed his eyes, and she glanced down long enough to see his finger twitch on the trigger. Then she returned her attention to the fight.

This could get messy.

Before the rush and thump of fast moving shifters reached them though, an ear piercing whistle sounded through the hotel. It seemed to reverberate off the walls, echoing around the high ceilings and then rushing out the door again.

"The signal," one of the women cougars with a gun shouted.

Cary braced for something horrible. Blinked.

And had to blink again.

Blurs of motion, a few hisses…

And the cougar shifters vanished.

The adult leopards who'd been in the fight, looked at each other, confusion plain in each expression. Then a handful of them gave chase, while the rest hurried to the children.

Lucas rushed past Cary to scoop up Miguel and hug his other three as they crowded around him. Over the top of Miguel's head, he said to Cary, "What the hell just happened?"

"The fact that they all disappeared at once following that whistle? Good question. No idea."

She glanced toward the main door and instinctively took up a protective stance in front of the kids again when someone ran in, until she realized it was one of the Jones siblings she hadn't officially met yet.

He hunted the room. "They're gone?"

Sherri, who Cary hadn't noticed was in the mix of the fight, went up to the younger man and they bent their heads together in discussion.

Lucas frowned, then said to Cary, "Apparently, they vanished from the main ballroom at the same time as they abandoned the fight here." He looked at her and mouthed, "What the hell?"

"Very good question," she murmured.

That was the weirdest attack she'd ever had to deal with. Everyone had been scared and very serious. There were guns involved. And a lot of violence across the room. Lots of yelling and screaming. But…

She looked around.

Nope. No one was actually hurt—or if the adult shifters had been, they'd all healed up already.

Given the bastard cougars had been standing there with *guns pointed at children*, she didn't believe for a minute they weren't intending on killing someone.

"Can you hear if anyone was hurt in the ballroom?" she said to Lucas, nodding toward where Sherri and the unnamed Jones brother were still talking and gesturing toward the room.

"Sounds like a few humans got injured but mostly in their rush to escape. The cougars didn't target them."

"That is…weird, right? I mean, they've made no bones about hurting kids and humans in this vendetta. So what gives?"

"Got me," he said. "But Owen has just said it's chaos in the ball-room still, and Deacon and Maria have their hands full settling things down."

Miguel pushed at Lucas's shoulder. "Daddy, I have to go pee," he murmured close to Lucas's ear but not so quietly Cary couldn't hear him.

"Oh, yeah, I forgot," she said. "He said that during the attack." She smiled encouragingly at Miguel. "And he did a very good job of wait-ing. He was very brave."

Miguel smiled at her, hesitant but proud, then pushed urgently at his dad again. "It's gonna be an emergency really really soon."

Lucas gave Cary an apologetic look and ushered all his kids ahead of him toward the bathrooms out in the hallway. He paused only briefly to say something to Owen and Sherri before hurrying out with a bouncing Miguel.

Moving at human speed now, Cary noticed. Habit because he would be encountering humans? She wondered how Deacon and Maria were going to explain the fast shifter movements during the attack to their human donors.

Once she was assured all the kids were in the safe care of more adult leopards, she remembered she needed to use the bathroom too. Inconvenient, but since Deacon was busy, it seemed a good time to take care of that before she joined him to see if she could help clean up the mess.

The corridor outside the ballroom was a cacophony of bodies and shouting voices, demands and screams, and Cary noticed, a few women collapsed on the ground, being fanned by angry or anxious-looking partners. Fainting seemed a bit dramatic, but she supposed most humans didn't witness a shifter fight every day.

She pushed her way through the crowd, hunting for Deacon just in case, but she couldn't see him through the melee. She didn't see Maria or Evan either. But given the press of people all talking at once, she wasn't really surprised.

She emerged from the bathroom to even more churning and chaos, if that was possible. The bathroom had been blessedly silent, so maybe it was just the noise after the peace. But it was so messy and crazy, Cary wasn't even sure which direction to try to find Deacon.

She pressed back against a wall as a group of people in hotel uniforms hurried past, then stepped out into the swirl of movement, searching the crowds for a familiar face.

A tap on her shoulder.

She turned to face the person trying to get her attention.

That was the last thing she knew before blackness engulfed her.

*C*ary woke with a pounding head, a mouth full of cotton, and a very bad feeling about her current circumstances. She blinked open her eyes before she could stop herself, panic clawing at her gut.

Where the hell was she? What had happened?

Wherever she was, it was blessedly dark because her head screamed at her for allowing in as much light as she did. Wincing, she tried to reach up and touch her temple. Something clinked. A heavy weight on her wrist made her panic ratchet up another level. She squinted at the metal cuff attached to a long chain.

Shit.

She sat up, instinctively and too quickly. Her head protested and the darkness round her swam.

Damn it. Heal body, heal.

She needed to get out of…well, whatever the hell mess she was in, and she couldn't do that if she couldn't stand up without her head exploding. She waited out the dizziness. Then, working to hold panic at bay, took in her situation.

The bed under her was one of those rudimentary camping things with a metal frame and a thin mattress. The room seemed to be a nondescript space, dark but for a little night light plugged into a wall socket opposite the bed. In that faint light, the walls looked pale, the floors wooden but rough. There were no windows, the overhead light was a single bulb hanging from a ceiling socket, and her ordinary human sense of smell picked up the heavy layer of dust.

She sneezed, which made her vision swim again.

When the spots dancing in front of her finally stopped, she assessed herself. Outside of the headache and swimming vision, she didn't feel any other injuries. No cuts or bruises. Or if there had been any they'd healed already.

She must have taken one hell of a blow to the head, though. She reached up with the hand not chained—realizing as she did that only one of her wrists had a cuff around it, so yay! She was only partially chained to a wall—and felt around for a lump, wincing when her fingers brushed over a definite sore spot on the back of her skull. No blood, but then again, that could have healed already.

This was one of those times she was really *really* grateful for her ability to heal fast. Given the feel of that lump, she might well have been dead otherwise.

She was still wearing her fancy dress, her beautiful high heels, now flats, were tossed into the corner of the room along with her leather jacket. No sign of the miracle wine producing clutch, which was a shame. She frowned as her memory tried to fill in the blanks.

The attack, which was really weird and suspicious. Everyone was mostly okay. She'd had to use the bathroom. And then…

Blank.

She only knew she'd likely made it all the way to the bathroom because she didn't still have to pee. And her dress didn't feel like she'd had an accident.

Hey, a bright side.

She groaned and then winced at the sound. Sound echoed in this mostly open and blank room. Not good for her head.

Who the hell had hit her? And kidnapped her? Why?

And oh shit, what was she going to do since she didn't have anyone to protect?

Had the wizard somehow found her? He was one of the few

enemies currently after her who knew how her powers worked. Once the attack was over, and she wasn't protecting kids anymore, she was vulnerable.

But if it was the wizard, why wasn't she dead already? Not that she wasn't grateful to be alive. Still, Sheldon and his wizard mentor obviously wanted her killed not kidnapped.

Unless their plans had changed?

She gave the chain set into the wall an experimental tug. Yeah, that wasn't going to pull free easily. Maybe she could squeeze her hand through the cuff. She'd still be in a, presumably, locked room, but she'd at least be able to move around. And get her jacket. This place was cold.

The cuff was a thick, old fashioned kind, not the sort of the thing police officers used. Unfortunately, it was also sufficiently small that she couldn't scrunch her hand up enough to slip out. Maybe with something slippery like oil or butter, but all she was doing now was scrapping her wrist raw.

Damn.

What the hell time was it? How long had she been here?

Panic and fear started to creep in past her confusion, filling her chest and gut with the sickly, sticky feel of terror. She'd known she might end up dead this year. She just hadn't anticipated it happening while she wasn't doing her job.

She really had to stop making so many enemies.

To keep the fear at bay, she went back to working on the cuff, picking at it, trying to make her hand as small as possible, tugging at the chain, testing the wall around the bolts. Anything to make it feel like she was *doing* something.

Thoughts of Deacon stopped her cold in the middle of one more tug at the bolt.

Double shit.

They weren't near each other. His leopard got really upset when that happened. And he was surrounded by his own people with little control over his animal side or his magic. And she was wallowing in a blank room somewhere while he could be hurting people without meaning to and…

Was it weird she was more worried about him in that moment than herself?

Yeah, probably, but actually worrying about him and not herself helped calm her panic and let her think. She was used to worrying about other people. It was her job. And she could focus when she was doing her job.

She rubbed the back of her neck with her free hand and realized she was still wearing Jasmine's necklace, the little good luck charm dangling at the hollow of her throat. Well that was something anyway. If Angie was right, and it did have a little magic to it, Cary sure hoped that magic worked for her now. She needed all the good luck she could get.

Okay. Maria could help keep Deacon from tearing things apart. And he'd be focused on finding her, but hopefully that didn't drive him to hurt anyone while he hunted. Knowing Deacon would be hunting for her, even if only to save his own sanity, was reassuring. Someone would know she was gone, so this couldn't go on for a long period of time.

He'd call in reinforcements. Maybe Marianne had put some sort of tracking system into Cary's coat? They'd never discussed it, so probably not, but it was officially getting added to the list of options for her coat going forward because that would have been very useful in this situation.

Live and learn.

She hoped.

What else?

She continued to brush her fingers over her Fatima Hand charm and stare at the door across from the bed. It was surely locked, but since she was chained to a wall, maybe her kidnapper hadn't bothered? That would make getting out easier if she could get the cuff off.

She studied the bolt on the wall again, then tested the length of the chain. She could stand from the bed, which was handy. Flipping the mattress up, she looked for any bit of thick wire or metal she could pull out that might serve as a screwdriver. The bed was pretty flimsy, though, made of lightweight aluminum. Still, she looked at the various parts of the frame. Nothing felt strong enough, mostly stuff she could bend herself, which didn't bode well for being able to loosen the thick wall bolt.

Sighing, she looked longingly at her jacket. There was a cursed dagger in there still. She could use that about now—as a screwdriver.

Would it affect her and suck her into its curse if she pulled it out? There was no one for her to protect here but herself, but there was also no one around to trigger her jealousy—especially the kneejerk chemical reaction she had to Sasha. So…maybe it could work?

Getting to the jacket was the tough part. The chain didn't extend that far across the room.

She put the thin mattress back on top of the light frame of the bed and sat, contemplating her choices even as she continued trying to squeeze her hand out of the cuff.

What had she learned in six years that might help here?

Not much, frankly. That was embarrassing. But her entire educational effort before this had been learning about different types of bad guys and all about the preternatural world so she could protect other people. Mostly protect them in the moment, too. Not a lot of hunting people down and rescuing them from having been kidnapped involved in her job to date.

Definitely no lessons on how to get herself out of this kind of jam. Shit.

Okay, what else could she do before she went nuts? She thought about Deacon again and her worry rose. She really needed to get to him soon. If they were going to break up at some stage, they'd have to plan for it and do it right so no one got seriously injured. This was not the best way to end a mate bond that could turn one partner into a raging, magic-wielding beast.

Her heart hurt at the thought of her and Deacon ending things. She didn't want to. She was in love with him even if she couldn't admit it out loud yet. But boy had this trip thrown their already strange relationship for a loop. She couldn't even be sure what he wanted anymore and that left her hollow and sad.

Which was not a great state of mind for getting herself out of the trouble she was currently in so she really really needed to think about something else.

Like seeing Deacon again. The rest would work itself out. She just had to survive and escape.

But how?

She was still contemplating that question when the door across from her opened.

"You look comfortable," Sasha said, smiling that deadly feline smile of hers. "And you look like shit."

Cary's gut tightened and her pulse sped. "Sasha," she greeted carefully. "What's going on?"

"I'm breaking your bond for you, you stupid human," she said. "So Deacon can be with his real mate. Me."

Sasha had kidnapped her. Not the wizard. Not Sheldon.

Sasha.

Which meant Cary couldn't count on Deacon knowing she was in trouble.

Oh boy.

34

"**H**ow is Deacon?" Cary asked, keeping a careful eye on the shifter in front of her. Sasha hadn't bothered to close the door yet, but the room beyond the door was black. Cary could only tell that it was an interior space, but otherwise couldn't see or smell or hear anything that gave her a clue to where she was.

"Upset, of course," Sasha said with an elegant hand wave. "It's difficult when one's mate leaves you." Her eyes narrowed. "I should know."

"So, you really think he's your mate?" Cary had to work to keep her voice calm. Her body was trembling with the rush of adrenaline and fear. In her head, she was screaming against what Sasha was doing, had done, but antagonizing the woman wasn't going to help.

For once, Cary wasn't interested in irritating the bad guy.

"He *is* my mate," Sasha hissed. "There isn't any thinking to it. He just can't—" She cut herself off, glaring at Cary.

"He just can't smell it," Cary supplied.

All her worst fears came crashing in, and to her supreme irritation, all her sympathy for Sasha did, too. Boy, did she not want to feel sympathy for this woman right now. When she'd been kidnapped and was being held against her will while her mate was out there some-where thinking she'd left him and possibly losing his mind.

That thought was enough to squash most of her sympathy.

Sasha lifted a lip in a faint snarl. "He told you?"

"That you don't have a scent? Yes. I thought it would be useful for a shifter, in a world where you can't hide your emotions normally."

"That's been handy," she said, tilting her head in a little shrug. "Lately anyway. But it's also been a horrible bane to my existence among my people."

"Yeah, Deacon mentioned that too." Cary narrowed her eyes. "He didn't realize your mate wouldn't be able to smell you."

"No one has considered that," she said, her lip twitching like she wanted to snarl. "But it hardly matters. I know who he is."

"Are you sure? I mean, the bond can't really happen one-sided, can it?" She winced inwardly. Oops. Not a good question to ask if she wanted to keep Sasha calm.

"Of course I'm sure," Sasha said, letting the snarl out now. "He's mine. He's always been mine. Some part of him knows it or he wouldn't have been with me."

Oh, Cary wanted to point out that he'd been with any number of women over his long life but that seemed just as unwise as her last question so she bit her lip.

Unfortunately, while Sasha might not release a scent, she most certainly still had a scene of smell. And she could read Cary's easily.

"You think I'm just one of many?" Sasha said. "But you're wrong. The others were passing. The others were a blip."

Well, if the woman was going to know what she was thinking anyway... "What makes you think he could have slept with them if you were his mate?"

"You think he hasn't slept with other women while he's been with you?" Sasha mocked. "How very naïve."

That one might have struck more of a cord if Deacon hadn't had such a hard time being away from her. He literally hadn't had time to sleep with another woman since Cary had met him.

Except for that time he'd been home for a week and had claimed to remain in leopard form most of the trip.

Sasha had probably been around during that visit. And he'd definitely spent more time with Sasha than her during this trip.

The jealousy bug bit hard again. But something in Sasha's implications didn't sit right. Something in it sounded just wrong enough that despite her suspicions and jealousy, Cary wasn't buying it. Not enough to give in to her own insecurities.

Not yet anyway.

"He's not the kind of man who can only sleep with one woman," Sasha continued, watching Cary carefully. "I accepted that a long time ago. As his mate, I must understand him and give him his freedom."

"Yeah, I'm not just fucking him," Cary said, keeping her tone quiet but watching Sasha as closely as Sasha was watching her. "I might have," she added. "Just fucked him and been done with it, I mean. But he's the one who keeps insisting I'm his mate."

"You're *not*," Sasha hissed. "I am. I have been. He knows it."

"Okay. But I'm not a leopard, and so I'm not really up on how this mate thing works. Maybe you can explain it to me. Cause Deacon seems a little confused about all this."

"Don't insult him," Sasha snapped. "He's the most perfect man to ever live, and I will not have you saying anything against him."

Wow. The woman had it bad. Really really bad in so many ways and on so many levels.

Cary raised her hands, palms facing Sasha in a show of peace. "Fair enough. But really, I don't understand. How can he be your mate and still think I'm his mate?"

"He's just confused. You've bewitched him."

"I went through that with him already," Cary mumbled. She most certainly hadn't bewitched anyone. She wouldn't even know how. But maybe keeping that part to herself right now would be wise.

"So, you're rescuing him from his confusion?" Cary asked.

What she really wanted to ask was why she was still alive. She had no illusions about Sasha's willingness to kill her. She was pretty sure Sasha keeping Cary alive had nothing to do with her.

"I am," Sasha said with that sly smile. "He knows you overheard those two women assuming I was his fiancée. He thinks you've left him."

Cary narrowed her eyes. Her pulse was pounding hard, making it hard to stay outwardly calm, and she knew Sasha would smell her spike of panic. Still, the woman had just given her a very interesting bit of news.

"You planted those women," Cary said. "You sent them in to say those things to upset me."

"Upsetting you was just a bonus. I needed them to be able to tell Deacon they'd seen you and had been talking about me being his fiancée. They were so sorry for the confusion. It was almost sweet."

Sasha's level of sarcasm was impressive. Even to Cary.

"The attack…" Cary tried to think past all her swirling emotions. Boy, concentrating was tough when you were both pissed and terrified. She forced her brain to work. "That was convenient. And no one, or not many people, were hurt. The cougars with guns, threatening the kids, didn't even try to use the guns. They just stood there…" Cary raised her brows. "They also mentioned a 'she' who told them shooting me would be useless." She let out a long breath. "You are the 'she' in question."

She wasn't asking.

Sasha shrugged. "I needed the chaos."

"Why?" That was a question Cary was hoping she'd answer. The villain's need to explain and monologue was a very helpful cliché when they did it in real life.

"You are never alone," Sasha said. "Even when you are alone, you're alone surrounded by people who would notice you were missing." She glanced down at Cary's jacket, frowning a little. Then picked it up.

Cary swallowed down her panic, not even sure why it was spiking, but instinct had her leery of Sasha having her hands on that coat.

"In the chaos, it took hours before anyone noticed you were gone," Sasha continued, but she sounded distracted now, her focus on Cary's jacket. "Deacon might have been aware, but he was too busy fixing the mess to go looking for you. Michael was the first one to bring it up. Then Lucas." Sasha glanced at her. "You could have Michael, you know."

"What?" That felt like a non sequitur.

"Michael. Instead of Deacon. They look almost the same. Once your bond with Deacon is broken, you can have Michael instead."

"Uh," Cary said, because for a few seconds she couldn't form words. "You know that's not how it works. Right?"

Sasha shrugged, returning her attention to the jacket, her fingers running over the side pockets now. Cary's heartbeat jumped. Shit, Sasha would hear that, wouldn't she?

"You're sure Deacon is okay?" Cary asked, again, in an attempt to keep Sasha from searching pockets.

Still distracted, Sasha said, "Maria is keeping him calm."

"You know, I mean, I assume you know, it's dangerous to do this to him," Cary said. "He's not your average leopard."

Sasha gave her a pitying look. "Of course I know all about my mate, stupid woman. Why do you think you're still alive?"

Cary considered that for a bit, working through the implications. Then hesitantly said, "Because killing me would do him more damage? The change would be too sudden and he might not be able to recover from the loss of his mate. But having the bond broken slowly, through me leaving rather than dying, means he can recover." Cary raised her brows. "That's a diabolical plan, Sasha. But I can't say it's a bad one."

Sasha snorted, and to Cary's irritation, even that sounded elegant. Your kidnapper should not sound elegant and beautiful when they were snorting at you. This was almost worse than facing off against vampires and their stunning sexuality. Except, she'd only ever done that when she'd had someone around to protect and the vampires hadn't had personal reasons to kill her. So yeah, maybe this was worse.

Except, at least for now, Sasha didn't want her dead.

"So, you're breaking my bond with Deacon," Cary said slowly, hoping to force Sasha's gaze up from her jacket. The leopard had started running her fingers over the lining. "But you're offering me Michael in exchange." And wouldn't Michael be delighted to know he was being offered up as a second class alternative to his twin. "But if I get around Deacon again, won't the bond reform?" She honestly didn't know the answer to that question. Did Sasha even know?

"Once it's broken, it will stay that way," Sasha said, though she didn't look as confident as she did a moment earlier. She narrowed her eyes and stared at Cary a moment. "Maybe you shouldn't have Michael. That would place you too close to Deacon. No, you should just stay away from us all. Go back to that faery who's in love with you. You can have him."

Cary was pretty sure Jaxer would object to the phrasing of that even if he wasn't opposed to the end result.

"That's all you want?" Cary asked, skimming past the Jaxer comment. "For me to stay away from Deacon?" That was better than Sasha wanting her dead. It wasn't something she intended to do or be bribed into, but still, it was better when the bad guy didn't want to just kill her outright.

Sasha's fingers brushed across the inner pocket of Cary's jacket, and her gaze narrowed in on the sealed opening. She wouldn't be able to feel the dagger in there, but Cary was intensely aware of it, so close to Sasha, and fed by jealousy.

Marianne had designed the pockets in Cary's coat to seal and unseal with a touch, but she hadn't linked that touch to Cary specifically. Cary wasn't even sure that was possible—even though Marianne kept surprising her with what she was able to do with fabric. Which meant, if Sasha decided to open that pocket, she'd be able to. It didn't feel like there was anything in the pocket, so maybe she wouldn't bother.

It had never crossed Cary's mind someone might steal her coat since she either had it on or it was in her house. And she didn't typically carry around dangerous things in her pockets for this long, so that hadn't been an issue before.

The fact that she hadn't considered this option before now seemed extremely shortsighted. And stupid. Very very stupid.

Sasha looked Cary right in the eyes.

Cary knew her scent and heartbeat were giving her away. She

couldn't help it. Panic was running through her system. Frantic now. Even stronger than in the moments after she'd awoken to find herself chained to a wall. This was a kind of panic that no snark or calming breaths would ease.

And Sasha could smell every stinking bit of it.

The shifter's eyes narrowed as she glanced between Cary and the inner pocket. "Your faery lover said you had something in here. It feels empty, but it's not, is it?"

Cary didn't try to lie. Lying to shifters was a waste of breath. And she could barely breathe now as it was.

"What is it?"

"Dangerous," Cary said honestly. "Not something you want to touch. Trust me."

Sasha raised her brows at that, a mocking gesture that Cary had to give her.

"Yeah, okay, I know. Trust between us isn't exactly at an all-time high right now. But honestly, I'm not being tricky or trying to deceive you. You can smell that much. You really really don't want to open that pocket and mess with the thing inside. It's very dangerous."

"So am I," Sasha murmured.

"And this is worse. For your own sake, leave it alone."

Cary had a fleeting wonder if she'd be able to protect Sasha from the dagger. If Sasha took it out, would that trigger Cary's Protector magic and enable her to get the dagger back without anyone getting hurt? Or would her magic continue to lay dormant because Sasha wasn't a threat to anyone *but* Cary? Even with the dagger.

Oh, she really didn't want to test that theory.

Because if her magic didn't get triggered by Sasha holding the dagger…

Cary would be that awful things next sacrifice.

Shit.

35

Cary and Sasha held gazes for a very long moment, Cary's pulse pounding in her throat. She didn't try to hide her worry, and only hoped Sasha's keen sense of smell picked out the details, that Cary was actually as worried about the shifter as she was worried for herself.

"Please," Cary said quietly, "don't open that pocket. For your sake. Don't open that pocket."

"What is it?" Sasha asked, her gaze intent.

Which Cary took as a good sign because she wasn't looking at the pocket where the dagger was hidden. "It's a cursed blade. It feeds on jealousy. And obviously there's a lot in this room. It will take over your mind and make you do things you wouldn't normally do. It will feed on the blood you give it, and then it will feed on you. Please. Don't do that to yourself."

Sasha's gaze narrowed. "You're lying to me."

"No. You can smell I'm not. Right?"

"Scents can trick a shifter," Sasha said, her lip lifting in a snarl. "They rely too much on their sense of smell. And it can fail them at the most important moments."

Cary understood exactly what Sasha was implying—that Deacon's sense of smell had failed him in recognizing his mate—but she was way too worried about Sasha pulling out that dagger to argue with her.

"Sasha, you know I don't like you," Cary said, "and I know you don't like me. You've kidnapped me and are trying to separate me from my mate, which leaves no room for a future friendship. We absolutely have no reason to trust each other, and I have every reason to lie to you. But I'm not lying about this."

She winced. "I'm a pretty bad lair anyway. Even if I was trying to lie, you'd know it. No one ever believes my lies."

She held Sasha's gaze, willing her to believe. "This isn't a lie. The thing in that pocket is extremely dangerous and it will destroy you and everything around you if you touch it." She lowered her voice. "It could make you kill Deacon. Do you want that?"

Sasha glanced back at the pocket. And Cary's heartrate tripled. Had she just made a mistake? Suggested something Sasha might actually want?

"He's never acknowledged our bond," Sasha said quietly, almost to herself. "And then he leaves me for another woman. Claims she's his mate. But *I'm* the one. It's supposed to be me. We're supposed to rule together. Side by side. King and queen of our people. *Our* people."

She brushed the jacket pocket, the movement of her fingers making Cary's nerves twitch.

Cary wanted to leap forward and grab the jacket away so much she started working at freeing her wrist from the cuff again. This was bad. This was very very bad.

A tingling along her spine, the sense that someone was in danger and needed her help... That sensation she felt when her particular brand of magic was required.

She tugged at the cuff, right at the place where it locked together.

The cuff came away in her hand like it had never been closed.

Cary kept the cuff where it was as she studied Sasha, buying herself some time to plan now that she was free to act.

Who the hell was she supposed to be protecting here? Deacon wasn't around, but clearly Sasha's thoughts had turned her into a danger to him. Even if Sasha tried to kill Cary now to get her out of the way so she could get at Deacon, Cary's powers would work. Bad guys couldn't kill her to get to someone else. That was the wonderfully tricky part about Protector magic. To kill Cary, a bad guy had to want to kill Cary and only Cary.

Unfortunately, it looked like she'd focused Sasha on killing someone else. And while it meant her powers were now working, she was horrified Sasha was contemplating killing Deacon.

Shit shit shit.

"Maria's fault," Sasha muttered. "She could have told him."

Whoa, what?

Cary wanted to ask aloud, but was afraid to call Sasha's attention back to her too soon.

"She knew and she didn't tell him," Sasha said, as she slowly eased open the jacket pocket. "Maria isn't a good enough queen. I'll be better. I've always known that. But Deacon has to rule with me. Only me. No one else. Our people. If he won't rule beside me, if he won't admit I'm his mate, I have no choice, do I? I have no choice. He can't be with someone else. He can't. He's mine."

Cary watched the very tip of the dagger start to emerge from the pocket. It was still in the scabbard, but there was nothing stopping Sasha from taking it out of the scabbard once she removed it.

Sasha's eyes narrowed. "A knife. Well, that's..." She looked up, staring right at Cary. "Perfect."

Ah hell.

"Sasha," Cary said slowly. "Please. You need to leave that knife inside the scabbard. It's very important you don't touch it."

"Begging for your life?" Sasha asked.

"Begging for yours," Cary said.

Sasha snorted. "My life. What life? Maria's errand girl? Pitied by my people because my own mate doesn't know me? I had it all planned. And it would have worked. I would have been queen. Deacon my mate. But you had to show up. You had to fuck up everything."

"Yeah, sorry about that," Cary said mostly to stall. Sasha talking was good because she wasn't pulling the blade out of its scabbard. Yet.

"But really, Maria is going to live for a while yet. There was always a risk Deacon would find someone else, right?"

Oops. That wasn't maybe a good statement.

"Maria won't live forever. She's not a good enough queen. Deacon needed to be king. I was making that happen. You ruined it. All of it."

"Not sure how, but okay. Not the first time I've ruined plans." Although Cary really wanted to know how Sasha was making Deacon king.

"None of you understand," Sasha hissed, dropping Cary's jacket but keeping the dagger and scabbard in hand. She toyed with the hilt as she stalked toward Cary in slow, measured steps. "Not even Deacon. He ruined everything too. I was going to make him our leader. I was going to give him everything. And he threw that away for *you*? You of all people." She snarled. "You're just a human. Weak and worthless. Vicious and mean."

"Weak and worthless I will accept," Cary said, keeping her gaze on Sasha's, the way Lucy had taught her. "At least next to a shifter. But no one has ever accused me of being vicious before."

"You kill and slaughter. All humans do. You rip parents from their children. You destroy lives."

Because Cary was watching, she knew Sasha wasn't completely in the room anymore. Her thoughts were in some other very dark place, and she wasn't thinking of Cary.

Cary's heart hurt for her—so inconvenient this sympathy!—but she didn't let down her guard. Whatever inner demons haunted Sasha, the woman was still a threat.

Was it weird to be grateful Sasha wasn't just a threat to her?

Yeah.

But also pragmatic.

Cary's Protector instincts were humming. That dagger in Sasha's hand wasn't just dangerous to Cary. Sasha was going to use it against Deacon. Against Maria. Against maybe even herself now. And it was now officially Cary's job to prevent that.

But it was very weird trying to figure out how to protect the bad guy from herself.

Especially since she was holding the thing that was the threat.

Sasha's gaze dropped to the knife again, as if Cary thinking about it had reminded her of it. Damned shifter sense of smell. Her thoughts might well have reminded Sasha.

Slowly, in painful increments, Sasha eased the dagger back from the scabbard, inch by inch revealing the blade. The runes danced across the steel, folding and melting at a stomach-churning pace.

Cary felt the dagger's triumph in her bones, as a deep vibration that might have been a laugh if it had come from a person and not an inanimate object. Although, inanimate was probably the wrong word for that dagger.

Light from the blade painted Sasha's beautiful face a ghostly blue, and her eyes sparkled.

"Ah, Sasha," Cary sighed.

"You never told me," Sasha said. "It'll give me everything I want. I'll be their queen. It'll give me everything."

"Yeah, not how it really works." Cary loosened the cuff around her wrist and let it drop.

Sasha's gaze darted toward the restraint. "Well," she said. "Whatever your powers are, they're strong. That was designed to hold a shapeshifter."

"As you like to remind me, I'm not a shifter of any kind."

"And yet you opened the cuff. But you're not a witch."

"Not a witch," Cary confirmed, scooting to the edge of her bed, keeping her attention on Sasha's face.

"Once I kill you, the dagger says I can have everything I want," Sasha said again, her gaze unfocusing and turning inward. "Everything but Deacon. He's no longer worthy. I have to kill him." A tear dripped down her cheek. "And Maria. She won't die. The cougars can't reach her. I'll have to kill her too. It needs blood. Cary, it needs blood."

"Mm hmm," Cary murmured, her heart hurting at the pain in Sasha's expression.

But not enough that she missed the significance of her comment. If she'd heard right, and it wasn't just the dagger talking, Sasha had tried to get the cougars to kill Maria.

Something she'd have to think about later, once she saved Sasha from the cursed blade, and herself.

A flash of anger swept Sasha's gorgeous face, creasing her brow, narrowing her eyes, her full mouth pinched and her nostrils flared with her snarl.

"You," she hissed at Cary. "It's all your fault. You're the one who caused all this. Your blood will feed the blade."

"Yeah, no." Cary slowly came to her feet as Sasha started to stalk toward her.

"Then *his* blood. He's cheated on me and lied to me for too many years. And then he accepts *you*. He's not good enough for me."

"Sure sure." Cary edged away from the bed so she didn't have any obstacles in her way.

Sasha tracked her, followed her movements.

"But you know, I'm not going to let you kill Deacon and Maria, right?" Cary said. "No killing other people on my watch."

"You'll be dead," Sasha snarled. "You can't stop me."

Even if the cuff hadn't come away, proving her Protector powers were finally working, that admission would have been all Cary needed. Even though the people she was protecting weren't actually here at the moment, she was definitely standing between them and death.

Despite knowing better, Cary's gaze flicked down to the knife. The blade's runes continued to churn and dance, melting over the top of each other and down into the steal like rolling lava.

She needed to get that knife out of Sasha's hand. The woman's pale knuckles were white now, her grip was so tight. She wasn't going to drop the dagger. Cary doubted the dagger would let her release it at this point anyway.

But she shouldn't have looked away from Sasha's face.

Cary missed the telltale signs, all the things Lucy had been teaching her to watch for—those clues to someone's next action were all in their face, their eyes, the subtle movements of their shoulders. Getting distracted by the weapon they held was a mistake.

A mistake Cary had just made.

36

Sasha moved so fast, Cary felt like she blinked and there was a raging shifter standing right in front of her with a knife hovering over her.

Holy hell.

She gasped, but that was the only reaction she managed. Lucy's hard training fled Cary, leaving only her innate ability to freeze like a deer in headlights behind.

Cary froze, staring up at the cursed dagger as it vibrated just above her head.

She issued a few profanities under her breath. "I need to train a lot more," she muttered at the end of the string of words that did help relieve her shock and fear enough for her to breathe again.

"Why won't you die?" Sasha snarled. "You have to die. It's the only way!"

Cary still couldn't quite bring herself to look away from the dagger, even though she knew she should. But it was just so close, right there, hovering over her, waiting to drop, waiting to eat her blood and fear and jealousy.

Gross.

She finally blinked and forced herself to look at Sasha. The woman's expression was twisted up with her rage, her eyes glowed yellow as her leopard waited near the surface. Cary hadn't seen Sasha in her leopard form yet, or even seen her this close to losing control.

Both disconcerting and terrifying.

"You have to die," Sasha said, her voice lowering, an inhuman guttural quality filling it now, like she was already starting to shift. "If you don't die, if they don't die, I can't rule."

"You want Deacon dead? You love him so much you've arranged a lot of this, only to kill him?" Cary held Sasha's gaze, trying to see the woman past the animal trying to break free. Trying to see some sanity past the cursed blade's effects.

"He betrayed me," Sasha said. "He cheated on me with you. He worries about you. He's a weak leader. We need someone strong. Our people need me."

Sounded like Sasha had jealousies that went beyond just her jealousy over Deacon's other women. Which meant the damned dagger had a lot to work with.

Not good.

"Sasha, you need to let me take that dagger from you, okay?" Cary said quietly, keeping her tone even. "I'll make sure it stops hurting you and we can be done with this."

"It's not hurting me. It's going to give me everything. I just have to kill you and Deacon and Maria first. Then it will all be mine."

"But wasn't Deacon one of the things you wanted? Why would you kill him? Does that make sense to you?"

She didn't hold out much hope that Sasha would see logic in her current state, but keeping her distracted seemed like a good idea, because she was still trying to push that dagger down into Cary's skull and that wasn't good.

Cary desperately wanted to reach up and grab the knife, try to take it physically from Sasha. With her Protector powers working—thankfully!—she should be able to get the knife away. But given Sasha's speed and strength, Cary wasn't sure her own abilities would do her much good. Sasha could race out of the room with the knife before Cary could blink.

And Cary wouldn't be able to follow that fast.

At least, she didn't think so.

She'd never had to actually chase a shifter before. Mostly she did what she was doing now—froze and stood still. In fact, she usually wanted the bad guys to run away because it meant the people she was protecting were safe. But the knife was a new kind of bad guy to fight. And the people she was protecting weren't in the room.

Her hand twitched, the need to grab the knife strong. She made a fist and held still. She needed to keep Sasha—and that damned weapon—here. Which meant she couldn't just lunge at the woman. She couldn't do anything that might make her leave.

"Tell me about the cougars," Cary said, hoping to get back to some bad guy monologuing. If it worked, it was a great stalling tactic.

"Shut up and die," Sasha hissed, using two hands now in an attempt to plunge the dagger into Cary.

So much for bad guy monologuing.

Sasha's face contorted in rage as the dagger just hung above Cary, vibrating, but unable to break through and kill. With a scream, Sasha leapt away from Cary, springing halfway across the room in a move that no human could have made. She crouched low, her eyes blazing yellow now, her leopard right below the skin.

Cary expected her to shift at any moment, but if she did, she'd have to drop the dagger. That would be a good for both of them. Although, maybe not good for Cary since Sasha wanted her out of the way even without the dagger driving her to murder.

The leap had taken Sasha to one side of the room, leaving the way to the door wide open.

The unlocked, unguarded, easy to exit door.

She glanced at the way out, glanced at Sasha, then made a run for it.

When Sasha laughed, Cary spun to face her, standing in front of the only way to get out of this room.

"You think you can get away from me?" Sasha said, her voice guttural and deep. "Go ahead. Do it, prey. Run. I would love to chase you down and kill you." She flipped the knife in small circles, the hilt rolling in her palm, making its blade flicker in the room's light.

Cary raised her brows. "Oh no. I didn't move in front of the door to get out. I'm here to keep *you* in." And she closed the door behind her.

Sasha's eyes narrowed.

This time, Cary saw the attack coming.

The jump and scream and sheer viciousness of Sasha's attack was as impressive as anything Cary had ever seen. And she'd seen some pretty impressive acts of violence and rage over the years. Especially recently. Which should probably be a warning sign of some kind.

Sasha slashed at her with one hand contorted into a clawed shape that must have simulated her leopard's paw. With her other hand, she thrust the knife at Cary, over and over in a blur of speed, hissing and growling. The blade flared blue, then red as the creepy blood sprang from the steel and crawled along the surface toward Sasha's unprotected hand.

Oh shit.

Cary jumped toward the shifter, despite her angry attack and grabbed her wrist. "Sasha, you have to let the knife go. Now." Cary roared this last over the sound of Sasha's cursing and screeching outrage.

She still didn't know what happened when that creeping blood touched skin, but she really didn't want to find out this way. There was just no way it could be good.

Sasha fought off Cary's attempt to take the knife even as she continued trying to stab Cary with it.

Which made the whole process a lot more complicated than it had been with the previous user of the damned dagger.

"Sasha, damn it, stop fighting me," Cary muttered. "You have to let this thing go. Look at it. Look at the blood dripping down toward your hand. That's not my blood!"

Sasha ignored her. And because she was a shifter, their fight was ridiculously one-sided, even with Cary's magic working to help her keep up.

Cary clung to the thrashing woman for dear life, reminded in that moment of the saying about having a tiger by the tail—that it's most dangerous to let go.

Sasha flung them both around the room at speeds that made Cary nauseous and with a strength that made Cary feel very human and weak.

But she didn't dare let go.

The blood on the dagger dripped and dripped, pooling in a sickening umbrella over Cary's hand where she was trying to block it from Sasha. But the enraged leopard wasn't helping.

The blood didn't move like normal liquid or seem to obey the usual physical laws of the universe. It was thick and viscous and slow moving. But relentless.

More and more, flowing to cover Cary's hand, still not able to touch her.

It was like the blood was trying to get around her to touch Sasha's skin. And Sasha's continued fight had Cary worried the damned blood might succeed.

It wasn't getting flung around the room, which was fortunate, because Cary didn't want to accidentally step in the stuff. But the more it built up around her hand, the more she worried.

"Sasha. Stop. Fighting. Me." She growled at the woman and tried to hold her in one place. But that was like trying to stop a freight train by grabbing a handhold outside one of the cars. Cary just got dragged along for the ride.

This was particularly difficult in a ball gown.

More than once, Cary lost her balance and slipped, the only thing holding her upright her grip on Sasha's wrist. And the sure knowledge that if she let go, Sasha was lost to the cursed dagger.

"I'm going to kill you," Sasha screeched.

"Yeah, yeah, you've said that already. Let the knife go. I'm not going to let it take you." Geez, it was hard to protect someone when they wouldn't cooperate with being protected. "Sasha, stop and listen."

For an instant, when Cary looked into the shifter's glowing yellow eyes, she thought she saw some recognition, some realization that this wasn't a good situation.

Then Sasha blinked, the glow intensified, and Cary found herself flung off her feet completely, flying through the air as Sasha attempted to throw her off. Her grip on Sasha's wrist held, which sent them both tumbling into a wall so hard Cary lost her breath.

And her grip loosened, dropping away.

She scrambled to take hold of Sasha's arm again, putting her hands between the woman and the dripping blood, but she wasn't fast enough. A single drop got through.

Sinking into Sasha's skin.

Sasha screamed. Not the enraged, angry screams of earlier, but a tortured release of pain.

Cary panicked. She shook with fear and horror, not even sure what to do in that moment. All she could think was she needed to get the dagger out of Sasha's grip, now.

The screaming went on, piercing Cary's ears, making it impossible to focus. She tugged at the dagger, fighting against Sasha's superior strength, but it was like trying to claw a cement block out of the sidewalk with her bare hands.

"Sasha," Cary shouted over the woman's screams, "you have to let go! I can't get the knife away. Please, you have to release it."

Sasha's head thrashed back and forth, her eyes rolled back so Cary couldn't even see the yellow glow anymore.

Cary kept calling her name even as she pulled at her fingers, trying to pry them one by one from the dagger. The blood that had been flowing down the blade reversed itself, soaking back into the steel with a sick sucking noise that made Cary want to gage. The runes underneath the flowing blood had turned red. Cary was too frantic to try reading them, but she did notice they'd stopped moving.

If she wasn't so desperate, she might have even been able to decipher them.

The screams stopped so abruptly the following silence made Cary's ears hurt. She looked up to see Sasha staring at her with eyes gone completely black. No whites, no iris color, just a solid sphere of black.

That couldn't be good.

In a voice that wasn't her own, Sasha said, "We are one now, and I will have my blood."

"Oh boy," Cary muttered, still prying at Sasha's fingers. "Sasha, if you're still in there, you have to fight this. There's only so much I can do from the outside."

Her powers kept her in contact with Sasha and the dagger when she would have otherwise been tossed easily aside. And she was pretty sure she wasn't going to end up sacrificed on that blade because she still had people to protect from it.

But she'd never fought someone melded to the thing Cary was trying to protect them from. She had no idea how to get *between* the bad thing and the good guy when they were tied up together.

Sasha smiled, a silky, evil expression that wasn't like any look Cary had seen on her face before. She raised her free hand, and claws burst out of her fingertips.

Not like a normal shift. Blood flowed from her hands like she'd been wounded. Definitely not something that would occur as she went from her human to her animal shape.

The claws were long and thin and sharply pointed. Sasha looked at them, then swept them down toward Cary's throat.

Without thinking Cary gasped and leaned away from the attack, still clutching desperately to Sasha's wrist. She knew her powers would stop the attack, because Sasha was still obviously in trouble, but given the newness of this particular situation, Cary's rusty self-preservation instincts kicked in.

Fortunately.

Because the claws clipped close enough to her throat to raise the hairs on her skin.

Oh oh. How did that happen?

She felt a flare of heat at the hollow of her throat but couldn't afford to look down. Panic bubbled in her blood. So she did the next thing that came to her without thinking about it.

She dropped to one knee, still holding Sasha's wrist, letting the full force of her weight drop with her.

The sudden change jerked the shifter off balance just a little, but a little was all Cary needed. She spun on her knee, putting her back to Sasha, and jerked her hands down and forward, hard. As Sasha stumbled forward, Cary lifted up, taking the woman's weight on her back as she lifted Sasha off her own feet, then she spun again, the momentum of the move, sending Sasha sideways onto the ground.

Cary, still holding the woman's wrist, flipped Sasha so she was on her stomach and held her wrist high above and behind her, at an angle that would dislocate a normal human's shoulder. She put her knee in the middle of Sasha's back and wrapped her own arm around Sasha's arm, high. Using her upper body to lever Sasha's arm around, she twisted until the other woman cried out, then Cary twisted her wrist a little further.

Sasha's grip loosened. Just enough.

Cary snatched the knife out of Sasha's hand before she could tighten her hold again.

Everything seemed to still, the silence in the room deafening. Cary held her breath, waiting for some sign that the spell was broken, that Sasha was okay, that the dagger was no longer a threat.

When Sasha relaxed under her, and started to weep, Cary let out the breath.

She eased away from the shifter, releasing her hold. Sasha's arm dropped but she remained on her stomach, her face pressed into the floor, crying.

"It's okay now," Cary said quietly. "You'll be okay now." She hurried to the discarded scabbard, thinking only of getting the dagger contained again. The thing had caused enough trouble for one day.

She heard Sasha move and glanced over her shoulder to check on her even as she leaned down to scoop up the leather scabbard. It took Cary a split second to realize something was wrong with Sasha's face.

Her eyes were still black.

The shifter smiled. The evil expression that wasn't her own.

Cary gasped. And then the room's solid door shattered apart, sending shards of wood flying.

38

Cary ducked, covering her face with her arm as wooden shrapnel scattered past her. She blinked over her arm at the hollow doorway. A huge shape leapt through the darkness and into the middle of the room, landing between Cary and Sasha.

"Deacon?"

He looked at her over his shoulder, his eyes bright yellow in the dim light, glowing brighter than she'd seen them before. His jaw looked a different, stretched and wider, and his hair stood out around his face, moving as if in a breeze.

She'd never seen him quite like this before, and she'd seen him in some pretty deadly situations. But now, he looked wild, beyond any sense of control. She wasn't even sure he recognized her when he looked at her.

His nostrils flared, taking in her scent, and then he faced Sasha again. A growl so deadly and resonant it made the hairs on Cary's arms stand up.

To her horror, claws burst out of Deacon's fingertips. Unlike Sasha, though, his hands didn't bleed. He just had wickedly deadly claws in place of finger nails now—like a cat. Sharp, long, their tips glittering dangerously.

Most leopard shifters couldn't do that.

In the time it took Cary to take all this in, Sasha had risen to her feet. Her black eyes gleamed, her smile that evil look that made Cary's blood run cold.

Sasha tilted her head to one side as she studied Deacon. "I knew you'd come," she said in a voice much deeper than her own. "So much wonderful emotion. Such hot, thriving jealousies. I will eat well tonight."

Well, that didn't sound good.

Cary came up on the balls of her feet to run, just as Sasha lunged toward Deacon. The shifter was way too fast, and Cary would never get in front of Deacon in time, but she could get between them even if they were fighting—hopefully.

Except Sasha never reached Deacon. She froze, in mid-motion halfway to him, just…froze. Like someone had hit a pause button on a movie.

Cary froze too because she wasn't sure what was happening and had no idea what to do. Sasha's body started to vibrate, visibly, shivering and quaking. Blood dripped from her nose, splatting onto the wooden floor.

Oh shit.

"Deacon? Deacon, if you're doing that, don't. Don't kill her. She's under the dagger's curse."

He didn't seem to be listening. And she couldn't tell if the vibrating and nose bleeding were something he was doing or something the dagger was causing.

She looked away from the two shifters and focused on putting the jealousy dagger back into its scabbard. It fought her again. Twitching and jumping in her hand. It was also vibrating. Cary risked a glance up at Sasha. The two seemed to be vibrating at the same rate.

Was that Deacon or the stupid knife? He didn't seem to be doing anything, just standing there staring at Sasha, his claws out.

Only one way to tell.

She fought the blade, forcing the tip of the knife inch by inch into the scabbard, pushing it down until the hilt snicked into place.

A pulse of energy burst through the room, a shockwave that knocked Cary onto her ass. Followed by a moan of anger she didn't hear but felt in her bones.

Scabbard and secured dagger still in hand, she climbed to her feet. Sasha's eyes were still black. Blood was still dripping from her nose. And the vibrating had gotten worse.

Yeah, that wasn't good.

Cary dove between Deacon and Sasha, not even sure who she was protecting now. Maybe both of them. From each other.

"Deacon." Cary tried to get him to look down at her, but he kept his full attention on Sasha. His lip lifted in a snarl, a low hiss Cary hadn't noticed before falling from him. "Deacon, if you're doing this to her, stop. The jealousy dagger got to her. It's not her fault. Don't kill her."

He didn't look at her. He flicked his hand, still tipped by those wicked cat's claws, and Sasha screamed.

"Deacon, please. Please, don't do this."

She stepped closer but was afraid to touch him. She couldn't see any of the man she knew in his expression. Not the slightly out of control man she'd fallen for or the overly controlled, distant man she'd been living with here. She couldn't see anything human in him at that moment, despite him still being mostly in human form.

He looked savage, wild. Deadly.

Sasha made a choking noise. Cary glanced back. Blood dripped down her nose and from the corners of her black eyes, pain filled her expression. Except for the way her body shook, she still wasn't moving.

"Deacon, stop. Please. You have to stop." Cary faced him, dropped the dagger and stepped on it so it wouldn't move, then put her hands on his cheeks.

The gesture brought his gaze to hers. Nothing that looked like human emotion moved through his expression.

"Deacon," she murmured, lowering her voice. "Please stop. If you kill her, it will hurt you. I don't want you hurt. For me. For your mate. Please, stop hurting her." She stroked the hard line of his jaw, willing him to listen to her, to hear her.

She continued to murmur pleas, as she watched his jaw line change, returning back to normal so that he almost looked like himself again. His eyes continued to glow, but he blinked them finally. The claws on his hands retracted. A shudder shook through his big body.

He blinked again. "Cary?"

"There you are," she whispered. "I'm here. Don't worry. Everything is all right." She pulled him into a hug and his arms tightened around her like a vise. Even in this state, he was careful not to hug so tight he might hurt her, though, and that made her smile. "I've got you," she murmured. "You're safe."

He released a strained sounding huff of air like a laugh. "I'm here to save you," he said. His voice sounded harsh and gravely.

"Thank you," she said. "That was very nice of you."

He laughed harder this time, his body shaking, and he hugged her closer. She snuggled in, soaking up his warmth and the deliciously comforting scent of him.

She didn't even bother to move when she heard Sasha curse, felt the air currents of the other shifter's movements. The thud Sasha made when she hit the wall behind them sounded painful, though.

Cary glanced back. The woman was sprawled on the ground at the base of the wall, knocked away from her attack by Cary's shield.

She looked up at Cary with her black eyes and snarled. "This isn't over. I will feed!"

She made as if to rise and then stopped, again mid-motion, in an awkward position that no one could hold purposefully for long.

"Deacon, don't hurt her," Cary said, looking back up at him.

"Just keeping her quiet," he said. He cleared his throat as the harshness of it made his words difficult to hear. "I won't kill her."

"Thank you." Cary cupped his face in her hands again. "It's not her fault. It's the dagger." She nodded to the scabbard she'd dropped at her feet.

"It's contained," he said.

She heard his question. "It dripped blood onto Sasha, and a little got past me into her skin. She's still being affected by that even though the dagger is secured." She made a face. "And I have no idea how to fix that."

"I can help," a quiet, feminine voice said from the doorway.

Maria walked in, looking a lot less controlled and put together than usual. She was wearing simple black pants and shirt, her hair was in wild disarray around her shoulders. There were circles under her eyes and creases around her mouth and between her brows.

She looked around the room and released a long breath. "No one is dead."

Cary's mouth quirked. "Just barely," she said.

Her comment caused Maria to smile, but only a little. She looked at her son. "How are you?"

"Bad," he said. "But better than I was a few minutes ago."

"Thank the gods for that," Maria murmured. She looked at Sasha, still frozen like a statue in that awkward position. "I should be able to contain her for now. You can release her."

Cary watched Sasha finish her forward movement and then freeze again, her attention turned toward Maria. The vicious anger in her expression didn't diminish at all, and her eyes remained that solid black.

"How can you help her?" Cary asked Maria.

"I'll keep her safe in a containment cell and attempt to work the curse out of her blood. It will take time," she said to Cary's raised brows. "Keeping her safely contained is the only way we can take that time."

"I'll see if my bosses have any suggestions or anything that might help."

"Thank you," Maria said. "I would appreciate any assistance they can offer. The work I'll be doing with her will be delicate, and if there's an easier process I won't object."

"Are you okay?" Cary asked.

She smiled faintly again. "I've had better days."

Deacon winced, but didn't comment.

"I'll leave you two to collect yourselves," Maria said. She turned to leave, Sasha following in a stiff, automaton sort of gate that gave Cary the creeps.

When she was sure Maria was safely out of earshot—shifter earshot—she said to Deacon, "I'm not sure if I should tell your mother this before she works on Sasha, in case it affects what she does, but Sasha's been trying to have her killed by the cougars."

Deacon shrugged. "Yeah, we know."

"You know." Cary dropped her chin to stare at him. "And you've just let her get away with it?"

"My mother was in no real danger from them."

"Deacon, Sasha was her assistant. Who knew everything Maria did at all times. Why the hell didn't you stop her?"

"Sasha has always been a special case for my mother, and she didn't want to accept the betrayal at first. Once she was certain Sasha was behind the escalation in the cougar aggression, she still thought she might somehow save her."

"Sasha arranged to have kids kidnapped and almost got humans killed outside your clinic. I'm not sure it was a good idea to let her go that long."

"The kids and clinic shooting were the final straws for my mother. She had intended to call Sasha out as soon as the charity ball was over."

"And then the ball got attacked."

He made a face. "That was a surprise. She hadn't see that one coming."

"So she *can* make mistakes," Cary said. For some reason, it was a relief to know Deacon's mother wasn't infallible.

"A mistake that nearly got you killed." The growl was back in his voice.

Cary waved away his concern. "I was fine once Sasha threatened to kill you."

"What?"

"Once you were in danger from her, I had to protect you. My powers started to work. I was good. Then she started playing with the dagger and I had to protect her from the dagger..." At Deacon's frown, she said, "It's a long story. I'll explain it all on the way out of here." She blinked. "Where is here, by the way?"

"A small house halfway back to Portland. Sasha kept it for when she needed privacy."

"She brought me to her own house? That doesn't seem smart."

"She assumed we wouldn't guess she'd taken you. She was careful to ensure she didn't have your scent on her. And she tried to convince me you'd used the chaos of the cougar attack to leave me because you'd overheard some bullshit from some random humans."

"I did overhear exactly what she set me up to hear," Cary said. "And it had an impact."

"I'm sorry she did that to you."

"I'm sorry I bought it." She glanced around the windowless room, thinking Sasha must have put her in a basement, and then wondering where Sasha found a house with a basement. "What time is it exactly? I was unconscious. I have no idea how much time has passed."

"You were gone all night and half a day. It's the early afternoon."

"Damn. But that could have been worse." Unless it had been worse. "You didn't hurt anyone did you? I mean, you looked pretty messed up when you got here. Was I away too long?"

"Messed up?" His lip lifted in the beginnings of a smile.

"Yeah you were."

He shrugged. "I suppose I was. I don't remember much after I realized you were gone. I didn't kill anyone. It was close, though. A few of the leopards too close to me when Sasha told me you'd left will need some time to heal."

He wouldn't meet her gaze and her heart hurt for him. He was going to carry that guilt on his own shoulders rather than passing it off to Sasha where it belonged.

"Your mother helped?" she asked quietly.

He nodded. "And she'll need time to heal now too."

Cary let out a long breath. "You should know, I would never have left without talking to you first."

"I did know that."

"Good. I was worried."

"Why?"

"We haven't exactly been in sync lately. I thought you might believe her."

He cupped her cheek, his hands perfectly ordinary human hands now. "I know you too well for that. Even when we're not in sync."

"I'm glad to hear it," she said, meaning that more than she realized. "How the hell did you find me?"

"You're my mate. I can track you no matter where you are."

"You can?"

He shrugged. "It's not something most leopard mates can do. But I'm different."

Cary snorted.

"And Sasha should have realized."

"She didn't know the extent of your powers, though, right? I mean, no one does but a few family members. And you mostly refuse to use them."

"She still should have known she'd never be able to keep my mate from me."

He sounded so fierce and protective Cary shivered—in a good way. Which she'd probably be embarrassed about later.

He scowled. "This seems like a morbid question, but why didn't she kill you?"

"Oh, she was just trying to break our bond. She is very convinced you're *her* mate. Seriously convinced. And she didn't want to hurt you by killing me. At first anyway. Somehow in all the talk of betrayal and with the dagger adding to the mood, she decided everyone had to die. Fortunately."

"Fortunately?"

"Yeah. Without that part, I was helpless. Once she decided everyone needed to die, I had to protect you all." Cary shrugged. "It's nice when the bad guys get carried away and shoot themselves in the metaphorical foot."

Deacon shook his head, then settled his forehead against hers, resting there for a long moment. "I never thought I'd see the day I'd be grateful for your job."

She snorted. Cupping the hand he still had on her cheek, she rubbed his fingers. "So. You can do partial shifts, huh? Haven't mentioned that before."

"Part of the magic. I never do it."

"Uh huh. And you can sense where I am? The way you can with other leopards even though I'm not a leopard?"

He winced a little. "Didn't mention that before either, huh?"

"No. No, you didn't. Probably should have," she said.

"Sorry?"

The fact that he was asking if he should apologize shouldn't have made her want to laugh. Maybe she was delirious from all the stress of the last day.

"Are you mad?" he asked.

"I'm still deciding. Right now, I'm too tired to know for sure."

"Can I convince you not to be mad before you're rested enough to know?"

That did make her laugh. A laugh which went on a little too long, and confirmed she was absolutely delirious.

With a sigh, she shook her head. "Let's get out of here. I think I need a nap—that's not induced by a smack to the head."

"Better put your jacket on first." He glanced down and for the first time Cary looked at her dress.

Her *borrowed* dress.

"Oh man," she moaned. The poor, once beautiful gown was now filthy and it looked like she'd burst every seam in the thing. "I owe Nicky a new dress." She made a face. "I hope it wasn't too expensive. Maybe Marianne can make a replacement for me and I can sweep her shop floors to pay her back."

"Don't worry about the dress. I'll replace it for Nicky."

Cary raised her brows. "Thanks. It's good to have a rich boyfriend."

"Does that mean we're still a couple? You've been a little uncertain on that point."

"I'm not keeping you just for your money, if that's what you're implying." She let out a breath and said more seriously, "A lot has happened in the last twenty-four hours, but the one thing that hasn't changed, not in this entire weird adventure, is how I feel about you. I want you in you in my life, Deacon. The rest we can work out."

"Good," he said. "Because I love you."

For a full thirty seconds, she could only stare at him. "You've never said that to anyone before."

"No, I haven't."

"You just said the words."

"Yes, I did."

"You mean them, too."

"I do."

"Why now?"

"Because I need to let you know before you get killed."

"Well, that's romantic." She made a face.

He chuckled. "I need you to know," he said quietly. "Even when I don't show it. Or when we get…out of sync." He smiled faintly. "I need you to remember. I love you."

"Well…" She smiled. "Good to know."

He pulled her into a deep kiss, and she savored the truth of his words, all his emotions right there in that kiss.

And yes, she sang the song to herself as she kissed him back. It was a little too perfect to resist.

When she lifted her head, and met his beautiful golden-eyed gaze, a lovely peace she hadn't known for days filled her chest.

He glanced down and tilted his head to one side. "This is new." He touched the hollow of her neck and the charm there.

"Oh." Cary glanced down. "Yeah, that's the present from Jasmine Hashemi that Angie brought down. Remember the girl we saved the last time we tried to go on a date?"

"I remember. She knows Angie?"

"Long story." Cary waved that away. "It's just a token good luck charm. But Angie says there's actual magic in it."

"Good luck magic?"

"Yeah. And it must work, too, because I'm alive, and no one died, and Sasha only got cursed a little bit, which I'm pretty sure we can fix." She winced. At least she hoped they could fix that part.

Deacon lifted the charm to study it. "Remind me to thank Jasmine personally."

"Angie warned we'll get invited to dinner when we see her family again. She also said we should absolutely accept that invitation."

"It will be my pleasure." He smiled.

It was his slow, sexy, irresistible grin. With it, the last of her emotional confusion from the week melted away.

Which was only to be expected. Everything and everyone melted under that sexy Deacon smile.

She hugged him close. "Let's go home," she said.

As she scooped up her discarded jacket and shoes, she remembered something. "Wait, can we go right home or is your family still doing that dinner thing tonight?" She carefully slipped the jealousy dagger into her protective inner pocket. She really had to get rid of this thing.

"That was canceled when you went missing," Deacon said.

Was it bad that she was relieved? "I guess I can meet your siblings another time."

She really just wanted to get home and hug her dogs. And take a nap in her own bed. With Deacon. Which meant maybe it wouldn't start out as much of a nap. But that was good too.

"They all still want to meet you," he said as he helped her into her jacket and she did her best to hide all the places the dress no longer covered. "We'll reschedule."

"When?"

"A week. Time for things to settle down but before they all scatter again."

She sighed. At least she'd have a week at home before having to face his whole family. "I guess one more night out of town won't irritate the Nags too much. I did do my job while I was here after all." She patted her jacket over the pocket holding the dagger.

Deacon put a hand on the small of her back, guiding her out the door. She grinned at the gesture.

"They'll come to us instead of making us come here," he said. "It's safer for me to stay away from most of our people for a bit longer. Especially after…"

She squeezed his hand when he took hold of hers.

"We'll have dinner at my place," he said. "You can finally see it."

"So your entire family is going to descend on Portland in a week."

The entire Jones clan. Full of shapeshifting leopards roaming around her city. Where she couldn't escape them. Or run away and hide in her own home without it being rude.

"It'll be fun," he said.

Fun? Sure. Fun.

Oh boy.

THANK YOU

I hope you've enjoyed this Cary Redmond adventure! If you had fun watching Cary hang out with her best friends, you might like the short stories with their first meetings, all available now. Also, for those of you curious about the other *attempted* Deacon and Cary dates, look for those short stories starting in June 2020. Book four in the series, The Trouble with Baby Gods and Vampires, will be out in the fall of 2020. For an excerpt from that book, keep reading!

Updates on all my new releases, and a free, exclusive short story in my Tiger Shifter paranormal romance series, are available by signing up for my newsletter: http://eepurl.com/OxQQL. If you're over-whelmed with newsletters, you can get the updates at my website at http://www.katsimons.com, or follow my author page at your favorite vendor.

Thanks again for continuing on this adventure with Cary!
~Kat

THE TROUBLE WITH BABY GODS AND VAMPIRES

A CARY REDMOND NOVEL, BOOK 4
EXCERPT

1

Cary Redmond grinned at the vampire in front of her, frankly relieved. This was what she knew how to do. And after the last week with her boyfriend's family—they'd used the spring equinox as an excuse for a full family visit—this was a lovely break.

Although, she had been dealing with a lot of vampires in the last month. Since the beginning of February actually. She should probably be a bit more worried about that. All these vampires defying the Master's laws was…odd.

"I'm sure you know the rules," she said to the one she faced now. He was tall and thin and preternaturally beautiful with pale skin, silver white hair cut in a short, spiky style, and a face so chiseled and perfectly symmetrical he could have graced magazine covers and underwear ads. "In this town, no feeding on the unwilling," she said. "That's the deal."

"Gabriel is changing the 'deal'," the vampire snarled.

"Not that I've heard," she said reasonably. "And, you know, I would have heard. People talk about these things."

He lifted his lip in a look that was super condescending.

Cary just smiled. "You're looking at me and thinking I'm gullible and naive and don't know anything at all. But you'll notice how I'm *looking* at you, right? In the eyes? Like, maybe there's more to me than a little human blood?"

The vampire wasn't a spring chicken. He was past the century mark at least. And his initial attempts to toss her aside had required her to stand firm because she actually felt the tug of it. That meant he was a really powerful vampire, whatever his age. That was the only time she felt a vampire's attempts to move her. The only times she had really bad reactions to those attempts were when she met a Master vampire—which was blessedly rare. The last time she'd met one, she'd nearly thrown up on his shiny shoes.

Gabriel was the current Master of Portland, and when he'd over-thrown the previous Master, he'd declared he'd uphold all the laws she'd put into place to keep the hive safe. One of those rules—one that Cary had negotiated with Ariel personally because they'd both agreed, although likely for different reasons, that vampires shouldn't drink innocent kitten blood—was that the vampires in Portland only drank from willing people. *People*. Not kittens. Only those who could consent to the bloodletting.

Vampires didn't need to kill to live. Some liked to. All of them could. And the young ones sometimes had a hard time controlling that urge. But for the most part, they could carry on quite easily without killing anyone.

And in Portland, for the safety of everyone involved—not to mention the kittens!—vampires lived off the willing. In this town, there were more than enough willing to feed the hive.

Unless Gabriel had been allowing an increase in new vampires.

Which might explain why she'd been having to get between these guys and unwilling victims so much over the last few weeks.

She narrowed her eyes. "You're not making more vampires than you can support are you? Because that's not okay."

"What is it to you, human?"

"Hey, I live here too. We all need to utilize our resources, and over-burdening any of them is irresponsible."

The vampire blinked at her, his jaundiced-yellow eyes iridescent.

Eyes that would have been mesmerizing if not for the trembling human man Cary was protecting from being eaten.

The poor guy was not the kind that usual came into contact with vampires, that was obvious at a glance. And he wasn't even the kind of man she usually ended up protecting. To be honest, she mostly figured grown ass men should be able to take care of themselves. She had her prejudices. But in this case, the guy had just been minding his own business, locking up his fishing supply shop, and ready to head home.

"Do you think Jim here wants the waterways in the area over-fished?" she asked the vampire. "No. You know why?"

"Cause I'd go out of business," Jim muttered.

"Right," Cary said. "He'd go out of business. Overextending our resources is bad for everyone." She glanced back at Jim and nodded.

He returned the gesture, a little frantically, his eyes wide. Jim was a lanky, tall, bearded older man who looked like he was a lot more comfortable by a lake than walking around a city. He wore a flannel shirt under his heavy army surplus coat, his boots and jeans neat and clean but well worn. He had a nice, comfortable face with character wrinkles around his eyes and across his brow. She had a hard time guessing his age—because she was really bad at that—but she'd figure around his late fifties, maybe early sixty.

A far cry from the Goth kids and clueless tourists that usually fed the vampires. And the tourists were only allowed because the ones that agreed thought it was some sort of performance art specific to Portland, thanks to a little vampire mesmerism.

"So as Jim has clearly stated," she said to the vampire, who was trying to reach through her Protector shields to strangle her, "it's a really bad idea to make too many vampires. Has Gabriel been falling down on his job?"

Master vampires were supposed to keep hives under control, to sustainable numbers, and generally in line so no wars broke out. Falling down on those responsibilities usually led to another Master overthrowing the weaker one and taking over.

Cary wouldn't have thought the previous Master, Ariel, had been weaker. After their meeting, Cary had been terrified of her. Which meant Gabriel was even scarier. She really really didn't want to have to meet Gabriel if she could at all avoid it.

But if something was amiss in the hive and it was driving vampires to feed on the unwilling ordinary Jims of the city, it might fall to her to intervene. And wow did she *not* want to do that.

"You're meddling in business that doesn't concern you, woman," the vampire said, his voice very deep now.

"Yeah, you keep saying things like that, but really, if I have to keep getting between you guys and unwilling people, this is going to cut into my time. A lot. And that very much does concern me." She glanced back at Jim. His skin was very pale beneath his dark beard. "Bad guys always say stuff like that, though. I'm not sure why they can't think of more original lines. But it's always 'you're meddling in things you shouldn't' and 'this doesn't concern you' and 'you're a dead woman' and 'this isn't over, bitch'." She made a face. "I get those last two a *lot*. It's sometimes hard not to take personally."

She faced the vampire again. He was shaking his hands as if they'd gotten hurt. She frowned. "What did you just try to do? You really should stop before you catch on fire. That happens you know. Vampires try too hard to get at me and they catch on fire." To Jim, "The smell is really gross. It'd be better if he didn't do that."

"Wouldn't..." Jim swallowed audibly and lowered his voice. "Wouldn't it be bet-better if he was... You know?"

"Dead?" Cary frowned a little at the vampire. "Depends really. I don't know him." To the vampire, "Do you feed from unwilling a lot? Or is this just some new, desperate thing you've engaged in for some reason that I might have sympathy for and could therefore forgive you and send you on your way without you being dead? Again." To Jim, "Technically, he did die already. That's kind of how the vampire thing works."

"Didn't know they were real," Jim muttered.

"Yeah, that's generally better for all concerned," she said. To the vampire, "Are you going to answer my question or just keep trying to break through my shields to strangle me? I mean, I'd *rather* you didn't just randomly burn to death, but if you're determined, I guess I can't stop you."

"Gabriel will want to see you," the vampire growled, taking a few steps away from her. "After I tell him of your insolence."

She laughed. Really hard. "Me? I doubt he gives two flying fucks about me." Over her shoulder, "Sorry about the language."

"Understandable," Jim said.

"I'm an insignificant bug as far as the Master of the city is concerned," Cary said. "If you go to him complaining about a human woman preventing you from breaking *his* laws, I think it'll go worse for you than for me."

The vampire's eyes narrowed. She couldn't begin to read his expression. He was way too old for that. Outside of the anger he'd been purposefully showing her earlier—probably to try and scare her—he kept the rest of his thoughts to himself.

On the whole, she figured that was probably a good thing. She really didn't want to know for sure what he was thinking since it likely involved bloodletting, and specifically, her blood.

"I won't indulge you with the usual 'bad guy' parting line," the vampire said.

"You want to, though, don't you?" she said with a grin. "You are just itching to tell me 'this isn't over,' aren't you?"

He frowned, ever so slightly, and her grin widened.

"When—" he emphasized the word, "—Gabriel commands you appear before him, don't make him wait. That will go even worse for you."

"Yeah, good luck with getting him to have any interest in me at all."

"Oh, he's interested in you," the vampire assured. "Cary Redmond."

She blinked and he was gone. So fast, a breeze ruffled her hair. In the wake of his departure, her heartbeat hammered hard.

He'd known her name. He knew who she was even though she'd only said her first name aloud to Jim when trying to calm him down.

A strange vampire knew who she was, and said the Master of Portland was interested in her.

Oh oh.

~

Don't miss
The Trouble with Baby Gods and Vampires
Book 4 in the Cary Redmond series
Coming Soon!

BOOKS BY KAT SIMONS

THE CARY REDMOND SERIES

1 – The Trouble Black Cats and Demons

2 – The Trouble with Ghouls and Serial Killers

3 – The Trouble with Leopard Queens and Shifter Wars

4 – The Trouble with Baby Gods and Vampires COMING SOON

CARY REDMOND SHORT STORIES

When Cary Met Jaxer

When Cary Met Pickles

When Cary Met Marianne

When Cary Met Lucy

When Cary Met Angie

TIGER SHIFTERS SERIES

1 – Once Upon a Tiger

2 – Along Came a Tiger

3 – Here There Be Tigers

4 – Her Tiger To Take

5 – To Tempt a Tiger

6 – Down Will Come Tiger

7 – To Catch a Tiger

8 – What a Tiger Wants

9 – Taming Her Tiger

Tiger Shifters Series Vol 1 (Books 1 - 3)

Tiger Shifters Series Vol 2 (Books 4 - 6)

ABOUT THE AUTHOR

Kat Simons earned her Ph.D. in animal behavior, working with animals as diverse as dolphins and deer. She brought her experience and knowledge of biology to her paranormal romance and urban fantasy fiction, where she delights in taking nature and turning it on its ear. Her Tiger Shifters series combines romance and the otherworldly with heart-pounding action adventure. Her latest urban fantasy romance series follows the adventures of Protector Cary Redmond as she tries to manage her personal life while saving the world. A lot.

After traveling the world, Kat now lives in New York City with her family. She is a stay-at-home mom and a full time writer.

For more on Kat and her future books:

Website: http://www.katsimons.com
Newsletter: http://eepurl.com/OxQQL